BIRTH OF LEGENDS

STEEL CITY SERIES: BOOK 3

N.J. COLESAR

Copyright © 2019 Entanglement Interactive LLC
All rights reserved.

ISBN-13: 978-0-9989280-4-3
Hardcover: 978-0-9989280-8-1
eBook: 978-0-9989280-5-0

This book is a work of fiction. Names, characters, businesses, organizations, places, events, and incidents either are the product of the author's imagination or are used fictitiously. Any resemblance to actual persons, living or dead, events, or locales is entirely coincidental. Some locations described within the story are real places. Certain details may have been altered to better support the story.

Author: N. J. Colesar
Cover Art: Vanette Kosman

Publisher: Entanglement Interactive LLC

For information visit:
www.ENTANGLEMENT-INTERACTIVE.com

10   9   8   7   6   5   4   3   2   1

STEEL CITY SERIES

THE SHEARING
ORIGINS OF MYTH
BIRTH OF LEGENDS

To my children,
A few words of advice.

Be kind to everyone. Even the people you don't like.

Make your dreams a reality, even if it seems impossible.

And don't be afraid to ask for help.

CONTENTS

PROLOGUE I
PART I
CHAPTER 1 1
CHAPTER 2 10
CHAPTER 3 18
CHAPTER 4 27
CHAPTER 5 37
CHAPTER 6 47
CHAPTER 7 66
PART II
CHAPTER 8 77
CHAPTER 9 88
CHAPTER 10 100
CHAPTER 11 112
CHAPTER 12 125
CHAPTER 13 138
CHAPTER 14 154
CHAPTER 15 169
CHAPTER 16 183
CHAPTER 17 194
CHAPTER 18 212
CHAPTER 19 228
CHAPTER 20 238
PART III
CHAPTER 21 253
CHAPTER 22 263
CHAPTER 23 279
CHAPTER 24 294
CHAPTER 25 309
CHAPTER 26 320
CHAPTER 27 334
CHAPTER 28 347
CHAPTER 29 360
CHAPTER 30 369
CHAPTER 31 381
CHAPTER 32 394
EPILOGUE 401

PROLOGUE

The darkness was nearly complete as the shadows filtered between the faint moonlight that penetrated the leafy canopy above. The trees stood as black sentinels as a chorus of eerie shrieks and chilling howls echoed through the forest. Shapes moved beneath the trees, for on this night an unprecedented gathering took place.

A pack of small reptile-like Chupacabra with dark, leathery skin and sharp spines running down their backs huddled together and were nearly invisible in the darkness.

Nearby, a group of squat frogmen crouched against some large boulders as ghostly apparitions floated all around the gathering.

A pair of hodag paced between the trees. Each had a wide mouth with rows of gleaming fangs and a pair of horns sprouting from their wide heads. They had thick, short legs with huge claws and a long, bladed tail that slashed restlessly through the air.

Further back in the woods, a mysterious humanoid creature observed silently. It had tall wings poking up from its back and eyes that glowed red in the darkness.

Curled around a tree near the frogmen was a creature of monstrous proportions. Over twenty feet long, the gowrow was pale with two long tusks and large, webbed feet that ended in wickedly curved claws. A row of horns ran down its back and ended in a long, spiked tail.

Suddenly, a bipedal creature with red skin and the head of a goat glided out of the darkness on leather bat-like wings. Its forked tail guided it until it landed on its hooved feet near a large pile of brush. A low growl issued from the brush and a pair of golden eyes glared at the red devil.

The devilish creature regarded the threatening eyes for a moment before casually moving away. A pair of large, scaly beasts, each with a single eye in the middle of their forehead, watched the encounter and hooted with laughter. Metallic beaks filled with razor-sharp teeth gleamed in the faint moonlight as their numerous tentacles waggled in amusement.

An ugly little creature that was covered with warts and other blemishes cowered nearby and the devil saw it looking at him.

"What are you looking at, Squonk?" the devil growled.

The poor little creature whimpered in terror and suddenly dissolved in a puddle of tears.

The devil laughed, "That's what I thought."

The others all snickered until their laughter was abruptly cut off when four new creatures slunk out of the shadows. The newcomers were humanoid and covered in thick fur. They had the distinct appearance of wolves.

"Dewayo!" the one-eyed beasts shrieked angrily.

"Snallygasters!" the four wolf-like dewayo growled back and bared their fangs.

The two groups of monsters faced each other and were both about to attack when a foul stink of corruption filled the air.

Three figures shambled out of the darkness between them and both groups recoiled from the newcomers. Like human corpses, the emaciated creatures had pale, grey skin stretched tight over their skeletal bodies.

"Now isss not the time for killinggg," one of the gaunt creatures hissed with tattered lips.

"And who made you wendigo boss?" the red devil scoffed.

The three wendigo rounded on the devil. "The Golden One summoned usss all here," one of them hissed.

"I do not answer to this...*Golden One*," the devil sneered back contemptuously.

"Then flyyyy back to that Jerseyyy cessspittt where you belonggg," a wendigo retorted.

"Maybe I will," the devil glared balefully at the desiccated creatures. "But not until I remove your foul stink from this earth."

"That won't be necessary," a mighty voice boomed in the darkness.

An enormous figure glided out of the night. Cloaked in clinging darkness, the newcomer moved into the center of the assembly and a glint of gold flashed in the moonlight as he addressed the creatures gathered around him.

"I take it you are the Golden One?" the devil asked scornfully.

The figure's cloaked head nodded. "I have been known by that name."

"Good," the devil growled. "Then you can tell us why we are here."

The shadowy Golden One did not immediately reply as he cast his hidden gaze around at the gathered monsters. "For revenge." He clenched his fist. "You are the true masters of this world. It is time to step out of the shadows and take what is rightfully yours!"

"The humans are too many," one of the frogmen rumbled. "They will hunt us down and kill us all if we reveal ourselves."

"Not any longer," the Golden One countered. "I am sure you have all noticed the changes that have recently taken place." To which most of the monsters nodded their agreement. "The door to other worlds has opened and the humans are beset on all sides by creatures not of this realm. But this is *your* world; you know it better than anyone. Rise up and make the humans pay!"

"For what cost?" the devil scowled. "Surely you expect something from us."

"I ask only one thing." The Golden One opened his hand and a glowing disk-like object revolved in the air above his palm. "Should you find one of these, return it to me immediately."

The devil eyed the object with distrust. "What is it?"

"Insurance," the Golden One replied. "The humans will be looking for them as well. They will use them for protection. But if they do not have them…" The huge figure left the implications hanging in the night air.

But the devil wasn't convinced. "And what if we give these things to you? Will you then become the master of this world and hunt us down once our usefulness has ended?"

"Never," the Golden One boomed. "You are slaves to no one. Once the humans and their allies are dead, this world will become Chaos and you will be perfectly positioned to take it."

"We will never work with snallygasters!" one of the dewayo wolfmen growled at the serpentine beasts.

The Golden One chuckled darkly. "And you don't have to. Do as you will, but if you find anything of interest, bring it to me. Let your true nature free. Chaos is the source of all things and all things will return to Chaos."

The devil crossed his hooved arms across his chest defiantly. "And if we refuse?"

"You are still free to do as you will," the shadowy figured replied, but then a dark menace filled his voice. "But should I discover that one of you found something and withheld it from me, know that there is no place on this world or any other that you could hide, and there are fates worse than death."

"Spare me the threats," the devil scoffed. "I have seen hell. It holds no fear over me."

"I am sure it would not," the Golden One replied, "but I do not speak of hell." The devil's eyes narrowed, but the shadowy figure did not elaborate.

"And what do we get if we deliver one of these objects to you?" one of the snallygasters hissed.

The darkness seemed to grow around the Golden One. "Is not the destruction of the humans enough? You desire a reward as well?" he growled menacingly.

"Yesss," the snallygaster hissed. "This isss obviously important to you, so you will have to pay for it."

The Golden One was silent for a long moment before he finally spoke. "Very well," he growled. "You may name your price once you have delivered the object to me. If it is within my power, it will be yours."

"Exccccellent," the snallygaster hissed, and the other monsters voiced their approval as well.

"It is agreed then," the Golden One boomed with an air of finality. "Go now and retake what is rightfully yours. Sow the seeds of Chaos and bring this world to its knees!"

The gathered monsters roared their approval, and one by one vanished into the night.

PART I

CHAPTER 1

IT WAS A BEAUTIFUL DAY IN PENNSYLVANIA. A warm, autumn breeze blew through the rolling hills as some of the trees were just beginning to change color.

Nestled into the point between three connecting rivers sat the sparkling city of Pittsburgh, its new walls and towers gleaming in the evening light. Tall banners of black and gold fluttered from the ramparts, proudly declaring the city's allegiance.

The thick, banded walls and towers that now protectively ringed the city were a stark reminder of just how drastically the world had changed in less than a year.

When the Large Hadron Collider suffered a catastrophic malfunction, the vast release of energy had torn the protective Veil Between Worlds asunder, pulling all manner of creatures to Earth, in what became known as The Shearing.

Hideous beasts and vicious monsters of all shapes and sizes now prowled the world, and the unsuspecting humans had become their prey. But abominable enemies were not the only things that had been pulled to Earth.

Magic had poured through the rents in the Veil and flooded the world with power. Many individuals discovered they could wield this newfound power and used it to defeat the vile beasts that were threatening to overrun the planet. But the humans were unskilled in the use of magic and they could not hold back the ever-growing tide of bloodthirsty enemies.

Unexpected allies had arrived in the form of the sturdy dwarves and the mysterious elves. The human survivors of The Shearing had eagerly accepted the aid of the stranded elves and dwarves, and in return, the humans of Pittsburgh provided a home for their displaced allies.

That is not to say that there wasn't conflict.

The elves were notoriously secretive and they butted heads with the stubborn dwarves constantly. Both sides competed to prove that their way was superior. But when they managed to put aside their differences, they could achieve amazing things, like building the great city wall.

The construction had gone remarkably quickly thanks to a combination of human technology, dwarven skill, and elven magic. The wall had given all three races a common goal and helped to bond them together. But now that the huge outer wall was completed and only a few smaller, inner walls were still being finished, the groups had separated and were focusing on fortifying their own sanctuaries.

The dwarves carved deeper into Mt. Washington to expand Varnirborg as their blocky fortress along the ridge took shape, while Herrs Island and Neville Island were all walled off and became safe havens for the elves.

The humans mingled with both the elves and dwarves equally and acted as a kind of glue that held the two competing races together. But more binding than the humans was the growing threat of annihilation from several hostile armies that were slowly converging on Pittsburgh.

To the south was a shadowy force that was only glimpsed at night and left nothing alive in its wake. To the east, a growing horde of monsters controlled by the orcs, and their Warlord Stormtusk, was an unstoppable tide that brought ruin to all who tried to oppose them. And to the west was the Horned Legion of The Destroyer; countless kefali zealots who desired nothing more than to bathe the world in chaos.

****

"But what are they waiting for?" Liz McAllister asked, as she pulled a stray lock of hair away from her face.

A sword suddenly slashed at her and Liz barely got her own blade up to block.

"Who cares?" Mike Strazney shrugged, as he prepared for another strike. "So long as they are leaving us alone, I won't complain."

Liz and Mike circled each other, practice swords raised, in one of the small dueling circles on the lawn outside of the Cathedral of Learning as the sun began to set. They had been sparring for over an hour and Liz was drenched in sweat. To her great annoyance, Mike didn't seem to be sweating at all.

Before Mike could launch a new attack, Liz struck.

Her two short swords were a blur as she unleashed a whirlwind of slashes at Mike. But as quick as she was, Mike was faster and he parried every strike with his longsword.

The apparent ease with which Mike blocked her attacks made Liz angry and she redoubled her efforts. Her strikes came even faster, until something suddenly snapped inside her.

Her tiredness abruptly fled and she was filled with renewed energy. A strange sensation filled her and time itself seemed to slow. Her own movements were at their usual speed, but Mike was moving as if he were under water.

She had felt this way once before, during the battle in the bailey of the giant fortress. Since then, she had been unable to duplicate the awareness, until now.

A thrill of excitement coursed through her and she launched herself at Mike.

Somehow, Mike managed to block her first three strikes, but her fourth got through his defenses and she was rewarded with a satisfying thud as her practice blade connected with Mike's chest. Empowered that she had actually hit him, Liz swung her other sword at Mike, but it struck a shimmering blue shield just before it reached him.

"No fair," Liz complained. "I never win."

Mike rubbed his sore ribs. "You won that time," he groaned, and the shield vanished.

"You were probably going easy on me," Liz argued.

"Usually," Mike admitted, "but I had been fighting in the SCA for years before all this craziness turned my hobby into an important skill. But this time, you beat me fair and square. I saw something about you change before that last series. It was like you got faster and more confident in your movements."

"I did get a strange feeling there," Liz admitted.

That got Mike's attention. "What kind of feeling?"

Liz shrugged. "I dunno…I felt energized and like everything was going in slow motion, except for me." Liz shook her head. "I can't explain it."

Mike grinned. "Sounds like you were in The Zone."

"The Zone, eh?" Liz laughed. "Is that the technical term?"

"It is," Mike nodded with a dopey grin. "A similar slowing sensation hits me most every time there is a fight, so I started calling it 'being in The Zone'."

"I'm sure the elves and dwarves have similar experiences," Liz said. "You haven't asked them what they call it?"

"Heck no," Mike snorted. "They get to name everything. This one's mine."

"You're ridiculous," Liz laughed at Mike's logic. But she couldn't argue. It did seem like their allies always had a name for everything. She had even noticed that the elves wouldn't call the city Pittsburgh, instead only referring to it as the Steel City.

"You never get in The Zone when you're shooting?" Mike asked.

"Well, yes," Liz admitted after a moment's thought. "But being in the Shooting Zone feels different than being in the Fighting Zone. It feels more natural in the Shooting Zone."

"Well, with any luck you will shoot any baddies before they can get close enough for you to need a sword," said Mike. "Besides, you are the best shot in the whole city, remember?"

"I wouldn't go that far."

"I would," Mike said. "Even the snipers can't make some of the shots you do."

That last part was true enough. Liz's skill had greatly improved in the past weeks and she had won the last shooting competition, beating the best sharpshooters in Pittsburgh, including a team of elite Scout Snipers.

But that was before all the firing ranges had been closed and the use of firearms was suspended in an effort to conserve ammunition while the new factories stockpiled more.

Now, everyone was even more focused on martial and magical training.

A surprising percentage of humans had discovered they had some kind of power. Not necessarily magical, but some ability nonetheless. Many of those powers were on display all around them as humans, elves, and dwarves filled the lawn inside the newly completed curtain wall that encircled Cathy and her grounds.

"Well, guns only work when you have bullets for them," Liz said. "And with as many monsters that they say are coming for us, then I will need to be able to survive without my gun."

"I would say you are well on your way to rivaling the elven Blade Dancers," Mike said. "You have gotten really good, really fast."

"I can't be that good if you always beat me," Liz smiled.

"That's because I'm just *that* amazing," Mike smiled back. "And modest, too."

Liz playfully rolled her eyes. "Oh, whatever. You have the unfair advantage of having an enchanted dwarf mace to help you."

"Interesting." Mike inspected the long sword in his hands. "This doesn't look like an enchanted dwarf mace."

"No, it doesn't," Liz admitted seriously, but then the hint of a grin appeared. "But then, you also lost."

"Ouch!" Mike clutched his heart as if he had been stabbed. "That hurt."

"You're a big boy," Liz laughed. "You will get over it."

"I dunno." Mike waved his practice sword around threateningly. "That was an insult to my honor," he grinned. "I demand a rematch."

Liz set her feet. "It's your funeral," she said, as she readied herself for another bout.

"We'll see about that," Mike said, then suddenly launched a vicious two-handed cut at Liz's head.

Liz slid away just enough for the blade to whistle dangerously close to her face before she stepped in and slashed wildly at Mike before he could recover.

She wasn't quite quick enough though, and Mike was able to pull his longsword back and block both of her shorter blades.

"Nice try," Mike grinned, "but you will have to do better than that."

Liz growled as she launched herself at him again. She swung her short swords from opposite directions in the hopes that Mike couldn't block them both, but instead he didn't even try. Instead, Mike twisted away and swept his longsword back, catching both her blades and knocking her off balance. She recovered quickly and waded right back in, swords striking like snakes.

Mike blocked each of her lightning-quick attacks and they traded blows for several moments, neither able to find an opening and finish the contest.

Liz slashed low at Mike's leg, but he sidestepped and when Liz pursued, he twisted away again, whipping his sword behind him as he went. The flat of his blade slapped into Liz's rump.

"Youch!" Liz cried, and she quickly stepped away and rubbed her sore backside. "You are going to pay for that," she growled, as she set her feet and readied herself for another attack.

"Bring it on!" Mike laughed eagerly.

Liz charged ahead and the strange feeling returned. Mike's movements slowed and she felt a rush of energy. She grinned and leapt forward, blades flashing in the waning sunlight.

Mike backpedaled and desperately fought to keep her striking blades at bay.

Liz smiled as she saw her attacks getting ever closer to their marks and she knew this duel would soon be over. She slashed at Mike's head with one blade and he just barely got his longsword up in time to block, but now his middle was wide open and her other swords darted in for the kill.

Suddenly, his sword was there and knocked the killing stroke away. Frustrated, Liz struck faster, hoping to overwhelm him. But his movements were no longer slow. He moved just as fast as she was, perhaps even quicker.

"Two can play this game," Mike teased through gritted teeth.

Without waiting for a reply, he struck. Liz avoided the strike and stabbed at his broad chest. Mike sidestepped the thrust and chopped at her shoulder, but she got a blade up and deftly deflected the blow. Liz forced herself to move faster and fell deeper into The Zone.

Her attacks were faster than he thought, but Mike matched her every move and together they danced a deadly ballet.

The duel went on in a hypnotizing blur of flashing blades, until suddenly Liz got her swords on either side of Mike's, and she gave a violent twist.

Mike's longsword flew from his grasp and clattered to the ground.

Liz grinned and moved in for the kill.

Faster than the eye could follow, Liz's swords descended on the unarmed Mike.

But before the strikes could land, Mike somehow got his hands around Liz's wrists and held her in place.

His grip was like iron and Liz knew she had no chance of breaking away, so instead she drove her knee up, aiming for Mike's groin.

At the last moment, Mike shifted his hips and Liz's knee slammed into the meat of his thigh.

"Playing dirty now, are we?" Mike chuckled darkly.

"Exploiting a weakness is not dirty," Liz growled, as she struggled in Mike's grip.

Mike clamped down harder on her wrists until it became too painful to hold her swords anymore and she was forced to drop them from her nerveless fingers.

Liz growled, and suddenly pressed in and planted a foot on Mike's knee and then actually ran up his chest. She twisted back in the air and broke free of his grip to land in front of a stunned Mike.

"That was a neat trick," Mike laughed, clearly impressed.

Liz smiled back. "Just remember that I can walk all over you."

"We'll se-" Mike started to reply, but then Liz suddenly kicked at his face and he quickly brought his hands up to block. Before he had recovered, Liz drove in hard, fists and knees flying.

Mike countered her attacks and the two were locked in a brutal, physical contest. Liz managed to land a few blows to his shoulders and chest, but her strikes were ineffective against his muscled bulk.

Thinking quickly, Liz dropped down and swept her leg out and knocked Mike off his feet. He landed hard on his back, but before he could recover, she pounced on him. Sensing victory, she straddled his chest and rained fists and elbows down on his exposed head and face.

Mike got his thick arms up and managed to block the worst of her attacks, but he was trapped and taking a beating.

Mike abruptly heaved upward and with an immense show of strength, he lifted Liz off and twisted in the air. Liz landed on her back with Mike's heavy body pinning her down.

Liz flailed desperately and tried to hit Mike, but he easily pinned her arms down and trapped her beneath him. Panic suddenly filled her and she struggled wildly for a moment until she realized it was futile.

A strange scent filled the air and Liz was surprised to realize that it was Mike that she was smelling. Her senses were heightened while in The Zone, and things became crisper and more pronounced in her altered state. She had known she could see and hear better, but this was the first time she had smelled anything.

He had the faint smell of leather and metal on him, but more than that, there was a strange, but not unpleasant, odor that she assumed was Mike's personal aroma.

She was suddenly aware of the closeness of their bodies and she could feel the heat radiating off of his muscled body like a furnace. His scent surrounded her and she realized that she liked the feeling of him on top of her.

She looked up into his dark brown eyes that were only a few inches away from her own when she became aware of the sounds of cheering.

Still pinned, Liz tore her eyes away and looked around.

It seemed they had attracted a crowd. All around their dueling ring were cheering faces that were applauding Mike's victory.

Liz disliked being on display and especially in such a compromising position.

"You can let me go now," Liz breathed.

Mike smiled and released her wrists before pushing himself up and waving to the crowd. Liz quickly picked herself up and retrieved her practice swords.

"Another round?" Mike asked.

"No." Liz strode over to the rack on the outer edge of the ring and put the weapons on it. "I'm getting hungry. What do you say to getting some supper?"

Mike shrugged. "Sounds good to me. Let's go find Ted and Jack. I haven't seen either of them much these last few weeks."

"Neither have I," Liz admitted. "I never go into the workshop to see what Ted is tinkering with and Jack has been acting strange ever since we got back from the giant's fortress."

"He never did go to the healers, did he?" Mike asked, as he joined her by the weapons rack and hung up his long sword.

"Nope." Liz shook her head. "I'm worried about him."

"I know," Mike replied, as the two of them made their way out of the practice ring and through the dispersing crowd. "But Jack has never been much of a people person. He probably just wants some alone time."

"But it's been weeks," Liz argued. "There must be something else… maybe he's missing Emily?"

Mike snorted derisively. "I doubt that."

"Well, I am," Liz admitted. "She has been gone a long time. What if something happened to her out there? She could be in trouble and we would never know!"

Mike gave her a look that said she worried too much. "She is probably out doing Druidy things with those crazy brothers. You know how she likes the company of animals more than people anyway."

Liz couldn't argue with that, but it was still concerning that Emily had vanished weeks ago and they had heard nothing about her since. Add to that Jack acting strange and avoiding everyone, so she knew something was wrong there, but he refused to talk to her about it.

Liz sighed, "So, where are we going to find them?"

"Ted will be in the Verkstad, working on whatever it is he has been messing with. As for Jack," Mike shrugged, "your guess is as good as mine."

CHAPTER 2

They found Ted a short time later, deep in the bowels of the fortress-like workshop of the Verkstad, within the industrial section of the city dubbed the Foundry District, just as Mike had predicted.

It was a long walk, winding through burning forges, cluttered worktables, piles of metal, and all manner of partially constructed objects. The whole place looked like some mad scientist's lab, with electricity arcing in one corner as heavy machinery beat on a huge bar of steel in another. The sound was deafening, from the rhythmic pounding of hammers to the growl of electric saws.

A heavily muscled dwarf stomped by and Liz was surprised to notice that the dwarf's leg was copper below the knee. Thick cables attached the metal limb to the flesh and a jet of steam hissed from the artificial appendage with every step.

All around, shirtless dwarves toiled over glowing metal and hurried through the chaotic workshop in a dizzying frenzy of activity. Somehow, none of the dwarves ever collided and everything seemed to flow remarkably smoothly inside this veritable storm of construction.

The vast majority of those working inside the Verkstad were dwarves, but there were a few humans scattered about and Liz even spotted a lone elf working on something in a dark corner.

In the back corner of the building, they found Ted's private workshop that was separated from the rest of the Verkstad by heavy stone walls. It was quite a distinction. Only the Overseer of the Verkstad, Master Runesmith Nadal Ivaldisson, and the elderly Rune Lord Eitri Starmantle had the luxury of a private workshop. But thanks to the Heroes of Awesome status as the ones who rescued King Varnir Anvilborn's son, Ted had been given special access to the dwarves' materials and given his own personal workshop.

Ted looked up from his desk as Mike and Liz entered his large lab.

If the Verkstad resembled a mad scientist's lab, then Ted's office was a mad scientist's wet dream. Jars and vials of organic material that Liz didn't want to try to identify cluttered one entire wall. Next to the jars was every type of tool that Liz could imagine. From screwdrivers and hammers, to table saws and other machinery that she didn't even know the purpose of. A large forge glowed hot in one corner and sparks flew from a large, robotic arm that was doing something to a weirdly bent piece of metal.

Electricity arced between two tall coils of wire that were connected to some instrument that was making the most annoying ticking sound. On a wide table in the center of the room were several large computer monitors, each depicting something different. Liz couldn't even begin to guess what was on them, but it looked like schematics and simulations for something… or multiple somethings.

Tall vats of multi-colored liquid bubbled away in one corner while a pair of mannequins dressed in pieces of dwarf and elf armor stood guard. Not all the pieces were of obvious elf or dwarf origin, however, and Liz suspected they were of Ted's own design.

But the most interesting thing in the room was several laser beams of varying sizes and colors that spanned one long table that was connected to a complicated-looking machine. On the top of the machine was a small energy field with some kind of partially liquid material that was suspended in the air and slowly rotating within the basketball-sized energy field.

The suspended liquid wasn't the only thing floating around Ted's workshop. Thick, metallic plates were scattered all around the shop and above each plate floated a chunk of metal. Each metal was different in size and shape. Some of the plates had several metal bits floating above them, with a few even floating one atop the other.

Liz just shook her head as a small grin crept onto her face. It wouldn't be Ted's workshop without something floating around.

Perhaps more interesting than the mad scientist's lab was the mad scientist himself.

Ted Koldun was hunched over a table near the center of the inventor's fantasy. He wore a white lab coat over a leather apron. Thick goggles with layers of magnification lenses gave him a weird, robotic bug appearance, and his long beard was parted down the middle and tied back to his ears.

He looked ridiculous, but Liz guessed that the style was more conducive to keeping his beard from catching fire or getting ripped out by one of the many machines scattered about. But the goggles and parted beard were not the strangest things about him.

Just below the elbow, his left arm was bronze.

Over a month ago, the Heroes of Awesome had battled one of the legendary nephilim inside a dark, twisted fortress. During the course of the battle, Ted had gotten into a magical duel with the nephilim and one of the demigod's spells had exploded, taking half of Ted's arm with it.

But thanks to a grateful dwarf king, the dwarves had forged him a new arm made of bronze. At first Ted had refused, saying that such a device would only weigh him down. But the dwarves assured him that it would function just like his real one.

Dubiously, Ted had finally agreed and was fitted with the surprisingly life-like construct. Besides the metallic sheen and a few flexible tubes running into the skin above his elbow, the new arm looked exactly like his missing one. But more importantly, and surprisingly, was that the artificial limb actually worked!

To everyone's surprise and delight, especially Ted's, the bronze appendage moved and articulated just like a real hand. Ted was overjoyed and said that he could hardly tell that it was synthetic. It could feel things and it responded to his every command. From that moment on, Ted had retreated into his workshop to work on God-knows-what every hour of the day.

Liz was worried about him. He looked like he hadn't slept in days and he ran around like a man possessed. Despite his haggard appearance, the few times Liz had seen him, Ted always seemed in high spirits. He was obviously excited about whatever he was working on, but he wouldn't tell anybody what it was. Mike had been spending a lot more time in here as well, so Liz suspected that he knew what it was, but he wasn't talking either.

Books and scrolls were piled around Ted, and he had one particularly ancient-looking scroll rolled open before him.

Ted smiled when he saw them enter and his magnification goggles made his eyes look enormous.

"Why, hello there!" Ted beamed and waved his arms around the room grandly. "Welcome to the Imagitorium."

"The Imagitorium, eh?" Liz eyed the lab suspiciously. "I suppose that is a word for it."

"A darn good word, too," Ted chuckled, as he bent back over his scroll. "Now, what can I do for you?" he asked, without looking up.

"Well," Mike poked one of the floating bits of metal, "we came to see if we could pull you out of the rabbit hole long enough to shove some food in you."

"Hmm?" Ted looked up and blinked owlishly. "What's this about a rabbit?"

"It's supper time," Liz sighed.

"What?" Ted looked confused for a moment. "Oh, yes! Where does the time go?" He bent back over his scroll. "Just give me a few minutes to finish this translation…"

Mike poked another bit of floating metal and it clattered loudly to the floor.

"And don't touch anything," Ted grumbled without looking up.

Mike picked up the metal and sheepishly placed it back in the air above the metal plate.

"What are those things anyways?" Liz asked, as she eyed another floating metal scrap.

"Hmm?" Ted mumbled and glanced up. "Oh, those are magnets. I am experimenting with different metals and how they react to different magnetic strengths."

"Why?"

Ted blinked in confusion. "Because they're *magnets*."

Apparently, that was supposed to make sense and Ted went back to his scroll. Liz wasn't about to press the issue and continued to wander through the maze of strange objects.

Half-finished armor and pieces of various weapons were scattered all over the workshop floor. Liz even saw a pile of junk that she realized was actually car parts. What Ted could possibly want with an old shock absorber was anyone's guess.

"Hey, Ted," Mike said from across the room. "What is this?" He held up a small, metallic cylinder that had what looked like a sword's crossguard welded to it.

Ted glanced up and scowled when he saw what Mike was holding. "Put that down before you hurt somebody," he grumbled, and bent back over his scroll. "It will be a weapon if you two will ever let me finish this translation."

"Well, soooorry." Mike absently picked up another strange device. "Last time I checked it was *you* that came to *me* asking for help."

Ted sighed dramatically. "That is only because you are better with the forge than I am." He adjusted one of the lenses on his goggles. "That and those frustrating dwarves still won't show me how to make one of those blasted runes."

"You chose to learn dwarvish instead of runes," Liz chuckled.

"And a fat lot of good it's doing me now," Ted growled, and waved at the scrolls around him. "I can translate these, but it doesn't do me much good since I can't actually make the runes. I can only tell Mike what it says and let him make them for me."

Liz could see the frustration in his eyes. "Why don't you just have Mike show you how to make them?"

"I've tried," Mike admitted.

"Yes," Ted grumbled, "but I don't seem to have the *gift* for it."

"How is that the dwarves fault?" Liz asked.

"Because," Ted scowled at the old scroll as if it was the paper's fault. "I bet there is some trick to learning it that they haven't shown Mike, just so he can't teach me."

"I'm sure that's it." Liz nodded along, but inside she doubted the dwarves would hold that back. There probably was no trick and it was a gift, just like Ted's magic or her own healing powers. She did feel bad for him though. Ted was under the impression that there was nothing he shouldn't be able to learn, and to have something so close, but completely unattainable to him, must have been maddening.

Liz decided to change the subject. "So, what are you working on?"

Ted stayed hunched over his scroll. "I am making a heat-resistant, plasma-bladed poleaxe. Or at least that is the plan anyways. I am having difficulties, however, in maintaining a consistent energy field for the blade." He held up the scroll for Liz to see. "One of the Runesmiths gave me this and said it may help, but the instructions are for the crafting of a Superior Rune of Suppression and I will need Mike here to do the actual crafting of it."

"And like I already told him," Mike said, "I don't have the skill to craft a Superior Rune yet. Nadal is *still* trying to recreate the Superior Rune of Impact on my mace."

"Crafting a known pattern is sure to be far simpler than deconstructing an active example for the purpose of recreating it," Ted argued.

"That may be true," Mike offered, "but that doesn't change the fact that I probably won't be able to make your silly Superior Rune, even if you translate it."

"*When*," Ted muttered over the scroll. "*When* I translate it. And I have every confidence in your budding Runesmith abilities."

"I'm glad one of us does," Mike muttered.

Liz picked up a glass orb that seemed to have faint lights twinkling inside it. "And what if this rune doesn't work?" she asked, as she rolled the orb around in her hands.

"Then I will go to plan Y," mumbled Ted.

Liz chuckled. "Plan Y? What happened to plan B?"

With his nose still in the scroll, Ted sighed. "Plans A-X have already been failures. This needs to work before I run out of alphabet."

"I'm sorry," Liz replied sincerely. "Is there something I can do to help?"

Ted looked up at her and smiled sadly. "Unless you can create a stable, razor-sharp blade of plasma affixed to my poleaxe…"

"I don't think so," Liz replied.

"I thought not." Ted looked back down at arranged parts on his table in disgust.

"Why are you so determined to get this plasma to work?" Liz asked, as she carefully sat the glass orb back down.

Mike waved the question away. "He thinks that Brigit's spear has a plasma blade on it."

"It does," Ted argued, "and when I ask the elves about it, they refuse to talk. And the dwarves are little better; offering ways such a weapon *could* be made but assuring me that no such thing is actually possible."

"Brigit?" Liz looked at Mike. "That's the elf Warden, isn't it?" she asked, and Mike nodded. "What is so special about her plasma spear?"

"Just that such technology is currently beyond us," Ted said excitedly. "But if her spear does have a plasma blade, or some other unknown substance, that could revolutionize known science! Not to mention the practical applications of such knowledge."

"Like making weapons with it," Liz said.

Ted snapped his fingers. "Exactly."

"You do realize that her spear is probably magical and therefore doesn't have any new technology for you to learn?" Liz said carefully.

"I am positive that her spear is enchanted," Ted answered to Liz's surprise. "I could feel the power radiating off of it when we met in that awful castle."

"So why don't you just enchant your poleaxe?" Liz asked.

"It *is* enchanted," Ted replied. "But I have been unable to discover a way to maintain the plasma in a superheated state and confined to such a small area while being affixed to a hand-held weapon."

"He is trying to combine technology and magic to create a more powerful weapon," Mike finished for him.

"Precisely," Ted beamed, and then bent back over the scroll.

"Good luck with that," chuckled Liz.

Ted snorted disdainfully. "Luck doesn't exist. But thank you."

Mike meandered over to Liz while she inspected a misshapen lump of stone that looked like it had been formed to look like a cloth.

"What happened there?" Liz pointed to the oddly shaped stone.

Mike grinned. "Ted was trying to make a Deadening Hood, but instead he turned the cloth to stone. Apparently, he got the Stone Skin spell wrong."

Liz made a face. "And what is a Deadening Hood?"

Mike shrugged. "Another one of those mythical items that Ted is determined to bring back to life. The story goes that a Deadening Hood is a cloth head covering that is impervious to nearly all types of damage."

"I see," Liz replied quietly. "But that sounds like a basic protection spell the elves use on all their armor. And even if you can't damage the hood, wouldn't the force of say, a hammer, still crack your skull?"

"Ahh!" Mike held up a finger dramatically. "That is the tricky part. You see, the Deadening Hood is not only hard as steel, but also as light and flexible as cloth. Not only that, it also nullifies the force of whatever hits it, so the impact doesn't hurt you either."

"Interesting," Liz muttered. "How did he even hear about such a thing?"

"Some old spell book, of course," Mike smiled. "It is part of some legendary elven armor that they call Null Armor. Not very creative, I know, but I guess it is supposed to be crazy hard to make. So, naturally, Ted wants to make some."

"Naturally," Liz smiled, as she looked back at Ted's hunched form. She was glad the mad scientist was on their side. If he ever got even half of his designs to work, his enemies would be in for a surprise.

"OK," Ted groaned, as he stood up and stretched his tall frame. "That's done. Now I just need to read it to you while you make the rune."

"After we eat," Mike countered.

Ted looked like he was about to argue but thought better of it. "Very well… lead on."

"We have to find Jack first," Liz insisted, as she made her way back through the maze.

"Oh, I know right where he is," Ted replied. "I was out gathering some materials an hour ago and I saw him over by the Boxing Ring."

"What was he doing over there?" Liz asked, as she and Mike joined Ted by the workshop door.

"Fighting," Ted laughed. "What else?"

CHAPTER 3

It was a bit of a hike from the Verkstad to the Boxing Ring, and there was a huge crowd cheering on the two combatants inside the ring when they finally arrived.

Mike pushed his way through the mob with Liz and Ted following close behind. A chorus of angry mutterings greeted him, but those mutterings were quickly silenced when they saw the size of the man who was coming through.

A few of the onlookers actually moved aside willingly when they recognized the Heroes of Awesome approaching. Mike found it amusing that they had become minor celebrities after the battle with the giants. They had been credited with killing the nephilim and thus destroying the portals that had sustained the demonic legions of Fomorians. The allied force of humans, elves, and dwarves had defeated the giants and claimed victory thanks to the Heroes of Awesome, or so the story went.

In fact, it had been the three Wardens that had actually killed the mighty nephilim while the Heroes of Awesome either lay dying or paralyzed under the nephilim Anak's spell. But the Wardens had demanded that their existence be kept a secret and thus the Heroes of Awesome were given all the credit.

Mike knew that Liz felt guilty about not telling the truth, but he was just fine with soaking up some well-earned praise. They may not have killed the vile demigod, but they had held it off long enough for the Wardens to show up and kill it, and that was no minor accomplishment.

In the weeks since, Mike had been given command of several missions to hunt down rogue packs of goblins and whatever other manner of creature that was unfortunate enough to get too close the city. He had met with brilliant success, and his mastery of tactics and strategy had impressed both the elf and dwarf commanders enough that they had actually begun to ask his council when preparing for battles.

Mike thought his inclusion into the command structure was amusing, given his lack of any actual training. He blamed his vast amount of video game experience for his success, although he had to admit that strategic thinking did seem to come naturally to him. The only thing Mike liked more than expertly deploying troops was being in the middle of the fight.

General Adams was the ranking military commander in Pittsburgh and protection of the entire city fell on him. The general was a bold leader who preferred to seek out and destroy any hostile force at the first opportunity. This strategy aligned with the elves' mindset, who were also very offensive in their planning. But Mike and the dwarves preferred a defensive strategy that had the enemy coming to them where they could be trapped and destroyed with little danger to their own troops.

The reoccurring argument was what to do about the three hostile forces, each working their way slowly toward Pittsburgh.

General Adams and the other human commanders wanted to sally forth and destroy the growing orc horde to the east. The horde was believed to be the largest and thus the most dangerous of the three armies.

The elves, on the other hand, believed that the kefali were the most dangerous and the entire city should march on The Destroyer and his Horned Legion at once.

The dwarves agreed with the humans that the orcs were the greatest threat, but they wanted to stay safe behind the new walls and let the orcs smash themselves against it.

Mike agreed with the dwarves that a defensive stand would serve them best, but he wasn't so sure that the orcs were the most dangerous. He was more concerned about this mysterious shadow army that was creeping around to their south. Nobody had actually seen this army, just the empty towns that were left in its wake.

Technically, General Adams had command of the allied forces and he would have marched out to destroy one of their enemies weeks ago if it hadn't been for King Varnir Anvilborn.

The dwarf king refused to allow his Clan to be part of any "suicide mission" as he called it. And without the combined strength of all three allied armies, General Adams didn't have the troops to launch an offensive.

And so, they sat there, launching small-scale strikes against hostile forces while strengthening their defenses.

The waiting also gave rise to an increase of less-productive activities, such as the one unfolding before them in the center of the Boxing Ring.

When Mike finally pushed his way to the roped-off edge of the ring, he saw the source of the crowd's excitement.

Two figures stalked each other inside the ring. One was a young man of average height and the other was a stocky dwarf. Both were shirtless and circled around each other with fists raised.

Mike wasn't surprised when he saw that the man in the ring was Jack.

Jack was a rather handsome young man who wasn't nearly as broad as Mike, but still cut an impressive figure. His lean muscles glistened with sweat as he circled his opponent, but his usually crisp appearance had decayed over the last month. His Marine haircut had grown out into a shaggy mane and an un-kept beard had sprouted on his face. Dark circles under his golden eyes made him look like he hadn't slept in days, and for all Mike knew, he hadn't.

Mike still found Jack's golden eyes unsettling. Ever since they had changed during the battle in the giant fortress, Jack had been acting strangely. But he refused to see a healer and had taken to avoiding everyone, with the exception of challenging people in the arenas, of course.

His opponent was a heavily muscled dwarf that was covered in runic tattoos and sported an elaborately braided beard. His bulging muscles rippled as he moved and his massive fists weaved threateningly in the air.

The dwarf smirked as Jack suddenly drove in, fists flying. Jack moved surprisingly fast, and he managed to land several blows to the dwarf's head and chest before the dwarf got his large arms up to block.

The rapid hammering didn't seem to affect the dwarf in the least. He allowed Jack to pound on him for several moments before finally throwing a punch of his own.

There was a frenzy in Jack's attacks that Mike had never seen before. Yes, Jack was always a bit wild, but it was a controlled wild, as if he was dancing to his own crazy beat. But what Mike was seeing now was a complete disregard for any type of skill, relying instead on ferocity.

The dwarf's strike was blindingly quick and slammed into Jack's face with the force of a hammer blow. Jack's head snapped back, and he crashed to the ground and the crowd cheered.

Mike was shocked. Normally, Jack would never have let such a simple attack hit him; he was far too skilled for that. Perhaps his obvious lack of sleep was impairing him worse than he realized.

Somehow, Jack struggled back to his feet and motioned for the fight to continue. The dwarf shrugged and raised his heavy fists again.

Jack came on hard and fast, forcing the dwarf backwards, landing several solid hits. But punching the dwarf was like hitting a brick wall. Jack pounded the dwarf in the face repeatedly, but the dwarf only smiled up at him before blasting Jack in the chest with a ham-sized fist.

Jack doubled over as the wind was forced out of him. With their faces now even, the dwarf slammed his forehead into Jack's face. Jack's knees gave out and he crumpled to the dirt at the dwarf's feet. The crowd went wild.

"I told ye there be no chance o' ye beatin' me," the dwarf laughed over him.

Jack spat blood as he struggled to his feet. "We'll see about that," he growled, and raised his fists again.

The dwarf looked surprised. "Askin' fer another beatin' eh?" the dwarf smiled and set his feet.

Mike could see that Jack was furious at being knocked down twice and he was on the dwarf in a flash. Jack rained blows on the hapless dwarf from every angle.

The way Jack was fighting reminded Mike of watching a wild animal backed into a corner. There was no method or reason behind any of it, just blind desperation.

The stocky dwarf took the beating stoically, hardly seeming to notice Jack's fists that hammered into his wide, bearded face. That is, until Jack hauled back and delivered a devastating roundhouse punch that made the dwarf stumble away in a daze.

"Oy, ye shouldn't o' done that," the dwarf rumbled dangerously.

Jack came on again, but this time the dwarf wasn't fooling around. He blocked Jack's wild strikes and punched Jack hard in the face.

Jack kept his feet and the dwarf hit him again.

A look of surprise crossed the dwarf's face when Jack came at him again.

The dwarf's heavy fist collided with Jack's chin. Jack landed flat on his back and the crowd cheered.

The dwarf stomped up to Jack and raised a meaty fist above his head. "Ye ain't gettin up this time…" But before the dwarf could strike, Jack suddenly pulled his knees to his chest and kicked up with all his might.

Both feet connected with the dwarf's chin and his wide head snapped back violently. The dwarf's eyes rolled back in his head and he crashed to the ground in a nerveless heap.

The crowd erupted in cheers; all except for a group of dwarves who cried out that kicking didn't count. But the cheering of the crowd drowned out their complaints.

Mike ducked under the rope and approached his battered friend with Liz and Ted close behind.

"Cutting that a little close, weren't you?" Mike chuckled.

Jack waved the comment away dismissively. "I had him right where I wanted him the whole time."

"Sure, you did," Ted laughed. "What possessed you to fight him anyways?"

Jack retrieved his shirt and put it on. "I haven't been feeling the greatest and I thought a little scrap would help clear my head."

"And did it work?" Mike asked. He was surprised Jack had even admitted to not feeling well. Jack prided himself on being tough, so he must have felt truly terrible to even mention it. And now that he was close, Mike saw just how rough Jack was looking. His skin was pale and bloodshot eyes peered out from his battered complexion.

"No," Jack scowled. "Now, I have a bloody headache."

"Here, let me help." Liz moved toward him and held out a hand, but Jack jumped back like she was contagious.

"No, thanks, honey." Jack eyed her suspiciously. "I will be just fine."

"Fine." Liz lowered her hand. "Feel like crap. I don't care."

Mike knew that was a lie. Liz always cared when someone didn't feel well. It's who she was.

"What do you say to getting some food with us?" Mike offered. "We are headed to the cafeteria right now."

"I don't think so," Jack muttered. But Mike put his arm over Jack's shoulders and started walking, leading his scruffy friend along with him.

"Wonderful," Mike said cheerily. "A little food will do you good."

Jack scowled but allowed Mike to herd him along.

Cathy's cafeteria was packed.

Humans, elves, and dwarves filled the large space and the noise of hundreds of voices was deafening.

Mike, Liz, Ted, and Jack were seated around a small table filled with food that was off in the corner when Mike nodded toward a large table full of angry-looking men and women. "I don't understand why the New Puritans even bother coming here," Mike said just loud enough to be heard by his friends, but not loud enough for anybody else to overhear. "If they don't like elves or dwarves, why do they sit and eat around them?"

"Because they are making a statement," Liz answered. "They want the elves and dwarves to know they are here and that they don't like them."

Mike chuckled between bites. "That's funny because *nobody* likes the New Puritans."

Ted nodded his agreement. "They need to get over the fact that humans aren't the only sentient race on earth anymore."

Liz rolled her eyes. "That's not what it's about."

"Oh, really?" Ted sat up a little straighter at the prospect of a debate. "And have you had a conversation with one of these so-called New Puritans?"

"Actually, I have," Liz replied smartly. "They believe that the races should have little to no contact with each other, except for the purpose of avoiding extinction, which they think is what we are doing here now. But once the hostile races are defeated, they want humans, elves, and dwarves to go their separate ways."

"I'm guessing they don't like that the elves and dwarves have been given areas around the city for their own use," Mike said.

"Not at all," Liz confirmed. "And they especially don't like that some humans have been sexually active with elves and dwarves."

Jack suddenly barked a laugh. "They really wouldn't like me then," he chuckled, and tore into the steak on his plate with his bare hands.

"Ugh," Liz groaned. "Nobody wants to hear about your conquests."

Mike leaned in eagerly. "Don't listen to her. Let's hear the details."

Liz groaned again as Jack grinned wolfishly. "You know those two elf twins that hang around the Sword Ring?"

"The blonde Blade Dancers that have the ribbons on their swords?" Mike asked.

"That's them." Jack tore into the steak. "Let's just say none of us got much sleep for a few days."

To everyone's surprise Ted joined in. "What method did you use to attract the female elves?" he asked earnestly.

"Um..." Jack shrugged. "Just walked up to them and expressed my interest."

"Interesting..." Ted muttered to himself.

"Since when do you care about girls?" Liz asked. "Especially *elf* girls?"

Ted suddenly looked embarrassed, but Mike had an answer. "It's because he has a thing for Brigit."

Jack nearly choked on his food. "The Warden?" he mumbled, with a mouthful of steak.

"Shhh," Ted whispered to Jack. "And I do not have *a thing* for anyone." He grumbled at Mike. "I simply find her interesting and wish to learn more about her."

"That's called *a thing*," Mike laughed. "That is the exact definition actually."

Ted looked uncomfortable and Liz came to his rescue. "So, Ted, I've been wondering, why is your arm bronze anyways? I'm sure there are better metals to use."

Grateful to have a different topic, Ted eagerly answered. "There are better metals, yes. But all of the others are deemed more important for the war effort. So, all artificial limbs are bronze."

"I see..." Liz looked thoughtful. "I've been noticing a lot of dwarves with bronze parts recently."

"Yes," Ted nodded sagely. "There is a growing movement inside the Clans that actually embraces replacing organic parts with fabricated replacements. They distrust modern robotics and prefer a combination of gears and steam, augmented with runes, to produce a unique appendage." Ted leaned in conspiratorially. "I've even heard that some dwarves voluntarily remove perfectly healthy limbs to acquire a steam-powered appendage."

Liz looked appalled. "They do that on purpose?"

"Indeed," Ted nodded. "This growing cult of so-called Steam Dwarves has even been experimenting with adding weapon systems to the artificial limbs. Some of their designs are rather ingenious actually."

Mike could hear the admiration in Ted's voice and wondered how long it would take for him to add some destructive instrument into his own arm.

"I'll never understand dwarves," Liz breathed.

"Oh, it's not just the dwarves," Ted said.

"Of course," Jack growled. "We humans love our toys."

Ted looked meaningfully around the table "Not just humans."

"You're joking," Liz gasped. "Elves?"

Ted nodded.

"You lie," growled Jack. "Those goodie goodies would never attach some fake part to themselves."

"Normally, I would agree," said Ted. "But I've seen one with my own eyes and I know of two more elves that have grafted on artificial limbs." There was stunned silence around the table. "These few elves have embraced modern robotics and enhanced it with magic," Ted added. "Their work is the basis for some of my own projects."

"I'm sure the other elves love that," Liz said in disbelief.

Ted chuckled. "You could say that. As far as I know, these 'Synth-elves' are now outcasts of elven society."

"That's horrible," Liz said.

"Now, don't feel too bad for them," Ted added. "They have been sort-of adopted by the dwarves. It seems some of our bearded friends believe these Synth-elves prove that technology is superior to magic. Besides," Ted fiddled with his soup, "wasn't it some elves that stole Emily away?"

"It was," Liz nodded, "but that doesn't mean all elves deserve to be outcasts. And if I know Emily, she went willingly. She never did like being around a lot of people."

"But she has been gone for a month," Mike pointed out between bites. "Who knows what's happened to her."

"I'm sure she is fine," Liz said easily, but Mike could tell she didn't quite believe it. "She went with the Druids and they will keep her safe."

"Sure, they will," Jack growled sarcastically. "They will use their amazing, magical powers to take care of everything."

Mike noticed that the food hadn't helped Jack's appearance. If anything, he seemed more pale and sickly... and there was something strange about his unsettlingly golden eyes...

"That's not how magic works," Ted replied testily.

"Well, I wouldn't know that, now would I?" Jack growled angrily. "I'm not some wonderful wizard with power at my fingertips."

"Jack, that's not-" Liz started to say, but Jack suddenly stood up and stormed away, pushing his way through the tables, knocking people over.

"Should one of us go after him?" Mike said, as he watched Jack storm out of the cafeteria.

"I will," Liz said, and she began to gather up her plate.

"Better give him a minute to cool off," Mike offered. "He seemed pretty upset and we all know how Jack can explode when he gets angry."

"You are probably right," Liz sighed. "I think I'll get myself some ice cream and then I'll go after him."

Mike and Ted both chuckled. "You and your ice cream." Ted shook his head, amused, with a grin still on his face.

Liz scowled at both of them. "Neither of you have any room to talk. Mike, you eat more chocolate than most women and Ted, you drink more than is healthy for anybody." She stood up and went over to a large machine at a nearby serving station where she grabbed a bowl and pulled a lever. Ice cream poured out and twirled around her bowl until she released the lever.

"Drinking is good for you," Ted argued.

"Not the stuff you are drinking," Mike chuckled. "Just ask your liver."

Liz sat back down with her heaping bowl of ice cream.

Ted shrugged innocently. "You just don't know what's good."

"I sure do," Liz grinned, as she dug into her bowl. "And it's called ice cream."

CHAPTER 4

His insides burned.

Jack stumbled out into the cool summer breeze and took a deep breath. It felt good to be out of the confining cafeteria, but there were still too many people around.

What is wrong with me? Jack wondered in agony. *Must have been something in the steak.*

His skin felt like it had been dipped in acid and it was only sheer determination that kept him from wildly scratching all over. His burning insides also kept his mind off the irritated skin by keeping him focused on something even more painful.

Jack gritted his teeth and growled in agony as he stumbled away from the Cathedral of Learning as quickly as his tortured body would let him.

He trudged across the large yard and it seemed like an eternity before he finally made it through the thick gatehouse in a haze of pain. He didn't even notice the people who flinched away from his gaze and stared in shock at his back as he passed.

Jack clenched his jaw in a grimace of pain as a sudden wave of nausea threatened to overwhelm him.

With a determined growl, Jack forced his feet to keep moving.

He realized that everyone looked different... brighter, and clearer. Even though he had excellent eyesight, the change made it seem as though he had been half-blind before and now he had put glasses on.

A sudden scent made Jack turn and sniff the air.

What was that?... Squirrel?

Jack's mouth watered and he took a step in the direction of the smell before he got ahold of himself.

Squirrel? Since when did he know what a squirrel smelled like? And why would it smell good enough to eat?

Jack suddenly began to panic.

What was happening to him?

His insides burned.

His skin was on fire.

Sweat poured off him in buckets.

His senses were on overdrive.

Everything seemed new and wonderful. Like he had been dead but was now alive.

He had been reborn!

...No....

...It hurt...

...Pain...

Blinding pain swelled up and almost washed him away.

Jack howled and charged down the street, not knowing where he was going and not caring. All he wanted was an end to the agony.

He had been feeling strange for weeks, but the last few days had been miserable. Fever and chills came in waves, and one moment he would feel fine and the next he was doubled over, retching all over the floor.

A headache had begun a day ago until his head pounded so badly that he thought his skull was going to split open.

He wished it would.

He had hoped that getting into a fistfight with the dwarf boxing champion would either knock him out or at least dull the throbbing.

It hadn't.

Then, Mike had suggested eating and Jack had hoped a little food would ease some of the discomfort growing in his middle. Instead, the meat had only made the discomfort worse and it had blossomed into the burning that now coursed through his entire body.

But for some reason he couldn't stop eating. The meat had tasted so good. Even though it had increased the burning inside him, he hadn't wanted to stop and he had been disappointed that the meat wasn't raw.

Raw?

Since when did he like his meat raw?

It wasn't the meat that had driven him away. It was the noise. The noise of the cafeteria had grown while they ate and it very nearly drove him mad. It had been all he could do to not cover his ears at the deafening roar that echoed inside the chamber and reverberated inside his skull.

Jack continued his blind flight and didn't notice when he entered the woods.

He scrambled over sticks and rocks, but he couldn't escape the pain. His insides burned and his senses screamed as he desperately tried to get away. But there was nowhere to run.

He stumbled and fell, his joints suddenly going limp.

Jack forced himself back up, only to fall again. The strength had left him and it felt like his body was not his own.

He tried to move, but his muscles refused to respond.

Was that a worm?

Jack had his face planted against the soft ground. He swore he could actually hear the worms burrowing below him.

I'm going mad.

That was the only answer that made sense to his fevered mind.

He was going mad and he was going to die alone in the middle of the woods where nobody would ever find him.

That was no way for a soldier to go.

No.

That was no way for a Marine to go.

Jack roared in anger and brutally forced his body to obey.

He stood up and although every movement was agonizing, he pressed on. There was no destination in mind, but something drove him onward, deeper into the forest.

As he struggled to keep moving, Jack's vision began to turn red and everywhere he looked was clouded by a haze of rage and pain.

His muscles abruptly seized up and contracted all at once.

Jack crashed to the ground in a quivering heap.

Moaning, he crawled on all fours as excruciating spasms wracked his battered form.

His body quit responding altogether and Jack howled in agony as his vision went dark.

****

Liz was afraid.

She had followed Jack's trail into the woods, but after nearly an hour of searching she hadn't found him. With darkness rapidly approaching, Liz decided she needed help.

Jack's movements had been easy to follow outside of the Cathedral.

She had talked to several people who had seen a sick man matching Jack's description stumble through the gate and down the street. People along the street also said they saw him wandering along until he started to growl and shout before running off.

Liz grew more worried as the reports on Jack's condition got worse. They said he appeared delirious and was hunched over and clutching at his stomach as he shambled down the streets in obvious agony.

A few individuals reported that his appearance was very pale and he had a wild, almost feral, look in his eyes. One woman even said that he had sprouted hair along his neck and back as he ran by.

Liz didn't believe that last bit, but whatever was wrong with Jack sounded horrible and she needed to find him as soon as possible.

A pair of elves had seen Jack charge into a nearby park, but that was the last time anybody had seen him. So, Liz went into the forested park and began her search in earnest.

But as the evening wore on, Liz was no closer to finding him.

She had found the place where she believed he had entered the woods, judging by the broken twigs and disturbed leaves. However, his trail soon went cold and she lost all trace of where he may have gone.

A wolf howled in the distance.

Now, Liz was no stranger to the woods and could track just as well as some of the scouts, but somehow Jack had vanished without a trace.

She restarted her search from his entry point several times, but on each occasion, she still lost his trail.

Tired and frustrated, Liz finally left the woods to get help.

As darkness set in, she found both Mike and Ted working in Ted's workshop and not long after, she had both of them outside, in the park where Jack had vanished.

The sky was painted in brilliant streaks of red and orange as the last rays of sun began to set behind the hills and together, the three friends desperately searched the woods for any sign of Jack.

****

Repeating flashes of darkness and feelings of weightlessness left Jack disoriented and weak as he rolled around in a daze.

Where was he?

How long had he been in this endless nightmare of pain and confusion?

Why did he taste blood? Was it his, or someone else's?

His insides burned.

Again, the world turned black and the ground fell away beneath him. The weightlessness only lasted a moment before he smelled dirt and could hear the wind rustling through the trees.

Jack struggled to open his eyes and when he finally managed to pry them open he was surprised to discover it was nearly dark.

Agonizing pain shot through Jack's body and he howled in pain. His skin felt like burning ants were running all over him and he thrashed wildly trying to dislodge the imaginary insects.

Jack struggled to his feet and deliriously stumbled through the woods. His foot caught a protruding root and he tripped. Luckily his claws dug into the tree and he kept himself from falling.

Claws…?

Since when did he have claws?

Jack's bleary eyes looked down and saw his hands were far larger than they should have been and long claws tipped his hairy fingers.

Panic flooded him and Jack took off blindly into the woods, trying to escape this painful nightmare. He crashed through the trees, heedless of where he was or where he was going. All that mattered was to get away; far away.

But the faster Jack ran, the more the pain engulfed him. Until he crashed to a stop and convulsions wracked his tortured body.

Blood filled his mouth.

Jack spasmed uncontrollably, all alone and in the middle of nowhere, as the first stars began to appear high above him.

****

A shadow detached itself from the growing darkness and glided silently through the trees toward the sound of agonized howling.

Three more shadows materialized out of the gloom and ghosted along behind the first, leaving no trace of their passing.

****

"I think I found something!" Liz shouted excitedly.

She was halfway up a small hill that was far deeper into the woods than she had previously traveled.

"I don't know how you can see anything," Mike grumbled from the base of the hill. "It's nearly pitch black out here."

Liz had to agree, but thanks to space between two trees and the light of the emerging full moon, she was able to make out a person-sized patch of earth that was torn up like some kind of struggle had taken place.

Any number of animals could have dug up an area like this, but there were a few definitive marks that could only have been made by a human hand.

"It's not *that* dark," Ted said from below the other side of the hill, across from where Mike was.

They had been sweeping through the woods in an ever-expanding arc. Liz could see both of them from the ridge, but they couldn't see each other.

"Says the guy with a torch," Mike said loudly.

It wasn't really a torch, but Ted had one of his prototype poleaxes and this one had a large piece of glass that was shaped like an egg, built into the head. It gave off a fiery glow that resembled firelight and illuminated several yards in all directions.

Ted chuckled from around the hill. "It's not my fault you were not smart enough to bring a light with you."

"I was hoping to find him before it got dark," Mike grumbled, as he searched through the darkness.

"How's that working out for you?" Liz asked with a grin, and she pointed her flashlight down at him.

Mike winced at the sudden light and covered his eyes with his arm. "I was doing just fine until you ruined my night vision."

Liz laughed and moved the light away. "What night vision?"

"None now," Mike grumbled, and they continued their search around the small knoll.

The hill came to a gentle end and the three of them could see each other again. They continued their search through the darkness in a ragged line.

An agonized howling suddenly echoed through the trees and everyone froze.

"There aren't any wolves around here." Ted said grimly, as he scanned the darkness before them.

"I'm not sure that was a wolf," Liz replied anxiously.

There was a crash and a thump as Mike tripped in the darkness.

"Too bad you didn't bring your own light," Ted said, and his lighted poleaxe flared up dramatically to emphasize his point.

Mike scowled at Ted. "Actually, I did bring my own light," Mike replied testily.

"Well, let's see it then." Ted said with a smirk.

Leandros wouldn't approve... Mike thought before he bowed his head and closed his eyes. After a moment, he raised his head back up and took a deep breath before opening his eyes. When he did, his eyes burned with an ethereal blue fire that shone white-hot.

"There." Mike's voice resonated with a strange tone as power coursed through him. "Now I can see."

"Showoff," Ted grumbled, and went back to his search.

Mike grinned and started stomping through the woods again, but this time he wasn't tripping over any roots and he moved like it wasn't dark at all.

"Is that a good idea?" Liz asked Mike, as they tramped through the trees, his eyes burning like two fallen stars in the darkness.

"Probably not," Mike shrugged, unconcerned. "But I'm not much help bumbling along in the darkness."

Liz agreed with Mike's assessment, but that didn't mean his solution was a good one. "Isn't that dangerous?" she asked.

Mike's laughter was deep and resonating. "Of course. The Paladins and Guardians both agree that the Holy Fire is to only be used in emergencies." Mike's burning gaze turned to Liz. "I would call finding Jack an emergency."

"How long can you hold it?" Liz asked nervously. She knew enough to understand that the power Mike was holding was dangerous and could consume him if he wasn't careful. Some of the War Priests claimed to be able to wield a similar power and they spoke of its many dangers.

Another agonized howl echoed through the trees.

They were getting closer to whatever it was.

"Long enough," Mike answered, before he turned and strode boldly into the darkness, his eyes alight with blue flame.

****

Darkness consumed him.

Pain was all he knew.

It was everywhere. Every breath was fire; every movement sent burning knives through his body.

There was no escape.

Jack howled in anguish as he battled the darkness and the pain.

He was a Marine and whatever was happening to him he was going to beat it. He had bent the orc soul sword to his will. He had broken the Lector Priest's mind-control spell. He had even resisted the taint of the mighty nephilim. Surely, he could overcome whatever ailment or evil spell that was inflicting him now.

Jack growled in agony as his growing claws tore large gouges in the soft earth.

The first light of the full moon illuminated Jack's tortured form and his body convulsed violently.

Jack looked up at the moon and howled in rage and pain.

In the moonlight, his eyes shown like burnished gold.

****

Four shadows emerged from the darkness and floated toward the moonlit patch of forest where a tortured figure thrashed and moaned.

They stopped and remained motionless in the gloom just beyond the reach of the moonlight. They watched the tortured man for a moment until two more shadows materialized out of the darkness.

One of the new shadows was small, but the other new shadow was enormous and its inky blackness practically radiated violence.

Faint whispers passed between the shades until the smaller of the new shadows moved toward the tortured man.

When the shadow moved into the faint moonlight, it revealed only more blackness.

****

Jack saw the shadow detach itself from the darkness under the trees and soar toward him, but his contracting muscles wouldn't allow him to move. He managed to roll onto his side and bare his fangs as he growled helplessly at the approaching shadow.

The darkness closed in and loomed above him as it blocked out the meager light from the moon.

Jack tried to grab the pistol on his belt, but his hands were locked in clenched fists.

The shadow descended on him and Jack fought desperately to overcome his pain and force his spasming muscles to obey. His tortured body screamed at him as the veins in his face and neck bulged under his mighty struggle.

But his efforts were futile.

The pain was nearly overwhelming and his body was not his own.

A black, clawed hand reached out from the shadow and Jack howled in rage at being so helpless.

Something in the shadow's hand glittered in the moonlight.

Jack howled in agony as a new wave of white-hot pain suddenly shot through him.

The shadow's hand hovered above Jack's thrashing head and a faint powder fell from it. The glittering dust landed on him and he sneezed.

Jack rolled onto his back and his body abruptly began to seize violently. His back arched painfully high, until only his head and toes were still touching the ground. Jack howled in agony before his golden eyes rolled back in his head and everything went dark.

****

The five other shadows glided forward and surrounded Jack's unconscious form.

The largest shadow bent down and scooped up Jack's body and cradled him easily, as if Jack weighed nothing.

"Put him down!" a powerful voice thundered.

The shadows all jumped and looked around in confusion for the source of the mysterious voice.

Several yards away the air began to shimmer, like the heat off the road on a sunny day, and revealed three figures bathed in light.

The shadows shrunk back from the sudden brightness.

"I said, put him down," Mike's voice echoed with power. His eyes blazed with blue flames as he stepped forward and pointed his mace threateningly at the gathered shadowy figures.

Liz had her pistol trained on the towering shadow that held Jack's limp body and Ted stood between them with his poleaxe radiating the bright light.

When the shadows didn't move, Liz drew a slender short sword with her other hand. "We won't ask again."

Ted had the words to a spell on his lips when the smallest shadow suddenly stepped forward.

The concealing darkness that masked the identity of the small shadow began to unravel. It faded away like wisps of smoke to reveal the figure beneath.

Liz's mouth dropped open and Mike nearly dropped his mace in surprise.

The figure grinned impishly. "What took you so long?"

CHAPTER 5

"Emily?" Liz stared in wonder at her friend. "We were afraid that you were dead."

Emily smiled back and put her hands on her hips. "Do I look dead to you?"

Liz had to admit that she definitely did not look dead. Emily was wearing much the same thing as when she had run off with the Druids. Knee-high boots with a scandalously short mini-skirt and a tight leather corset that showed off way too much skin in Liz's opinion.

Emily had her compound bow in hand and the elaborate Endless Quiver peeked out from over her bare shoulder. The only thing that was really different about her was instead of Emily's usual black fedora she had a dark scarf wrapped around her head.

"Thankfully, no," Liz replied. "But it's been a month since you disappeared. What were we supposed to think?"

"Sorry, mom." Emily rolled her eyes playfully. "I'll be sure to call you the next time I'm on a dangerous, super-secret mission."

Liz scowled, but couldn't keep the smile from her face. "So, where have you been?"

"That is a long story," Emily answered uneasily, "and one that I will tell you all about, just not right now." She glanced back at Jack's unconscious form that was still being held by the huge shadow.

"You can stop pointing that gun at us now," Emily chided with a grin.

"Oh." Liz looked embarrassed and quickly lowered the weapon. "Sorry."

But Mike wasn't so quick to lower his guard. "Who are your…friends?" he asked suspiciously, as his burning gaze turned to the five figures behind Emily that remained cloaked in shadow, even to his enchanted sight.

Emily looked back at the shadows and said. "No point in sneaking around now. May as well show them."

At first Liz thought the shadowy figures were not going to listen, but then their clinging darkness began to evaporate in smoky tendrils.

Three of the shadows revealed themselves in the light of Ted's poleaxe to be a trio of strange-looking elves that Liz actually recognized.

Rubadub was of average height and dressed in soft leathers. A band of metal encircled his left bicep and blue markings were painted all over his exposed skin. A wolf-headed silver torc hung around his neck and a leather strap held back surprisingly dark green hair where two small deer antlers poked out from his green mane.

Robadoo was hunched over and his facial features closely resembled Rubadub. His hair was short and wild like a ratty bird's nest with feathers sticking out of it. A thick, feathered cloak hung across his shoulders and a feathered skirt encircled his waist that led to calf-high wrapped sandals. Clutched in one hand was a long, wooden staff topped with a large bird's skull and stuffed wings. Blue paint markings covered his body just like the other elf, only his pattern was wildly different. An eagle-headed silver torc hung around his slender neck and small bones pierced his long, pointed ears.

Rabidad resembled the other two and they were obviously brothers. Rabidad was taller and much more heavily muscled than his brothers. A large bearskin cloak hung from his broad shoulders and blue markings were painted all over his body. A silver torc encircled his thick neck, similar to the others, only his had bears heads on it. Each of the brothers held a tall walking stick with a pinecone on the end.

Liz was not really surprised to see the three elves. They were Emily's Druid instructors, after all, and it had been with them that she had disappeared in the first place.

But the other two figures *did* surprise her.

The smaller of the two shadows revealed a body covered in thick black fur and the strangely feminine face of a bear. Her snout was going white and thick globs of white paint were plastered to her matted fur.

Behind the old bear woman was a towering monster encased in heavy spiked armor. The massive beast had long, pointed ears atop a wide skull with an elongated snout full of curved fangs and the menacing, golden eyes of a ferocious wolf. Jack hung limply in the armored beast's grasp.

"Pipaluk?" Liz breathed, "Lorcan?" She could hardly believe what she was seeing. "What are you doing here? I thought you took your tribe and left."

The old bear woman smiled. "We had," Pipaluk answered. "We searched all across the land, but we quickly discovered that there was no safe place for us on this world. We were moving south when we came across Emily and her Druid masters. From there it was decided that we would aid them in their quest to discover the identity of the mysterious army moving to our south in exchange for a safe haven."

"We offered to bring you back with us," Liz noted.

"Indeed," Pipaluk nodded. "However, at the time we had hope of finding a way back to Nibiru... but after a moon's turn of searching, we could no longer afford to wander aimlessly in the hope of returning to our lost home."

"And did you discover this mysterious army's identity?" Ted asked.

"That is not my place to say," the old bear woman answered, and looked to the Druids.

"All will be revealed in time," Rubadub countered. "But right now, we have more immediate concerns, such as the state of your friend here." He motioned to Jack's limp body.

"What did you do to him?" Mike growled dangerously. The burning light faded from his eyes, but he still hadn't lowered his guard and watched the elves and kefali with equal suspicion.

"I have put him to sleep," Pipaluk answered. "Your friend was in terrible pain, so I gave him something to help ease the Change coming over him."

Dread filled Liz.

"Change?" she asked, with a hint of panic in her voice. "What change?"

Pipaluk made a brief motion and Lorcan brought Jack forward and gently set his unconscious body down. Mike, Liz, and Ted carefully approached and looked down on their friend.

Liz recoiled in horror and Ted whistled in amazement.

"My God..." Liz breathed.

Jack's body had ballooned out and his clothing had torn in several places where tufts of dark fur had sprouted. His hands and feet had grown, and each appendage had grown wickedly curved claws. But the real horror was what remained of his face.

Jack's handsome face had become a mangled mess of flesh and fur. Fangs jutted out from his twisted mouth and his spine bent at a funny angle. His features were so twisted that it was hard to tell that it was their friend lying there.

Mike scowled at Lorcan. "What is happening to him? How did this happen?"

"I believe *what* is happening is quite obvious," Ted commented, as he bent down and got a closer inspection of Jack's disfigured body.

Mike and Liz both gave him a confused look and Ted sighed heavily. "Honestly," Ted pointed at Jack. "He was howling and growing claws and fangs and is even more hairy than he already was." Ted pointed up to the sky. "And there is a full moon...which means..."

"Werewolf," Mike finished.

Ted gave a satisfied nod. "Exactly."

"But how?" Liz asked. "Wouldn't he need to have been bitten or something? Like by another werewolf?"

Ted shrugged and Mike just stared hard at his stricken friend.

"I believe I can answer that," Lorcan growled.

"It was during our skirmish inside the Isfet camp," the huge Warg explained. "The foul Lector Priest had Jack and me under his evil spell. However, to my shame, Jack was able to break free of the vile mind control, while I was not. We battled each other and during the course of the duel I bit his arm." Lorcan's ears drooped in shame. "I was not strong enough to overcome the spell and it is my fault this has happened to him."

"But you aren't a werewolf," Ted argued. "You are kefali."

"Where do you think such an ailment originates?" Pipaluk asked.

Ted snorted derisively. "From another werewolf, of course."

"True," the old bear woman nodded, "but where did they get it?"

Ted scratched his beard thoughtfully. "Are you saying that werewolves originated with people who were bitten by kefali?"

"Not just any kefala," Pipaluk answered, "but those bitten by Cynocephali, like our large Warg friend here."

"So, only Cynocephali make werewolves," Liz surmised.

Pipaluk looked down at Jack with concern in her eyes, or was it sadness. "Yes and no," the old bear woman answered, "but I will explain later. We must get him confined to a safe location before my medicine wears off."

"Just give him more," Mike said. "I have a lot of questions."

"I am sure," Pipaluk nodded, "but now is not the time because more medicine will not work. The disease will build immunity to it soon and then Jack will awaken and the Change will overtake him. With any luck, he will be locked away someplace safe before that happens."

"Do you have a place?" Liz asked. "You were going to take him somewhere before we arrived."

"No," Lorcan growled. "We were going to move him deeper into the forest and after he has fully Changed, I would subdue him."

Liz made a face that said she didn't approve of that idea.

"How about the jail?" Ted offered suddenly. "A jail cell should hold him."

But Emily was shaking her head before he finished. "That's in the city. The guards would never let Pipaluk or Lorcan through the gate."

"What about that cloaking spell you used?" Emily offered.

Ted shook his head. "Won't work. The walls are protected from cloaking spells."

"What about-" Emily began, but Ted cut her off.

"We cannot teleport inside either," he explained. "The walls are warded against it."

"Why don't we just let them get captured?" Rabidad, in his bearskin cloak, asked suddenly. "Will the guards not take us to this *jail* then?"

"Probably," Liz admitted, "but they might throw us all in if we show up together. I don't know about you, but I have no desire to see the inside of a jail cell."

Ted snapped his fingers excitedly. "I've got it! We can do the old 'pretend we are bringing new prisoners in' trick and then bust them out again once our mission is complete."

Liz rolled her eyes. "Ted, this isn't some movie that we can just waltz into a prison and then break out of."

"Then let's hear a better plan," Ted grumbled.

"There is a small park next to the jail," Emily said suddenly, as she turned to the Druid brothers. "Could we treewalk him there?" she asked.

The three brothers exchanged looks. "Yes, yes," Robadoo's head bobbed along as he talked. "As long as the wards do not stop us. Yes." The feathered Druid cocked his head and eyed a nearby tree. "Only one way to find out," he chirped, and then took a quick hop-step and vanished into the tree.

A moment later he reappeared with a large, crooked grin upon his face. "Yes, yes. The way is clear. It seems not all paths into the city are blocked."

Ted scowled. "I must tell the mages of this. It wouldn't do to have our enemies able to simply treewalk past our defenses."

"You can tell the mages whatever you want," Liz said, "but after we get Jack inside."

"Fine then," Ted replied. "Let's get going."

Rabidad in his heavy bearskin bent down and gently picked Jack up. "We do not all need to go," he rumbled. "I can make this journey on my own."

"No," Emily said, "I am going too. The rest of you can stay here."

"She is right," Rubadub added. "There is no need for all of us to go and reveal our kefali allies." The deer-antlered Druid said, "Remain here. I am sure you have many questions. Do not fear, your friend will be in good hands."

Jack groaned in the large Druid's arms.

"Quickly!" Pipaluk urged. "The medicine has almost worn off!"

Without hesitating, Rabidad took Jack and vanished into the nearest tree with Emily close behind.

"Alright," Mike rounded on the two kefali. "Explain to me *exactly* what is happening to him."

Before either of the kefali could answer, Rubadub stepped forward. "I can answer that."

"You know what's happening to him?" Liz asked.

Rubadub's antlers brushed some low branches as he nodded. "In an age long past, we elves considered ourselves the only sentient race in existence, until the Kefali Invasion. You see, the kefali had discovered a way to cross the Veil Between Worlds and they used this knowledge to invade and conquer other worlds in the name of Ma'at."

"They were under the false impression that it was their job to bring Order to the universe," Rubadub snorted scornfully. "Although it was a long and bitter war, our forefathers taught them the error of their ways."

"The kefali's sudden invasion caught us by complete surprise and they were able to capture numerous island nations before we even knew what was happening. Their lightning assault even allowed them to nearly overrun the whole of Themiscyra." The elf Druid sounded amazed. "If it wasn't for the mighty Amazons, all of Themiscyra would have fallen."

"But the horde of kefali did not wait to finish off the largest of our islands," Rubadub grinned. "Instead, they pressed on and attempted to sail across the Southern Sea to Hyperborea. Now, with Gaea being a world of countless islands, we elves mastered the art of shipbuilding and sea battle long ago. The kefali horde had gathered every ship they could find and amassed an enormous fleet, but by this time our forefathers had realized the danger and had begun to mobilize a resistance."

"Our hastily assembled fleet was dwarfed by the might the kefali had gathered, but we attacked anyway," the Druid said proudly. "Although there was no chance of winning such a battle, our seafaring skill and proficiency in the Art wreaked terrible losses on the kefali and half of their fleet was destroyed by a force a fraction of their size."

"It was not half," Lorcan growled. "There were more losses than there should have been, but it was not nearly half."

Rubadub waved the interruption away. "Regardless, the result was the same. The sea battle slowed the kefali down enough that a unified army had gathered at the White City and when the horde finally arrived, they were handily defeated."

Lorcan snorted. "Your idea of history is somewhat warped, elf. It is true that you were eventually victorious, but it was a close thing. If not for the intervention of your Pantheon and the defection of The Destroyer, we would have won."

Liz knew that Ted and Mike were eating this up, but she had more important things to do than listen to some bit of contested history. "This is all very interesting," she said, "but what exactly does this have to do with what is wrong with Jack?"

"I am getting there, my dear," said Rubadub. "I am nearly finished."

The huge Warg grumbled something under his breath, but Rubadub ignored it.

"Now, where was I?" The antlered Druid looked thoughtful for a moment. "Ah, yes. After *handily* defeating the kefali at the gates of the White City, the war ground to a standstill. The kefali dug in to the places they had captured and continued to gain reinforcements through the Veil. Years went by with neither side able to break the other, and it was during this time that the Druids of that Age came to understand and even befriend some of the kefali species."

"You must understand, the kefali that invaded ranged from small, rodent-like creatures to towering behemoths that dwarfed even our Warg friend here. But the vast majority were the Dog Soldiers of the Cynocephali." Surprisingly, Rubadub looked at Lorcan for confirmation.

"That is true," Lorcan growled. "We Cyno have the largest standing army and have traditionally formed the backbone of any Ma'at force."

Rubadub nodded his thanks. "Originally, the Druids began studying the different species of kefali to learn their weaknesses. But soon they were also searching for a cure to the mysterious ailment that had afflicted some of the elven warriors… these elves would transform into mindless, kefali beasts during a full moon."

"You say 'kefali beasts'," Ted said. "Don't you mean Cynocephali beasts?"

But it was Pipaluk, not Rubadub, who answered. "As I said before, it is the bite from a Cynocephalus, and more specifically a Warg, that creates what you call a werewolf. However, every kefali House has the potential to infect another with WereDisease, although such an occurrence is extremely rare since we kefali have a natural resistance to the disease."

"So, the disease Jack has is called WereDisease?" Liz asked.

"Indeed," Pipaluk answered, "and I am afraid there is no cure."

"So, every full moon he is going to change into a werewolf?" Liz groaned.

"Perhaps," Rubadub answered. "Or he may never return to his human form and become a permanent hybrid."

Liz couldn't believe what she was hearing. Jack was infected with an incurable disease that could leave him a mindless beast for the rest of his life.

The strange darkness Liz had discovered inside Jack when she had healed him once suddenly made sense. She hadn't been able to remove it and he had brushed it off as nothing, refusing to see the more skilled dwarven or elven healers.

"There is nothing we can do?" Liz asked desperately.

"I am afraid not," Rubadub answered sadly. "There were tales of Master Healers being able to cure the disease if caught within a day or so of infection, but there is no proof to those tales. Even if there were, your friend is far beyond that point. The best you can hope for is that he will return to his human form and only become a hybrid for the three nights of the full moon's cycle."

Liz refused to believe that there was no help for Jack. "But you said that kefali are resistant to the disease," Liz said to Pipaluk. "That means it can be treated."

But the old Baribal shaman shook her head. "Many have tried throughout the ages to find a cure. None has been successful. The best we can do is briefly slow it down, like I did for your friend there," Pipaluk said. "There is no cure. I am sorry."

"Nothing is impossible," Liz argued. "Impossible just takes longer."

Rubadub smiled. "Spoken like a true healer."

"I *will* find a cure," Liz growled.

"And it is my sincerest hope that you do," Rubadub said. "But be wary. Many a healer has wasted their lives searching in vain for a cure."

"The search for a cure can begin later," Mike rounded on the Druids. "What I want to know is what the Hell you have been doing with Emily for the last month."

"Training," Robadoo chirped. "Training her while we searched for the mysterious army to the south."

"And did you find them?" Mike asked.

"Oh, yes, yes." Robadoo cocked his head and stared at Mike with one eye. "We found them, we surely did."

"And…?" Mike pressed.

Robadoo shivered and cowered back so Rubadub answered. "We discovered our greatest fears," the antlered Druid said grimly. "We found the Shadowed Ones."

CHAPTER 6

"Well, that sounds ominous," Ted muttered.

"Is that supposed to mean something to us?" Mike asked.

"No," Rubadub answered. "It will not... not yet. But it means something to the elves."

"You will learn soon, soon," Robadoo chirped. "There is a meeting in the Grove tonight where we will reveal what we discovered about our enemies. You shall come, too. Yes, yes."

Rubadub nodded. "That is a good idea, brother. The Great Mother has seen fit to bring us together on such a momentous night; it must surely be for a reason."

"What is so momentous about it?" Ted asked.

"The Council is meeting in the Grove this night to learn what we discovered and to decide on a course of action," Rubadub said. "And any time you can coax a dwarf king out of his hole is a momentous occasion," he added with a smile.

"This meeting sounds *super* exciting," Liz said sarcastically, "but I will not be joining."

"Why not?" Mike asked.

"Because," Liz replied, "Jack needs help and I need to find a cure. I can't do that if I'm sitting around listening to the council debate what to do.

You guys have fun. I am going to the jail to see what I can do for Jack."

Mike knew there was no arguing with her. "Fine," he grumbled. "At least let one of the Druids treewalk you there."

"Me, me!" Robadoo bobbed happily. "I can take you. Sure, sure!"

"Alright." Liz shivered just thinking about treewalking. "Let's get this over with."

She took the bird-like Druid's hand and followed him into a nearby tree where they both vanished.

Mike turned away from the tree that Liz had disappeared into. "That brother of yours is a strange one."

Rubadub grinned. "He puts on a good show does he not? Thankfully, he only lays it on thick when there are others around or else I would have strangled him long ago. But yes, he is a rather strange bird." The antlered Druid looked up at the dark sky. "We had best be moving. The meeting will be starting soon and we cannot be late. We are the main attraction after all."

****

Liz waved goodbye to Robadoo as he stepped back through the tree that they had just come out of and disappeared.

She turned away from the tree and looked out from the small park she found herself in, to the tall jail across the street.

The jail was a 10-story, plain looking building of red brick with few windows that sat on a street corner looking out over a small park and beyond to the glittering lights of downtown.

Liz quickly crossed the dark street and entered the light as she came up to the jail.

Inside the heavy front doors was a small anteroom that had a pair of guards on either side of the smaller, inner door.

The guard on the right was a heavily armored dwarf with an intricately braided beard and a long, white cloth hanging from his belt like a loincloth that had a weird grid pattern running down its center.

The other guard was a tall female elf in silvery mail and armed with a round shield and short sword. She had a dark blue tabard on that had a silver, three-armed spiral over the chest.

Liz had learned a little bit about the policing structure of the elves and dwarves over the last few weeks. Turns out the dwarves didn't really have any kind of justice system. The local enforcers, called Judges, would deal with any lawbreakers immediately. There was no court or trial, just the Judge who acted as police, judge, jury, and (if the situated called for it) executioner. The local clan chief would be called to resolve major disputes, but overall the dwarves policed themselves.

The elves' judicial structure on the other hand was a bit more complicated… but not by much. Their version of police officers was called Arbiters and they reported to the local Magistrate. It sounded as though they were called upon only rarely, with the local lord stepping in only to hear the most serious crimes. Similar to the dwarves, the elves also preferred to govern and police themselves.

Neither guard made any move to stop her as she strode purposefully past them and through the inner door.

Inside there was another small room with several hallways stretching off in different directions with an enclosed desk positioned at the nexus of the hallways. Seated at the desk, behind a layer of glass, was a heavyset human police officer.

"Can I help you?" the officer asked when Liz walked up to the desk.

"Yes," Liz said. "An elf should have come in a little while ago carrying a sick man. Did you see them?"

"Ah, yes," the officer replied. "Large fellow with a bearskin cape, right?"

"That's correct," Liz said. "Where did they go?"

"The elf wanted the most secure cell we have so I sent them to 10," the officer said. "The fellow he was carrying didn't look too good and I said the hospital was a few blocks up, but he insisted on a cell." The officer looked worried. "Whatever that guy has isn't contagious, is it?"

"Only if he bites you," Liz replied.

The officer paled. "Maybe a cell was a good idea then. He looked a little feral."

"He was awake?" Liz asked with a bit of panic in her voice.

But the guard was waving his hands. "No, no. He wasn't really awake, more like drunk… or on some heavy drugs. Let me see…" The officer looked over at a computer next to him and pressed a few keys. "Yep, he is still only semi-conscious, and the big fellow and small girl are still watching him."

Liz breathed a sigh of relief. "Good. Now, how do I get there?"

The guard pointed down one of the halls. "I will open this door and you will find some elevators. Get in and press '10'. I will then approve the request and you will go up. Take the first right and the guard there will let you through. Your friends will be in the last cell on the right."

Liz followed the guard's instructions and she found Rabidad and Emily standing inside Jack's cell, where Jack himself was curled into a tight ball on the floor and moaning softly.

"How is he?" Liz asked nervously.

"Getting worse," Emily replied grimly.

"The medicine is wearing off and I believe it won't be long before he completes the Change," Rabidad added.

"Then I don't have much time." Liz bent down and put a hand on Jack's sweaty forehead. Golden light flowed out of her hand and seeped into Jack for several moments, but nothing happened.

Determined to heal him. Liz closed her eyes and delved deeper into Jack.

The writhing darkness surrounded her, like a captured storm, straining to get out. As she watched, tendrils of blackness snaked by and wound around every fiber of Jack's being. To Liz's horror, the blackness merged with Jack until the two were fused together.

Liz poured every ounce of healing power she could summon into the bonded material, but they remained completely fused.

Desperately Liz searched for a solution. At this rate, Jack would be completely consumed by the disease in a matter of minutes. Then she had an idea. If she couldn't break the darkness away, maybe she could at least stop more of it from reaching him.

She thought she heard a faint voice in the distance, but she couldn't make out what it was saying.

Liz turned her attention to the writhing tendrils of blackness that had yet to find purchase on Jack's soul. The golden light collided with the blackness and the inky stain retreated. Liz cheered as the darkness fled, but her cry of joy turned to one of frustration as the darkness rose up like a black tidal wave and drowned out her light.

The darkness roared around her and what little remained of Jack was completely consumed.

Liz desperately fought against the howling maelstrom until she was suddenly ripped away and violently snapped back into her own body.

"What the-" Liz started to say, but Rabidad had her by the shoulders and roughly pulled her out of the cell and slammed the door closed.

Liz was disoriented from being torn out of the Delve so suddenly and it took her a moment to comprehend what she was seeing.

Huge golden eyes glared down at Liz and the massive beast, trapped inside the cell, let out a bone-chilling howl.

****

The light from Ted's poleaxe made the shadows dance crazily as the small party made its way through the dark forest.

Rubadub and Robadoo led the way with the two kefali close behind and Mike and Ted bringing up the rear. Robadoo had returned shortly after taking Liz to the jail and they had set off immediately for the Druid's Grove.

They had only been walking for a short time when two shapes appeared out of the darkness. The two figures were pacing along a stretch of trees and angry mutterings could be heard as Mike and the others drew closer. When the figures saw the newcomers, they stopped their pacing and turned to face them.

As Ted's light touched them, Mike saw that one figure was covered in chainmail with an elaborate metal disk over his chest. A snarling dog-shaped helmet with full aventail completely covered the figure's face, but Mike knew his identity.

"Alpha Gadhar." Mike slightly inclined his head to the leader of Canis Madra.

"Mike Strazney." The alpha returned the greeting. "And Ted Koldun. We meet again."

Behind the armored Canis was a large Baribal wrapped in pipe-bone armor with many strange feathers and painted markings on his thick, black fur. He looked somewhat familiar, but Mike thought all of the bear-like creatures looked alike.

Before Mike could ask who the Baribal was, Gadhar rounded on the Druid brothers. "What sort of trick are you two playing at?" he growled angrily. "You tell us to meet you at this… grove place and show us how to get there, but then we cannot enter!"

"Nonsense," Rubadub replied calmly. "You can enter whenever you choose. You must simply cross the Panic Line."

"The what?" the alpha growled. "I see no line."

"Of course, you do not," Rubadub laughed. "But you felt it, did you not?" The antlered Druid grinned. "The feeling of eyes watching you, of something getting closer, of uncontrollable terror…"

Gadhar growled menacingly. "Do not play games with me, elf."

"I do not," Rubadub replied coolly. "That is the Panic Line, the protective barrier and only way to enter the Grove."

"How do we cross?" the Baribal beside the alpha asked softly.

"Strength of Will will see you across," Robadoo chirped.

Alpha Gadhar's eyes narrowed dangerously under his helm. "We have tried that, elf," the large Canis nearly spat the word. "Now, see us across to this silly meeting or we are leaving."

"You are no fun," Rubadub pouted, but his eyes twinkled mischievously. "Very well," the antlered Druid said grandly, and went behind a tree. He returned a moment later with four gnarly staves, wrapped in vines and each topped with a pinecone. He then proceeded to hand one to each of the gathered kefali.

Lorcan sniffed the pinecone suspiciously. "What is the purpose of this?" the huge Warg growled.

"To get you across the Panic Line, of course," Rubadub answered.

"What about us?" Ted asked and motioned to himself and Mike.

"Ahh," Rubadub grinned. "We shall see if you two are worthy to enter the sacred heart of the Druids."

"That doesn't quite seem fair," Ted complained. "Why do they get a free pass and we have to make it ourselves?"

Rubadub laughed. "Because they have an important message to relay to the Council, while you two are, as you humans say, just along for the ride."

"Let's get this over with," Gadhar growled, and took the pinecone stick and marched back into the tree line. The other kefali followed and the two Druids shared a mischievous grin before heading in after them.

Mike looked at Ted and his tall friend shrugged before heading off into the darkness and taking his light with him.

With a heavy sigh, Mike followed the others into the trees.

He hadn't gone very far before an eerie feeling came over him. Mike had the distinct feeling that someone was watching him. He glanced over his shoulder but didn't see anything.

Then, he noticed the unnatural silence that had befallen the forest. No birds sang, no leaves rustled, there was no sound except for Mike's breathing and the heartbeat pounding in his ears.

After two more steps, the hairs on the back of Mike's neck stood on end and a shiver of dread passed through him. There was something evil out there. He was sure of it.

Ted had frozen in place and was glancing around nervously as sweat beaded his brow. Mike could also see Lorcan and the other kefali ahead of them, each was snarling, with gritted teeth, as they struggled forward. It was as if they forcing their way through some unseen torment.

Mike had a good idea of what they were feeling. The watching eyes seemed to close in on him with each step and the feeling of irrational terror became unbearable.

There was *definitely* something evil watching him.

Fear seized Mike and the overwhelming desire to run away filled him. At that moment, he wanted nothing more than to be as far away from this horrible place as he could be.

With a supreme effort of will, Mike squashed the terror and brutally pushed it away. He knew it was the Druid's spell and that there was nothing out there. But even so, he struggled to keep his emotions in check.

Mike took one purposeful step in front of the other until he caught up to Ted, who was still paralyzed by fear. Mike grabbed Ted roughly by the arm and practically dragged him along with him.

After what seemed like an eternity, the unnatural terror faded as Mike and Ted finally made it across the invisible barrier.

Ted took a relieved breath and sagged against a tree. "That was... unpleasant."

Mike laughed and clapped his friend on the back. "You can say that again."

Ted smiled weakly. "That was… unpleasant."

Rubadub appeared from between the trees and grinned at them. "I am impressed," he said. "I can see now why the Great Mother chose you." The antlered Druid motioned for them to follow as he turned away. "Few non-Druids are able to cross the Panic Line without the aid of a thyrsus."

"A what?" Ted asked, as he and Mike followed the green-haired Druid through the trees.

"A thyrsus," Rubadub replied, as they met up with Robadoo and the four kefali. He motioned to the pinecone-topped staves the distraught kefali were desperately clutching like some kind of life raft. When Robadoo tried to take the thyrsus away from Lorcan, the huge Warg clutched the small-looking staff to his large chest and growled menacingly until the Druid backed off.

"They were a gift from Dionysus," the antlered Druid explained, as he swept up the others and led them all deeper into the forest. "But it was not until after the Kefali Invasion that they were used to cross the Panic Line, for before that there was no such line. Our Sacred Groves were only lightly warded from unfriendly eyes until the kefali came. With all of the Groves in Themiscyra under assault, it became necessary to better protect them. However, we had no such means and with all the mages busy battling the kefali sorcery, we were on our own. So, we turned to the gods for help and thankfully our prayers were answered."

"But it was not *our* gods who answered," Robadoo chirped.

"Indeed." Rubadub pushed through a thick tangle of branches. "It was actually one of the gods of the kefali."

"Lies," the alpha growled. "None of the Blessed Ma'at would abandon the Divine Order."

"Come now, Gadhar," Pipaluk chided. "This would not be the first god to leave the Ma'at, nor the last, I am sure."

"But who would abandon such a noble undertaking?" the alpha growled.

"Ahh, but I never said it was one of the Ma'at," Rubadub said.

"Then who was it?" Gadhar growled.

Rubadub laughed. "It was the Great God Pan."

"Pan!" Pipaluk and Gadhar choked together.

"Impossible," Pipaluk breathed. "Everyone knows that the Great Pan died in the last days of the war with the elves. With the demise of the Great Pan, it has fallen to Silenus and Faunus to watch over the forests."

"Then everyone knows wrong," Robadoo chirped, "for the Great Pan faked his death and remained behind when the Ma'at fled."

Pipaluk shook her head in denial. "Why would he do such a thing?" she asked softly.

"I do not know," Rubadub replied, "but the fact remains the Great Pan answered our prayers and supplied us with the knowledge of how to create the terror-barrier, that we call the Panic Line, to protect our groves."

Alpha Gadhar started to say something, but Rubadub cut him off and earned an angry glare from the large Canis. "Shh… Now is the time for silence," the antlered Druid said softly. "We are nearing the Heart of the Grove."

****

The beast that had been Jack thrashed and roared inside the cell and its rage was terrible to behold. There was a wild light in its golden eyes and no sign of the man he had once been behind the wolf-like features.

Liz was grateful that Rabidad had pulled her out of the cell when he did. She hadn't realized that the medicine had worn off and Jack had fully transformed while she was still trying to heal him.

With a deafening roar, the wolfman tore at the thick metal bars of the cell with tooth and claw, desperately trying to escape. When it became apparent that the effort was futile, the huge beast gripped the bars with its clawed hands and pulled.

A drunken dwarf was seated glumly in the next cell and laughed as the wolfman pried at the thick bars. "Good luck with that," the dwarf belched. "I been tryin' ter do that all night."

Almost as if the beast understood him, the wolfman gripped the bars and heaved with all its might.

Then, to everyone's horror, the thick steel bars started to bend!

"Loki's balls…" the dwarf gasped, suddenly sober.

Rabidad put a thick hand on Liz's shoulder and protectively pulled her further away from the cell. "Stay behind me," the large Druid rumbled grimly, never taking his eyes off of the wolfman.

Each bar bent several inches away from the other before the straining wolfman's freakish strength finally gave out. The beast howled and tried again, but whatever force had given it strength had fled and the wolfman couldn't make the bars budge.

The huge beast raged inside the cell, tearing large gouges in the walls and completely destroying the inside of the small prison. But even with all the ferocious rage, Liz couldn't help but feel only sadness. She had seen her friend be completely consumed by a virtual sea of darkness that she had been unable to stop, even though she was counted among the most powerful healers in the entire city.

Perhaps the others were right. Maybe the disease was incurable.

No. Liz refused to believe that.

Everything could be healed. She had to believe it.

The huge beast roared and battered the cell until its rage finally played out. The panting wolfman collapsed in a furry heap and curled into a protective ball in the furthest corner of the cell.

Emily looked up at the large Druid. "Now what happens?"

"Now we wait," Rabidad replied.

Golden eyes glared at Liz from inside the cell. "For what?" she asked.

The large Druid sat down on one of the chairs across the hall. "The sun."

"And what will that do?" Liz asked as she took a seat next to him while Emily nervously paced across the hall.

"With the sun will come the truth," Rabidad replied grimly. "Either your friend will change back into his human form and only become a hybrid during the full moon or he will not and will remain a mindless beast for the remainder of his life."

****

A ring of enormous stone pillars encircled a gigantic stone slab in the center of the moonlit clearing. High above, countless stars glittered like a sea of diamonds across the night sky, while numerous torches cast a fiery glow inside the monolithic structure.

Standing around the huge slab was the Allied Council of Pittsburgh.

Representing the humans was General Adams whose dark skin blended in with his pieces of black orcish armor. He was in quiet conversation with two of his military commanders.

The commanders were Major Sanders, who was slightly overweight and had a passion for using aircraft or drones for support whenever possible, and the grey-haired Colonel Wheeler, who had the unique ability to walk through solid objects. Four dour-looking Marines stood guard a few paces behind their commanders.

Nearby, Archmage Talsin's dark blue robes appeared almost black in the firelight. He stood at the head of elven representatives along with the petite Supreme Sorceress Braelynn, in her tight, white gown, and the Arch Battlemage Gwydion, who was resplendent in his polished oricalcum armor. Four heavily armed female Blade Dancers of the Korybantine Guard lounged lazily nearby.

At the furthest point away from the elves, but still inside the stone ring, was the dwarf King Varnir Anvilborn and his retinue.

The king's coppery beard was tied in an elaborate series of braids and he was encased in an exquisite suit of ornate armor that was covered in glowing runes of power and the legendary Axe of Perun was strapped to his broad back. The king was flanked by the red-bearded Master Cleric of Frigg, Fugal Brightrobe, who looked like anything but a cleric with the long scar running down his face, and the grey-bearded Rune Lord Eitri Starmantle, whose worn leather apron appeared dull next to the other finery around him.

Standing still as statues behind their king were four identical Huscarl Rune Knights, completely encased in their heavy rune armor. Their hands were folded over the hilts of their heavy war hammers and the runic heads rested easily at their steel-shod feet. Mike noticed that one hammer was far more elaborate than the others, but he didn't have time to consider it further.

The gathered dignitaries representing the three allied races gathered in around the stone table when a figure emerged silently out of the darkness. The figure was robed from head to toe in a dark green material that resembled mossy bark and carried a gnarled thyrsus. When the newcomer removed the heavy cowl, it revealed a dark-haired elf beneath.

"High Druid Belenos," Archmage Talsin said, once the hood had been pulled back. "I do hope you have a good reason for summoning us all out here in the middle of the night."

"Indeed, I do, Archmage," Belenos replied with a bow. "And I thank you all for coming on such short notice." He began, "As you all know, there are three hostile armies beyond this city. Two of them we knew the identity of. The first is the massive horde of orcs and their thralls that are led by a mighty warlord called Stormtusk to our east. They have taken over several villages and are using the captured human factories for some unknown reason."

"The second force is to our northwest and is comprised of kefali in the so-called Horned Legion of Isfet," Belenos said grimly. "We know their leader calls himself The Destroyer, but little else is known about him. They are searching for something and it is believed that once they find it, they will come here to destroy this bastion of civilization."

"But the third force has remained an unknown," the High Druid said, "until now." An excited buzz arose from the gathered leaders at the news. "That is the reason for this meeting," Belenos explained, and motioned with his free hand.

Out of the darkness two more figures emerged. One was tall and had dark green hair with small, deer-like antlers poking out and the other was hunched over and covered in a feathered cape.

"These are the Druids Rubadub and Robadoo," Belenos said introducing them, and the brothers nodded a brief greeting in turn. "This last moon turn they have been searching for the identity of the southern army that had so eluded our scouts."

Belenos moved aside to allow the other Druids to explain. But before they could begin, Archmage Talsin interrupted. "Pardon me," he said softly, "but I do believe there are a few more of you hiding back there." The Archmage smiled. "Why don't you all come out here and join us."

The Druid brothers turned to each other questioningly and Robadoo shrugged, so Rubadub waved the others forward.

Six shapes emerged out of the gloom.

Alpha Gadhar and Pipaluk appeared slowly and were followed by Lorcan and the other Baribal with Mike and Ted bringing up the rear.

"Kefali!" Arch Battlemage Gwydion cried in alarm as power crackled to life around him. "We are betrayed!"

Faster than thought, the four Korybantes sprang into motion with blades drawn. The Marines snapped to attention and trained their rifles on the newcomers as the elves charged in.

"STOP!" Mike bellowed, as he and Ted jumped in between the charging Korybantes and the kefali. Seeing two humans in their path, the elven Blade Dancers pulled up short and looked questioningly back to their leaders for direction.

"Well, that was unexpected," Braelynn murmured.

The dwarf Huscarls hadn't budged and their king remained seemingly unconcerned with the events unfolding around them.

"How could you let the Isfet in here?" Gwydion cried angrily.

"I do not believe they have," Talsin replied calmly. "If I am not mistaken, these kefali are Ma'at."

"Ma'at!" Gwydion nearly choked. "That is even worse! The Ma'at seek to conquer everything! Tell me that isn't so!"

"It is not," Pipaluk boldly responded. "It is true that many Ma'at wish to bring the Divine Order, but we are not so fanatical as they. Our only wish is to defeat the traitorous Isfet and return to Nibiru in peace."

"You see?" Talsin said with the hint of a grin playing on the edges of his lips. "These are Reformed Ma'at. Nothing at all to worry about."

"Reformed Ma'at my ears!" Gwydion spat. "They will stab us in the back the moment they get the chance."

"Perhaps," Talsin conceded, "but I still wish to hear what they have to say."

"This is folly, Talsin," Gwydion growled. "These beasts should not be allowed to live."

The Korybantes eyed the kefali behind the two humans and Mike was afraid they were going to ignore the Archmage and attack.

"I said nothing of letting them live," Talsin replied simply. "I merely wish to hear their explanation before any killing happens."

Gwydion looked about to order the guards to attack when the dwarf king suddenly spoke. "I also wish ter hear what these creatures have ter say," King Varnir rumbled. "It no be every day that a Son o' Fenrir appears before ye," he said, without taking his steely gaze off Lorcan.

"Fine," Gwydion snapped, and the Korybantes immediately backed off a step but kept their blades in hand.

The small Sorceress Supreme turned to the High Druid. "What is the meaning of this Bel?" she asked gently. "I know the Druids and kefali have somewhat of an unusual understanding, but this seems bold, even for you."

"My apologies, Lady," Belenos bowed. "I did not intend to startle anyone. I had planned to reveal the kefali later, after our news was delivered." He motioned to the dog-like kefali. "This is Alpha Gadhar, pack leader of the Canis Madra and behind him is Lorcan the Warg." Belenos introduced them. "And this is Pipaluk, Elder Shaman of the Hoonaw Tribe Baribal and behind her is War Chief Sikoba, also of the Hoonaw Tribe."

"A pleasure," Braelynn said curtly. "Best get to the point before any blood is shed."

"Wise words, my Lady," Rubadub replied respectfully. "As the High Druid said, my brothers and I had been sent to discover the identity of the mysterious army reported to the south. It took us a long time to locate their trail, but eventually we found them," the antlered Druid said proudly. "You see, they only moved at night and because of-"

"Get to the point Rubadub," Belenos interrupted.

"Yes, High Druid," Rubadub said, before turning back to the assembled Council. "We discovered, to our dismay, that the army to the south is in fact the Shadowed Ones."

Commotion erupted among the elves at the mention of the name and the Korybantes abandoned the kefali and surrounded their leaders protectively, as if expecting enemies to jump out at any moment.

The elven representatives all talked at once.

"It is as we feared," Braelynn breathed.

"That is impossible," Gwydion muttered, as the three talked amongst themselves.

The dwarf king cleared his throat loudly. "And just who be these Shadowed Ones?" King Varnir rumbled over the panicked elves.

The elven council members quieted down and the diminutive sorceress answered. "The Shadowed Ones were once elves," Braelynn stated grimly, "but they have abandoned the Light and now walk the Shadowed Path."

For the first time, General Adams spoke. "And what do you mean by they were 'once elves'?"

Braelynn looked at the two Archmages and Talsin nodded.

With a deep breath, the Supreme Sorceress began. "At the dawn of elven civilization, we were all unified in the worship of the Light. In those days, each city-state battled their neighbors for dominance and each sought to carve out an empire across the seas. But none could gain more than a few islands before they were overthrown. That is, until King Radamanthas."

"By all accounts, he was a very charismatic ruler and a marvelous speaker. So much so, in fact, that Radamanthas actually convinced several cities that he had the power to unify the elven people simply by speaking to them. Upon hearing him speak, many cities swore their allegiance to him immediately."

"But while many city-states fell to King Radamanthas simply by the power of his words, some did not. And those that did not were subject to the vast armies of Radamanthas' closest friend and ally, King Taranis. Now, where Radamanthas was a politician, Taranis was a brutal warlord and together they quickly created one of the largest empires on Gaea.

"Seeing the combined might of Radamanthas and Taranis, two more of the most powerful rulers of the age also joined them. Queen Scatha and the Harvest King, Laomedon, added their cities to the growing empire, to create the largest, unified kingdom that we have ever known."

"However, news of horrible atrocities committed by the Four began to reach the other rulers and soon the true nature of the Four became apparent. It is unknown how or why, but sometime during their conquests they abandoned the Light and succumbed to the Shadow."

"Many did not believe that such mighty rulers could be what some were accusing them of and the doubt may have gone on for much longer if it wasn't for the Battle of Nysa Valley, where their corruption was revealed."

"During the battle, Queen Scatha launched an assault on the Nysa defenders when she was suddenly struck down. But her sorcerous powers brought her back from the lands of the dead and she arose as the even more powerful Lich Queen. With her 'newfound' necromantic powers fully revealed, she brought all of the dead back to serve in her undead armies. It is said that by using powerful blood magic she created the first vampires to act as her generals for all eternity."

"With the true nature of the Four revealed at last, the War of the Shadow began in earnest with the fate of all Gaea hanging in the balance. But even with the unification of the remaining city-states, the might of the Four could not be overcome. The war dragged on for centuries with the

Four slowly consuming everything that stood in their path and giving them the title of the Harbingers, for they brought death and destruction wherever they went, and none could stand against them."

"With nearly all the world fallen to the Shadow, the remaining free cities were desperate to find a way to stop the Harbingers before the elven race was utterly consumed. All hope seemed lost as the undead hordes pounded on the grand walls of Vlaanderen until the mighty Archdruid Dagda consulted with the Oracle and learned that the Harbingers could not be defeated, but they could be trapped."

"And so, the Dagda joined with the Grand Archmage Janus Urelius and the most powerful mages, Druids, and clerics left of the age and together they cast the Great Binding that locked the Harbingers behind the Seven Seals forever."

"A tale worthy o' the Loremasters," King Varnir rumbled, "but what does that have ter do with anythin'? Are ye saying that these Harbingers have returned?"

"Thankfully, no," Belenos answered, "but that is not the end of the tale. You see, with the Harbingers trapped, we needed to protect the Seals so that they could never return. It fell to the Druids to be the Watchers of the Seals." Belenos touched the silver torc around his neck reverently. "Every Druid wears a torc that allows them to feel any nearby Seal, with the Dagda's master torc granting him alone the knowledge of each Seal's exact location."

"Get ter the point, elf," King Varnir rumbled.

Belenos scowled but continued. "I should not reveal this, however, the safety of this world and every other hangs in the balance." The High Druid seemed at war with himself as he struggled to find the words. "The Shadowed Ones are making their way to this city because one of the Seven Seals is here and they wish to destroy it and free the Harbingers."

"What?" General Adams asked as shouts of surprise and disbelief filled the air. "How is it here? And how could they even know where it is?"

"I do not know," Belenos admitted once the commotion finally settled down. "All we know right now is that the Shadowed Ones make for the Steel City for the sole purpose of destroying the Seal and they have allied themselves with the Horned Legion and orc horde in order to achieve their goal."

"Damn," General Adams cursed. "There goes our hope that the three armies would fight each other before turning to us."

"We can no let the Seal be destroyed," Eitri Starmantle spoke for the first time. "If these Harbingers be as dangerous as ye say, protectin' the Seal must be our primary concern."

"So, where is it?" Colonel Wheeler pointedly asked the High Druid.

Belenos shrugged. "I know not," he replied. "As I said, only the Dagda knows the location of every Seal. We can only feel the presence when one is nearby."

"Well, ye best get ter feelin'," King Varnir rumbled, "and find that Seal afore our enemies do."

"I agree," General Adams stated. "We must secure this object before it falls into the wrong hands."

"And what happens once we find it?" Ted asked.

"Then the Druids will guard it with their lives," Rubadub said proudly.

"Yes, yes," Robadoo chirped in agreement.

"If this Seal is as important as you say," General Adams said, "then we should all have a hand in protecting it."

"I second that," King Varnir rumbled.

Belenos looked unhappy, but eventually nodded. "Very well. Once the Seal is recovered it will be protected by us all *until* this crisis has passed."

"It is decided then," Gwydion said. "But what do we do with *them*?" He motioned to the four kefali that had remained silent.

"We have news of our own," Alpha Gadhar growled. "And you would do well to listen."

"My apologies," Gwydion bowed mockingly. "Please enlighten us."

Ignoring the comment, Pipaluk stepped forward. "As you are all aware, The Destroyer has been searching for something these last weeks." The old shaman looked around the council meaningfully. "I am here to warn you that he has found it."

"Found what?" Gwydion snapped.

"Powerful allies," Pipaluk replied gravely. "The Destroyer has enlisted the aid of wendigo and other monsters of this world."

"Wendigo.... as in the evil cannibal spirit?" Ted asked.

"The same," Pipaluk confirmed. "We do not know how he convinced the wendigo spirits to join him. Our best guess is that the wendigo have taken human hosts and have no cannibalistic urges toward the kefali, allowing The Destroyer to bind it with the promise of all the humans here in your city."

"And how do we kill it?" General Adams asked, straight to the point.

"Destroying its physical body should suffice," Pipaluk answered.

"So, nothing special is required?" Ted asked. "No silver bullets, holy water, or any of that sort of stuff?"

"How should I know?" Pipaluk grumbled. "I've never even seen a wendigo before."

The elves scowled at the old shaman as if it was her fault she didn't know exactly how to kill the evil spirit and the looks on their faces made the dwarf king laugh.

"Bwahahaha!" King Varnir chuckled. "I like this one. She speaks the truth." His laughter subsided and he grew suddenly very serious. "I have a feelin' that givin' us a warnin' about a beast that ye don't know how ter kill was only part o' yer reason fer bein' here this night. So, tell me bear-creature; what is it that ye want from us?"

Pipaluk was taken aback by the sudden turn of events and looked to the alpha for help, but the dwarf king growled. "Do no look at the spawn o' Fenrir fer answers. Speak yer mind and do so quickly."

The old shaman met King Varnir's eyes and held them. "We wish to join you in the coming battle against The Destroyer and his allies."

Gwydion started to speak, but King Varnir rolled over him. "And what will that assistance be costin' us I wonder?" the dwarf king rumbled, never taking his steely gaze off the old shaman. But Pipaluk didn't back down.

"We seek a safe place for our people inside your walls until such a time that we can return home," Pipaluk answered honestly.

"Ahh," King Varnir nodded sagely, "there she be."

"Impossible!" Gwydion spat. "Kefali cannot be trusted. No elf would ever let such a creature into their city."

"Well," General Adams said, "it is a good thing that this isn't an elven city."

The Arch Battlemage's mouth dropped open as he stared at the commander of the human armies in disbelief. "You can't seriously be considering their offer!" he gasped. "They are *kefali*." He said the last word like a curse.

The general ignored Gwydion and instead looked to Mike and Ted. "Are these the same kefali that assisted in the rescue of King Varnir's son?"

"Yes, sir," Mike replied.

"And do you trust them?" General Adams pressed.

"With my life, sir," Mike answered truthfully.

General Adams nodded and turned to Belenos. "And what do the Druids think?"

"I would not have brought them here if I did not see the Light in them," Belenos replied.

"And what of the dwarves?" General Adams addressed the king.

"I owe a debt ter these beasts fer saving me son," King Varnir rumbled. "If they wish ter die beside us in the comin' battle, then I welcome them."

"Talsin?" General Adams looked to the Archmage expectantly.

The Archmage slowly looked around at the gathering. "It seems as though we are outnumbered." Talsin looked to Gwydion who forcefully shook his head "no" and then to Braelynn who just shrugged her small shoulders.

After a long pause, the Archmage tilted his head back and stared up at the night sky. "Very well," Talsin finally breathed.

Gwydion slammed his hands on the stone table. "This is foolishness!" he bellowed, before turning on his heel and storming out of the ring of standing stones.

There was an uncomfortable silence after Gwydion left.

"Should I go after him?" Braelynn asked softly.

"No," Talsin responded. "He needs time to accept our decision." The Archmage looked to where Gwydion had vanished into the darkness. "He has hated the kefali a long time. It will not be easy for him to accept their help... but he will see the truth eventually."

"It be decided then," King Varnir intoned.

"Indeed," said the General. "If there is nothing else, preparations need to be made for our new allies," General Adams said, as he looked at those gathered around the table.

"Actually," Ted suddenly said, "we need to talk about the city's wards."

CHAPTER 7

The next day arrived cool and overcast.

As the light slowly increased, it found Mike seated at one of the jail's waiting room chairs with Liz sitting next to him, sleeping on his shoulder. Emily was sprawled out on a long bench nearby with Rabidad's bearskin cloak draped over her. The large Druid himself was nowhere to be found, having returned to the Grove after Mike arrived at the jail late that night.

The drunk dwarf in the next cell had been taken away a short time later when he wouldn't stop complaining about the "wet dog smell" and the huge werewolf's constant growling at him.

As the faint light of dawn filled the room, Liz's eyes slowly opened.

She didn't move right away, enjoying Mike's closeness. His thick shoulder wasn't the most comfortable pillow ever, but he radiated heat and in the cool jail it was a very pleasant position.

Liz closed her eyes again and listened to the silence around them.

Silence?

Liz's eyes popped open again.

Why was there silence? When she had fallen asleep it had been to the moaning and growling of a very unhappy werewolf that constantly scratched and bit at the walls and bars of its cell.

Liz suddenly sat up and looked to Jack's cell. Hope filled her at the prospect that Jack had returned to his human form with the sunrise and would only become a werewolf during the nights of a full moon.

The jail's lights had been turned off late that night and had yet to be turned back on, casting all of the cells in shadow.

Liz peered into the darkness of Jack's cell but couldn't see anything beyond the hint of a dark shape huddled in the back corner.

Eager to find out how he was, Liz started to stand up until Mike placed a restraining hand on her leg. The unexpected contact caught her by surprise and a startled squeak escaped her lips.

"Don't do that," Liz whispered angrily, and punched Mike in the arm.

"Shhh," Mike held a finger to his lips and nodded toward Jack's cell. When Liz turned, she saw two golden eyes glaring at her from the darkness.

A low growl echoed down the hall and to Liz's dismay she saw long, white fangs snarl from behind the bars. All she could make out were the baleful golden eyes and white fangs from the shadows, but that was enough to dash her hopes that Jack would be human again.

"Oh, no…" Liz moaned.

The werewolf suddenly howled.

Emily jerked awake, falling off the bench and landing with a thump on the cold stone floor. Cursing, she eventually untangled herself from the bearskin cloak and stood up.

Once freed, Emily adjusted her head scarf before she looked back at the cell and Liz could see the sadness in her eyes when Emily realized that Jack was still a monster.

"So much for him coming back in the daylight…" Emily said gloomily. "Now what do we do?"

"We find a cure," Liz replied without hesitation. "There must be something we can do for him."

"But you heard the elves," Emily argued. "There is no cure."

"I refuse to believe that," Liz retorted. "The elves aren't the only ones around here that could have a cure and just because they haven't found one yet doesn't mean one doesn't exist."

Mike and Emily shared a look that said neither of them believed there was much hope for finding anything that could help.

"And just how exactly do you plan on finding this cure?" Emily asked. "It's not like there is a book called 'werewolf cure' just sitting around and the Internet still isn't working so we can't browse for an answer."

"Actually," Mike said, "since you have been gone, we have been getting some spotty Internet access. It's not much, mind you," he added, "but it is working sometimes."

"Really?" Emily perked up a bit and carefully adjusted her headscarf. "What else have I missed?"

"Well…" Mike thought a moment. "Radio is working, and phone calls will sometimes go through, but it is spotty like the Internet. The reports we have been getting back haven't been good though."

"It looks like the same thing that is happening around here is happening all over the world," Mike said. "I guess most of Europe is holding out pretty well considering, with most of the people moving into all the old castles and fortresses over there. But other places haven't been so lucky."

"Many of the reports are conflicting though," Liz added. "We will hear that a city is destroyed one day and that it is still there the next. So, we can't be sure how much information we get is even accurate."

"Like New York City," Mike nodded. "One day, we received a warning over the radio to avoid the city because it had been completely overrun by swarms of ratmen. But the next day, we received another message that said NYC was perfectly safe and any survivors could find a safe haven there."

"But not all of them have been conflicting," Liz added.

"No," Mike agreed. "Everyone seems to agree that DC is gone."

"Gone?" Emily asked. "How can it be gone?"

"That story varies," Mike replied.

"Yeah," Liz said, "we have heard everything from all the citizens going crazy and killing each other to it being taken over by snake people. Nobody can agree on how, but they all agree that DC is overrun."

Emily looked aghast. "Then who is running the country?"

"There is no country," Mike said grimly. "It's everyone for themselves."

"But it's not all bad news," Liz said. "There have been whole towns that didn't even know anything strange was happening."

"Really?" Emily laughed. "How could they not know?"

Liz shrugged helplessly. "I guess there were no monsters or anything so life went on as it always has. The phones and Internet were out of course, but nobody thought much of it until it lasted for weeks. And it wasn't until shipments stopped coming in that they realized something was seriously wrong."

"That's crazy," Emily laughed. "You can't tell me that somebody didn't go out and see what was going on."

"Oh, people did," Liz replied, "but none of them came back, so everyone just adjusted and kept doing what they had been."

Emily shook her head in disbelief. "I guess anything is possible."

Mike was staring into the cell at the dark mass that was their friend when he said. "So, where have you been these last weeks?"

"Like I said," Emily replied defensively, "I was with the Druids looking for that mysterious southern army that we discovered was actually bad elves."

"Yes, we heard that," Mike rounded on her, "but it wouldn't take weeks to find an army that close and get back. Not even one that only moves at night."

"You would be surprised," Emily muttered. "But you are right," she breathed nervously. "That wasn't the only thing that happened while we were out there."

Emily gently touched her headscarf and a strange look crossed her face.

Curiosity piqued, Liz asked. "What happened?"

There was a long pause and Liz was afraid Emily wasn't going to answer, but then she took a deep breath and said. "We were following the army's trail when we came across a-"

Whatever she was going to say was interrupted when a bell chimed. At the far end of the hall, the elevator doors suddenly slid open and four burly dwarves stepped out.

They were heavily armed and encased in silvery plate armor as they strode down the hall. Each wore a white monastic scapular with a bloody handprint emblazoned on the chest. Their faces were hidden behind full helms that left only their eyes visible and as they got closer, Liz could see their eyes narrow dangerously when they saw the beast's furry form huddled in the corner of the cell.

The werewolf sniffed the air and must have caught the dwarves' scent because he suddenly howled and began thrashing wildly inside the cage.

Surprisingly, the jail guards actually let the dwarves through the steel doors and into the hallway. The howl spurred the dwarves onward and they drew their weapons as they stormed down the hall.

Seeing the naked steel, Mike got to his feet and planted himself between Jack's cell and the oncoming dwarves. Liz and Emily quickly flanked Mike and blocked the hallway just as the dwarves reached them.

"Can we help you?" Liz asked as nicely as she could. She had a bad feeling about the sudden appearance of the dwarves and their drawn weapons didn't bode well for their intentions.

"We received word that a human be cursed by Fenrir," one of the dwarves rumbled, and his helmeted head turned and regarded the raging wolfman in the cell. "It seems the rumors be true."

"He is not cursed," Liz retorted. "He only has a disease and now that he is safely locked away we will find a cure for him."

The four dwarves laughed.

"There be only one cure for Fenrir's Curse." The dwarf lifted his large axe meaningfully. "And we o' the Hands o' Tyr be here ter bestow it."

"That won't be necessary," Emily replied. "He is in good hands here."

The lead dwarf snorted. "Ye think that cage will hold him fer long?" The dwarf shook his head sadly. "Ye know nothing about the Curse. Every night he will grow stronger until he breaks free o' that cage an' rips everyone around him apart. And those unlucky enough ter survive being bitten will be cursed as well."

"Do ye wish ter damn the whole city because ye're too weak ter do what be necessary?" the dwarf snarled.

"No one is going to be damned," Mike replied coolly, as he drew his ancient mace and unslung his shield. He never seemed to be without them these days. "But neither is anyone getting your so-called 'cure'."

The dwarves bristled and readied their weapons. "Now, no be doin' anything foolish, humans," the leader rumbled dangerously. "We know he was yer friend, but he can no be helped. He be a danger ter everyone."

"He isn't a danger," Emily shot back. "Not while he is caged like some animal."

"But he *be* an animal," the dwarf rumbled stubbornly. "Let us put him out o' his misery."

"I'm afraid that's not going to happen," Mike said, and the four dwarves grumbled angrily, but Mike stood his ground. "He is safe inside that cell and if he somehow manages to break free, then, and only then, will he be dealt with. So long as he is inside that cell, you will not touch him."

"Foolish humans," the dwarf spat. "He will escape and then it will be too late. Now stand aside!" the dwarf demanded, as the four dwarves took a step forward.

Mike eyes suddenly blazed with blue fire, and Liz drew both her pistols and trained them on the approaching dwarves. Emily raised her scepter and the eyes of the skull pulsed with an eerie green light.

Unperturbed, the dwarves came on.

To Liz's surprise, a similar blue fire erupted in the eyes of one of the dwarves while the hammerhead of another was suddenly wreathed in lightning. The leader's axe burst into flame as a gyrating rune appeared in the air before the fourth dwarf.

The beast inside the cage howled and went berserk at the sight of the fire.

The jail guards watched on in amazement at the events unfolding behind them, afraid to interfere with such powerful warriors.

"Do not do this, dwarf," Mike's voice echoed with power. "We do not wish to harm you."

"Harm us?" the dwarves laughed. "We no be fearing any human rabble."

"We are not rabble!" Liz trained one pistol on the lead dwarf with his flaming axe and the other on the rune-wielding dwarf. Emily leveled her glowing scepter at the dwarf with the crackling war hammer while Mike faced off against the dwarven Guardian.

Mike raised his ancient mace and runes burst to life along its flanged head. Tendrils of power gathered around the glowing weapon and began to swirl around the head.

The dwarves' advance suddenly faltered as they noticed the mace for the first time. "Rikr Foerah," one of the dwarves breathed. "Ye be Michael Strazney," the lead dwarf said in something close to awe, as he looked from Mike to Liz. "And ye must be the great healer Elizabeth McAllister." The dwarf turned his gaze to Emily. "And ye can be none other than the witch, Emilia Strega." The four dwarves suddenly seemed less eager to challenge the three humans before them.

"I'm a *Druid*," Emily replied hotly, "and it seems you know us, but we don't know you."

"Aye, all know the mighty Heroes o' Awesome." The flames on the dwarf's axe spluttered and went out. The other dwarves followed his lead and released their powers as well. "They saved Prince Brokkr from the filthy kefali and defeated one o' the wicked nephilim."

The power clinging to Mike's mace faded away and the fire in his eyes went out. "And who are you?" he demanded.

The leader removed his helmet and revealed himself as a young dwarf with a spiked mohawk and a curly brown beard. "I be Raenods, Captain o' the Hands o' Tyr and these be me Hands." The other dwarves removed their helmets as their captain introduced them.

Ingemar Fiddlesticks clutched the war hammer and was the largest of the four dwarves. He had an unruly mop of black hair and a beard that nearly obscured his entire face.

Kjell the Scorched was a Rune Priest and obviously got his name from the horrible burn marks that covered the left side of his face. What little beard he had left was bright red, making it look like his face was still on fire.

To Liz's great surprise, the last dwarf to be introduced was the Guardian who actually turned out to be a female.

Astrid of the Broken Spine had long, blonde hair that was tied up under her chin and fell across her chest in a tangle of knots. With her helmet on, her hair looked like a beard and in her heavy plate armor she could easily be mistaken for a male.

"A pleasure to meet you all," Liz said, once the introductions were finished. "But we still aren't letting you kill Jack."

Captain Raenods stared at the raging beast in surprise. "That be Jack Treno?"

"Yes," Mike replied. "He was bit by a kefali during the raid that rescued Prince Brokkr and he contracted what the elves call WereDisease."

"I be sorry," Raenods said. "The loss o' such a mighty warrior will be keenly felt."

"He is *not* lost," Emily hissed angrily, and the scepter's skull eyes began to pulse with an inner light. "Say it again and I'll kill you where you stand."

Raenods held up his hands in a placating gesture. "I mean no offense, lass. But the fact remains, yer friend Jack has been consumed by the Curse. There be no comin' back from that."

"We'll see about that," Liz replied sharply. Everyone's insistence that WereDisease was incurable was really getting on her nerves and she was more determined than ever to save Jack. She just had to keep him alive long enough to find a cure. Which wasn't going to be easy since Liz was sure that these four dwarves were not the only ones that would want to see Jack's head on a plate.

Liz could see the captain was about to argue, but she cut him off. "Look, just give us a few weeks to look for a cure," she pleaded. "Just because there isn't one on your world doesn't mean there isn't one here."

Captain Raenods stroked his beard in thought. "Aye, lass. Ye may be right," he finally answered. "All o' Clan Anvilborn owes ye a debt fer savin' ar' prince, so we will give ye until the next moon ter find a cure," he rumbled to Liz's vast relief. "But be makin' no mistake, we will return and give yer friend Tyr's Peace if he be still a beast."

"Thank you," Liz breathed. "That will be plenty of time."

The dwarf captain nodded curtly. "Very well," Raenods rumbled, as he abruptly turned away with the other three dwarves on his heels. "One o' the Hands will remain beside this lifting device ter ensure he does no escape." The dwarf captain said as he stomped away.

He turned back one last time. "The next moon," he rumbled, before entering the elevator with Astrid and Kjell beside him. Ingemar and his massive hammer could just barely be seen through the metal bars as he took up a position beside the elevator as the doors slid closed.

"Do you really think you can find a cure in a few weeks?" Emily whispered, so that neither the dwarf at the end of the hall or the guards could hear.

"I hope so," Liz whispered back grimly. "But if we don't, we are going to need to get Jack out of here before they come back."

Emily scowled and looked at the dwarf guarding the elevator. "That's not going to be easy with that hairy ape down there."

"I will take care of the guard if that time comes," Mike said softly. "We will need a place to move him to."

"Yes," Liz agreed. "You should go look for one while I go search for a cure."

Emily planted her hands on her hips. "And what about me?"

"You stay here and make sure those dwarves don't come back while we're gone," Liz replied.

"Oh, great," Emily moaned. "I'm the babysitter."

PART II

CHAPTER 8

The days ticked by much faster than Liz could have thought possible.

Other than taking her rounds with the healers and practicing her blade work, Liz spent nearly every waking hour pouring through old books from the Cathedral of Learning's vast library and asking any elf or dwarf that she could get to talk to her about a cure.

She had even approached some of those few, brave kefali that had dared to enter the city after the Council's decision to grant them a safe haven. The majority of elves were not happy about it, but so far there hadn't been any serious incidents.

But those Baribal Kaakuush and Canis Madra that had actually spoken to her were very unhelpful. Pipaluk maintained that there was no cure and her medicine wouldn't work again.

So, she had turned to the root of the problem.

Lorcan.

Liz had confronted the huge Warg when she had finally located him in the Grove. He revealed that he hadn't even considered the possibility that Jack could have gotten WereDisease from him. Apparently, the disease was so rare among the kefali that they didn't even have a name for it. It had actually been the elves that named it WereDisease after the first elf that had been infected.

The dwarves in particular were very closed mouthed about "Fenrir's Curse" and Liz could get almost nothing from them except that those with the Curse were killed immediately.

During her investigation, she did learn that the Hands of Tyr were a militaristic branch of the Church of Tyr and they believed it was their duty to purge the taint of Fenrir from the world. Besides that, she learned nothing even remotely helpful.

The elves were little better. Every elf she talked to maintained that there was no cure for WereDisease and that a quick death was the best option.

One senior healer said there was a rumor that WereDisease could be healed if caught within the first few days of being infected, but even then, it would take a powerful True Healer to even hope to have any success.

That news gave Liz the spark of hope she needed to continue her desperate search. If it could be healed early, then that meant it wasn't incurable after all. Granted, it was only a rumor of a legend since many of the elves thought WereDisease had gone extinct since shortly after the Kefali Invasion thousands of years ago, but it was hope.

Liz looked at the clock on the wall and then closed the old book on the table in front of her. She was seated in a small study room off of the main library inside Cathy with stacks of books heaped around her.

Liz rubbed her eyes wearily. Another promising book that turned out to be little more than a fairytale. Most of the countless books she had gone through had been completely unhelpful, focusing on the ways to identify and kill werewolves.

Even more frustrating than not finding a cure, was the conflicting accounts on how to deal with a werewolf.

One book told her that garlic was a werewolf repellant, while another book said that garlic didn't affect werewolves at all and was for vampires only. Yet another old tome said that werewolves were immune to physical injury and only fire could harm them. But the next book she read stated that fire had no different effect on werewolves and that it would take an enchanted or blessed item to do the werewolf any harm. But there was one thing that all accounts seemed to agree on.

Silver.

It seemed that the one common weakness of werewolves was silver. Whether it was a silver stake, silver cross, silver dagger, or silver arrow, it was the silver that harmed the werewolf. It seemed as though the silver was poisonous to werewolves and it was the only universally accepted method of killing one.

Killing one, however, was not what Liz wanted to do.

She didn't want to use the silver as a weapon, but it did give her an idea. If something about the disease couldn't survive being in contact with silver then maybe she could refine some silver into a cure. It was a narrow hope, but the only thing she had.

Liz stood up and gathered her things.

Further investigation would have to wait. She was due for a training session with the Battle Priests for another round of war healing.

The training session took place at one of the general training areas within the Cathedral grounds.

Every training area was in use, both inside the Cathedral of Learning and outside as the residents of Pittsburgh prepared for war.

Word had reached them the day before that The Destroyer and his Horned Legion were finally on the march and headed for the city. It was estimated that it would take at least a few days for the massive Isfet army to traverse the hilly landscape around the city.

The mysterious shadow elves were still somewhere to the south, but nobody could say for sure where they were or how soon they would get here. It was assumed they would time their arrival to coincide with that of the Isfet legion.

The nearest and most immediate threat was the vast orc horde, but for some unknown reason they seemed content to hold the towns and factories that they had already taken.

Liz's thoughts were interrupted when a staff slammed painfully into her ribs.

"Concentrate," Ipheto chided, as she stepped back and twirled her staff easily.

Ipheto was a pretty blonde elf and a High Priestess of Demeter. Her pale blue robes swayed softly as Ipheto circled Liz. Despite her gentle appearance, Liz had discovered that this priestess was an expert with a staff.

"I know you worry for your friend," Ipheto said, "but in battle, all of your friends will be in danger. You cannot let it distract you." As she said this, Ipheto drove in, her staff becoming a whirling blur.

Liz met the charge and blocked the first three strikes with her own staff. But this was not a martial contest. The real training was about to begin.

Arrayed around the two combatants were seven dwarves. Each held a long dagger as they watched the contests. Suddenly, one of the dwarves drove their dagger into their own arm. Blood fountained as the dagger was jerked back out.

Liz said a quick prayer without slowing the duel and the wounded dwarf healed up without a trace. As Ipheto struck again in a whirlwind attack, two other dwarves jammed daggers into their arms. Somehow, Liz battled back the furious assault and still managed to heal the two dwarves.

"Very good," Ipheto said, "but you will need to do better than that." She launched a flurry simultaneously as four dwarves stabbed themselves.

Liz's staff met Ipheto's at every turn and a soft, golden light descended on each of the wounded dwarves.

No sooner had the wounds healed than the other dwarves began stabbing themselves. As Liz desperately fought off the darting staff, she healed each wound as it appeared, but there was no end. As soon as one was healed, they stabbed themselves again.

All seven dwarves were bleeding freely as Liz battled the elf priestess and called down the healing golden light over and over again.

Liz focused more on the injured and healed several of them at the same time, but took a stinging hit to her thigh for the trouble. Growling angrily, Liz threw herself into the battle with righteous determination. She wasn't about to let this challenge get the better of her.

Strike and heal, strike and heal; the process repeated for what seemed like an eternity, but Liz never got any closer to healing all the dwarves while keeping Ipheto at bay.

Her clothes were soaked through and sweat was running into her eyes making it hard to see. Her arms burned with fatigue and she knew she was slowing down. Ipheto's attacks kept getting closer as Liz battled and healed with all her remaining strength.

Frustration mounted as Liz realized she couldn't heal the last ones before the first stabbed themselves again. It was a never-ending cycle that she was powerless to stop.

The blurring staff darted in and grazed Liz's temple, knocking her back and drawing a bright line of blood.

"Yield," Ipheto breathed heavily. Liz was glad to see the priestess was breathing nearly as hard as she was. "You cannot heal them all. You are not strong enough."

"We'll see about that," Liz growled, and threw herself at the elf.

A resounding crack split the air as the two staves connected over and over again. If Liz couldn't heal them all, at least she was going to win this fight.

With the words of a prayer on her lips, Liz suddenly drove in with her staff. Ipheto saw the strike coming and moved to block it. But the strike was a feint, something she had picked up from her duels with Mike. Instead of following through with the staff, Liz ducked down and swept her leg around and knocked Ipheto's feet out from under her.

The High Priestess landed with a surprised thud on her rump as Liz finished her prayer. A brilliant golden light filled the air and all seven dwarves were healed at once.

"Impressive," Ipheto said from her seated position. "It seems you have proven me wrong yet again."

Liz smiled and helped pull the priestess to her feet. "I'm just full of surprises."

"Indeed," a deep voice rumbled. One of the surrounding dwarves stepped forward and Liz was surprised to discover Fugal Brightrobe. The Master Cleric of Frigg was an exceptionally short dwarf with a long scar running down one cheek. "Such a feat should take many years ta master," Fugal rumbled, "but ye done it in less n' one." The dwarf shook his head in wonder. "If I hadn't seen it with me own eyes I would no believe it."

"These humans do pick up things remarkably quickly," Ipheto agreed.

Fugal eyed Liz thoughtfully. "Ye sure ye won't join the Church o' Frigg?" the dwarf asked. "Ye would be most welcome inter our order."

"No, thanks," Liz answered with a smile. She had given the same answer to the persistent cleric for what must have been the hundredth time. "You know I serve another."

"Aye." Fugal hung his head in defeat. "The Creator be lucky ter have ye. But should ye change yer mind, Frigg would welcome ye with open arms."

"I'll keep that in mind," Liz promised with a grin.

With the training session completed and a motion from Fugal, the gathered dwarves sheathed their daggers and began to disperse.

"Your power grows daily," Ipheto stated. "You should consider Master Brightrobe's words. Joining an order would be beneficial to your continued development." The High Priestess looked meaningfully at her. "Demeter could use a follower such as you."

Liz smiled ruefully. This was a common argument. Both the elves and dwarves found it odd that the majority of humanity worshiped the Supreme Being that they simply called the Creator. They couldn't understand why humans would put such devotion into a being that was so far above everything that the prayers of one, pathetic, mortal soul would be inconsequential. They maintained that the Creator had the whole of the multiverse to maintain and could not be bothered with such trivial requests and meaningless adoration that would ultimately go unnoticed.

Liz couldn't understand how the elves and dwarves could acknowledge the existence of a supreme Creator yet worship these lesser "gods". Didn't they know that God loved all of his creations, no matter how small? It was a debate she didn't feel like having right now; she had more important things to do, like helping Jack.

"I appreciate the offers," Liz said, "and I will think on them. But right now, I need to get back to finding a cure."

"Ye be wasting yer time," Fugal rumbled. "There be no cure fer the Curse except fer the axe."

"Master Brightrobe speaks true," Ipheto said. "There is no cure for WereDisease."

"Maybe on your worlds," Liz replied stubbornly. She was getting tired of people telling her there was no hope and no cure. "But we are on Earth. And there may be something here that you both don't have."

"It is possible," Ipheto mused thoughtfully, "but highly improbable."

Liz smiled. "So, your telling me there's a chance."

"I wouldn't -" Ipheto began, but Liz cut her off.

"Great!" Liz beamed. "That's all I needed to hear."

****

Emily took a deep breath as she looked out through the trees. It was good to be out of the confining jail and back in the woods again. The days had dragged by as she spent most of her time watching Jack rage inside his cage. She would talk to him and feed him, but she never got any response besides threatening growls and snarls. Although, yesterday Emily could have sworn she saw a brief hint of recognition in his feral gaze when she had come back from lunch. It could have just been her imagination though.

Her ability to understand animals and "hear" their thoughts allowed Emily a glimpse into Jack's shattered mind. Jack wasn't really an animal, but he was close enough that she could sometimes hear pieces of words. The whispers she got were mostly just incoherent babbling and bloodthirsty rage.

There wasn't anything she could do for him now, so she forced him from her mind. The Druids had given her a mission and she was going to see it completed.

She could hear the song of birds and the rustling of a squirrel as he bound through the leaves. Light filtered down through the colorful leaves as Emily heard what she had been listening for: the faint sound of singing.

"I've got something," Emily said, and a tall elf stepped out of the brush nearby.

Cora was a Priestess of Artemis, but they called themselves huntresses and she didn't look at all like your normal elven priestess.

Cora was clad in a soft, leather vest and skirt with tall, leather boots. She had dark, nut-brown skin and black hair pulled back in a long ponytail. In her hand was a beautiful longbow and a quiver of arrows was slung across her back.

"Yes," the huntress replied, as she scanned their surroundings, "I can hear it as well."

"What is it?" Emily asked, as they set off together toward the sound.

"It is hard to say," Cora admitted. "Many creatures can sing or produce a call that we think of as singing. One should always be wary of such sounds in the forest. It is generally a seductive means to lure prey into a trap."

That explanation didn't make Emily feel any better as they picked their way carefully through the forest in search of the mysterious source of the singing.

The two of them were out in the woods just west of Pittsburgh after a scout returned late from his patrol and reported that a beautiful young woman in the middle of the forest had seduced him. According to the scout, they had made love for several hours before the scout had passed out from exhaustion and later awoke all alone beside a small pond.

The Druids thought the matter was worth investigating and had sent Emily and Cora out to discover if there was in fact a woman in the woods, or if the scout was merely telling tales to account for his tardiness.

But the scout had said that he had been lured by the sound of singing, which Emily and Cora were now also following. It seemed that one part of the scout's tale had been true.

Emily hadn't met Cora before today, but had quickly decided she liked the bold huntress. The pair had many things in common, including their love of the forest and an affinity for bows.

Cora was curious about Emily's compound bow, but refused to try it, believing that one should never use another's bow. Emily thought that was a strange idea, but from what little she knew of the Priestesses of Artemis, that was one of their least-strange beliefs.

It had been Emily's great surprise to discover that every huntress was, in fact, a virgin like their goddess. She couldn't understand why someone would willingly choose such a lifestyle. Life was to be enjoyed fully and to do otherwise was foolish.

The singing grew louder as the pair carefully crept through a tall stand of oak trees. They passed by a small pond and verified another piece of the scout's tale.

The entrancing song came from just ahead of them when sudden movement in the trees made Emily and Cora duck for cover behind a large oak. The song never wavered and after a tense moment the crouched pair peeked out around the tree and saw the source of the enchanting song.

There, sitting in one of the lower branches of a great oak tree was a beautiful, young maiden. A crown of woven oak leaves decorated with acorns kept her lush, brown hair out of her face, but besides that, the maiden was completely naked.

Her sun kissed skin was marvelously tan from countless hours spent outdoors. Her legs were long and shapely as she dangled one playfully from her perch. Despite being nude, she reclined in the tree branch with her hands behind her head like it was the most comfortable recliner.

As the maiden stared longingly up into the swaying branches, she sang in a language that Emily recognized as Elvish but couldn't understand the words. The music was hypnotizing and there was something alluring about the nude figure that Emily couldn't explain.

Cora breathed a sigh of relief at the sight of the nude maiden. "Thank the Goddess," the huntress breathed.

"What is it?" Emily whispered, unable to tear her eyes away from the sight before her.

"That," Cora whispered back, "is a dryad."

"A tree nymph?" Emily finally tore her gaze away as the pair hid behind the tree. "What do we do about it?"

"You come say hello," a musical voice replied.

Emily and Cora froze behind the large oak and didn't move.

"Oh, come now." The musical voice's laughter sounded like wind chimes. "You can't hide behind that oak forever. Besides, I would love some company."

Cora slowly stood and Emily followed her lead. Together, they stepped out from behind the tree and revealed themselves to the dryad, who was still reclined on her branch.

Cora bowed to the dryad. "I am Cora, Huntress of Artemis. And this," she motioned to Emily, "is Emily, apprentice to the Druids."

The dryad's large eyes sparkled mischievously as she regarded the pair. "Welcome to my Stand," the dryad replied playfully. "You may call me Melody."

Melody untangled her hands from behind her head and stretched luxuriously, her back arching and her perfectly shaped breasts catching the sunlight. She grinned impishly and then leaned forward and sprawled out on the branch seductively. "Now, what brings a Chosen of Artemis and a Watcher to my humble abode?" the dryad purred.

Emily was entranced by the beautiful creature before her and it took her a minute to realize it had asked them a question.

Cora, however, did not seem to be fazed by the dryad's otherworldly allure. "One of our scouts reported he had been seduced by something during his patrol," the huntress answered. "We came to find out what had forced itself upon him."

"Forced?" Melody pouted teasingly. "I did not force myself on anyone.

I assure you all force was entirely consensual and highly satisfying." The dryad licked her lips. "Perhaps I can show you…"

"I'm afraid not," Cora replied coolly. "There are armies on the move and they are headed this way. It would be best if you got as far from here as possible before they arrived."

"Armies?" Melody laughed. "Whose armies?"

"Kefali," Cora replied grimly.

"Ahh," Melody purred. "It has been a long time since I enjoyed the company of a kefali." The dryad closed her eyes and ran her hands up and down her curvaceous body. "Some of them are like rolling around in a soft, warm blanket. And they are hard in all the right places," she added with a devious grin.

"That is enough," Cora growled, and Melody pouted playfully.

"I am serious," the huntress continued. "They are not the only ones moving through these woods. The kefali are in league with the Shadowed Ones."

The dryad's eyes flashed and she hissed angrily at the mention of the fallen elves. "How could this be?" Melody hissed. "They were all banished after the war."

"We don't know," Cora answered, "but we know at least some of them escaped and are here on this world."

"A pity," Melody pouted. "I was just beginning to like this place. So full of potential."

Emily finally found her tongue. "You could come back with us."

The dryad's gaze turned to Emily and a playful light entered her huge eyes. "I appreciate the offer, Druid, but my place is here in the wood." Melody shifted and gave Emily a full view of her bare assets. "The huntress doesn't know how to have fun, but I see a kindred spirit in you." The dryad uncoiled and stood up on the branch, giving Emily a show. "I have never tasted a human female before," Melody breathed. "I am sure we could find a little time alone before these armies arrive…"

Emily fought the pull she felt to rush over and join the dryad in her tree. "I appreciate the offer," Emily forced out. "Maybe next time."

"Join me." Melody's body moved seductively through the branches. "I can show you pleasures you couldn't even imagine."

Emily took an unconscious step forward before she caught herself.

With a mighty effort of will, Emily pushed aside the desire she felt for the alluring creature.

"I'm afraid not," Emily replied, free of the dryad's influence.

Melody's face fell. "Very well," she pouted, before she brightened up again. "At least I shall have something to look forward to on this strange world." Melody pulled herself up onto a higher branch. "I look forward to our next encounter," the dryad purred, and she started to sing as she pulled herself up even higher until she disappeared into the colorful leaves and her song faded away.

"That was… different," Emily said, as she stared at the canopy of rustling leaves high above.

"I'm impressed," Cora admitted, as the pair turned and started back out the way they had come. "Few can resist the call of a nymph."

"You did," Emily replied.

"Yes," the huntress said, "but Artemis has taught us to resist such temptations. You have no such defense."

"But Melody was a girl." Emily shook her head in wonder. "I don't like girls."

"It makes no matter," Cora replied. "Nymphs all appear as female but they make no distinction between mortal genders. They will seduce any mortal that happens to cross their path and use them for their pleasure."

"I felt a similar sensation when we encountered the nephilim," Emily admitted, as they picked their way back through the forest. "But there was a difference between them. With Melody, I felt desire, but also that I was desired." Emily struggled to explain the strange feelings. "But the nephilim was just pure lust that was forced upon me. That probably doesn't make any sense, but there was a difference."

"Of course, there was a difference," Cora answered gently. "The nephilim are vile creatures that were born of evil and that use their influence to overwhelm, and eventually kill their victims to power their dark magic. But Melody and her kind are peaceful creatures that merely takes one's own desires and magnifies them until you are susceptible to their charming influence."

Emily shivered, caught between repulsion and attraction for the dryad.

"Let us hope we do not encounter Melody again," Cora stated.

Emily trudged through the forest beside the elf. "Yes, let's hope."

CHAPTER 9

Sweat gleamed on Mike's bare chest as he struck the glowing piece of steel with a heavy hammer. Sparks flew with each strike as the hot metal was pounded into shape.

There was something satisfying about taking a block of steel and turning it into something usable. There was a fundamental joy in creating something with your hands that just couldn't be put into words. At least that was what Mike thought as he looked at the piece of hot metal taking shape on the anvil before him.

He was in Ted's workshop while Ted was hidden behind a black welding mask in the far corner with sparks cascading around him. Apparently, Ted had discovered some kind of breakthrough on whatever he was working on and hadn't left his workshop in several days.

Ted was being his secretive self and Mike had given up on probing for clues on what he was working on. It didn't help that Ted had a bit of an odor building up about him from so many days locked in this room, so Mike was just fine keeping his distance. Besides, Mike had an idea about some of it since Ted had asked him to create a few runes, but Mike couldn't guess how some of them went together.

The Rune of Expansion had been particularly hard to master and Nadal had laughed at him for even trying to learn such a complicated rune. But the Runesmith's laughter had ended a couple days later when, to Nadal's disbelief, Mike successfully crafted a Rune of Expansion.

Ted had then asked for a dozen more such runes and Mike had made them, but he still didn't know what Ted wanted them for. Shrugging helplessly to himself, Mike put the half-formed lump of steel back in the forge.

The rain of sparks in the far corner ceased and Ted removed his mask. Without moving his left arm from the table, Ted put his magnification goggles on and selected a delicate tool from a nearby tray before hunching back over his work.

Mike couldn't see what Ted was doing with all the junk piled up between them, but whatever it was seemed to have his friend excited. The occasional puff of smoke, clatter of banging metal, and grunt of exertion was all that Mike noticed as he pulled his glowing piece of steel back out of the forge.

A large, steel mitten gauntlet that encased the entire hand and stretched all the way to the elbow sat on the workbench next to Mike. He had finished the gauntlet the day before and was now working on hammering out the final pieces. After learning a few new runes thanks to Ted's projects, Mike had approached Nadal about an idea he had been tossing around.

With having several wooden shields shatter on him, Mike wanted a new steel shield, but he didn't want to carry such a heavy item around on his back. The answer came in the form of the Rune of Expansion and the Rune of Compression.

Mike hadn't known either rune even existed until Ted had asked him to make them. Both runes were Master Runes and Nadal had assured him that learning even one would take months at best. Mike had met the challenge head on and crafted them both inside two weeks.

Granted, they were not Master quality, but after a few tests they did function and Mike considered that a success. Seeing how the runes actually worked had given Mike an idea on how to make a new shield that solved his problems.

After consulting with several smiths and procuring the required metals, Mike had forged the extended gauntlet and several long pieces of steel.

Mike drew out the last piece and hammered it into shape. Once he was happy with the shape, Mike dropped the hot steel into the oil to harden it and then finished the last alterations before beginning to assemble the pieces to the gauntlet.

The runes he would need were already sitting on a table, complete and ready to be applied. Now, attaching a rune wasn't ideal. An attached rune didn't have the same power as an inscribed rune did, but with the enemy closing in, Mike didn't have that luxury because the process of inscribing would add days to the process. And if he messed up, he would have to start all over again.

Time seemed to fly by as he worked, lost in the joy of creating. Before he knew it, even though hours had passed, Mike's project was finally completed.

Sitting on the workbench was a large kite shield made of several steel plates that fit seamlessly together. The shield was attached directly to the gauntlet to make one solid device.

Now, was the moment of truth.

Mike slid the elongated gauntlet shield on and gave it an experimental wave. It fit like a glove and had a good balance. Overall, Mike was pleased with his creation. However, the real test was about to begin.

Activating the rune inside the gauntlet with a thought, a blue tinted energy field sprang to life above the steel shield. Mike breathed a sigh of relief as the rune held. He hadn't been sure this part would work, having taken a Rune of Holding and filling it with the protective Aegis energy that Guardians and Paladins were known for.

Now Mike wouldn't have to use his own energy to summon the Aegis on his shield; it was now part of the shield itself.

Mike was glad his experiment had paid off, but the biggest test was yet to come.

With another thought, Mike dismissed the Aegis.

He closed his eyes and took a deep breath. "Please let this work," he muttered fervently.

With another thought, the shield suddenly quivered and then abruptly collapsed in on itself. The metal plates folded neatly and vanished inside a thick ridge along the top of the gauntlet.

After a careful inspection of the gauntlet, Mike held his arm out and there was a metallic *shhhink* sound as the metal plates unfolded and reformed into the kite shield. A huge grin split Mike's face as he collapsed and reformed the shield several times.

"Hey, Ted," Mike called across the room.

Ted looked up from his project; magnification goggles making his eyes look comically large.

Mike raised his gauntleted arm so Ted could see, then opened and closed the shield.

"I'm impressed." Ted's response sounded like he was anything but. "However, I believe you will find *my* modifications a bit more… useful."

"Alright, hot shot," Mike laughed. "Let's see it."

"Very well." Ted removed his goggles and stepped away from his workbench. "The systems should be functioning enough to give you a demonstration."

As Ted emerged, Mike noticed the large addition that Ted had welded and bolted to his artificial arm. The device arose from the back of Ted's forearm and extended its entire length until a thick, flexible pipe spanned his wrist and connected it to a square device attached to the back of Ted's hand. Several small, flexible pipes connected the blocky construct to the arm itself and a few pipes also went from the hand to the arm device.

A small firing range had been wedged into one corner of the lab and the black scorch marks along the stone walls spoke of unconventional use.

Mike planted himself at the firing line of the short range. "So, what is it supposed to do?" he asked, as Ted placed a ballistic gel dummy on a small wooden pedestal for a target. The dummy had a reinforced leather vest on and a chainmail coif over its head. Once the dummy was in place, Ted hauled another ballistic gel dummy beside the first, but this one wore a steel breastplate and full steel helm.

Ted grinned and raised his modified copper arm. "Prepare to be amazed."

The device began to hum and as Mike watched, the flexible tubes started to glow as some bright fluid began to flow through them. Steam vented from the device as the hum grew louder.

There was a sudden burst of energy and a shimmering blade of liquid light erupted from the device on the back of Ted's hand.

The blade was approximately two feet in length and maybe four inches wide at the base before it narrowed to a razor-sharp point. Light shimmered off the liquid material as some invisible force contained it.

It looked like Ted had managed to figure out how to make a plasma weapon after all.

"Impressive," Mike said stoically, unwilling to give Ted the satisfaction of seeing how impressed he really was. "But, does it work?"

"Does it work?" Ted scoffed. "You tell me."

Ted suddenly slashed at the leather dummy. The smell of burning leather and plastic filled the air as the blade cleanly split the unfortunate dummy in half.

Another slash bit deep into the metal armored dummy, carving a blistered path from the shoulder to the center of its chest. Hot metal dripped on the floor as Ted extracted the hissing blade from the ruined dummy.

"Needs a bit more power to cut all the way through the metal plate," Ted muttered, as the plasma blade retracted back into the device. "But soon it will part steel like a hot knife through butter."

"I thought you were going to put a plasma blade on your pole axe?" Mike asked.

"Oh, I did that days ago," Ted replied dismissively, and waived vaguely to another corner of his workshop. "This is far more than a mere plasma blade."

"A *mere* plasma blade?" Mike laughed. "What could be better than that?" he asked, as Ted joined him at the firing line.

Ted raised his arm and aimed at the ruined gel dummies. The hum intensified as energy crackled and spit around his wrist-mounted device.

A wild grin crossed Ted's bearded face. "A cannon."

The weapon roared as a bolt of searing plasma erupted from the device and shot across the room. The bolt exploded in a brilliant flash of light that left a smoldering puddle where the dummies had been.

"You have *got* to make me one of those," Mike laughed, as the smoke and stink of melted gel wafted over them.

"Eventually," Ted promised, still grinning madly. "The design needs a bit of work yet," he admitted. "So far, I've only been able to get three shots off before it overheats."

Mike put his hand on his friend's shoulder. "Ted, if you need more than three shots with that thing to kill an enemy, then you have bigger problems."

"Indeed, my friend," Ted chuckled, "but there is no such thing as overkill."

"Amen to that!" Mike laughed. "But how does that thing do against a magical shield?"

Ted looked thoughtful. "That is a good question… care to test it?" He motioned for Mike to move to the still-smoking crater at the end of the range.

But Mike was shaking his head before Ted had finished. "I may not be the sharpest knife in the drawer, but there is no way you are getting me down there to be your next test dummy."

"But it's for science!"

"No," Mike chuckled. "How did you get it to work anyway? I thought you couldn't keep the plasma stable enough to form a blade."

"I couldn't," Ted admitted, "but this isn't a pure plasma blade," he explained. "It is kind of an alloy of different particles that I was able to contain and shape into a superheated plasma cutter using a powerful electromagnetic field and a laser." He tapped part of the large device affixed to his copper limb. "While a refrigeration unit keeps the whole thing from overheating and melting my arm off."

"With the help of a few well-placed runes to compensate for small size, it was relatively easy. But, making it shoot… *that* was the hard part."

"I had to find a way to contain a buildup of the plasma alloy and then fire it with enough force to be deadly. Thankfully, I was able to use the same electromagnetic field to catapult the plasma charge, using technology similar to a railgun. And, of course, I had to augment the device with runes and enchantments to keep the device small enough to fit on my arm."

"What do you even need a cannon for?" Mike asked. "You can already throw fireballs and all kinds of other spells."

"Wielding magic takes energy," Ted explained in his professor voice. "If I can perfect this weapon then I can save my strength for more important spells during battle. Also, this should discharge at a higher rate than any spell I could summon."

"I see…" Mike said. "But I still have one very important question. When do I get one?"

Ted laughed. "This is still just a prototype. Once I have a fully functioning device and finish my other projects, then I can make you one."

"Well, what are you wasting time talking to me for?" Mike replied. "Get back to work!"

****

Liz's heart pounded in her chest as she carefully reached through the darkness between the thick, steel bars. She held her breath as her hand inched ever closer to the mountain of black fur on the other side. Emily stood behind her, virtually invisible in the deep shadows as she chewed nervously on the corner of her headscarf.

The mountain of fur suddenly shifted and a startled squeak escaped Emily before she could control herself. Liz froze, arm outstretched, just inches away from the shifting black mountain.

After a tense moment that felt like forever, the mountain settled and Liz finally let out a shuddering breath. Inching forward with her face pressed against the cold bars, Liz reached as far as she could until her fingers brushed the wall of thick fur.

The darkness around her vanished and was replaced by an even darker, more sinister blackness that rolled around her, as she stood alone in a haunted wasteland.

Liz was horrified at the sight around her.

Everywhere she looked she only saw more darkness. Heartbreakingly, there was no trace of Jack. There was only the beast.

She delved deeper, desperate to find something that remained of her friend.

As she soared through the black clouds of Jack's consciousness, Liz thought she heard a faint voice calling out to her.

"Jack!" Liz shouted into the darkness.

But there was no reply; only the same faint calling that was too quiet for her to make out the words above the howling wind.

Liz tried to follow the faint sound, but no matter what direction she went, she never got any closer. It seemed to come from everywhere and nowhere. Liz searched desperately, her determination driving her ever deeper. But eventually the faint voice faded away and Liz was left alone, lost in the blackness with only the howling winds to accompany her.

Sadness threatened to overwhelm Liz as she realized that her last hope for saving Jack had quite literally faded away. If she had managed to touch Jack sooner, then maybe she could have reached him before it was too late.

She was about to move deeper when an invisible force suddenly tugged at her.

At first Liz thought that Jack was trying to communicate with her, but a second tug and she realized that it must be Emily trying to get her attention.

Liz opened her eyes to the different kind of darkness. The jail's lights were still off and the hallway was still shrouded in shadows.

The only light was at the far end of the hall where the guards stood watch with their backs to them on the other side of the door.

"We aren't alone," Emily whispered urgently, when she saw Liz's eyes flutter open.

The huge mass of fur shifted and Liz quickly removed her hands from between the bars. No sooner than her hand had left the cell than a pair of angry golden eyes flared into existence. The great werewolf uncoiled and arose like some feral titan.

The werewolf growled, deep and furious, but Liz suddenly realized that he wasn't growling at them. The huge beast eyed the shadows behind Liz and Emily and she slowly turned to see what had caught the beast's attention.

At first Liz didn't see anything but shadows, until a hooded figure slowly emerged from the darkness.

"Who the hell are you?" Emily said, after she had pulled a small knife from her boot. "And how did you get in here?"

Emily had left her bow and scepter in the waiting room, not expecting to need them while inside the secure building. Luckily, Liz still had her pistol strapped to her thigh and she slowly drew it but didn't immediately point it at the newcomer.

The hooded figure was very short and extremely wide. At first Liz thought it was some kind of kefali based on the dark hair that concealed its body. But she quickly realized that the newcomer was actually dressed from head to toe in heavy furs.

The figure slowly reached up and Liz saw there were long, steel claws on the figure's heavy gauntlets as it pulled back its hood and revealed the mangiest dwarf that Liz had ever seen.

His beard and hair were a tangled mess, and what little of his face that Liz could see was crisscrossed with numerous scars. But it wasn't the scars or wild appearance that caught her attention.

The dwarf's golden eyes glittered in the faint light.

"I be Rangvald," the mangy dwarf growled, "and I be here fer yer friend."

"What do you want with him?" Liz replied cautiously, still without raising her pistol. She didn't want to start a fight if she didn't have to. Despite his feral appearance, Liz didn't feel threatened by the savage dwarf.

"I be here ter help 'em," Rangvald growled.

"And why should we trust you?" Emily challenged.

"Because I be a Priest o' Fenrir," Rangvald replied. "An' the Great Wolf has blessed yer friend with a portion o' His mighty strength, but the mortal form be unprepared fer such a wondrous gift."

"Gift?" Emily scoffed. "You call that a gift?" She motioned to the towering werewolf who hadn't taken his eyes off the dwarf.

Their golden eyes met.

"Indeed, I do," Rangvald replied reverently.

"You said you were here to help him," Liz said cautiously, a spark of hope forming within her. "Does that mean you have a cure?" But her hope was quickly shattered.

"A cure!" the wolf priest spat. "There be no cure fer those touched by the Great Wolf."

"Then what do you want?" Emily growled angrily.

"Ter free his mind o' course," Rangvald growled back. "The Spirit o' the Great Wolf has consumed him, but if I be no too late, n' he be possessin' o' a strong mind, then maybe I can help yer friend subdue the Spirit and regain his body."

"And just why would you do that?" Liz asked suspiciously. She was thrilled that there was a chance for Jack to return to them, but she didn't trust this strange dwarf's motives. There was something he wasn't telling them, she was sure of it.

"Because the Great Wolf needs His followers ter be possessin' their own minds," Rangvald rumbled. "Only those strong enough ter master Fenrir's Spirit be worthy o' His eternal gift."

Liz didn't like the sound of an "eternal" gift. "And what happens if he isn't strong enough?" she asked, afraid of the answer. So far, it had seemed that every chance Jack had to overcome this disease had failed.

"Both body an' soul be consumed, until only a pure avatar o' Fenrir's Spirit remains," Rangvald replied. "Such avatars be considered the most holy o' beings within the Cult o' Fenrir, but they be wild and uncontrollable, a living incarnation o' the righteous rage o' the unjustly imprisoned Great Wolf."

"I thought he was already lost," Emily replied hopefully. "When he didn't change back after the first full moon we thought the change was permanent. Are you saying that he isn't consumed yet?"

"It be depending on the willpower o' the blessed," Rangvald replied. "Some are consumed instantly upon receivin' the Spirit, while others conquer it even before they know that the Spirit be upon 'em."

"How will we know if he is still in there?" Liz asked dubiously. She had gotten her hopes up too many times to completely believe what this strange dwarf said.

"There be only one way ter find out," Rangvald said, as he strode past Liz and Emily to stand before the cell door. "Ye need ter let me in," the mangy dwarf rumbled.

"You can't be serious," Emily laughed in disbelief. "If we open that door he will tear you apart and then come after us!"

"Then gather yer weapons," Rangvald replied solemnly. "I need ter be in contact with 'em ter perform the Fenrisúlfrian Rite."

Liz and Emily shared a look before Emily shrugged. "It's your funeral," she said, as she went over and retrieved her bow and scepter from the nearby waiting room.

Inside the cage, Jack was acting strange. His large, golden eyes hadn't left the mangy dwarf since he had appeared and there had been none of his usual rage at being confined. Instead, he stood quietly in the center of his cell, watching every move that Rangvald made.

This whole idea was foolish, but Liz was desperate to help Jack and if this strange dwarf said he could by going into the wolf's den, then Liz wasn't about to let the opportunity slip by. All they needed to do was keep the door open long enough for Rangvald to enter and then lock it back up behind him.

"Wait," Liz said suddenly. "We need one of the guards to open the door. But if we go over there then Kjell will see and try to stop us."

"Who be Kjell?" Rangvald rumbled.

"He is a Hand of Tyr," Liz replied, and to that Rangvald bared his fangs angrily. "He has been guarding the elevator door since they learned about Jack."

"We canno let the Hand interfere," Rangvald growled. "He must no be knowin' that I be here."

"Don't worry." Emily walked up to the keypad next to the cell door and grinned impishly. "I know the code."

"How do you know that?" Liz asked without thinking. "Oh, wait. I don't want to know do I?"

"Probably not," Emily winked suggestively.

"Are you ready?" she asked the ugly little dwarf.

"Git on with it," Rangvald replied distractedly, golden eyes locked on to Jack's through the bars.

Liz took up a position several yards behind the mangy dwarf and readied both pistols as Emily typed in the code.

This is a bad idea, Liz thought too late, as Emily pressed the last key and the door suddenly slid open.

Liz trained her pistols on the huge werewolf as the door banged open, but to her surprise the beast didn't immediately try to lunge out. Instead, the towering werewolf's golden eyes were locked onto the mirrored eyes of Rangvald as the short dwarf quickly stepped into the cell.

Emily hit another key and the cell door abruptly slammed shut with a loud bang.

One of the guards looked back at them, but Liz doubted he could see much of anything down the dark hallway. The guard must have noticed something was off because he grabbed a flashlight before opening the heavy door and stepping into the darkened hallway.

"What's going on down there?" the guard shouted as he turned the flashlight on and started down the hallway.

Emily gave a panicked look at Liz, as the guard's light got closer.

Just then a siren began to wail outside in the distance.

A moment later another siren started up, and then another. Soon, the night was alive with the sound of warning sirens going off all over the city.

"What is that?" Emily looked around in confusion. "Did we set off some kind of alarm?"

"No," Liz replied grimly, as she started off down the hall toward the door with Emily in tow, all thought of Jack and the strange dwarf suddenly forgotten. "We are under attack."

CHAPTER 10

"Well, that's enough for me," Mike said, as he picked up a towel and proceeded to wipe the sweat off his bare chest. "It's getting late and I have training in the morning."

Most everyone else in the Verkstad had left hours ago, but Mike and Ted were still in the workshop, each trying to get as much accomplished on their respective projects as possible. Mike had a hard time walking away from a task once he started it, but even he couldn't work at the forge day and night. His muscles were tired from all the hammering and he was eager to find his bed.

Ted, however, was still surrounded in a cloud of smoke and sparks as he continued his ceaseless tinkering. Every once in a while, Ted would mutter something under his breath, but other than that he had been silent since the weapons test.

Mike finished toweling off and pulled his shirt on just as the first siren sounded in the distance. As more sirens picked up the call, Ted looked up in confusion. "What did I set on fire this time?"

"Nothing," Mike replied grimly, as he strapped on his weapons belt that had his ancient mace dangling from it. "Those alarms are telling us that we are being attacked."

"Attacked?" Ted's magnified eyes blinked owlishly behind his goggles as what Mike said slowly sunk in. "Who is attacking us?"

Gunshots and shouts of alarm could be heard over the howling alarms.

"That's what I'm going to find out," Mike said, as he picked up his newly crafted gauntlet and carefully slid his hand inside. Mike clenched his fist and looked at Ted. "You coming?"

The possibility of getting into a fight wearing only jeans and a tee shirt wasn't the most appealing idea, but Mike didn't have any of his armor with him, just the shield gauntlet that he had been working on.

It would have to do.

"Of course." Ted put down his tools and grabbed a molded cuirass off the wall behind him. With the cuirass on and white lab coat overtop, Ted picked up a strange-looking staff out of one corner and joined Mike at the door.

Mike eyed the bizarre staff in Ted's hands as they made their way through the nearly empty forge. It was a blocky contraption with ribbed pipes and coils of wire wrapping around the long shaft and he couldn't help but notice that it resembled the device affixed to Ted's arm. There was no obvious weapon on the staff, with only a blocky protrusion of steel and wire to mark the top of the shaft. Near the base, Mike thought he could see some bare wood poking out, but there was so much material covering it that it was hard to tell.

As they made their way out of the huge Verkstad complex, they came across several other humans and dwarves that were also rushing out to see what the sirens were about.

Once outside in the darkness, everyone scattered, each person having a different destination in mind. Mike headed unerringly down one street with Ted following close behind.

"Where are we going?" Ted asked, as the sounds of shouts and gunshots grew louder. A strange sound high above them made both Mike and Ted stop and look up.

Mike didn't see anything, but he could have sworn it sounded like wings above him. Low-hanging clouds blanketed the night sky, making it impossible to see anything that may be above them and blocking the moonlight to cast everything in an even deeper darkness.

"We are going to HQ," Mike answered, as he started off again, still cautiously watching the cloudy night sky. "If anyone will know what is going on, it will be there."

Ted was about to say something when an explosion lit the sky several blocks away. More shouts and gunshots erupted all around them and people were now running in every direction, some half-dressed, others in full armor, but nobody seeming to know what was happening.

More wing beats buffeted the air above them, but when Mike looked, there wasn't anything there. As they purposefully marched through the dark streets, the distinctive clang of steel on steel reached their ears. Shouted orders and bloodthirsty roars mingled with the clash of steel.

"Do you hear that?" Ted asked, as the sounds of battle got louder.

"Indeed," Mike replied eagerly, and gripped his mace tighter. The anticipation of combat grew with every step and Mike had to force himself not to charge into the unknown.

But it was difficult.

Mike never felt more alive than when he was surrounded by enemies and was battling for his life. The rush of emotions was intoxicating. Excitement, joy, rage, pain and fear - yes, especially fear - all warred within him and became one emotion in the heat of battle. When his life was hanging by a thread, Mike couldn't feel more alive.

As they hurried down the dark street toward the sounds of battle, the heavy beat of huge wings suddenly soared over them and a moment later, six black figures landed on the ground before them. Mike and Ted came to an abrupt halt as the crouched figures slowly stood.

They were all dressed head to toe in black. The only thing Mike could see about them was their red eyes through a narrow slit. Each newcomer was easily as tall as Ted and much heavier. Corded muscles stood out from the black material that tightly covered their bodies.

The glint of steel appeared as the newcomers drew various weapons. Twin swords, sais, and katanas were all in evidence in the faint light.

"Ninjas," Ted breathed.

The huge, black-clad ninjas suddenly sprang at Mike and Ted without warning.

The heavy katana descended on Mike, but just before the razor-sharp blade landed, Mike raised his gauntleted left arm and his shield sprang to life just before the blade hit.

Unprepared for the sudden jolt, the ninja was caught by surprise and Mike's return swing crushed the ninja's ribs and sent him flying backwards.

One of the ninjas hurled a trio of shurikens at Ted, but he ignored them and concentrated on the spell he was saying as the other ninja charged him with twin ninjato swords. The flying shurikens bounced off a shimmering, golden field before reaching Ted, just as he finished the words of a spell.

Darts of purple energy flared out from his outstretched hand and buried themselves in two of the ninjas before they could react. A third ninja took a glancing blow from one of the darts as he charged Ted with a pair of long sais. Each sai was like a two-foot long needle with a handle and the slender blades jabbed at Ted. He blocked them with a twirl of his modified staff and the duel was on.

Mike found himself caught between two ninjas as he desperately blocked their lightning quick strikes, but was unable to mount any kind of offensive of his own. When he did find any opening, the ninjas nimbly danced away from his swing, having seen what his mace could do.

In the darkness, it was difficult to see the black-clad ninjas and it was only by the faint glint of their weapons that Mike was able to see some of the attacks at all. But Mike was in his element and he smiled as he battled his deadly assailants.

Dodging aside from one ninja's strike, Mike retracted the shield and caught the blade of the other ninja with his gauntleted hand. Surprised, the masked ninja was unprepared when Mike gave the blade a mighty jerk and as the ninja stumbled, Mike brought his mace down on the unfortunate assailant's head.

The other ninja's blade stabbed at Mike's unprotected back, but just before reaching him, it was turned aside by the protective Svalinn Field.

Mike felt the impact on the Field and immediately spun around. As he did, the shield reformed on his arm. He punched out with the shield and rammed it into the ninja's throat.

As the huge ninja clawed helplessly at his ruined windpipe, Mike looked up in time to see Ted fling the last of the ninjas across the street with a word of power. The flying ninja slammed into a wall with a sickening crunch before falling to the ground with a dull thump.

"That was fun." Mike looked at the bodies sprawled around them. "I've never fought ninjas before."

"I don't know that we have," Ted said, as he bent over one of the large, black-clad corpses. "I don't believe these were real ninjas."

Mike looked down at the bodies at his feet. "They look like ninjas to me."

"Of course, they do," Ted chuckled. "Do you think the two of us could have defeated six ninjas so easily?"

Mike shrugged his broad shoulders. "We're just that good."

"Pshh," Ted scoffed. "We may be more skilled than most, but I find it highly improbable that we could overcome true martial arts masters with such relative ease."

"Then what is your explanation?" Mike shot back.

"Undecided," Ted replied distractedly, as he crouched down beside one of the bodies. "But I do have several working theories." He reached down and pulled the black mask off the nearest body and revealed a wide, green face with a thick nose and small tusks protruding from the lower jaw.

"As I suspected," Ted muttered. "Orcs."

Another explosion in the distance lit the night and revealed several dark shapes flying over the city. All around them were the chaotic sounds of battle and it felt strange to be so alone in the dark while battles raged unseen around them.

"What does that mean?" Mike asked, as he came to stand beside his crouched friend.

"It means," Ted replied, "that the orcs have somehow managed to launch a surprise attack on the city that we are ill prepared for."

"Well, come on then." Mike hauled Ted to his feet. "We have a city to save."

Together, they continued down the dark street as roars and the clash of weapons grew louder until they rounded the next corner and the source of the chaotic din was revealed.

The street was a war zone.

A host of the black-clad, orc ninjas filled the street as they battled a heavily armored company of Steel Legion Knights from the local chapter of the Armored Combat League along with a band of Scadian Knights.

There were no battle lines in the frenzied melee, just a mad brawl in all directions. But a moment's analysis told Mike that the humans were holding off the larger orc force, which Mike didn't find surprising considering the ACL Knights and Scadians were among the most well-trained and well-equipped human warriors. Like Mike and Ted, the Knights had years of medieval combat experience and were accustomed to the confusing ebb and flow of battle. The Knights were proving it now as they were slowly cutting through the larger orc ninjas.

Weapons wreathed in power and magical shields aided the Steel Legion Knights' skill in arms to give them an advantage over their un-augmented enemies.

Mike and Ted wasted no time joining the fray and a few minutes later the last orc fell.

As the victorious Knights cheered, a short Scadian approached Mike and Ted through the throng. His ornate Gothic plate was immaculate and Mike marveled at how no blade ever seemed to reach the formidable warrior.

"Duke von Jensin." Mike clasped the newcomer's armored hand warmly. "It is good to see you."

"What are you doing here?" the duke asked not unkindly. "Did you finally accept my offer to join the Peerage?" he added hopefully.

"Sorry, Duke." Mike shook his head. "We just saw a fight and couldn't let you have all the fun."

"Ah, well," von Jensin said, and paused as the sounds of gunshots and roars intensified. "We must find the rest of our company" the duke added. "Will you join us?"

"I am afraid we cannot," Ted answered. "We are headed for HQ to find out what exactly is happening and how we can help."

"A good plan," von Jensin said. "Once we have recovered the remainder of our company we make for the Cathedral. Should you have need of our swords, you will find us there."

"Thank you," Mike said, and with that the duke turned on his heel and shouted orders to move out. The Knights expertly formed ranks and briskly marched away. Mike and Ted didn't watch them go. Instead, they headed off in the opposite direction where the still-distant military HQ was located.

"We need to hurry," Mike said unnecessarily, as they picked up their pace to a jog. They hadn't gone more than a few yards when five more ninjas dropped out of the darkness before them.

Ted groaned as they came to an abrupt halt. "We don't have time for this." He raised his artificial arm and the hum of building power grew. Two crackling bursts of plasma erupted from the device above his wrist and struck the lead ninjas. The resulting explosions vaporized the orcs and left nothing but singed meat and smoking bits scattered across the street.

"Well, that worked," Mike muttered.

But they hadn't taken two steps when out of the darkness a dozen more black-clad orcs dropped out of the sky around them. Suddenly, Mike and Ted found themselves surrounded. The pair shared a look and Mike grinned eagerly.

Just then, an enormous shadow descended from the clouds like some awful specter of death. Huge, leathery wings that nearly spanned the width of the street billowed out as the huge creature landed with a jarring crash behind the orcs.

Two long, clawed arms pushed the scaly, serpentine body upright and a wicked looking barb weaved dangerously on the creature's tail. Large, hungry eyes glared out from a reptilian face filled with countless, curved fangs. To Mike's surprise, there was a saddle strapped to the creature and an orc seated upon its back.

"I hope you've got a few more shots in that cannon of yours," Mike muttered, as he gripped his mace tighter.

Steam vented from the humming weapon. "So do I," Ted breathed.

The wyvern suddenly released an ear-splitting screech and the orcs charged.

****

Liz cursed and rammed another magazine into her pistol as an additional group of the black-clad, orc ninjas appeared out of the darkness.

She and Emily had rushed out of the jail, and to their surprise, had found the guards desperately fighting a group of huge ninjas.

Liz and Emily threw themselves into the conflict; Liz dropping black-clad attackers with well-placed shots while simultaneously healing the wounded guards as Emily rained a virtual hail of arrows into the mass of ninjas.

With the combined firepower of the guards, Liz, and Emily, the ninjas were quickly cut down. However, more had come out of the darkness before the last had fallen and these ones were not alone.

An enormous wyvern dove out of the black clouds and scattered the defenders just before the next wave of ninjas entered the fray.

The battle had become more chaotic and disorganized after that, with small pockets of resistance warring with larger groups of black-clad attackers at every corner.

More wyverns had appeared and now there must have been dozens of them soaring below the dark clouds. If that was how many could be seen, Liz was afraid to consider how many must still be hidden in the clouds.

Liz had a small group of guards around her, but she had lost Emily in the maelstrom after the first wyvern had scattered them. Once the guards had realized that Liz was a healer, they had rallied around her and she had unintentionally become their de facto leader.

Although these black-clad orcs were thought of as ninjas, they didn't fight with the skill normally associated with the legendary assassins.

When Liz mentioned this, one of the dwarf Judges had told her that the enemy they faced were nothing but rappa; unskilled ruffians that were usually meant as a distraction while the real shinobi completed their true mission.

Liz didn't like the sound of that.

If these *rappa* were just the distraction… then what were the orcs really after?

A huge, misshapen wyvern suddenly swooped by, soaring much lower than the others that wheeled and shrieked in the dark sky above. It was bloated and misshapen, with what looked like large growths sprouting from its scaly hide.

To Liz's surprise, one of the lumps suddenly detached and fell from the beast's body. Other lumps shifted and within moments nearly a dozen dark masses dropped from the wyvern and landed on the pavement near Liz and her companions.

The shapes stood and revealed more of the black-clad rappa, only these were smaller than the hulking attackers they were used to.

The rappa charged Liz and her guard companions, but there wasn't anything that could be called a battle. With several well-placed shots, Liz and the armed guards dropped every rappa before they could close the distance.

Liz noticed something odd about that last group of rappa and made her way over to one of the bodies. Her companions formed a protective ring around her as she knelt beside one of the fallen attackers. The black-clad body was much smaller than the usually bulky orc warrior. The proportions were also wrong. Usually the orcs had longer arms and smaller heads with protruding jaws, but the covered rappa had none of that.

Liz reached down and pulled the hooded mask away.

A sick feeling filled Liz at the sight that greeted her. Quickly glazing eyes stared accusingly at her from a face of pale skin with a mop of curly brown hair.

"Oh, no…" Liz breathed as the human face looked up at her.

She had never killed another human before and the mere thought of doing so made her ill. But now, lying before her, were several of her fellow humans, dead by her hand. She couldn't be sure that this one had been killed by her, but deep down she knew. It had been her hand that ended this man's life and the thought made her sad.

Liz had killed countless beasts and monsters since The Shearing had brought all manner of creatures to Earth, but they had all been aliens, easily dismissed as not human and not of this world, and thus not as important. But now, for the first time, she had killed one of her own kind.

She was surprised at how much the realization affected her. Liz told herself that this was nothing more than another enemy, but she couldn't bring herself to believe that with those accusing eyes staring at her.

A quick inspection found all of the black-clad corpses that had dropped off the wyvern together were also human.

What would make humans join with such monstrous creatures like orcs?

Liz couldn't understand it. Unless it was some form of mind control… Liz had plenty of experience with that. But since when did orcs allow humans to fight for them? As far as she knew, orcs didn't have a language that anyone could understand.

Liz was still bent over one of the human rappa corpses when a trio of wyverns suddenly landed around her and her companions. Surprisingly, each wyvern had an orc rider armed with a long, curved spear perched upon its scaly back.

Pistols were no match for the hard scales of the wyverns and Liz cursed again that she didn't have her MK13 with her. The only hope was hitting the beasts' eyes, but the draconic heads bobbed and weaved so erratically that hitting them was nearly impossible.

The lead wyvern rider spotted Liz and her knot of allies and motioned to his two companions. Together, all three wyverns converged on the hapless group.

Liz hopelessly raised her pistol and fired.

****

An arrow punched through the ninja's neck and another slammed into his chest a moment later.

A surprised elf spun around in time to see the stricken orc ninja collapse at her feet.

"Thank you." The blonde elf nodded curtly to Emily before another ninja rushed in. The elf's name was Camilla and she was an Arbiter. That was all the more Emily had learned since the two of them had found each other during the first chaotic moments of the battle.

Now, the two of them faced a pack of the black-clad orcs and Camilla wielded her longsword with stunning grace while Emily peppered the ninjas with a steady stream of arrows. The Endless Quiver that King Varnir had given her was proving its worth now as she unloaded arrow after arrow into the attackers. Orcs fell by the score, but more appeared all around them. It was like they were being born out of the darkness.

Others battled all around them; men and dwarves and elves, locked in combat with the rampaging orc ninjas that seemed to be everywhere. Spells cut down scores of the wild orcs, but there were so many that the losses didn't even register. It didn't help that the bloody wyverns would swoop down out of the night and pick off unsuspecting defenders and carry them off into the black.

Emily trained her arrow on one such flying wyvern and released. The arrow punched through the beast's eye and into its brain. The wyvern screamed as it died and crashed into a building in a shower of glass and bricks.

Nearby, Camilla twirled amidst a host of orcs, her blade flashing in the dim light as she cut a path through them. Emily followed behind, dropping orcs with precise arrows. That is, until one of the orcs deflected her arrow with a flick of one of his slender blades.

She drew and fired again, but the orc dodged aside and the arrow whizzed harmlessly by.

Emily was momentarily surprised.

Finally, a ninja with actual ninja-like skills. Emily had been wondering at the lack of ability these ninja-wannabes possessed.

Camilla must have noticed the difference as well for she eagerly turned her attention to the more skilled opponent. Blades clashed as Camilla's longsword met the slender short swords of the true orc ninja.

Where most of the orcish blades were curved, this ninja's blades were perfectly straight and surprisingly thin. Camilla's slender longsword looked almost brutish in comparison.

Sparks flew around the elf and orc as they weaved a deadly dance in the darkness.

Camilla kicked at the ninja's head, but the nimble orc twisted away and managed to slice a long cut along the elf's shoulder as it avoided the strike. Camilla didn't seem to notice the wound and rushed the orc with a dizzying array of attacks. But the orc and elf were evenly matched, and the ninja avoided every one of Camilla's attacks.

Emily had an arrow drawn and the fletching was rough against her cheek as she waited for an opening, but Camilla and the ninja's movements were so fast that she couldn't get a clean shot.

The ninja suddenly threw something against the ground and a cloud of smoke burst around them. Emily couldn't see what was happening inside the obscuring smoke.

She could hear the ring of steel as the orc ninja and elf Arbiter dueled inside the smoke. A grunt of pain issued from the darkness and the sounds of battle suddenly ceased.

To Emily's dismay, the orc ninja emerged from the smoke.

She was just about to release her arrow when the orc stumbled and she saw that blood ran freely down the ninja's chest.

Camilla stepped out of the rapidly dissipating smoke as the wounded orc fell to its knees. With calm efficiency, the Arbiter walked up behind the wounded orc and swiftly drove her longsword through the ninja's back.

The orc slid off the blade and fell dead at Camilla's feet.

Without warning, a flying wyvern suddenly appeared around the corner and soared low overhead. As it did, its wickedly barbed tail abruptly lashed out and stuck Camilla's head from her shoulders.

The huge beast didn't even slow as it wheeled by and disappeared down another dark street.

Emily stood in stunned silence and watched helplessly as her companion's headless body slowly toppled over.

But she didn't have time to mourn the sudden loss as more black-clad orcs rushed at her.

Shock was replaced with anger as Emily drew her skull-topped scepter and unleashed a withering hail of green energy into the surrounding orcs. Filled with rage and heedless of the danger, she drove into the swirling melee as black-clad bodies crumpled in the face of her punishing volley.

The orcs were being pushed back when three huge wyverns with orc riders landed amidst the carnage. The great scaly beasts screeched and lashed out with their barbed tails until the riders directed them towards the largest knot of defenders.

Emily's rage found a focus and she turned toward the trio of wyverns without a second thought. It had been such a beast that had killed her newest friend and she was going to make them pay.

Flashes of green light burst around her as she unleashed volley after blistering volley of green bolts into the unfortunate orcs, until she was finally close enough that a path opened up between her and the grounded wyverns.

The beasts were so focused on the group they were converging on that they completely ignored the larger battle around them. And who could blame them? There were few weapons around that would be of any real threat to the armored wyverns.

A wicked grin spread across Emily's face and her scepter's eyes blazed hungrily.

CHAPTER 11

A dozen black-clad bodies lay scattered across the narrow road, nearly invisible in the darkness. But the immense corpse that lay smoldering in the center of the street dwarfed them all. Its wings were bent and broken while the charred remains of its mammoth skull grinned sightlessly into the blackness. The unfortunate rider had been flung from the beast's back in its death throes and lay dead at the base of the building that it had slammed into.

"Aahhh, that stings," Ted grimaced in pain as he shook his smoking copper arm. The device attached to it spat sparks and vented steam as foul-smelling smoke wafted out from inside the warped casing.

"Well, who's the genius that overloaded his fancy new cannon?" Mike said, as he eyed the bodies scattered around him, making sure none of them was moving. Satisfied, he retracted the shield into his gauntlet and joined Ted as they climbed over the huge wyvern corpse that blocked their path.

"It worked though, didn't it?" Ted grumbled, as he stepped over the thick tail.

Mike looked at the blackened skull of the huge beast. "You could say that."

The supercharged blast from Ted's plasma cannon had incinerated the wyvern's head surprisingly well. Unfortunately, the cannon itself had ruptured from the powerful buildup and was now useless.

With the abrupt death of the wyvern, the so-called "ninjas" had been easy prey for the experienced duo.

"Luckily, that's not the only trick I've got up my sleeve." Ted's eyes twinkled mischievously as they strode across the leathery carpet of wyvern wings.

"I'm sure it's not," Mike chuckled, as they finally extracted themselves from the beast's remains.

Together, they strode down the dark, deserted street as the sounds of battle echoed eerily all around them. Strangely, this section of the city was pitch black, with none of the usual streetlights or glow from the windows to light their way.

"Why didn't you just use a spell on the wyvern?" Mike asked. "You are a wizard after all."

"Mage," Ted corrected, "and until we know what we are dealing with, I don't want to waste my strength."

"Seems to me that having a cannon that can melt the face off a wyvern would be a nice backup if we come across something worse," Mike argued.

"And rely on an experimental piece of equipment?" Ted scoffed. "I trust my own abilities to overcome any obstacle far more than a piece of technology, even one of my own devising."

Mike shrugged helplessly as they strode into the unknown.

Ted eyed the darkness warily as they neared the Command Center Complex. They had still not seen another living soul. "I don't like this…" he muttered. "Why isn't there more activity around here? Shouldn't there be soldiers rallying and people everywhere or something? And why are the lights off? I don't remember hearing about the power going out."

"I don't know," Mike muttered darkly. "Something is definitely wrong."

Out of the darkness, on either side of the street, the Command Center slowly appeared, with the Bridge of Sighs linking the two buildings above the street.

The Central Command Complex, or simply HQ, as it was commonly known, was the old Allegheny Courthouse and Jail. The large, granite blocks and Romanesque Revival architecture gave the complex a distinctive medieval feel. Located near the very heart of downtown, the castle-like walls of the old jail and high watchtower seemed out of place surrounded by modern steel and glass skyscrapers.

But the fortress-like nature of the buildings and central location was perfectly suited for use as a command center. The old jail had acted as a stronghold during the first chaotic days of The Shearing and had provided a rallying point for the city's police forces.

However, that heart seemed to be missing as Mike and Ted hurried through the darkness toward the silent complex.

They were nearing the main doors when they discovered the first bodies.

At first, Mike thought the four Marines were sleeping at their posts, but when they got closer, they found all four Marines had their throats slit from ear to ear.

Mike crouched down and inspected their guns. "Whoever did this snuck up on them," Mike muttered. "They didn't even fire a shot."

"Who could sneak up and take four Marines unawares?" Ted asked as he eyed the darkness.

The dull echo of gunshots inside the old jail sounded loud in the silence.

"I don't know," Mike said, as he grabbed one of the fallen soldier's M4 carbines and stuffed his pockets with every magazine he could carry. "But I say we go find out."

Electricity crackled around Ted's clenched fist. "Sounds good to me."

****

Liz shouted a warning to her companions as a barbed tail lashed out at them. The orc riders hooted eagerly and urged their winged mounts on as the great beasts snapped and clawed at their surrounded prey.

Ineffective bullets pinged off the hard scales of the wyverns, but the orc riders weren't so well armored and one of them fell from the saddle.

The riderless wyvern didn't seem to notice the loss of the orc upon its back and continued to advance on Liz and her companions beside its two brethren.

Numerous wyverns flew overhead and shrieked wildly as they disgorged more black-clad figures onto the already chaotic street. Fireballs and lightning reached up and blasted some of them from the sky, but for every orc or wyvern brought down, two more seemed to take their place.

One of the huge beasts in front of Liz rose up before her and she unloaded the last of her bullets into its scaly face. One of the shots found its mark and the wyvern shrieked in pain as one of its large eyes burst in a shower of creamy liquid.

A barbed tail flashed out of the darkness and stabbed a dwarf in the chest right beside her. The tail jerked back and pulled the skewered dwarf along with it.

An elf screamed as a wyvern bit down and ripped the unfortunate elf's arm off at the shoulder.

The defenders were being cut down all around her and Liz knew that this was the end. The wyverns had them surrounded and none of the defenders had the proper means to kill the armored beasts.

Liz drew her slender sword and slashed at a scaly tail as it sliced one of the guards in half. Her sword scraped along the hard scales, but she found hope when the blade cut through the smaller tail scales and found the soft meat beneath.

The wyvern shrieked and pulled back its injured tail as its fanged head swung around to face her. Cold malice glittered in its one good eye and Liz knew she was next.

The great beast reared back and prepared for the fatal strike when a bolt of green energy detonated against the side of its head. The wyvern shrieked and turned as more bolts burst along its body. The sudden assault caught the wyverns off guard and green explosions ripped into each of them.

The great beasts turned to face this new threat as the green energy continued to batter them. The explosions weren't doing that much damage, but the magical energy was breaking through the scales.

With the wyverns distracted, Liz quickly healed the most seriously wounded of her little band before pursuing the winged monsters.

The wyverns were closing in on the source of the magical assault and Liz was surprised when she caught a glimpse of their savior through the battle.

Emily strode purposefully through the melee, heedless of the danger as she continued her unrelenting assault on the incoming beasts.

Liz was impressed at Emily's bravery in facing three wyverns at once, but she also thought it was incredibly stupid. Her scepter was hurting the mighty beasts, but it wasn't enough to kill them. Soon, they would reach her and it would be over.

Determined not to let that happen, Liz searched desperately for a way to distract the wyverns from their antagonist. But she was out of ammunition and didn't have anything on hand that could move them from their course. So, without any other options, Liz charged ahead through the swirling battle and followed in the beasts' wake.

A black-clad rappa jumped out at her, but she stabbed it and kept moving without slowing. She had to find a way to save Emily.

Too bad she didn't have any idea how to do that.

To her great relief, Liz discovered that the group of guards had followed her and they closed in around her protectively as they gained on the slithering beasts.

As the three wyverns closed in on Emily, Liz realized to her dismay that they wouldn't get there in time.

But as Liz and her companions futilely chased the wyverns, a group of dwarves in white scapulars cut their way through the swarming rappa and joined Emily. One of the dwarves swung an unmistakable burning axe and Liz recognized them.

It was Captain Raenods leading a band of the Hands of Tyr.

The dwarves fanned out around Emily and formed a protective wall between her and the wyverns. Every weapon of the Hands either burned or crackled with magical energy. The wyvern riders slowed their mounts upon seeing the sudden magical might aligned against them, but the riderless wyvern charged ahead and met the dwarves head on.

The dragon-kin was a fearsome beast, but the dwarves reacted with practiced precision. The wyvern lashed its wickedly barbed tail and clawed at the dwarves, but they avoided its wild strikes and quickly surrounded it. Burning blades and pulsing hammers tore at the beast's flanks as it spun in circles, desperately trying to strike in every direction at once. The wyvern failed miserably and within moments the dwarves had hacked away the beast's two legs and severed the barb from its tail. The dragon-kin shrieked in agony until Captain Raenods ended its suffering with a single, mighty blow from his burning axe.

With the death of the wyvern, the Hands of Tyr turned their attention on the remaining two beasts. But the wyvern riders thought better of engaging the skilled dwarves and urged their mounts away. Winds kicked up as the mighty wings propelled the wyverns from the ground and soon the great beasts were lost to the cloudy darkness.

Liz and her companions battled the rest of the short distance through the rappa until they finally reached Emily and the band of Hands.

The two groups quickly joined forces, and no sooner had they combined ranks than a thunderous wave of gunfire erupted from a nearby street.

The unseen volley cut down scores of black-clad orcs and the gunfire continued as it slowly drew closer. The rappa nearest the street saw what was coming and began to flee, and those fleeing orcs were running straight toward Liz and her companions.

Liz, Emily, the jail guards, the Hands of Tyr, and the other acquired fighters braced themselves as a panicked tide of rappa fought desperately to get away from whatever was coming down the other street.

"Cut 'em down!" Captain Raenods bellowed, as he slashed at the orcs with his burning axe. "Let none escape!"

The Hands took up the cheer and soon all of the defenders threw themselves into the slaughter with renewed vigor.

Devastating spells and bullets decimated the orcs as more humans and their allies came out of the surrounding buildings and adjoining streets. Magical darts skewered the rappa and walls of fire incinerated whole rows of unfortunate orcs.

The steady rumble of gunfire grew louder until at last, the source of the rappa's distress was revealed. Spread across the entire street was row after row of human spearmen with ranks of infantrymen close behind. The humans were instantly recognizable in their gleaming coats of chainmail with black and gold tabards that had the distinctive steel castle emblazoned on their chests.

The Steel City Guard cut an impressive figure as they marched down the street, cutting down scores of black-clad rappa with every passing moment.

The defenders rallied with the appearance of their allies and the rappa were soon routed. Few escaped the slaughter and those that did were pursued by armed groups of angry citizens.

"Boy are we glad to see you," Emily said to the Guard commander when they found him after the road had been secured. "How did you know we needed help?"

"We didn't," the commander admitted. "We haven't received any orders at all. I took my company out and we have been clearing the streets, one by one."

"Shouldn't HQ be directing the defenses?" Liz asked.

"Yes," the commander replied grimly, "but HQ has been silent since the warning sirens went off. I sent a detachment to the Command Center, but I haven't received word from them, either."

"Maybe the radios aren't working again," Emily offered, but the commander shook his head.

"No, the radios are working just fine. We have been organizing ourselves so far. Every available unit is out patrolling the streets. We can't figure out any strategy to the orcs' attack. They seem completely random in their assault."

"Welcome ter war with orcs," Captain Raenods grumbled. "They rarely be doin' anythin' that could be called rational."

"But there must be a reason for all this," Liz said. "Why would you attack a city and be so disorganized? Surely there was some kind of goal."

"We thought the same thing," the commander replied, "but all the gates are secured and there is no trace of them beyond the walls. It seems that the scattered aerial assault is the only attack."

"But why?" Emily muttered. "Surely there was some point to all this." She motioned to all the corpses littering the street. "Why launch a surprise attack and send unskilled warriors to random locations?"

A cold realization suddenly hit Liz.

"A distraction," she breathed, remembering what the Judge had told her earlier about the shinobi. "All of this was to distract us from their real mission."

"But what could they want besides taking over the city?" the guard commander asked.

Liz looked around at all the carnage. "I'm afraid we'll soon find out."

****

Mike and Ted snuck through the shrouded Command Center. The thick stone walls were dark and foreboding as they crept through the stillness that was occasionally punctuated by the dull echo of gunshots deeper inside the complex.

Bodies of soldiers and command personnel littered the halls and Mike was hard-pressed to suppress his urge to rush off and find whoever had committed so many murders.

The brutal efficiency was obvious from the angle of the bodies and precise wounds. The attackers had struck with surgical precision and had moved through the complex so quickly that many of the soldiers hadn't even drawn their weapons before being cut down.

Mike and Ted were going down their third hallway before they saw the first signs of resistance.

Bullet holes marred the walls and one corner was a charred ruin from an explosion, but Mike didn't see any enemy corpses among the dead. Either the attackers had somehow made it through the hail of gunfire unscathed, or they had taken their dead with them once the defenders had all fallen.

Mike hoped that it was the latter and gripped his pilfered rifle tighter. He didn't relish the idea of fighting something that was immune to bullets and grenades.

Gunshots echoed loudly down the hall and Mike knew they were getting closer. Eager to find the enemy, the pair hurried through the broken hallways toward the sounds of battle.

The dark stone corridors seemed to go on forever and eventually Mike recognized that they were headed toward the very heart of the Command Center where General Adams and the other senior commanders oversaw the defense of the entire city and surrounding countryside.

With sudden clarity, Mike realized what was happening.

The cunning orcs had launched a decapitation strike to eliminate Pittsburgh's commanders while the wyverns dropped foot soldiers across the city to keep the defenders occupied. In one swift strike, the orcs would kill the city's leaders and leave the city vulnerable to an organized attack.

One thing still didn't make sense to him, though.

As Mike and Ted hurried through the darkness, Mike couldn't help but wonder. *Why now? Why the Command Center? Didn't the orcs realize that it wasn't just the humans that defended the city?* There was practically an entire kingdom of dwarves, including their king, here that would see to any defenses should General Adams and his commanders fall. And then there were the elves and their magic. Surely killing a few human leaders wouldn't make much of a difference in the coming battle.

Mike could hear the explosive bark of gunfire and the clash of steel up ahead, and he knew they were getting close.

There was something he was missing; something important that made the orcs attack here and now, and Mike was afraid what that reason could be.

With Ted right behind him, Mike turned the last corner into the central command station and finally came face to face with the mysterious attackers.

The command station was a large, multi-level room that acted as the brains of the entire city's defenses. Several walls were covered in televisions, fed live feeds from cameras positioned all along the city's new walls. Banks of computers covered one entire level of the room and an enormous holographic map of the city hovered in the center of the main chamber.

Several bodies of command personnel sat slumped over their stations, but thankfully it seemed many of them had avoided the surprise attack. Radios crackled as countless voices requested aid or called for orders that would never come.

Mike took this all in at a glance as his attention was drawn to the far side of the chamber.

Scores of orc ninjas milled about the chamber near a small hallway whose entrance was littered with black-clad corpses. A rough barricade of heavy tables and chairs could just be seen at the far end of the hallway and Mike was glad to see that someone had survived the surprise attack. But there must have been fifty or more orcs in the command room and he doubted that whoever was behind that barrier had enough ammunition to hold against such numbers.

A trio of ninjas suddenly charged down the hallway and was met by a thunderous burst of gunfire. At first the ninjas actually managed to dodge the bullets, showing a degree of skill far superior to any of the ninjas that Mike had faced so far, but the hail of gunfire was unrelenting. The ninjas couldn't avoid them all and were shot down before they had made it halfway down the hall to join the growing pile of bodies that was clogging the already narrow passage.

Then, an orc stepped out of the milling throng that was different than the rest. Where the other orcs were covered from head to toe in concealing black cloth, this one was dressed in deep, blood red robes and pieces of black-lacquered armor.

The orc growled something in its guttural language and a bubbling red mist gathered around its legs and began to creep down the hall.

As the red mist rolled over the bodies in the passage, they began to decompose at a horrendous rate. The corpses withered away beneath the mist and within moments there was nothing left but heaps of stained, black cloth.

Mike tried to summon a Svalinn Field, but the distance was too great. It was with a heavy heart that he realized he couldn't block the murderous gases progress. Soon, it would reach the barricaded room and kill everyone inside.

"Can't you stop it with a spell?" Mike whispered to his friend.

"If I use a spell, that sorcerer will feel my presence," Ted replied quietly, "and then we will have him and an army of orc ninjas coming for us."

Mike cursed softly. As much as he didn't like to admit it, they couldn't hope to overcome so many orcs.

They watched helplessly as the red mist billowed down the passage in a smoky wave and was just about to the barricade when it suddenly rolled up an invisible barrier. The mist swirled and thickened in the hallway but couldn't cross the barrier.

Mike breathed a sigh of relief. "I thought you said the sorcerer would notice you?"

"I didn't do that." Ted looked confused. "I thought you did."

Mike shook his head and watched the gas congeal around the barrier. It seemed there was at least one gifted person behind that barricade and for that he was grateful.

The gathered orcs seemed unwilling to enter the red mist that still clung to the hallway and for good reason.

That gave Mike an idea.

"What do you say we give those poor bastards down there a fighting chance?" Mike whispered with a mischievous look in his eye.

"Uh, oh." Ted knew that look. "What did you have in mind?"

"Something incredibly stupid," Mike grinned, and then whispered his plan into Ted's ear.

"You weren't kidding," Ted chuckled, as Mike finished outlining his plan. "But I think we should reconsider our options."

Mike looked down at the passage and saw that the red mist had nearly dissipated. Soon, the orcs would attack again and this time the poor souls trapped behind the barricade might run out of ammunition.

"No time. Besides, I've always wanted to do this," Mike said, and abruptly vaulted over the railing to the level below.

Ted rolled his eyes and prepared the necessary spells.

Mike dashed across the control room, weaving through the computer stations and yelling at the top of his lungs. "Leeeeeeroyyyyyyy!"

The sudden commotion had the desired effect as scores of huge orc ninjas forgot their cornered prey and turned their baleful gaze on the hollering Mike.

"Leeeeeerooooooyyyyyy!" Mike bellowed, as he charged the nearest group of ninjas and unloaded his M4 into the surprised orcs.

When the rifle clicked dry, Mike hurled the rifle at the closest ninja who deftly deflected the awkward projectile as Mike drew his mace and the concealed shield sprang to life.

The orcs were now fully aware of Mike and scores of them leapt forward with weapons drawn, eager to slay this reckless human.

Mike swung at the first ninja to reach him and was surprised at the skill at which his enemy avoided his attacks. A second ninja joined in and suddenly Mike was desperately battling for his life. These ninjas were far more skilled than the other ninjas they had faced and it took all of his considerable skill to keep their weapons at bay.

Blessed dwarf steel met tamahagane blades as Mike was slowly forced back as more ninjas charged at him.

Running out of time, Mike took several cuts to his chest and arms as he pressed in and caught one of the ninjas with a glancing blow from the powerful impact mace. The slight contact was enough to stagger the deadly orc and knock him into the other ninja.

Seizing the opportunity, Mike turned and fled as dozens of ninjas came boiling across the control room after him.

As Mike scrambled away, the sorcerer waved his hand and black blades erupted from his fingertips. The blades shot forward and trailed black streamers of smoke as they flew across the room.

The ninjas abruptly stopped their pursuit when the sorcerer spoke and Mike turned to discover the conjured projectiles streaking toward him.

Mike held his ground as the black blades impacted on the hastily summoned Svalinn Field several feet in front of him. The blades shattered against the invisible barrier and the armored orc hissed in surprise.

The sorcerer barked another harsh command and billowing black smoke erupted before him and coalesced into a massive, hellish creature.

The beast was crouched on all fours and had the shape of a tiger, but that was where the similarity ended. This monster was the size of a horse and Mike knew that its huge jaws could easily snap a man in two. Between its coal black stripes, its fur glowed with a hellish light; like its insides were made of molten fire and its soulless eyes were completely black.

The creature's baleful gaze found Mike and its roar shook the heavy, stone walls. The hellish beast lunged forward and crossed half the chamber in one mighty leap. With the evil tiger now with them, the horde of ninjas resumed their charge.

"Run away!" Mike shouted, as he turned and ran from the hell beast and bloodthirsty ninja army.

Ted appeared at the railing above as Mike pounded up the steps with the ninjas closing in. Ted raised his arms and shouted a word of power. A wall of force radiated out from him and flung the first several ranks of ninjas backwards, giving Mike some much-needed space.

But the demonic tiger pounced through the wave of force like it wasn't even there and landed with a thunderous crash at the foot of the stairs.

Lightning flared from Ted's staff as Mike joined him on the upper balcony. The crackling bolt struck the beast and it flinched away from the light, but the lightning danced harmlessly over its glowing coat.

"Well, that's not good," Ted muttered, before Mike grabbed his arm and spun him around as the huge demon tiger shook off the last sparks of electricity. Together, Mike and Ted raced away as the mighty beast easily leapt over the stairs and charged after them with a host of angry ninjas close behind.

CHAPTER 12

After a brief discussion with the Guard commander, it was decided that Liz and Emily would take a small detachment of the Guard to the Command Center to discover the reason for the radio silence while the remaining soldiers would continue to clear the streets.

Upon hearing of the special mission, Captain Raenods insisted that he and his Hands join the party. Liz and Emily weren't thrilled with that turn of events, but they decided that having such skilled warriors along wouldn't hurt, especially if Liz's belief that the distraction had something to do with HQ being silent.

To Emily's great frustration, there were no available vehicles anywhere in sight, so it looked like they were in for a long walk. She didn't relish the idea of trekking through the dark streets with roaming bands of rappa and wyverns flying around, but they didn't have much choice.

Thankfully, the armed Guards quickly dispatched the few groups of rappa that they did encounter before they could get too close.

Liz had acquired a rifle from one of the Guardsmen and she used it with amazing efficiency to take down several wyverns with remarkable precision. Emily took down one of the scaly beasts, but most remained out of range of her arrows. So instead she focused on picking off any rappa stragglers that tried to flee.

As their small band progressed through the streets, they picked up many citizens who added their strength to the armed party.

They had gathered dozens of followers, and were still many blocks from the Command Center, when a huge wyvern suddenly fell out of the clouds and appeared to be fighting with something that had large, feathered wings.

The beasts were locked in furious combat and the wyvern landed with a thunderous crash on its back in the middle of the street, blocking their path.

Bestriding the stunned wyvern was a beast with the golden-furred body of an enormous lion and the white wings, forelegs, and white feathered head of an eagle.

Emily immediately recognized a majestic griffin. They had encountered one before, several months ago on their initial trip to Pittsburgh.

The stunned wyvern struggled to fend of the razor-sharp talons and wickedly curved beak of the ferocious griffin until the golden beast clamped down on the wyvern's long neck and with a violent twist there was a resounding *crack* and the wyvern went limp.

The griffin dropped the dead wyvern and the great white wings seemed to glow in the darkness. The golden body shimmered as the magnificent beast moved off the dead wyvern and its huge eyes took in Emily and the small party before it as it gracefully climbed off the scaly corpse.

The Guard fearfully raised their weapons as the legendary creature slowly stalked toward them.

"Lower yer weapons, ye foolish humans," Captain Raenods barked. "That be a griffin."

The Guard followed the dwarf's orders and slowly lowered their rifles, but they still eyed the dangerous beast warily.

Shrieks and howls filled the air and everyone looked up as the soaring wyverns suddenly began to dive and twist away from smaller golden forms that appeared out of the clouds and dove at the dragon-kin.

Dozens of griffins appeared out of the overcast night sky and viciously attacked the vast wyvern host.

The defenders below cheered at the sight and Emily couldn't help but join in the applause. She looked back down at the magnificent griffin as it approached and she couldn't help but feel that this creature seemed familiar...

We meet again, Druid.

Emily jumped as the words sounded in her mind and she suddenly realized why this griffin looked so familiar. It was Eagle Feather, the griffin they had rescued months ago.

"What are you doing here?" Emily asked the majestic creature.

We have come to assist you, Eagle Feather replied.

"I can see that," Emily smiled. "But why?"

The griffin tilted its massive head and regarded Emily with one large eye. *Are you injured?*

"I don't think so…" Emily inspected herself. "Do I look hurt?"

Your scent is strange and the covering on your head…

"Oh." Emily touched her head wrap self-consciously. "I'm not hurt, I just like to wear it."

You humans are strange creatures.

Emily suddenly felt eyes on her and when she glanced back she found everyone in the party staring at her in amazement. It took her a moment to realize what the problem was.

They couldn't hear Eagle Feather.

Emily's Druidic powers allowed her to understand animals and that seemed to include legendary creatures like griffins. But to everyone else, it seemed as though she was having a one-sided conversation with herself. They probably thought she was going mad. Only Liz knew what was happening and Emily was grateful when she replied to their stares.

"Emily is a Druid," Liz explained to the gathering. "She can communicate with the griffin."

That seemed to pacify most of the group until they all looked up and pointed excitedly. Emily turned back to see what the commotion was and looked to the sky.

Out of the darkness, a second griffin glided on silent white wings and landed gracefully beside Eagle Feather. This griffin was far larger than even the huge Eagle Feather, and where Eagle Feather had a lush coat of golden fur, the newcomer's fur was such a pale yellow that it was nearly white.

The massive creature eyed Emily and her companions a moment before a deep voice resonated within her mind.

Greetings Druid, the griffin said, and regally bowed his feathered head. *I am Longmane, leader of this Flock. I am pleased to finally meet the ones who saved my daughter from the cursed wyverns.*

"It was our pleasure, mighty Longmane," Emily replied with a slight bow of her own.

We have come to assist you if we can, Longmane said. *Do you have need of us?*

An idea suddenly popped into Emily's mind. "Actually, yes. Did you fly over the Command Center on your way here?"

Command Center? Longmane tilted his great head in confusion.

Of course, the griffin wouldn't know what a command center was, Emily scolded herself. "It looks like a small stone castle surrounded by skyscrapers."

Ahh, Longmane nodded. *We did cross over a darkened area of your strange city that had a castle within the glass forest. Is that your destination?*

"It is," Emily replied. "Can you take us there?"

The mighty griffin eyed the large group of defenders and shook his massive head. *Even I cannot carry so many.*

"You don't need to," Emily replied excitedly. "Just Liz and me."

Longmane nodded his assent. *Very well. We will take you.*

****

Mike and Ted dove into a stairwell and pounded up the steps. Ted paused only for a moment to mutter a quick spell, locking the door behind them, before hurrying up after Mike.

A tremendous crash shook the walls as something huge slammed into the sealed door.

Mike and Ted picked up their pace as the heavy thumping continued until the door finally gave out and shattered under the extreme pressure.

The impossibly wide head of the hellish tiger squeezed through the ruptured doorway and somehow managed to get its massive bulk into the stairwell. With amazing dexterity, the great beast bound up the steps after its prey with scores of orc ninjas boiling up in its wake.

Mike and Ted reached the top of the stairs and found the heavy steel door was locked. Ted muttered something under his breath as he slammed the palm of his hand on the door and it suddenly sprang open.

Together, they rushed through and quickly slammed the door shut behind them. Another muttered spell sealed the door and then Ted noticed their surroundings. "Oh, great," he muttered. "We are trapped on the roof."

The cloudy night sky rolled high above and the sounds of gunshots echoed from all around them. The roof they found themselves on wasn't very large, and there were no visible ladders or other possible escape routes.

"We aren't trapped," Mike countered, as he peered over one of the edges, searching for a way off. "There has to be a fire escape or something around here." When he didn't see anything, he added, "Don't you have a flying spell or something?"

A heavy thud shook the door and a deep growl issued from inside the stairwell.

"Of course, I don't," Ted growled. "I have been focusing on battle magic, not flying." He eyed his own ledge and didn't see a way off. "I thought you knew where you were going?"

"How should I know where those stairs went?" Mike argued, as he peered over another ledge. "I was busy trying to get away from the giant demon tiger that wants to eat us."

Another heavy thud shook the door and it groaned under the strain.

"That's just great," Ted growled. "Now, we are trapped on an open roof with a magically-resistant demon and a horde of orc ninjas that want to kill us."

Mike stepped away from the last ledge, suddenly calm. "That sounds to me like an epic way to go out."

Another heavy thud shook the door and the reinforced steel started to bend.

Ted grinned and joined Mike across from the door. "Two heroes stand alone on a dark rooftop, surrounded by evil ninjas and demonic beasts."

Another heavy thud shook the door and one of the hinges broke off.

Mike smiled at his friend and readied his mace as the shield formed on his arm with a metallic clink. "I couldn't have written it better myself."

Power suddenly flared along Ted's modified staff and the blocky head blazed with life as a long, axe-like blade grew from one end and a long spike of liquid light extended from the other.

"A plasma poleaxe," Mike chuckled. "I should have known."

The steel door screeched in protest and finally gave way before the tremendous force behind it. The heavy door landed with a crash and the massive tiger-like demon bound through the opening. The great beast's too-intelligent eyes took in the situation and Mike could have sworn the creature smiled as it realized they were trapped.

Dozens of ninjas fanned out around them and with their backs to the ledge, Mike and Ted were quickly surrounded.

"Here goes nothing," Mike muttered, just before the demon tiger let out an ear-splitting roar and the surrounding ninjas burst into motion.

Mike summoned a barrier that blocked off one side and forced the attackers to bunch together as waves of fire flowed out from around Ted.

Blades clashed as Mike met the first wave of ninjas. He blocked and parried furiously as the ninjas pressed in with weapons that bit like striking snakes. Flickering blades darted in and scored countless cuts across Mike's unarmored body and his clothes were quickly stained red with blood.

Ted hurled a veritable hurricane of destructive spells around him, but for every orc that fell, another took its place and gained another step closer. Shurikens suddenly flew from the ninjas, but the golden bubble of light around Ted deflected the deadly projectiles.

The demon tiger roared again and suddenly drove through the orcs and barreled them out of its way in its quest to reach Ted.

A rainbow of magical spells broke over the mighty beast as Ted desperately tried to find some spell that could harm it. But nothing he did had any real effect and only seemed to anger the demon.

With his attention turned to the tiger, the ninjas seized the opportunity and closed with Ted. One of the ninjas raised his katana behind Ted's back and prepared for the fatal strike, but the ninjas suddenly flew off the roof as Mike's mace struck as he barreled his way through the throng to fight at Ted's side.

The evil tiger pounced and crashed into Ted.

The golden shield shattered as the massive beast bore him to the ground. Ninjas struck from all sides and Mike knew the end was near. But he wasn't about to go out without a fight.

Beaten and bloody, Mike roared in defiance as he called forth the Holy Fire.

His eyes blazed with blue flames and his vision became clearer. He could smell the coppery tang of his blood and the stink of orcs that mingled with the sulfur of the demon. Time seemed to slow as he fell deeper into the Zone.

Mike abruptly slammed his mace onto the rooftop at his feet and a shockwave billowed out around him, knocking the ninjas back.

Free from the orcs for the moment, he turned to the great beast that had Ted pinned and was trying to bite through the shaft of the plasma poleaxe that Ted had jammed between its jaws.

Glowing ribbons of mist coalesced around Mike's mace and streamers of pulsing energy spiraled around the weapon as Mike pointed it at the demonic creature. The mace flared with brilliant light and a beam of white-hot power burst from the ancient mace and struck the evil creature as it straddled Ted.

The holy energy lance erupted when it made contact with the demonic creature and the resulting explosion flung the massive beast across the roof where it skidded to a halt on the far side of the roof.

The orcs howled in rage and came on in a storm of slashing blades as Mike hauled a dazed Ted to his feet.

Ted steadied himself as Mike lunged forward and met the oncoming horde head on. Eyes blazing, Mike waded into the black tide and bodies were hurled in all directions as his mighty impact mace lived up to its name.

But even with the added power of the Holy Fire coursing through him and the influence of his mace, Mike was slowly being cut to ribbons by the sea of blades around him. He knew he couldn't stop them all but at least he could give Ted a chance to recover while taking out as many of the orcs as he could before they finally overwhelmed him.

A wave of heat washed over him and then Ted was at his side, plasma poleaxe blazing as he sliced through the surprised ninjas. Together they battled back to back as the ninjas pressed in around them.

A thunderous roar shook the rooftop as the demonic tiger somehow picked itself up and reentered the fray. The orcs made way for the mighty beast as it headed unerringly toward Mike.

A straight blade suddenly stabbed out of the throng and drove through Mike's left shoulder, just above his shield. Another blade sliced across his calf and Mike fell to a knee as the demon closed in for the kill.

Ted tried to turn and help his friend, but when he did, a spinning shuriken finally broke through his weakened shield and plunged into his arm. His hand went numb and he lost his grip on the poleaxe.

An orc drove in with a blade aimed for his throat, but it abruptly collapsed with a hole in its head, and a moment later Ted heard the bark of a gunshot.

More ninjas died as the mysterious bullets found their mark and the orcs looked around in confusion as arrows also began to fall among them with deadly accuracy.

Mike shielded his eyes as dust began to swirl around the roof as the wind grew stronger. An ear-piercing shriek above them made Mike look up and what he saw he couldn't believe.

Two huge griffins with white wings circled the rooftop like gigantic birds of prey and the beat of those mighty wings was what was causing the dust storm. What was more surprising than the sudden appearance of the griffins was the riders upon their backs.

Liz fired her rifle from the back of a huge, pale griffin while Emily showered arrows from a smaller, golden griffin.

The surviving ninjas turned and fled from the mighty spectacle as death rained down from above. A bare handful escaped to the stairwell, most being picked off as they made for cover. But there was one who didn't flee.

The great demonic tiger stalked toward Mike, seemingly oblivious as arrows and bullets pelted its blazing hide.

Mike gritted his teeth and forced himself to stand as the demon moved toward him. Ted yanked a bloody shuriken from his arm before collapsing nearby.

The huge cat crouched down and Mike painfully tried to raise his shield for the pounce he knew was coming.

Great, corded muscles bunched and the demon tiger sprang high into the air with its foot-long claws extended as it flew toward Mike.

Mike braced himself for the impact, but halfway to him a golden blur crashed into the demon and bore it to the ground.

The two great beasts broke apart and circled each other warily.

Suddenly, the hellish tiger roared in pain as pieces of it started to flake off. Within moments the beast started to fade away. The demon screamed one last time as it lost its hold on reality and abruptly vanished into mist.

The magnificent griffin circled the place where the demon had been a moment before and gave a satisfied snort before joining the pale griffin that had also landed on the roof. Liz leapt off the pale griffin and ran over to

Mike who had fallen to his knees while the great beasts had confronted each other.

Whispering a fervent prayer, Liz swiftly healed Mike before moving over and doing the same for Ted.

"Thanks," Ted groaned, as he picked himself up with the aid of his staff that no longer glowed with power. "But you ruined our epic death scene."

"I'm sorry," Liz replied with mock concern, "but the heroes had to swoop in and save the damsels in distress."

"Damsels?" Mike scowled, as his shield retracted into his gauntlet.

Liz ignored him. "What is going on here? Besides you two clowns trying to get killed."

Mike suddenly remembered the sorcerer and the survivors trapped inside the control room. "Come on!" he shouted and rushed toward the stairs with Ted following close behind. Surprised by Mike's sudden reaction, Liz stood there in confusion for a moment before hurrying after them.

Emily watched her friends disappear into the ruined stairwell from atop Eagle Feather. "Don't worry about me!" she shouted, as Liz vanished down the stairs. "I'll just stay here!"

****

Liz ran down the dark stairs as fast as she could to keep Mike and Ted in sight below her. She slung her MK13 over her shoulder and drew a pistol as she raced down another flight, and saw her friends open the door on the next floor and charge through.

Mike and Ted's urgency drove her onward and she barreled through the door after them, pistol first, as she prepared to be beset by enemies.

To her surprise and great relief, no enemies greeted her, only a dark hallway that Mike and Ted were running down.

"Wait for me!" she shouted, as she ran after the vanishing pair, but they didn't slow so she tried another tactic. "It's a bad idea to leave your healer behind!"

That got the reaction she was looking for as Mike and Ted both slowed to a stop while Liz rushed to catch up.

"Where are we going?" Liz gasped when she reached her friends.

"Central Command," Mike replied, before resuming his pace down the hall with Ted and Liz close behind.

They made several turns and Liz was quickly lost in the stony labyrinth of the command center. She was glad that Mike had an uncanny knack for directions and she was confident that they were headed in the right direction, even if she didn't have a clue where that was.

They turned down one last corridor, which opened up into a large, multi-leveled room that could only be described as a command center. But this command center looked like a bomb had gone off.

Bodies littered the floor and the walls were scorched black. Smashed control stations and unrecognizable fragments were strewn everywhere. A thick haze of foul-smelling smoke obscured the furthest corners of the chamber and Liz could see figures moving around in the gloom.

The three friends readied their weapons as they cautiously made their way into the smoke-filled room.

Voices emerged from the haze and Liz breathed a sigh of relief when she heard English and not the guttural rumblings of the orcs. But Mike and Ted didn't lower their guard and pressed on through the smoke.

"We couldn't see them through the clouds," a voice said, as they got closer to the obscured figures.

"Clouds?!" someone bellowed. "We have radar! Why aren't we using it? We should have seen this attack coming miles away!"

"Sir," a different voice spoke up nervously. "Our radar is calibrated for weather patterns and doesn't pick up much else. With the low cloud cover we couldn't see them until it was too late. But the radar at the airport could detect incoming aerial attacks."

The shapes resolved themselves into a group of human soldiers and command personnel all gathered around a furious General Adams.

"Then either get ours recalibrated or go procure the one at the airport," General Adams ordered angrily. "From now on, if a pigeon shits within a hundred miles of this city, I want to know about it!"

"Yes sir!" A soldier snapped a quick salute before hurrying out of the room.

Operators were seated at all of the remaining communication stations, issuing orders and gathering information as a flood of calls came in.

"Now, go find out what the Hell is going on in our city," General

Adams barked, and the personnel around him scattered to their assigned tasks.

The general noticed Liz and her friends for the first time and a brief look of surprise crossed his face before he motioned them to join him.

"So," he said grimly, "I take it we have you to thank for that little diversion?"

"We thought you could use a hand," Mike replied easily.

The general snorted. "You had that right. Those sneaky bastards caught us with our pants down," he said, and eyed Liz and her friends suspiciously. "How is it that you guys always seem to be in the right place at the right time?"

Ted shrugged. "Just lucky I guess."

"I'm sure," General Adams muttered.

"I fer one be glad they be so durned lucky," came a deep, rumbling voice out of the smoke and a moment later, two dwarves strode through the haze.

Liz recognized the speaker and was surprised to discover it was the copper-haired Prince Brokkr accompanied by a stern-looking bodyguard. Both were covered in blood and had weapons in hand.

"I be takin' luck o'er skill any day," Prince Brokkr rumbled.

"I second the dwarf," a musical voice said from beyond the smoky gloom, followed by the appearance of a trio of elves. "Luck cannot be learned."

Two female Korybantes flanked the speaker, a handsome Paladin with coal black skin and brilliant purple eyes.

"Commander Valerian," Liz breathed. "It is nice to see you again."

The Paladin's smile practically lit up the room. "Ah, Elizabeth. So good to see you, and it is Stratigos Valerian now."

"Congratulations," Liz beamed at the handsome elf.

"Thank you." Valerian inclined his head gratefully. "It was decided that someone needed to have command over all the elven forces and since I was the most senior commander, Arch Battlemage Gwydion elevated me to the honored position of Stratigos."

"Aye," Prince Brokkr rumbled, "and we were havin' a secret meetin' ter plan fer the comin' battle when an army o' orcs dropped in on us."

"Not a very secret meeting then," Mike noted, and General Adams scowled at him.

"Obviously not," the general grumbled. "I don't understand how they could have known about it. It wasn't decided until yesterday."

"Could they have used a spell?" Ted asked.

"No," Stratigos Valerian shook his head. "The wards prevent any scrying spells."

"Then we have a spy," General Adams growled.

"But who would spy for the orcs?" Ted asked.

"Humans," Liz said sadly. "There were humans fighting for the orcs in the streets. They were dressed the same and I didn't notice until I uncovered one."

"Why would anyone help the orcs?" General Adams asked with confusion plain on his face.

"Because people suck," Mike replied. "Are you really surprised that there are scumbags out there that would love to see the world burn?"

"But to join the orcs..." the general muttered.

Mike suddenly laughed. "I'm glad they joined the orcs. It will be good to kill the traitors."

"We really don't need any more enemies," said Liz. "I think three hostile armies is more than enough."

"I agree with Elizabeth," Valerian said. "We need more allies, not enemies."

"I may be able to help with that," Emily suddenly said, as she stepped out of the haze.

Prince Brokkr snorted. "An' how ye goin' ter do that?"

"I have a message from Longmane," Emily replied smugly.

The dwarf prince scratched his coppery beard. "And who in Loki's Balls be that?"

"He is the leader of the griffins," Emily answered.

"Griffins?" General Adams looked around as if expecting the legendary creature to appear out of the smoke next. "As in, body of a lion and head of an eagle, griffins?"

Emily nodded. "The same. And they are offering an alliance."

"Now, that be good news indeed," Brokkr rumbled happily.

General Adams didn't seem as pleased about the news. "Can we trust them?"

"O' course," Brokkr rumbled before Emily could answer. "We dwarves have fought beside the mighty griffins fer centuries. They be noble beasts and the most loyal allies anyone could hope ter find." The prince looked around at the gathering meaningfully. "But cross 'em and it'll be the last thing ye ever do, don't ye doubt."

"Colonel Wheeler!" General Adams shouted, and a man standing behind a row of communications personnel looked up.

"Yes sir?" the colonel answered.

"Someone give me the sitrep," the general barked.

"The enemy is in full retreat, General," Colonel Wheeler announced. "City Guard units are sweeping the streets as we speak, and the elves and dwarves report all orcs have been eliminated from their districts. There are also reports coming in from all over the city of griffins battling the wyverns in the air."

"A sign of good will from the griffins," Emily said quickly.

"Thank you, Colonel. Continue overseeing the cleanup," General Adams said. "That will be all."

Colonel Wheeler snapped a quick salute before turning back to the communications station.

"Now," the general rubbed his temples wearily, "I assume these griffins want something in return for their assistance."

"They do," Emily answered nervously.

"And what could a bunch of griffins want from us?" General Adams asked.

"What everyone in these crazy times wants," replied Emily. "A safe haven."

CHAPTER 13

"A safe haven?" General Adams chuckled darkly. "I don't think anywhere could be called *safe* these days." The general looked around at the ruined command center that was being revealed as the smoke slowly cleared. "We aren't even safe in the heart of our own city."

"Griffin riders be excellent scouts," Prince Brokkr rumbled. "Nearly every Mountain Clan employs at least a few o' the beasts fer such things. An' our smiths could be makin armor fer 'em ter boot."

General Adams sighed and looked around at the gathering. "And if we accept their offer, just where will we be keeping these creatures?"

"They would be most welcome among the Aos Si," Stratigos Valerian said.

"Pssh," Prince Brokkr chortled. "They be staying with the Clans o' course."

Valerian looked about to argue, but Emily cut him off. "Why don't we allow the griffins to choose where they wish to remain?"

"It seems that there are no objections to the beasts staying here?" General Adams asked, and when no one spoke up he said. "Very well, they can stay. But only under one condition; they must follow our orders and allow riders. Will that be a problem?"

Liz and Emily shared a look before Emily answered, "I will ask them, but I don't think that will be a problem at all."

"Good." The general gave a satisfied nod. "Now, if you will excuse me, I have a city to clean up." And with that, General Adams spun on his heel and began barking orders as he marched away.

"So, what happened after we left?" Mike asked, after the general disappeared into the smoke.

Valerian answered, "With the sorcerer distracted and most of his shinobi chasing after you, we launched a counter attack that took them completely by surprise."

"Aye," Prince Brokkr rumbled. "Twas a glorious sally that swept the filthy orcs away."

"I wouldn't say we *swept them away*," Valerian argued. "But after a short and furious skirmish, we overcame them and finally killed the sorcerer, who was the last to fall." The stratigos eyed Mike and Ted curiously. "But how did you survive?"

Brokkr rumbled his assent. "Aye. The last we saw o' ye, there be a mighty Hellcat and a horde o' shinobi chasin after ye."

"Hellcat?" Ted scratched his beard thoughtfully. "Is that what the demon tiger was called?"

"Aye," the dwarf prince nodded. "The old texts speak o' such creatures. They say Hellcats were created when Black Orcs would capture one o' the Great Cats and through the vilest o' witchcraft summon a demon ter possess the mighty beast. Once possessed, the Hellcat was bound ter an object that chained the demon ter the will o' the wearer."

"That's horrible," Emily gasped. "Who would do such a thing?"

"Orcs," Brokkr rumbled grimly. "But ye didn't answer me question." He looked at Mike and Ted. "How'd ye survive?"

Mike shrugged innocently. "We ran."

"To the roof," Ted added.

Liz put her hand on Emily's shoulder. "Where we saved them."

"Truly?" the dwarf prince rumbled with disbelief evident in his voice. "How did ye kill the Hellcat? The old texts say they be near impossible ter defeat, being resistant ter both spell and blade alike."

"We didn't kill it," Liz admitted. "It just kind of... vanished into smoke."

"Interesting," Valerian muttered. "If what you say is true, Prince Brokkr, then I believe this Hellcat lost its tether to our realm when you killed the sorcerer."

The prince nodded his bearded head. "That confirms the lore o' such things. But the beast be no truly defeated until the object it be bound ter also be destroyed."

"Then we must find and destroy this object at once," Stratigos Valerian said, and turned and strode away into the fading smoke.

The others quickly followed the tall elf though the wreckage of the command center until he stopped beside a large, headless corpse. Mike recognized the black lacquered armor and knew this to be the body of the sorcerer.

The elf Paladin bent down and began to carefully search the corpse.

He removed several bags of what looked like different colored sand, a handful of small animal bones, a few rings, three earrings, a pouch full of strange coins, an odd-looking bracelet attached to a matching ring by a small chain, and a serrated dagger with a golden hilt.

"What does this object look like?" Valerian asked, as he laid out all of the items before him.

The dwarf prince shrugged his heavy shoulders. "To the Nine Hells if I be knowin'. All the lore says is 'an object' be used ter bind em."

"Well, that's helpful," Liz muttered, as she crouched beside the handsome elf lord and examined one of the rings.

"Be careful my dear." Valerian took the ring and placed his hand on Liz's. "We don't know what spells may be woven into these objects."

Liz suddenly felt a strange sensation faintly blossom in the back of her mind, a feeling that she couldn't quite place.

"He's right." Mike abruptly bent down and pushed himself between the pair. "We don't know what kind of traps might be woven into them."

"Well, excuse me," Liz grumbled, as she readjusted from Mike's sudden intrusion. "How do you plan on discovering the Hellcat object if we don't touch them?"

"I'm sure the mages can divine their purpose," Ted offered.

"And how long will that take?" Liz asked.

Ted shrugged. "Minutes... days... years? Who can say how complex any of these items are?"

"Exactly." Emily suddenly spoke up. "We can't let that poor tiger stay possessed and trapped inside some piece of junk!"

"I agree," Liz said, and she bent down and picked up another one of the rings. This ring had a silver band set with a row of red gems and was much too big for her slender fingers. Before anyone could stop her, she rammed it on her finger. Everyone held their breath as they waited to see what would happen, but after a tense moment Liz breathed a sigh of relief. "See, nothing to worry about."

"That was incredibly foolish," Valerian scolded "and not to mention dangerous. It could have exploded and killed us all."

Liz's cheeks colored in embarrassment from the rebuke, but she didn't back down. "But it didn't. And if you want to go, then go. I will find this object and free the tiger."

Emily sat down beside Liz. "So will I." She removed her earrings and picked up one of the sorcerer's earrings. It was shaped like a black tooth and she jammed it into her ear.

Emily hissed in pain as the earring began to smoke. She quickly ripped it out and threw it back onto the floor.

The dwarf prince stomped a heavy boot on the discarded earring. "Ye be wastin' yer time," Brokkr rumbled. "Even if we were ter find the correct object, we will no be able ter free yer cat."

Emily scowled up at the dwarf while holding her injured ear. "And why is that?"

"Me ancestors spent a great deal o' time trying ter find a way ter free the beasts. But none was ever discovered."

"Perhaps the mages could be of assistance," Valerian offered.

The dwarf prince snorted, "If a dwarf can no unmake a thing, then it can no be unmade."

"Can't we just destroy it?" Ted asked and raised his staff meaningfully.

"O' course," Brokkr rumbled. "But if we be destroyin' it then the cat's soul will be dragged ter Hell along with the demon as likely as no."

"Then what do we do?" Emily asked, as she picked up the serrated dagger. "We can't just leave it trapped in there?" She rolled the dagger over in her hands but couldn't find anything out of the ordinary about it.

"I'm no fer knowin'," Prince Brokkr rumbled. "The possessed beasts never survived bein' separated from their bindin'."

"You said possessed," Liz said excitedly. "Can we have an exorcism or something to remove the demon?"

The dwarf prince looked dumbfounded. "I'm no fer knowin' if that ever been tried afore," Brokkr admitted. "Me ancestors were tryin' ter find ways ter defeat the beasts, no ter save em."

"She does have a point," Valerian added. "If these beasts truly are possessed, then theoretically they can be exorcised."

"I hate exercise," Emily muttered, as she put on another of the orc's rings.

"I know," Liz laughed, as she attached the bracelet to her wrist and slipped the attached ring over her finger. "But it's-" Liz suddenly gasped and her body went rigid.

"Liz!" Emily cried. "What's wrong?"

"I... found it," Liz said through gritted teeth, "and it's not happy to see me."

The handsome Paladin lord bent down and placed his hands on Liz's shoulders. "You must fight it," he said. "The demon will try to consume you like it has the beast."

Mike stepped in and pushed Valerian aside. "I think she knows that," he grumbled, as he gently helped Liz to her feet.

Liz squeezed her eyes shut and sweat beaded her brow.

"Are you alright?" Mike asked.

No reply came and Liz remained motionless.

"Liz!" Mike grabbed her shoulders and gently shook her. "Can you hear me?"

Liz's eyes suddenly popped open. "Of course, I can hear you," Liz snapped. "Now, stop shaking me. I'm trying to summon a demon here."

"Sorry," Mike mumbled, and slowly backed away as Liz took a deep breath and closed her eyes again.

Mike found himself holding his breath for what seemed like an eternity, but he was sure only a few moments had actually gone by, until the first wisps of smoke billowed up before Liz's outstretched arm. The black smoke boiled up into a dark cloud of swirling ash and the overwhelming stink of sulfur filled the air.

The roiling, black ash cloud swiftly resolved itself into the all-too-familiar form of the glowing Hellcat. Huge eyes, like pools of unending darkness, burned with an evil intelligence as it regarded the puny mortals gathered before it. A menacing growl rumbled up from deep inside its mighty chest as it hunched down and took a threatening step forward.

Mike's gauntlet shield sprang open and Ted's plasma poleaxe burst to life as they stepped in front of Liz to confront the demon. They were joined a moment later by Stratigos Valerian and his Korybantes on one side and Prince Brokkr and his Huscarl on the other.

Emily drew her bow and found a bead on the huge beast, but before she could release, Liz placed a gentle hand on her arrow. "Stop," Liz commanded calmly. "It won't hurt us."

The demon tiger bared its fangs and lashed its tail threateningly. "Coulda fooled me," Emily muttered.

Liz released Emily's arrow and pushed her way between Mike and Ted to stand alone before the awesome might of the possessed beast.

Mike started to step forward, but the dwarf prince held him back. "She'll be fine, lad," Brokkr rumbled. "As long as she be wearin' the bracelet, the Hellcat can no touch her."

Mike didn't like the idea of some flimsy piece of jewelry being the only thing standing between Liz and a demon, but he knew the dwarves understood orcs and demons better than anyone. So, if Brokkr said she would be fine, then she would be. But that didn't mean he had to like it.

Liz took a nervous step forward and everyone held their breath as she reached out a cautious hand toward the growling Hellcat.

The Hellcat's pitch-black orbs regarded Liz, as she stood alone and unprotected, before the possessed beast. Liz took another slow step forward and the demon's eyes narrowed dangerously.

She took another step and the demon suddenly bared its foot-long fangs. With an impressive show of courage, Liz only paused for a moment before she took a final step and placed her hand on the beast's massive head.

The mighty Hellcat froze when she made contact and a slight gasp escaped Liz's lips as her fingers connected with the coarse fur. She took a deep breath and closed her eyes as she took the massive beast's head in her hands. The Hellcat remained motionless, either unable or unwilling to move.

Golden light welled out from under Liz's hands and a moment later the beast's eyes began to close as its powerful body seemed to relax.

Liz spoke softly into the possessed cat's ear and the beast sagged even more under Liz's gentle coaxing.

Suddenly, the black eyes popped open and the Hellcat's earsplitting roar echoed through the chamber. The beast's muscles bunched as it desperately tried to push itself away, but its head was somehow held immobile by Liz's gentle touch.

The Hellcat roared and clawed at the ground as it fought to get away, but its head remained strangely motionless even though the rest of its body strained to escape. Everyone in the room backed away from the thrashing demon, giving the frenzied beast plenty of space.

With her chest just inches from the roaring jaws that could easily snap a man in two, Liz calmly continued to whisper into the Hellcat's ears as the golden light soaked into the black fur.

The demon's struggles grew more frantic and its huge claws dug long gouges in the stone floor, while its great head remained locked in Liz's embrace.

Emily abruptly cried out and fell to her knees, clutching her ears in pain.

"What is it?" Ted asked as he knelt down beside her.

"Can't you hear it?" Emily asked, through gritted teeth. "The cat… it's screaming."

Mike listened, but all he could hear was the roar of the possessed beast as it thrashed helplessly in Liz's hands.

The demon tiger's struggles were getting weaker as the unrelenting golden light flowed into it. The Hellcat sagged as it expended the last of its energy and as everyone watched, the beast's struggle slowly ceased.

A long moment went by before Mike noticed the first change.

The hellish light that pulsed between the beast's stripes began to fade as if the fire inside the mighty body was being smothered. The evil light dimmed and turned a dull grey before being blown away by some unseen breath of fresh air that revealed a brilliant, white coat of glossy fur that sparkled between the black stripes like new-fallen snow.

The sulfuric stink slowly faded along with the hellish light and within moments, the evil creature was washed away to reveal a majestic white tiger of immense proportions.

The beast's eyes remained black pools of utter darkness for several heartbeats after the rest of the demon's aspect was cleared away. But as everyone watched in stunned silence, the blackness began to drain away as if someone had pulled a plug and the evil inside was emptied. Two, huge, ice-blue eyes regarded Liz as the golden light slowly faded.

Liz gently released the mighty white tiger's head and she promptly collapsed.

Mike was the first to her and he quickly scooped her up protectively in his thick arms, as the huge tiger remained motionless. Liz smiled weakly up at him and put a reassuring hand on his chest.

"Loki's Balls," Brokkr cursed. "I was no thinkin' such a thing be possible."

"What thing?" Emily asked as she rubbed her temples wearily.

The dwarf prince eyed Liz with a look of something between fear and admiration. "The lass here exorcised the demon," he rumbled in amazement.

"Surely such a thing isn't unheard of," Ted replied, as he eyed the motionless beast wearily. "I'm sure you dwarves have exorcised your share of demons."

"O' course," Brokkr nodded, "but exorcisin' a free demon be one thing. Removing a demon that be strong enough ter dominate a Great Cat that also be bound to a material object ter boot..." The dwarf prince shook his head in wonder. "That should be impossible fer a mere cleric ter be doin' alone."

"Luckily," Liz breathed, as Mike gently set her on her feet, "I'm not a cleric."

Brokkr snorted. "Maybe no, but ye got the powers o' one."

"We can debate Liz's clerical status later," Mike interrupted. "The real question is, what do we do with that-" He motioned to the massive white tiger that was still staring at them curiously with its huge, ice-blue eyes.

"We free it," Emily answered immediately.

"I agree," Liz said, as she stood before the Great Cat. The large creature was so tall that she stood nearly eye level with it. "But why isn't it moving?"

"I believe," Valerian began, "that it hasn't moved because you haven't ordered it to."

"Ordered it?" Liz muttered, but didn't look away from the tiger as she took a step toward the beast and carefully ran a hand through the soft, thick fur of its neck. "You can move freely," she said softly.

The towering cat immediately turned and licked her with a huge, wet tongue that covered Liz's entire face.

Liz laughed as the tiger bore her to the ground and showered her with grateful licks that covered her in slime. "Stop. Stop!" she laughed, as she struggled to escape the giant beast's grateful embrace.

Emily watched the joyous struggle with a smile. "So, how do we free it?"

"I'm no fer knowin,'" Brokkr admitted. "The beast's soul be bound ter the artifact. Ter sever the connection will kill the beast."

"Surely there must be a way," Stratigos Valerian replied. "Every enchantment can be undone."

"It's been tried, elf," Prince Brokkr rumbled.

The stratigos scowled at the prince. "Perhaps by dwarves."

"Are ye sayin' elves could do somethin' me ancestors could no?" Brokkr growled dangerously.

"I'm saying," Valerian answered carefully, "that perhaps we elves have methods that might prove more effective, if given the chance."

"Bwahahaha." The dwarf prince suddenly roared with laughter. "Ter think elves would be knowin' more about demons than dwarves! Bwahaha."

The elf lord ignored the laughter. "I admit orcs and demons are not the province of elves, but magic is." The dwarf prince quit laughing. "If a dark enchantment bound this poor creature, then perhaps the mages could unravel it."

"It's worth a shot," Emily hurriedly said before Brokkr could reply.

"I agree," Liz said, now that she had finally escaped the grateful tiger's grasp. "But I don't want some random mage poking at this and accidentally killing her."

"Her?" Ted muttered, as Valerian held out his hand and said. "Give me the bracelet and I will take it directly to the Archmage."

Liz shook her head and clutched her arm with the bracelet to her chest. The huge tiger stepped protectively between Liz and the elf lord and growled menacingly at Valerian who hastily lowered his hand and moved away.

Liz smiled and petted the great cat as it snarled at the elf. "I am perfectly capable of taking this to the Archmage," she said sweetly. "Thank you though."

"Very well," Stratigos Valerian said curtly. "Now that this matter is settled, I must return to overseeing the defenses and assisting General Adams with the cleanup."

The elf lord took his leave as he and his Korybantes moved off to another area of the command center.

"An' I need ter inform me father what happened here," Prince Brokkr rumbled as a way of farewell. He and his lone Huscarl started to turn away when he paused and looked back at Liz. "Ye should be returnin' the beast ter the bracelet afore too long," he rumbled. "The enchantment will eventually weaken and force the great beast ter return anyhow."

"I will," Liz promised, and the dwarf prince nodded before marching away. "Now, if I just knew how to do that," she muttered softly.

Ted scratched his beard thoughtfully. "Probably the same way you summoned it in the first place."

"Hey, Em, can you tell me anything about her before I send her back?" Liz asked hopefully.

"Yeah," Emily replied. "Her name is Kiba'Nadare and she is tremendously grateful to be free of the Bakeneko's presence. She is also extremely tired."

Liz ran her hand through the soft fur one last time and sighed. "Alright, Kiba'Nadare, here goes nothing." She closed her eyes and a moment later a swirl of snow suddenly kicked up around the huge tiger. The snow increased and whirled around the beast in a small blizzard before abruptly fading away and taking the Great Cat with it.

Liz grabbed the bracelet with her other hand in surprise. "It just got really cold."

"Oh, shoot!" Emily hissed suddenly. "I left Longmane and Eagle Feather waiting for an answer on the roof!" Without waiting to see if anyone else was coming, she spun around and dashed back through the ruined control room.

Emily didn't need to worry because the two griffins were still waiting for her when she and her friends finally reached the roof a few minutes later.

You spoke with your leaders? Eagle Feather asked eagerly.

"Yes," Emily replied, slightly out of breath from running up the stairs. "They said you are welcome to stay here, but there are conditions."

What conditions? Longmane asked with a nervous snort.

"You must allow riders and follow orders," Mike answered, and everyone looked at him as if he had gone mad.

"What?" Mike looked around at his friends. "I was just answering the question."

"What question?" Ted asked. "Nobody said anything."

"He did." Mike pointed to Longmane. "Right, Emily?"

Emily nodded. "He did actually."

"Interesting," Ted muttered. "I forgot you could understand griffins… I wonder why…"

Mike shrugged. "Just lucky I guess. Now, back to the matter at hand." He turned back to the pair of griffins. "What do you say to those conditions?"

I have no objection to allowing riders; however, I do not enjoy the idea of taking orders from biped, Longman answered with the toss of his great, feathered head. *But if these are the conditions, then I will accept them until such a time as our enemies are defeated and my Flock can find a permanent home in this strange world.*

"Wonderful." Mike clapped his hands together eagerly. "Now that that's settled, what do you say we go hunt some orcs?"

Liz sighed wearily. "Haven't you had enough excitement for one night?"

"Every enemy we kill now is one less we have to fight later," Mike replied with an eager grin.

"You're crazy," Emily muttered, "but you do have a point."

Liz groaned, "Ugh, you sound just like Jack." Liz's eyes suddenly bulged. "SHIT!" she cried. "We left Jack alone with some strange dwarf! We have to get back. NOW!"

Liz started for the door, but Mike grabbed ahold of her arm with a grip like a vice. "Whoa. What strange dwarf?" Mike asked.

"He said he was a priest of Fenrir or something and he had golden eyes, too," Liz answered in a rush. "He said he could help Jack if he wasn't too late and we locked them in the cell together."

Mike released Liz's arm. "Why on Earth did you lock them in the same cell?"

"Because we heard the sirens," Emily answered. "I wasn't about to let two werewolves loose when we were already under attack."

Liz threw up her arms in disgust. "Why are we wasting time talking about this?" she growled, before turning and again heading toward the shattered doorway. This time Mike didn't try to stop her and instead followed her lead. Ted hurried after them and Liz had almost reached the doorway when Emily coughed meaningfully. "Ehem." Everyone turned back to see what the noise was about. "As much as I would *love* to walk all the way back to the jail, I have a better idea," Emily said, and threw her thumb in the direction of the two huge griffins perched behind her. "Who wants a lift?"

The dark, cloudy sky was empty of wyverns, but the occasional explosion and burst of sporadic gunfire still echoed through the cold night air. A few fires also burned, but it seemed that much of the excitement had died down and the city was returning to normal.

The two soldiers standing guard outside the jail nearly fainted when the two huge griffins suddenly dropped out of the sky and landed right in front of them, the force of their wing beats pushing the soldiers back into the wall.

Mike and Liz hurriedly slid off the back of Longmane as Emily and Ted quickly dismounted Eagle Feather.

"Thank you," Emily shouted over her shoulder, as she and her friends hurried up the steps and ran right past the surprised guards. As quickly as they had arrived, the two griffins bound back into the air, and with a few beats of their mighty wings vanished back into the darkness.

Mike bulled his way through the guards inside. Thankfully, one of the guards recognized Liz and let them through before a fight erupted.

The Heroes of Awesome piled out of the elevator as soon as the doors opened and charged down the dark hallway. Thankfully, there were none of the Hands of Tyr standing watch. The jail guards on this floor had been warned of their pending arrival and quickly opened the doors for them.

Mike swiftly strode down the dark hallway with Liz, Ted, and Emily close behind. They hurried by rows of empty cells until they saw the one with a large shape huddled in the center. Mike breathed a sigh of relief. At least Jack hadn't escaped. However, as they drew closer Mike clenched his mace tightly, still prepared for the worst.

The huddled mass shifted and a pair of golden eyes glittered in the faint light. As Mike and the others stopped before the cell door, the golden eyes narrowed and the hairy figure rose up from the darkness.

Ted slammed the butt of his staff on the ground and a faint light burst to life on the tip of the staff. The sudden light banished the darkness and revealed the wild figure standing in the cell before them.

"Took ye long enough," a mangy-looking dwarf with golden eyes snarled. He was short and had layers of heavy furs draped over shoulders that hung to the floor. Numerous fangs and wolf totems decorated his rusty chainmail armor and he wore heavy steel gauntlets adorned with long, steel claws. "Now, let me out o' this stinkin' cage," he growled.

"What did you do with Jack," Emily snapped back. "If you hurt him I swear-"

"Easy lass," the mangy dwarf chuckled. "The pup will be fine." The dwarf stepped aside and when he did it revealed a sleeping Jack, curled up on the floor and covered in a heavy fur cloak.

Amazingly, Jack looked like his old self, a bit worse for wear with a scraggly beard, shaggy hair and dark circles under his eyes, but thankfully human.

Emily quickly typed in the code and opened the door.

Liz was the first one through the opening and she immediately went to Jack and Emily joined a moment later. Mike knew Jack was in good hands and he blocked the doorway before the dwarf could escape.

The golden-eyed dwarf glared up at him. "Best be movin' lad," the dwarf growled deep in his throat.

Ted stepped up behind Mike's shoulder. "I don't believe you are going anywhere just yet."

The dwarf bared his fangs at the tall pair blocking his escape. "What do ye want?"

"Answers," Mike replied. "Who are you and what did you do to Jack?"

The strange dwarf scowled and Mike saw his eyes dart nervously down the hall to where the guards were posted. "Don't worry friend," Mike said, guessing the dwarf's thoughts. "We will have you out of here before the

Hands of Tyr come back. Now talk."

The dwarf accepted that with a curt nod. "As I told yer women folk, I be Rangvald o' the Cult o' the Great Wolf and I guided yer friend through the Fenrisúlfrian Rite. He be stronger than he looks. I was no thinkin' he would overcome the Spirit so late after receivin' the Gift." Rangvald looked back at Jack's huddled form. "He be one o' the Pack," the dwarf rumbled with pride.

"What happens to him now?" Ted asked.

"He needs rest," Rangvald answered. "And once he be ready, he'll be needin' ter learn how ter further control his Gift."

Just then the elevator at the far end of the hall chimed and the doors slid open and the disfigured Hand of Tyr, Kjell, stepped out.

Rangvald saw Kjell and bared his long canines in a fierce snarl before quickly pushing his way between Mike and Ted, who didn't try to stop him.

"How will he learn to control it?" Ted asked as the mangy dwarf hurried away into the darkness of the hallway.

"Don't ye worry," Rangvald rumbled, as he disappeared into the gloom. "He'll find me."

Ted glared at the spot where the strange dwarf had vanished. "I just love vague answers," he grumbled.

Mike looked back and saw that the guards had opened the gate and Kjell was storming down the hallway toward them. "He probably thinks it made him more mysterious or something," he muttered, as he turned to face this next dwarf.

Kjell stomped up to Mike and Ted and glared past them into the cell where Liz and Emily were still bent over Jack's huddled form.

"What are ye dolts thinkin'?" the dwarf bellowed. "The beast could escape!"

Just then Liz and Emily carefully helped Jack to his feet. He was covered in sweat, with one shaky hand clutched at the fur cloak that was the only thing covering his naked form.

Jack's golden eyes flashed at the dwarf's words. "Do I look like a beast to you?" he rasped angrily.

Kjell stared at Jack, dumbstruck. "Impossible," he breathed. "Ye were lost ter the wolf. I saw it with me own eyes."

"Well, I'm fine now," Jack rasped, as he shifted unsteadily under his heavy fur cloak. "Now, go away and find some other poor slob to bother with your yammering."

The dwarf's chest puffed up and his patchy beard bristled at the indignity. "Yammerin'!" Kjell thundered angrily. "Ye no good whelp! I'll-"

"Be going now," Mike calmly interrupted and placed his hand on the angry dwarf's broad shoulder. "I'm sure your captain will want to know what's happened here," he continued, as he forcefully turned Kjell around and steered the stammering Hand away from the cell. Mike knew the dwarf must have been truly rattled to allow himself to be pushed around so easily. Dwarves were amazingly strong, and Mike doubted that even he could make a dwarf go where he didn't want to.

When the Hand finally calmed down enough and came to his senses, Mike already had him several steps down the hall. Kjell angrily shook Mike's hand off and turned to glare at the large human.

"Don't ye lay a hand on me, human," Kjell growled dangerously. "And don't ye be goin' anywhere," the dwarf growled, and abruptly spun on his heel and stormed away. "Cap'n Raenods will be wantin' ter speak with that one," he snarled over his shoulder without looking back.

The guards hurriedly opened the heavy steel doors and the dwarf barreled on through and stomped directly into the open elevator.

Jack sighed deeply once the dwarf was out of sight. "If I had to hear one more 'ye' or 'yer', I might have torn his throat out," he growled. "It's like listening to a drunk pirate."

Mike grinned. "Aye mate-y," he said with a thick accent, "but we best be off afore he returns with the other Hands o' Tyr."

"Yes," Jack agreed quickly, "and we need to find me some clothes."

"Since when do you care about clothes?" Emily teased and she reached under his cloak and playfully slapped his bare backside.

"Hey!" Jack cried and jumped away, clutching at his cloak protectively.

"Aw, ya big baby," Emily teased. "Usually you like it when I do that."

"Emily!" Liz groaned. "Really?"

"What?" Emily shrugged innocently. "It's true."

Liz sighed. "I think Jack has had a rough enough day without you harassing him."

"I'm not *harassing* him," Emily replied with an impish grin. "He likes it."

"Normally," Jack muttered, as he carefully backed away from Emily.

"But right now, there are only two things I want - clothes and food. In that order."

Ted cleared his throat. "We can discuss these matters at a later date. What do you say we get out of here before those dwarves get back?"

"I second that," Mike quickly agreed, as Ted helped Jack out.

"How are we going to get him out of here?" Liz asked as she and Emily stepped out of the cell. "I doubt the guards will just let us walk him out."

"Trust me," Mike scowled down the hallway. "They will let us through," he muttered, as he patted his mace meaningfully.

"Good," Jack breathed. "I'm starving."

CHAPTER 14

The next day dawned cool and overcast. The few fires that had burned the night before had been quickly put out and Pittsburgh was calm once again. The attackers' bodies had been piled up and burned, leaving behind smoldering ash piles for the early morning light to find. The only other evidence that something had happened were the huge wyvern corpses scattered throughout the city.

Crews of dwarves worked on the large bodies, carefully cutting away the scales to be used later in crafting new armor and then finally stripping away the flesh to get the pearly-white bones underneath. Wyvern bone was a valuable item to the dwarves, who used it for numerous purposes ranging anywhere from an ingredient in advanced runes to simple jewelry. The meat was also put to good use in the dwarves' cook pots and smoke houses. The elves and humans turned their noses at the offered wyvern meat and the dwarves were happy to keep it for themselves.

Mike stood atop the Liberty Gate, looking out at the brilliant yellows and reds of the autumn leaves covering the rolling hills in all directions. He was clad in his full-suit of dented armor, determined to never again get caught without it, should another surprise attack occur.

A new silver eagle insignia was fastened to his breastplate, replacing the two silver bars that had previously adorned the armor. While General

Adams had survived the surprise decapitation strike, many of the other senior officers hadn't been so lucky. With many vacancies on the command council, General Adams had promoted Mike to the rank of Acting Colonel, technically leaving him outranked only by Major General Kelly and General Adams himself.

Mike wasn't too thrilled with the promotion. He knew it was more of an honorary title since he wasn't officially in the Army, but regardless, the title came with responsibilities.

He had been tasked with overseeing the wall defenses and that was why he was standing on the gatehouse, in chilly wind at the crack of dawn, when all he wanted to do was be back in his warm bed. Mike had considered refusing the promotion, but he knew there were few in Pittsburgh that had as much tactical knowledge in medieval strategies like he did.

Mike wished Jack were here with him. Where Mike understood medieval strategy, Jack understood modern warfare. Together, they could anticipate every move and counter it.

But Jack wasn't here.

After returning to their apartment, Jack had found some clothes and food then quickly passed out on the couch. Liz had refused to leave him alone and when Mike had left that morning she had still been there, sleeping in the chair by his side.

Mike sighed and pushed the thought from his mind, and instead turned his attention to the report that he had received upon his arrival at the wall.

The Destroyer's Isfet army was still snaking through the northwestern hills, apparently trying to gather as many allies as possible before the final push to the city. Mike couldn't understand what allies they could possibly be finding, but he was afraid that he would find out soon enough. Even with the Isfet's wandering course, they should still reach Pittsburgh in a matter of days.

"Who is this 'Destroyer' clown anyway?" Mike suddenly asked.

The pair of elves standing nearby didn't say anything for a long moment. One was hidden in the folds of his long robes while the other was resplendent in his silver armor.

The robed elf beside him shrugged helplessly. "I only know what the stories say," Regulus answered.

"And those are few," Leandros added.

The Battlemage and Paladin of Athena had joined Mike a short time ago and Mike was glad for their company. The elves knew the kefali better than anyone and if there was a weakness to be exploited, Mike wanted to know about it.

"I'll take any information you have," Mike said.

"Very well," Regulus breathed. "If this is truly the same Destroyer from the Kefali Invasion then we know his name is Malek and he is a powerful demigod. He claims to be the son of Apep, called the Lord of Chaos, whom you humans may know as Apophis."

Mike scratched his goatee thoughtfully. "As in the evil Egyptian Serpent God?"

"The same," Regulus nodded. "Although 'evil Isfet Serpent God' would be more accurate. But regardless of parentage, Malek the Destroyer was a demigod who led an army during the Kefali Invasion."

"I thought the Ma'at invaded?" Mike interrupted. "Why would they let an Isfet lead an army?"

Leandros laughed. "If Malek said he wanted to join the invasion, who do you think would be stupid enough to tell a demigod 'no'?" The Paladin chuckled at the idea. "As you humans say, it was a win-win for the Ma'at; get an enemy demigod on your side to kill your mutual enemies, and if those enemies somehow kill the demigod, then you lose that enemy as well."

"Either way," Regulus said, "Malek is said to be a mighty beast; half minotaur and half serpent that possess both immense physical and magical strength."

"Sounds lovely," Mike muttered darkly.

"I'm afraid little else is known about him," said Regulus. "It is believed among some that Malek used the war to slowly convert many of the Ma'at soldiers to Chaos. Until near the end of the war, when it is believed that he took his new Isfet forces away, abandoning the Ma'at armies and leaving them vulnerable to attack."

"Some prefer to believe it was purely through elven fortitude and cunning that we were able to finally break through the kefali lines and push them from our world," Regulus continued. "But some of us know better. It was Malek's betrayal of his fellow kefali that allowed our ultimate victory.

But where Malek went with his traitor army is unknown. He was never seen by the elves again…until now."

Mike shook his head in disbelief. "I thought this war happened thousands of years ago."

"Over twenty thousand, actually," Regulus corrected.

"How is that possible?" Mike asked. "Surely the same Destroyer isn't still alive today."

The Battlemage smiled. "Malek is a *demigod*. That means he is immortal."

"Immortal," Mike groaned hopelessly. "That's just wonderful."

Leandros laughed again. "Fear not, friend Mike. His immortality extends only to the ravages of time. He can still be killed."

"Yes," Regulus added, "and you have already defeated one demigod. Surely you can vanquish another."

"You're talking about the Nephilim," Mike said.

Just then the radio clipped on Mike's armor crackled to life.

"We've got incoming," the voice said excitedly. "A large, unknown force is approaching from the north, traveling down the I-279 corridor."

Mike quickly grabbed the radio. "Hold positions," he ordered. "Find out who they are."

A long, tense moment passed as static crackled until the voice returned. "It's dwarves," the voice said with obvious relief. "Repeat; a large force of dwarves is approaching down the I-279 corridor."

"Wonderful..." Regulus muttered under his breath. "More dwarves."

"How large?" Mike asked. It had been a long time since any sizable group had reached the city. Mike had given up hope that any more refugees would arrive before the enemy armies descended on them.

"I estimate around a thousand," came the reply. "Looks like hill dwarves, sir, and there are a few humans leading them... and sir?"

"What?"

The voice hesitated for a moment. "There are four tanker trucks with them."

"Tanker trucks?" Mike wondered aloud. "What's in them?"

"Unknown sir," the radio crackled. "The trucks aren't marked, but the dwarves have the trucks surrounded. They seem to be protecting them."

If the army had walked any distance, then the tankers could be filled with water. But after discovering that some of the attackers that night had actually been human, Mike was suspicious of everyone. However, he had no reason to doubt the dwarves. They hated the orcs with a passion and Mike couldn't believe a single one of them would betray their allies.

"Let them through," Mike ordered at last, "but stay alert. We don't know what they want yet."

"Yes, sir," the radio crackled, then went dead.

****

Liz groaned and stood, rubbing her sore back after a long night of sleeping in what she quickly discovered was a rather uncomfortable chair.

Jack was still asleep on the couch and Liz placed her hand on his head for a moment before giving a satisfied nod. She turned away and padded softly into Mike's kitchen, her bare feet making scarcely a sound on the cold, hard floor.

After a brief search of the cabinets, Liz was appalled at Mike's meager rations. He had hordes of noodles and countless meats, but there wasn't a single vegetable in sight.

Liz smiled ruefully to herself and dug through the pantry until she was able to scavenge enough components to make a decent breakfast.

She considered simply going down the hall to her own room, but she was loath to leave Jack here alone for any stretch of time. Besides, she knew he would also be hungry when he awoke, so she busied herself in the kitchen and hummed a merry tune while she worked. Liz enjoyed cooking. She wasn't quite sure why, but she found something peaceful about it.

She put a pot of water on the stove and it was soon boiling merrily. Liz poured the hot water into two large mugs and then dug around one of the cabinets until she found a small wooden box tucked away in the back. She opened the box and inside were a few bags of tea that she knew Mike kept on hand just for her because he wouldn't drink tea if his life depended on it.

As the tea steeped, Liz finished cooking breakfast. As she was setting the plates on the table she heard a low moan followed by a growl. A minute later, a very unkempt Jack shambled out and unceremoniously plopped himself at the table.

"Good morning," Liz said cheerfully. "How are you feeling?"

Jack grunted a reply as he lifted the steaming cup to his face and sniffed curiously. His nose wrinkled in disgust and he set the cup back down.

"I have to go," Jack muttered, and abruptly stood back up.

"You can't leave," Liz said curtly. "You need to stay here and rest."

"I haven't got time to rest," Jack growled, as he put his worn boots on. "I need to find that bloody dwarf so I can control this damn beast inside me."

Liz stood. "Let me try and heal you again," she pleaded. "Maybe I-"

"No," Jack snarled, then his voice softened. "I appreciate you trying, but I am cursed and there is nothing anyone can do. As much as I hate to admit it, my best chance is with that smelly Rangvald." Then Jack grinned. "At least I can turn into a wild rage monster."

"There is that, I guess," Liz sighed and sat back down. She knew Jack was right. She couldn't heal him and this wolf priest did appear to be the only one able to help him now. "How are you going to find him?"

Jack tapped the side of his nose meaningfully. "With this."

"You're going to smell him?" Liz asked doubtfully.

"Yes," Jack answered proudly. "It seems my senses have become more sensitive since I got bit. For example, I can smell a faint hint of the mint soap you used yesterday under the sweat. You also have a cut on your left side and two on your right leg."

Liz was surprised. She hadn't told anyone about the injuries and they were carefully bandaged. "How did you know about those?"

"I can smell the blood," Jack said, as he walked to the door. "But why didn't you just heal them?"

"Healers can't heal themselves," Liz replied, then after a moment added, "At least not one of my skill level."

That made Jack laugh. "You are one of the most gifted human healers in the city. Surely if anyone could do it, it would be you. Unless…" Jack paused a moment, considering. "Unless you want the scars to impress somebody…. like Mike maybe?"

"No," Liz snapped, and Jack laughed even harder.

"So, that's what a lie smells like," he chuckled to himself as he opened the door. "And I'm afraid to say that none of those cuts are deep enough to leave much of a scar, so you'll have to impress him some other way."

"Oh, shut up," Liz growled, and Jack laughed as he swiftly closed it behind him. Liz could still hear him laughing as he walked away down the hall.

Liz was still scowling at the two steaming cups of tea in front of her when her cell phone rang.

****

Emily carefully picked her way across the smooth rocks of the swiftly flowing stream. She was out far beyond the safety of the city walls and she couldn't be happier. A breath of hot air blew through the autumn leaves and Emily smiled. She loved autumn. There was something about the changing leaves and earthy smell that filled her with joy. But then again, she loved all the seasons. The seasons represented change and change was what drove life forward. Anything would become stale if it lingered around too long, especially the weather.

Skipping over the last few stones, Emily at last came upon the source of the stream, a tall waterfall. It was one of many in the narrow valley that she found herself in, but she knew beyond a doubt that this was the one she wanted.

"I'm here," Emily said to the waterfall.

There was no response.

Unconcerned, Emily sat down on the large river stone and waited.

It was a magical sight. The mist off the waterfalls gave everything in the valley a slight sheen of water that sparkled mischievously in the morning sunlight. Small rainbows glittered in the air all around and birds sang merrily from the trees. The last lightning bugs flickered in the dawn light and butterflies glided between the newly-opened flowers.

Emily sighed contentedly and laid back on the rock, soaking up the sun's rays and listening to the sound of crashing water.

"Greetings Kaolru," a deep, majestic voice rumbled.

Emily continued to lie on the rock, completely at ease. "You're late," she said, and closed her eyes, letting the sun's rays warm her skin.

"I had to be sure you were alone," the voice replied.

"Well, I am," Emily grunted, as she pushed herself up and faced the waterfall. "Are you going to come out of there?"

Silence was her only reply.

"Be that way," Emily grumbled, and crossed her arms under her breasts. "So, what did you want to see me for?"

"I have a gift for you," the voice chimed.

Emily eyed the waterfall skeptically. "And where would you have found a gift?"

"Does it matter?" the voice rumbled. "I do not give gifts lightly. Either come and accept it or be gone."

Emily held up her hands in a placating gesture. "Ok, ok, I'm sorry."

"Then come forward," the voice behind the waterfall chimed.

Emily hopped off the large rock and skirted the edge of the falls until she found a hidden gap between two large rocks. She ducked between them and vanished behind the falls.

The roar of the falls rumbled through the valley and anyone passing by wouldn't have known anyone was there.

Emily re-emerged a moment later with something clutched protectively in her hands. It wasn't until she was safely back on the large stone that she opened her hands to see what was inside.

Her breath caught as blue light sparkled from between her hands. Resting in her palm was a large teardrop-shaped pendant of blue crystal. Multi-colored striations glittered inside the metallic blue stone. The gem was set in a silver pendant that was attached to a length of fine, silver chain.

"It's beautiful," Emily breathed in awe.

"I am glad you approve," the voice behind the waterfall chimed happily, as Emily put the amulet around her neck and the gem nestled snugly between her breasts. "Wearing it will increase our connection and allow greater communication between us, even over great distances," the voice continued. "Should you have need of me, simply say my name and I will come."

"Good," Emily said, as she absently stroked the blue crystal. "I was getting tired of being summoned with no way of talking back."

"Have no fear, Kaolru," the voice seemed amused. "As our bond grows, so too will our ability to spirit speak. Eventually the need for the trinket will fade and it will be little more than a simple piece of jewelry."

"It won't work for anyone else?" Emily asked.

"No," the majestic voice replied. "We two are bonded. To everyone else that gem is just another piece of crystal."

"What about these?" Emily touched her head wrap self-consciously. "They are getting bigger."

"Of course, they are," the majestic voice laughed. "It is the physical representation of our bond. The greater it becomes, the longer they will become." The laughter in the voice faded. "How long do you plan on hiding this from your kind? Are you afraid they will reject you?"

"I don't know... maybe..." Emily muttered, unsure of how she felt. She didn't care what other people would think. She didn't like people anyways. But she was concerned with what her friends would think. She didn't have many friends, which was just the way she liked it, but she also didn't want to lose the few she did have.

"Your fears are unfounded," the voice said, as if it could read her thoughts. Perhaps it could. "For even if everyone rejects you, I will not. You and I are joined forever."

"Thanks. That just makes me feel so much better..." Emily mumbled, when a low growl suddenly issued from behind the waterfall.

"Kaolru!" the voice rumbled in earnest. "You must be away! Two of Fenrir's Children approach from the west. They must not discover our presence here."

"What about you?" Emily asked. But only silence answered her and suddenly she knew she was alone.

"Fenrir's Children?" Emily muttered to herself as she carefully danced over the stones, away from the falls. That name sounded familiar.

Curiosity overruled caution and instead of heading back to Pittsburgh, Emily listened to the whispering trees and followed their directions. Through the forest and around a rocky hill, the trees led her unerringly to her quarry.

Voices could be heard on the wind and Emily knew she was getting close. A short trek through a thick patch of mountain laurel brought her to a heavily forested patch of woods that was still partially dark, even though the sun was rising ever higher.

The voices became clearer and Emily was surprised to discover that they sounded familiar.

Emily slowed as the voices grew louder and she carefully picked her way toward them. Years of hunting and more recent instruction by the Druids had honed Emily's woodcraft to such a degree that she didn't make a sound as she stalked stealthily through the trees.

At last she came upon a dark stand of trees and carefully peered around a particularly large trunk where she finally saw Fenrir's Children.

****

"Again!" Rangvald barked.

Jack groaned from where he knelt on the ground, naked and drenched in sweat.

"Ye don't be havin' time ter rest," the mangy dwarf growled. "There be a war comin' an' if ye don't have the Spirit under control, the blood craze will consume ye."

"Blood craze?" Jack gasped. "That sounds fun."

"Trust me, brother," Rangvald growled, "there be nothin' fun about it. Now, embrace the Spirit!"

Jack pushed himself to his feet and closed his eyes. His muscles tensed and bulged as Jack strained against some unseen force.

Suddenly, dark fur sprouted all across Jack's body as his arms and legs began to extend. Corded muscle erupted under his skin and his hands swelled in size as claws protruded from his hands and feet. His face stretched and cracked as bones shifted and molded themselves into a long snout with a mouth full of razor sharp fangs. After nearly a full minute, Jack's howl of agony changed into one of victory as the transformation completed.

Where a man once stood, now a towering werewolf with coal black fur and fierce golden eyes now loomed.

"Good," Rangvald nodded his shaggy head approvingly. "Now, release it."

Werewolf Jack glared balefully at the dwarf, but after a moment his fur receded and Jack the man was standing there once more.

"Again!" Rangvald barked.

Again and again Jack called upon the latent wolf spirit inside him and to his surprise each transformation hurt a little less.

Rangvald watched carefully as he morphed over and over, looking for any sign that Jack was losing his control. But after more than a dozen transformations, the dwarf was finally satisfied that Jack wasn't going to lose himself in the wild spirit again.

Each change happened a little faster than the one before it and where once the change took over a minute, it now happened in just a few seconds. Jack no longer cried out in pain at each transformation. Instead, he welcomed it.

Becoming one with the wolf made him feel more alive. His normal senses were already greatly increased, but when he became the wolf it was stimulation on a whole other level. As the wolf, he could smell the worms in the ground beneath his paws, hear the beat of a butterfly's wings, see the hairs on a fly's back, and even taste the air for creatures that had gone by.

"How do ye feel?" Rangvald suddenly asked.

Werewolf Jack looked down at the mangy dwarf. "Great," Jack rumbled, and was surprised to discover that he could speak in his altered form. "Why don't you stay in his body all the time?" Jack asked. "It's so… superior."

"Because it be dangerous," Rangvald growled. "The longer ye be one with the Spirit, the greater yer risk o' losin' yerself ter it. It be unwise ter stay joined fer longer than necessary, a few hours at most. Any longer an' the hunger will grow ter be more than ye can bear. If the hunger takes ahold o' ye then ye will be consumed and I' be afraid there be no bringin' ye back again."

"So, I would be trapped like this forever?" Jack smelled the dwarf's urgency. "This doesn't seem like such a bad way to live."

"No," Rangvald growled. "Yer not understandin'. Ye would lose yer mind and become little more than a wild beast. That be our curse. Ter taste the true glory o' bein' one with the Great Wolf, but always needin' ter give it up, lest we be utterly consumed by it."

"I understand," Jack replied.

The mangy dwarf glared, unafraid at the towering werewolf before him. "Do ye?" Rangvald snarled. "I dun think ye do." The dwarf turned away and began gathering a few things into a leather sack. "But ye will soon find out."

Jack watched in confusion as Rangvald made ready to leave. "You're leaving?" Jack asked.

"Aye," Rangvald rumbled. "I have helped ye ease into the joinin', the next part be fer yerself alone. Stay joined with the spirit until ye feel the hunger begin ter gnaw at yer soul, then, and only then, must ye release it." The dwarf finished packing his meager belongings. "I have no desire ter watch ye stand around an' wait fer the hunger ter take ye. Besides, the female will be better company than I."

"Female?" Jack looked around in confusion. It was just the two of them, alone in the darkness of the forest.

Rangvald laughed and moved away. "Yer senses aren't as keen as they can be, pup." As the dwarf strode away, he raised his voice. "Come on out lass, yer friend will be needin' some company." Rangvald moved through the forest more quietly than Jack would have thought possible, even with his advanced hearing, the old dwarf hardly made a sound.

As the mangy dwarf vanished into the trees, the wind shifted and Jack suddenly caught a new scent in the air, one that he recognized instantly.

Werewolf Jack bared his fangs in what he hoped was a smile. "Come on out Emily. I know you're there."

A moment later, Emily stepped out from behind a thick tree and smiled sheepishly. "I didn't want to interrupt your little practice session."

Jack saw that Emily clutched her bow tightly, but he was glad to see she hadn't knocked an arrow. She trusted him that much at least. As she picked her way carefully through the trees, Jack's eyes were drawn to the sway of her hips and the bounce of her breasts.

A primal urge suddenly filled Jack and his vision swam.

"You know..." Emily stepped over a fallen log and straddled it suggestively, "there are all manner of dangers out here, orcs...nymphs...me..." She grinned wickedly. "I must admit I find the whole werewolf-thing attractive."

Emily carefully slid off the log and came down through the last of the trees where she sat her bow and quiver down. She smiled mischievously and slowly pulled her boots off.

Barefoot, she glided toward Jack, slipping out of the rest of her clothes as she came.

"This world is dull," Emily pouted, as she pressed her shapely body against his. Her scent was intoxicating.

Jack reached down and gently cupped her face in his clawed hands. "Good thing I have a cure for that," he whispered, as he bent down and kissed her. Emily eagerly returned the embrace and the taste of her lips was like the sweetest candy.

He gently licked the side of her neck and she moaned with pleasure. Her soft, pale flesh pressed against him and her heavy breath was hot against his face. Kissing her neck, Jack slowly opened his mouth and viciously sank his fangs into her slender neck.

Blood gushed from the wound and a coppery taste filled his mouth as Emily spasmed in his grip.

Jack snarled and threw his head back angrily as he pushed the vile thoughts away.

Where had that come from? Jack growled angrily. *It must be the hunger Rangvald spoke of. Perhaps it wouldn't be so easy to overcome after all.*

Jack looked up and saw that Emily had frozen in place halfway to him, a look of concern on her face. "It's okay, Jack," she said softly, and continued her approach. "We will beat it together."

"You should go," the werewolf snarled. "It's not safe to be around me."

Regretfully, Jack released the wolf sprit and his body returned to its weak, human form.

"I'm not going anywhere," Emily replied with an impish grin. "I can't leave a naked man all alone in the forest."

****

It was several hours before Mike finally caught his first glimpse of the newcomers as they marched down the highway.

The scout had been right; it did look like the small army had around a thousand hill dwarves with a few humans scattered throughout. And they were bringing four large tanker trucks along with them.

Mike watched their approach from atop the huge gatehouse until the army at last came to a halt just beyond the immense sealed doors.

Three figures detached from the larger host and approached the gate. Two were dwarves; one was a red-bearded hill dwarf, with his shaved head covered in blue tattoos and a wooden round shield strapped to his thick arm. The other dwarf was shorter and encased in exquisite armor that was inscribed with runes. A heavy blue cloak fluttered out from behind the dwarf as he removed his helm to reveal cunning eyes and a thick, black beard. The last figure was a bald human who was as large as Mike and had a short, red beard. He wore simple robes and walked with a slender quarterstaff.

Mike's face split into a grin as he recognized the figures below. "Open the gate!" he shouted, before eagerly heading for the stairs.

The reinforced steel doors were still slowly swinging open by the time Mike reached them and he hurried through the swiftly widening gap. He quickly passed through the cool dark of the vaulted gatehouse and strode onto the bridge.

As he approached the trio, the large robed man walked forward and grinned in a wide smile that matched Mike's own.

"Alex!" Mike laughed, as they embraced warmly. "It's good to see you!"

"Hello, big brother," Alex Strazney laughed merrily, and the two released each other. "It's good to see you, too!"

Mike eyed his little brother curiously. "What are you doing here? I thought you were staying in Clearfield with the rest of the family."

"I was," Alex replied, "but since you left there hasn't been much excitement. It seems some orc warlord down this way has gathered up nearly all the baddies around, making it relatively peaceful back home. So, when I heard that the dwarves were headed here with their delivery, I decided to tag along and see if I could find you."

"And find me you did," Mike smiled. "How did you manage to escape without our little sister following you?"

"Ah," Alex looked guiltily away. "I may have snuck out before she knew I was going…"

"Oh, boy. Rachel is going to be pissed when she sees you again!" Mike laughed and turned to the two dwarves behind Alex. "Lord Aurvang! Baldor! I wasn't expecting to see you here."

The heavily armored Lord Aurvang stomped forward and clasped Mike's forearm in a warrior's handshake. "Greetin's, Blódskuld. I hope we have arrived in good time."

Some of the mirth drained out of Mike. "If you are looking for a battle, then, yes, you have arrived just in time."

The dwarf lord nodded as if he had expected no less. "Good," he rumbled. "I did no want ter be missin' all the fun."

Mike chuckled and looked to the other dwarf. "Baldor, I didn't expect you to come back. I thought you didn't like being surrounded by Clan Anvilborn?"

The jarl snorted, "O' course I no liked bein' surrounded by mounties! That be why I brought some o' me Hardhelms back with me."

"I see that." Mike glanced over the dwarf's head and eyed the four tanker trucks intently. "So, what are those for?"

"That's Uberjuice," Alex answered proudly. "We've been making it since the dwarves converted some of the old ethanol plant into a brewery."

Baldor cleared his throat. "It no be true Uberjuice," the jarl corrected, "but it be the closest durned thing we can be makin' on this world."

"Why did you bring it here?" Mike asked.

Baldor laughed. "For the victory celebration o' course!"

"Aye," Lord Aurvang rumbled his agreement. "That and we be hopin' ter trade it fer some good steel and other supplies we be needin'."

"I'm sure we can work something out. Now, let's get everyone inside." Mike put his arm across Alex's shoulders and headed back toward the open gate. "We have a lot of catching up to do."

CHAPTER 15

"It took you three days to walk here?" Mike shook his head in disbelief. "Why didn't you just drive?"

"We wanted to," Alex replied with a laugh, "but we didn't have enough transports to fit all the dwarves, so we decided to walk."

Mike chuckled as he opened the door to his apartment and stepped in. His mirth vanished when he noticed two people seated at his kitchen table.

A faint prickle of emotion flared in Mike's mind as Liz looked up in alarm. She was seated at the table wearing a soft, white robe. Her hair was wet and she held a steaming cup of tea in her hands. Seated across from her, nearest to the door and with his back to them, was a man in military fatigues. The man turned around when they entered, and Mike was annoyed to discover it was Scout Sniper Jason Andrews.

"Mike!" Liz said, surprised. "What are you doing here?"

"This is my apartment," Mike said, as he stormed into the room with Alex close behind. "What's going on here? And where is Jack? I thought you were watching him"

"I...I was," Liz stammered, "but he took off as soon as he woke up."

Jason looked mortified and hastily stood up. "Col. Strazney, sir! I'm sorry sir, I had no idea this was yinz residence, sir. I-"

Mike raised his hands in a placating gesture. "Calm down Jason," he said before addressing Liz again. "You just let him leave?"

"What was I supposed to do? Hold him down and wait for you to show up?" Liz sipped her tea. "Look, I had made breakfast for us, but when he got up, he refused to eat and just charged out. Then Jason called and I invited him over so the food didn't go to waste."

"And you helped yourself to my shower," Mike noted.

Liz's cheeks colored guiltily and Mike felt a strange sensation in the back of his mind. "I didn't want Jason to show up and me not be here."

"You live right down the hall," Mike laughed. "Not that I'm complaining of course, you can use my shower whenever you want. But I don't care for surprise guests in my place. Sorry, Jason."

"Understood, sir. I will take my leave now." Jason quickly gathered his things. "Thanks for the tea, Liz," he said, as he scurried out of the door.

Mike chuckled as the door slammed shut. "He does know my rank is honorary, right?"

"I don't think it matters," Liz muttered. "Military types are funny like that, I think."

"Colonel?" Alex asked.

"It's a long story," Mike replied.

Liz noticed Mike's brother for the first time and she beamed. "Alex!" She jumped up and caught him in a big hug. "What are you doing here?"

Alex smiled as he slowly extracted himself from Liz's embrace. "We came looking to trade some fresh-brewed ale for whatever you can spare." Alex gave an exaggerated wink. "It has nothing to do with most of the dwarves also wanting to join in the battle that we hear is coming."

"Of course," Liz laughed. "Who wouldn't want to join in a battle where you are outnumbered a hundred to one?"

"The odds aren't that bad," Mike added dolefully. "I think it's more like ten, or maybe fifty, to one."

Liz rolled her eyes. "That's just sooo much better."

"Besides," Mike added, "we have guns. How bad could it be?"

Alex and Liz groaned in unison. "You just had to say it."

"Relax," Mike laughed. "It looks like we still have a few days before any of them get here."

Alex's eyes lit up. "Good. Then you can show me around."

Mike's smile faded. "I don't know about that. You should be ready to head back as soon as the supplies are loaded up and ready to go."

Alex faced his brother defiantly. "I'm not going back."

Expecting an argument, Alex was surprised when a small grin appeared on Mike's face.

"I figured as much," Mike said with a laugh. "And I know better than to try and convince you otherwise once you've made up your mind."

Alex gave a relieved laugh. "That is a trait we can both claim."

"It sure is." Mike's smile fell away. "You do realize that when this battle comes, there is a good chance that we will all die?" he said in all seriousness.

"Of course," Alex replied, "but there is also a chance that we won't."

Liz snorted into her cup. "And how do you plan on staying alive? I don't think you're going to kill many orcs with that stick." She motioned to the quarterstaff in his hand. "You're going to need something that's a little more… deadly."

Alex eyed the slender wooden quarterstaff in his hand.

"Liz is right," Mike said. "I'm sure Ted has something laying around that you could use."

"I suppose you're right," Alex agreed. "And it will be good to see Ted again."

"I can show-" Mike started to say when his radio crackled to life.

'*Col. Strazney. Report to HQ immediately,*' the scratchy voice said before cutting out again.

Mike groaned. "What do they want now?"

Alex looked at Mike in surprise. "When did you join the Army?"

"I didn't," Mike grumbled. "It's an honorary title."

Liz chuckled and finished the last of her tea. "Keep telling yourself that," she teased, as she got up and set her cup in the sink. "You better get going. It sounded urgent."

"Everything is urgent with them," Mike grumbled. "Hurry up and wait."

"Just go." Liz grabbed Mike by the arm and turned him toward the door. "I will show Alex around until you get back."

"I should make them wait," Mike pondered aloud, as Liz walked him to the door. "That would teach them they can't summon me on a whim."

Liz opened the door and steered Mike through it. He turned around and scowled as Liz blocked the doorway. "Don't be silly," Liz said, as she gently placed her hands on his armored chest and looked up into his dark brown eyes. "Now, be a good little soldier and report for duty." She gave him a quick shove and slammed the door shut before he could react.

Alone in the hallway Mike grinned to himself as he walked away. "I should have seen that coming."

****

Liz breathed a sigh of relief as she heard Mike's footsteps fade down the hall. She had been afraid he would be his usual stubborn self and try to stay. She turned and leaned her back against the door. "I'm glad that's over."

"I bet," Alex laughed. "So, do you invite other guys over to your boyfriend's apartment for breakfast often?"

Liz was taken aback. "Mike is *not* my boyfriend," she said quickly. "We are just friends."

"Riiight," Alex smiled, and then thankfully changed the subject. "Anyways, where are we going to first? It's been a long time since I was in the Burgh and you could say it's changed a bit."

"First," Liz opened the door and peeked out to make sure nobody was around, "you are going to stay here while I go back to my room to change. Then, I will take you to the Foundry."

"What's the Foundry?" Alex asked.

"It's where all the crafting happens," Liz replied distractedly. She didn't see anybody so she stepped out into the hall. "Now, stay here. I'll be right back." And with that she hurried down the hall, white robe flapping around her bare feet.

Alex didn't have long to wait. Liz reappeared a few minutes later fully dressed in jeans and a tank top with a black leather jacket over top. She had a pistol strapped to both thighs and a slender sword hung from her belt.

"Are you expecting trouble?" Alex asked at the sight of the weapons.

"Always."

The Foundry district was the manufacturing core of the city. Factories, laboratories, and warehouses sprawled across several blocks. The clang of hammers and whine of heavy machinery reverberated down the streets. The site was a beehive of activity with laborers hurrying back and forth carrying all manner of goods, from raw iron ore to finished suits of armor and crates of ammunition.

At the very heart of the Foundry sat the Verkstad. The old steel mill had been taken over by the dwarves and converted into the mighty fortress-like factory that Liz and Alex walked into.

"Impressive," Alex said softly, as he watched the flurry of activity around them in amazement.

Liz led Alex through the maze, and everywhere he looked, Alex saw something new.

In one corner sat a massive battle tank that had a score of men and dwarves clinging to it. Sparks flew as one man welded something to the tank's armored skirt as a dwarf chiseled glowing runes onto the barrel of its main cannon. Nearby, a pair of elves polished what looked to be a huge, silver statue of an elf warrior, complete with spear and shield.

In one roped-off section was a huge griffin that was being fitted with a new suit of armor. The metal was dark and polished to a brilliant sheen. Engraved runes flowed across the heavy plates and Liz couldn't believe that the dwarves had fashioned something so breathtaking so quickly.

Further into the twisting depths of the Verkstad was a woman flying around on what appeared to be a hoverboard. She zoomed overhead and Alex almost ran into an ugly dwarf that had several large metal studs driven into his brow. The dwarf snarled something in Dwarvish and kept going, dragging an impossibly large sled piled high with gears and pistons along behind him.

Finally, after almost getting cut in half by a stray laser beam and just barely avoiding having a barrel of liquid nitrogen dumped on them, Liz and Alex made it safely to Ted's workshop.

Alex stepped into the chaotic room warily. He knew that the dangers they had just faced were nothing compared to what Ted's personal lab would surely offer.

Multi-colored liquid bubbled along one wall and electricity danced between two tall, copper coils in the far corner. Tools and discarded parts were scattered everywhere and Alex wondered if some kind of bomb had gone off, which was entirely possible.

"Are you sure he's in here?" Alex shouted over the clanking and rattling noise all around them.

Liz shrugged and picked up a large wrench and banged it against a metal pipe that ran up the wall and across the ceiling where it branched off in multiple directions all across the room.

The pipe rang like a bell and after three good smacks a goggled head popped up from behind one particularly large pile of machinery.

"Do you mind!?" Ted shouted over the ringing. "I'm trying to concentrate here!" Then he disappeared behind the pile once more.

Liz and Alex shared a look and Alex said, "Do we have to go in there?"

"I'm afraid so," Liz sighed, and stepped into the disaster area with Alex close behind.

It took them several minutes to carefully pick their way through the tangle of cables, wires, pipes, and other constructs of unknown machinery until they finally found Ted working on some kind of small, bladed device. Liz didn't get a good look at it because as soon as they arrived, Ted quickly threw a dirty rag over it.

Liz was immediately suspicious, but she decided to ignore it. Let him have his little secrets. It was probably something science-y that she wouldn't understand or care about anyways.

"Alex!" Ted beamed. His eyes looked enormous from the magnification lenses he had attached to the thick goggles and Liz had a hard time not laughing at the comical sight. "It's so good to see you!" He clasped Alex in a firm handshake. "What brings you here to my humble abode?"

"Well," Alex returned the handshake warmly, "I hear there is a battle coming and you might be able to get me a better weapon than this poor thing." Alex held up the wooden staff meaningfully.

"Ahh, I see." Ted tugged on his sooty beard thoughtfully. "What sort of weapons do you prefer?"

"Two-handed," Alex answered. "I like something with a long reach."

Ted smiled. "A man after my own heart. You will like this then." Ted grabbed his heavily modified staff from atop a nearby pile of junk. He pressed a button on the shaft and the top section thrummed with power as the glowing blade erupted from the head.

Alex's eyes lit up. "Now, that's what I'm talking about!"

"I'm afraid this one's mine." Ted handed the poleaxe to Alex who handled the strange weapon with care. "I call it the Plazmax."

"Plazmax?" Alex inspected the shimmering axe head curiously.

"It's a poleaxe that I modified to have a plasma blade," Ted explained excitedly. "Now, it's not pure plasma you understand. Too unstable. No, this uses lasers and magnetism to contain the plasma and channel it into a razor-sharp cutting edge." Ted paused. "And there are a few runes and enchantments on it for the places I couldn't quite figure out," he admitted guiltily.

"I like it," Alex said, as he admired the hissing weapon in his hands. "But if this is yours, what do you have for me?" Alex saw a pile of pole weapons stacked in a corner. "How about one of those?"

Ted followed Alex's gaze and his already magnified eyes bulged in alarm. "Absolutely not! Those are the failed plazmax prototypes. I'm afraid the Mark I through Mark XXII are just as likely to explode as work. No, no…" Ted turned away and began rummaging around in a pile of unrecognizable parts on a nearby chair. "I know I left it over here somewhere…. Ah, ha!" Ted pulled something from the pile and held it up victoriously.

Alex's first thought was of the black batons the police used. It was a shiny metallic tube around two feet long that had a ribbed body with slightly thicker caps on either end.

Alex eyed the baton dubiously. "I thought I said something with a long reach?"

Ted grinned mischievously. "You did."

Suddenly, the small baton expanded, more metal ribs sliding out and stacking together until the baton hand turned into a staff as tall as Ted.

"Now, that's more like it," Alex said approvingly. "Only, it's still just a staff. Just this one is metal instead of wood."

"Ahh," Ted held up a finger knowingly, "but that's not all it does." Ted took the staff in both hands and held it out horizontally to the floor. Then with a twist of his wrists, the staff snapped in half and as he pulled the halves apart, Alex saw that a long length of chain connected them.

"Getting cooler," Alex said, "but now it's just a two-section metal staff."

"I'm not done yet," Ted laughed. "This isn't just any two-section staff. This is an enchanted, banded mithril staff, crafted by Forgefather Polynices himself," he finished proudly.

It was Liz's turn to eye the weapon dubiously. "Where did you get that? I seriously doubt the elves' Forgefather gave it to you."

"He did," Ted sounded hurt. "I helped him on… a small project… and he thanked me by giving me this staff."

"Riiight…" Liz didn't believe a word of it, but then again, anything was possible. "So, what kind of enchantment does it have?"

Ted's boyish grin came back like it had never left. "I'm glad you asked," he said eagerly. "Now, I haven't had the time to experiment with its full range of capabilities, mind you," Ted warned, before continuing with growing excitement. "You see, either end can be charged with whatever element you choose." The end of the half-staff in Ted's right hand caught fire and started to glow cherry red from the heat. The end of the half-staff in Ted's left hand formed large crystals of ice until an icy spear tip glittered in light.

Alex nodded approvingly.

The right staff's flames suddenly sputtered and died as clumps of rock bubbled out from the staff and formed a large hammerhead of pure stone. At the same time, the ice spear melted away and was replaced by arcs of electricity that snaked around the tip.

"That's cooler n' shit n' all," Alex said carefully, "but I don't have any magic or special powers. Will it still work for me?"

"Of course, it will!" Ted laughed. "The staff is enchanted. No powers are required by the wielder. All you have to do is picture in your mind what you want the staff to do, and it will… so long as it is within the enchantments' capabilities, of course."

Ted twirled the linked pieces around experimentally. "I call it, the Ribbed, Mithril Staff of Elemental Transfiguration." He snapped the two ends back together and handed the complete staff to Alex.

Alex took the slender weapon gratefully. "Why not just call it the Staff of Elements?"

Ted blinked owlishly then laughed, "I guess that could work too."

Alex noticed Ted's copper arm for the first time and pointed at the block of cabling sticking out of it "What happened to your arm?"

Ted held up the metallic appendage for him to see. "I lost it in a fight with a demigod," Ted replied airily, then he grinned. "That sounds cooler every time I say it."

"A demigod?" Alex looked doubtfully to Liz who nodded.

"It's actually true," Liz answered. "We fought a nephilim in his evil castle full of giants, and Ted lost his arm and we all almost died."

"That really happened?" Alex breathed. "We heard stories about it back home, but nobody really believed them."

"I don't know what you've heard," Ted said, "but there was a castle full of giants and demons protecting a nephilim while he tried to summon his father, Baphomet, from Tartarus."

"And you stopped him?" Alex asked.

Ted looked offended. "Of course, we did. You don't see any devils wandering around, do you? We *are* the Heroes of Awesome after all." Ted looked down at his copper arm thoughtfully before continuing. "After the battle the dwarves forged me this new arm and I added a few… improvements of my own."

"I see." Alex watched uneasily as steam hissed from one of the tubes connecting the device to Ted's arm. "Do I even want to know what it does?"

"It's a cannon!" Ted beamed proudly. "It fires high energy plasma bolts," he explained. "I even took down a wyvern with it… before it overheated."

Alex's eyebrow raised in surprise. "A wyvern? Really?" he asked, and Ted nodded smugly. "Well, I'm impressed. One of your inventions actually worked."

Liz laughed, "That's what I said!" and Ted scowled. She chuckled merrily at Ted's annoyance. "Oh, Ted, you know it's true. Just look at the heaps of exploded devices you have piled up in here."

Ted's scowl softened and turned into a rueful grin. "Genius can't be rushed," he shrugged innocently. "I was making fireballs for science. Now, enough about me." Ted eyed Alex's robes critically. "That's an interesting outfit you have on. Very monk-like, but it won't serve you very well in a real battle." Ted moved to another jumbled area of his workshop and started rummaging around in a different pile of junk, muttering to himself. "I'm sure I have another suit laying around here somewhere…"

"Don't worry about it," Alex said. "I'm quite happy with what I have on."

Ted looked up in confusion. "Impossible. Somebody will poke you all full of holes wearing that."

A sly smile snuck onto Alex's face. "They'll have to hit me first."

"Oh, really?" Ted stood and put his hands on his hips. "You think you're good enough to *never* get hit?"

Alex shrugged noncommittally. "Growing up with Mike, I learned long ago that getting hit can be a rather… unpleasant experience. Even without his stupidly overpowered mace, Mike still hits with the force of a sledgehammer. Over the years, I've gotten rather good at avoiding strikes."

Ted snorted derisively, "Dodging your brother is one thing, and being surrounded by orcs with swords is quite another."

"I'll be fine," Alex replied confidently.

Ted threw up his hands in defeat. "Hey, it's your funeral." He walked back over to his worktable. "Now, if there isn't anything else you need, I have some things I need to finish before I get interrupted by this pesky little conflict."

Liz smiled to herself. Leave it to Ted to describe a battle that will likely see the city destroyed and everyone dead as a "pesky little conflict."

"Alright," Liz said. "We are going. Just don't get in a hurry and blow yourself up."

Ted snapped his magnification goggles down and threw her a big thumbs-up. "Fireballs for science!"

****

HQ was a hive of activity as the remaining officers and staff scurried everywhere. Mike made his way through the winding corridors, as the increasingly frantic nature of the staff caused him to grow suspicious that something significant was going on.

When he finally reached the central command station, Mike was impressed at the change that had come over the large room since last night.

Gone was the heavy smoke, ruined bodies, and broken equipment. Bullet holes and scorch marks still marred the walls and floor, but the ruined computers had been replaced and nearly all of the monitoring stations were back up and running. Command staff filled the room with noise and it seemed like a completely different place from the night before.

"Colonel Strazney! Over here," a voice shouted from the floor below.

Looking down, Mike saw the plump Major Sanders wave at him before ducking into an adjoining room.

Mike took the stairs down to the main floor and made his way toward the room that the major had gone into. Four heavily armed Marines stood guard before the reinforced steel door, but they didn't try to stop him as he pushed the heavy door open.

Inside was a small, dark room with the only light coming from two of the flat-screens mounted on the far wall. Mike was about to ask what was so urgent that he had to come right here, but the words died on his lips when he saw who else was in the room.

On one side of the room, Lord Aurvang cut an imposing figure in his heavy rune plate, but he paled in comparison to the majesty of King Varnir standing beside him. Four elite Huscarl bodyguards from Clan Anvilborn stood silently along the wall behind their king and his companion.

Across from the dwarves was the noble Stratigos Valerian, resplendent in his sculpted armor and tall, crested helm. Arch Battlemage Gwydion stood at his shoulder, nearly invisible beneath the folds of his hood as four Korybantine Guard mirrored their dwarf counterparts.

In the center of the room were General Adams and his top-ranking officers, including Major Sanders. Everyone in attendance had their gaze locked on the two screens, both of which were showing a moving birds-eye view of some countryside. The speed and terrain were different on both displays and Mike guessed they were watching a live feed from two separate aircraft.

The heavy door clanged shut and General Adams looked back and saw Mike. "Ah, good. Everyone is here." The general motioned Mike forward. "You're just in time."

"What's going on?" Mike asked, as he joined the others before the flickering displays.

One of General Adams's aids that Mike didn't know answered. "We have been tracking the approaching kefali army with UAVs for the last several days," she said crisply. "Yesterday at 0300 hours, we lost visual as they entered the woodlands of Brady's Run. This morning, we found them again, moving south, where we believe they will try to cross the Beaver River somewhere between New Brighton and Rochester."

"That's awfully close to the Ohio," Mike said, looking at the map pinned to the wall. "You don't think they will cross there?"

"No," Stratigos Valerian replied. "Our enemies are working in concert; they will try to surround us. With the Shadowed Ones to the south, and the orc host to the east, that only leaves the north open. The kefali will descend on us and cut off any escape."

"We already guessed that," Mike said. "So, why this meeting? They are doing exactly what we figured they would."

"Precisely," Lord Aurvang rumbled. "Now be the time ter strike."

"Strike?" Mike looked between the military leaders of the three races and saw the same look of eager determination on all of them. "I thought we agreed that it was too dangerous to attack. Our best option is to consolidate our forces and use them to repel the attack at the walls."

General Adams stared hard at Mike. "That is the plan we agreed to publicly," the general said. "In reality, we received additional reinforcements from the 103rd Armor Regiment a few weeks ago and planned to use them on the offensive. So far, our strategy has been working. A Company is moving around what is left of Monroeville, harassing the growing orc host, while B Company is spread out above the North Hills, waiting for the kefali to make a move across the river where we will be waiting for them."

"And everyone agreed?" Mike couldn't believe what he was hearing. "How did I not know about this?"

"I opposed the idea," King Varnir rumbled. "It be folly ter endanger such marvelous machines in such a useless conflict when they could be better used fer defendin' me walls."

"They aren't *your* walls," General Adams replied curtly. "They're *our* walls, and that is why I left C Company behind to defend them." The general turned to Mike. "And you didn't know about it because you didn't have the proper clearance, but now that you are a Colonel you have access."

"That's just great." Mike looked up at the large screens and watched the landscapes move by. "What are we looking at?"

Another officer that Mike didn't recognize answered. "Two UAVs were launched, and we are currently waiting for them to establish visual contact with the enemy."

"And how long will that take?" Mike asked.

Major Sanders watched the screens expectantly. "They should arrive momentarily."

His words were proven true a minute later when one of the drones flew over a low ridge that opened up into a winding valley with a narrow gorge opening up into it. Along the ridge facing the gorge, Mike could see the blocky shapes of at least eight battle tanks spread out in a ragged line.

One of the drones gained altitude before hovering high above, giving the assembled leaders the full view of the valley and the line of tanks watching the gorge opening across from them. The other drone continued down into the valley and flew toward the gorge. That was when Mike saw them.

Moving like a living carpet across the entire width of the gorge, even tromping through the trickling stream that cut through the center, was the vast kefali army.

The Horned Legion was aptly named, Mike thought, for the majority of the warriors were the towering, bull-like minotaurs. But they were not alone. Marching along beside the minotaurs were all manner of beasts. Kefali that looked like snakes, lions, vultures, and numerous other animals were scattered throughout the massive army.

"My God..." one of the human commanders muttered at the imposing sight. "There are so many of them..."

"Yes," Stratigos Valerian replied grimly, "and this is just the vanguard."

The sprawling Isfet army didn't seem to be in any hurry and churned through the gorge like a glacier of death, knocking down the sparse trees and trampling everything in their path.

"Sir." One of the commanders turned to General Adams and touched her wireless headset. She listened to something for a moment before continuing. "The tank crews report that they are in position and awaiting your orders." She handed another wireless headset to the general and he put in on.

"This is General Adams," he said into the small microphone at his cheek. "Hold positions. Prepare to engage on my mark."

The legion of kefali continued its steady march through the gorge as it snaked its way toward the open valley and the waiting battle tanks of B Company.

General Adams sighed wistfully. "What I wouldn't give for just one bomber right now," he muttered almost to himself. "We could turn the whole gorge into a deathtrap."

"We have a few attack helicopters," Mike offered. "It would be like shooting fish in a barrel."

But one of the commanders was already shaking his head. "We considered it, but we thought it best to keep them on patrol around the city in case the orcs try another surprise wyvern attack."

"Besides," Major Sanders added, "it wouldn't do for us to potentially lose our only air support."

"We have the griffins," Mike countered, but the human commanders just laughed.

"I'm talking about *real* air support," Major Sanders chuckled. "Not a bunch of flying lions."

Lord Aurvang glared at the major. "Don't ye be underestimatin' the mighty griffins."

On the screens, the first kefali had reached the mouth of the gorge and were spilling out in the valley into an ever-expanding tide.

"I think it's about time to show these beasts what we're made of." General Adams looked to King Varnir who nodded his assent and then to Stratigos Valerian.

"The die has been cast," Valerian said grimly. "The Battle for the Steel City is about to begin."

"So be it." General Adams touched his headset. "B Company. Fire at will."

CHAPTER 16

"So, you're saying that you can heal *anything*?" Alex asked, disbelief evident in his voice.

"Pretty much," Liz answered. "I can't bring someone back from the dead... and I wasn't able to cure Jack, but I can heal almost any injury."

Alex shook his head in wonder as the two of them walked down the street toward the Healers Tent. "Amazing. And I can't believe that Jack is a werewolf, like a *real* werewolf. How cool is that?"

"I don't know that he would agree with you," Liz said seriously. Alex made a face and she laughed. "Yeah, you're right," Liz chuckled. "I'm sure he thinks being infected by some incurable kefali disease that turns him into a giant wolfman is the best thing ever."

"Who wouldn't?!" Alex replied with a grin, and Liz wasn't sure if he was kidding. "I hear these kefali are all different kinds of animals, so does that mean you could be something besides a wolf?"

"I think so," Liz replied. "Pipaluk said something about it once, but I don't remember the details."

Alex's face scrunched up in confusion. "Who's Pipaluk?"

"She is a Baribal shaman," Liz replied, but when she saw Alex's blank look, she continued, "which is a type of kefali that looks like a black bear."

"Cool." Alex looked lost in thought for a moment as he walked along with his new staff. "So, all kefali aren't bad?"

Liz laughed. "No, they aren't all bad… but I don't know that these ones are good either."

"What do you mean?"

Liz sighed, unsure how to answer. "When we rescued the dwarf prince from the kefali, we learned that they were called Isfet and that they were worshipers of Chaos. But there is another faction of kefali called the Ma'at that want to bring Order." She took a deep breath before continuing. "The Isfet are the ones threatening us now, but it was the Ma'at who invaded the elves, so I don't think we can really call the Ma'at our allies. We have a common enemy in the Isfet right now, so we are working together, but that's about it."

"I see," Alex replied thoughtfully. "So, what kind of animals do these…Ma'at look like."

"Well…" Liz said, "the ones that are here look like shaggy dogs and black bears mostly. With the exception of Lorcan who is the wolf that bit Jack."

"And the Isfet?"

"Bulls and lions mostly," Liz answered, "but I don't think it really matters what type of kefali they are. I'm pretty sure it's their religion, so any of them can choose to either believe in Isfet or Ma'at."

"And how many different types of kefali are there?"

"I have no idea," Liz shrugged helplessly. "I would guess that there are as many types of kefali as there are wild animals. From what I understand, the kefali organize themselves into families based on the type of animal they are descended from. For example, Pipaluk is a Baribal, but she is also a Kaakuush."

Alex's brow furrowed in confusion. "What's the difference?"

"Who knows?" Liz laughed. "I think Kaakuush is saying she is part of the bear family and Baribal is the specific type of bear, which in her case is a black bear, but I could be wrong. I find all the different names for the types of kefali confusing."

Alex smiled. "I'm sure we will learn them eventually."

"Maybe," Liz smiled back, "but that's not the worst part. The elves call the various species of kefali by different names. Like the bull-like ones are called minotaur by the elves, but the kefali themselves have a different name for them; Tiraan or something like that, I think."

"Interesting," Alex replied. "And each of them can infect you? So, you could be a werebear?"

"I guess so," Liz shrugged.

Alex suddenly laughed. "Could you imagine being bitten by a kefali rabbit?" he grinned. "Oh, no! Here comes the terrible werebunny!"

Liz chuckled along. "More like the ferocious werehare!"

They both shared a good laugh and Alex wiped a tear from his eye. "We shouldn't laugh," he said in all seriousness. "Those things could rip your throat out."

They walked for several blocks as Liz tried to fill Alex in on everything that had happened over the course of the summer. She was recounting their first encounter with a griffin when they turned a corner and came upon a large crowd gathered around a man preaching from atop a small stage.

"Oh, no." Liz groaned at the sight of the man.

Alex looked from the preacher to the cheering crowd in confusion "What is it?"

"Truthers," Liz scowled at the crowd.

"And who are they?" Alex asked.

"A bunch of fools that think all religions are part of a greater whole," Liz explained hotly. "They believe that there is one Creator above all that made the universe and that he is the God worshiped by Christians, Muslims, and any other monotheistic religion."

"Ok?" Alex's brow furrowed in thought. "So, what's wrong with that?"

"What's *wrong* is that they think that all of those religions worship the same God," Liz snapped angrily.

"Well, don't they have a point?" Alex said carefully. "A lot of religions do have similar stories and some nearly identical events."

Liz gave an exasperated sigh. "You sound like Mike."

They reached the edge of the crowd and began working their way around.

Alex shrugged innocently. "My brother and I don't agree on much," he smiled, "but we do share a common distrust of government and organized religion."

"But all those religions are so different," Liz argued. "You can't say that God is the same for all of them. There are fundamental differences that cannot be explained away."

"Yes, they are different," Alex conceded the point, "but the key word there is religion, and a religion can change a lot in two thousand or more years."

But Liz was shaking her head before he had finished. "Yes, but these Truthers are taking it to a whole new level by saying that the pagan gods are real and exist on the same level as angels."

They walked around the outskirts, but the gathering took up the entire street. So, Liz and Alex had to slowly push their way through.

"Interesting..." Alex looked thoughtful. "I had been wondering about that. I suppose it makes sense... if they all exist then there isn't really any reason to fight over which one is right. And it would explain how the elves' and dwarves' prayers get answered."

Liz rolled her eyes. "They would fight over who is more powerful or some other nonsense, I'm sure. Besides, all prayers get answered because God doesn't want anyone to suffer. He is our parent. Even when his children push Him away, He still loves us and will be there for us."

"Then why would you need a particular religion?" Alex asked. "If God answers everybody, then aren't these Truthers right?"

"No," Liz said passionately. "God answers prayers to stop suffering, but only true followers make it to heaven."

Finally, they pushed their way around the final edge of the crowd and into the open street once again. They continued down the street, away from the cheering onlookers.

Alex looked doubtful. "So, you're saying that God will answer your prayer if you believe in Zeus or Thor, but you won't get into heaven?"

Liz shrugged, "Something like that."

"Sounds like a dick-move to me."

Liz scowled up at him. "It's called free choice. It would be a dick-move to demand our love and loyalty. Instead, we are granted the gift to choose what we believe, instead of it being forced upon us."

"It's not really much of a choice when the options are either do what God says or go to hell," Alex muttered.

Either Liz didn't hear him or ignored the comment as she continued.

"It might even be that the gods don't even play a part in healing. It could just be that people with the power to heal find it easier to call on their own abilities when praying, thus attributing the healing to the god they called upon."

"Either way," said Alex, "the theological debate on which religion is right will never end. There can be no winners in such a dispute because nobody living knows what happens after death. It is a futile argument. One in which I shall not take part. All that matters is strengthening one's mind and body to be in perfect harmony. Only through meditation and self-reflection can one truly find peace."

"Finding eternal salvation isn't futile," Liz argued passionately. "It is our greatest mission to guide everyone to the saving light of God."

"We need salvation because we are all cursed with original sin?" Alex laughed and shook his head in denial. "I don't think so. Original sin is the greatest lie conceived by the early Church to gain followers."

"It is no lie," Liz replied. "If not for original sin, we wouldn't be living in this imperfect world in the first place."

"And some moldy old book told you that?" Alex snorted derisively but noticed that Liz was becoming upset, so he quickly changed his tone. "Look," he said in a placating manner, "I'm not saying you are wrong. There could very well be a paradise awaiting on the other side, but I'm not going to put all my faith in something that may or may not exist."

"But religion isn't just about getting to heaven," Liz said. "It also teaches compassion and how to live your life to the fullest. Religion has done great things to help people."

"It has also killed a lot of people," Alex added. "If everyone just quit trying to prove that their beliefs were the right ones, then the world would be a much better place."

"You can't blame the religion for everyone killed in the name of religion," Liz argued. "It is people's greed and lust that cause war and suffering. They just put a mask of religion on it to justify their deeds and to lure others to their cause."

"But what if these Truthers are right?" Alex asked. "What if heaven isn't some magical place reserved for Christians and is really a place for ALL the good people. Like some huge pizza in the sky."

"What?" Liz looked at him as if he had grown a second head. "A huge pizza in the sky?"

"Well... yeah." Alex shrugged sheepishly. "What if heaven is broken into slices. Each slice is different, but they are all still pizza. So, Christians have their slice and Jews their slice and so on. That way, God isn't a selective asshole and all the good people still get to Heaven."

Liz smiled at her large companion. "You would relate this to food."

Alex grinned back. "I do love me a good pierogi pizza!"

A large group of people appeared from around the corner a few blocks away and began marching toward them. They carried signs and someone was using a megaphone to shout something, but it was too muffled to understand from that distance.

"Aw, crap," Liz muttered darkly when she saw the approaching throng.

"Who are they?"

"Divisionalists," Liz answered grimly. "Basically, a bunch of Atheists that joined together into a kind of militia to challenge the Truthers. They believe that there are no gods or demons, and that all the powers and magic are the result of natural phenomena that manifests in certain people."

"That doesn't sound so bad," Alex said as the mob drew closer.

"It wouldn't be if that was it. But all they want to do is pick fights with anyone who tries to argue with them. And I don't mean a fight with words."

Alex guessed that there were over fifty Divisionalists headed their way and it was then that he noticed the variety of weapons in their hands.

"Hey!" Alex cried, as Liz abruptly grabbed his arm and roughly dragged him down a smaller side street. She pulled out her cell phone as she continued to move down the alley.

"What are you doing? Alex asked, as he tried to catch up.

Liz's ponytail streamed out behind her as she dashed toward the end of the street. She punched in a few numbers and put the device to her ear. "Calling the City Guard."

"You can still call 911?" Alex asked in disbelief. "I didn't think anything like that was working anymore."

Liz held up a finger as she talked into the phone. "Yes, I need a detachment of the Guard at the corner of Fifth Ave and South Craig Street. There is a Truther's rally there and around fifty armed Divisionalists headed their way..." Liz talked for a few more moments until she finally hung up and turned back to Alex. "Sorry, but I had to warn them before things get out of hand."

"Fine with me," Alex said, "but since when does 911 work?"

Liz and Alex turned off the side street and hurried down the one that ran parallel with the one they had originally been on. They could see the gang of Divisionalists marching across from them headed in the opposite direction.

"When phones started working again, 911 was one of the first services restored in the city," Liz explained. "It gave people jobs and helped coordinate defense efforts. Of course, calling anywhere is still spotty at best, but it goes through more often than not now."

"I see." Alex watched the mob across from them warily. "It's good to know that help can still be reached if you need it."

"Yes," Liz breathed a sigh, as the pack of Divisionalists was lost from sight down the other street. "Regaining emergency services was a top priority."

"But shouldn't we stay and help?" Alex asked with a worried look back.

"No," Liz answered briskly. "The Truthers can handle themselves. They are mostly a peaceful lot and there was more than one mage in that crowd. Thankfully, there are few hardcore Divisionalists, so large confrontations are rare."

"If you say so." Alex looked around at the buildings for the first time and noticed with some surprise that they had changed from the industrial center that they had started in to an almost residential area that they now found themselves in. "So, where is this Healers Tent anyways?"

Liz pointed off to their left where the towering majesty of the Cathedral of Learning dominated the skyline. "It's over there."

****

The thunder of the cannons shook the valley and the gorge erupted in fire and death as the high-yield shells exploded among the tightly packed kefali. The walls of the gorge collapsed under the bombardment and tons of stone broke free to crush the helpless warriors below. The poor creatures didn't stand a chance as the ground detonated around them and scores of shattered bodies cartwheeled through the air.

Glittering shields had sprung up across the Isfet army and offered some protection, but even they couldn't withstand a direct hit from the powerful 120 mm cannons.

Those kefali lucky enough to have already escaped the gorge roared in anger and charged through the valley, eager to take bloody revenge.

But a hail of gunfire met the mighty warriors of the Horned Legion as the tanks' gun crews opened up with an array of machine guns. Old .50 cals thundered to life and tore through the heavy-bodied minotaurs with ease as M240's sprayed death in a withering storm of fire. The howling Legion surged forward, heedless of the danger, and were pulverized into oblivion by the concussive blasts of cannon fire, crumbling stone, and a perpetual rain of bullets.

Back at HQ, Mike and the other leaders watched as the battle unfolded on the screens before them.

"Congratulations, General," one of the aids said excitedly. "Your plan worked perfectly!"

But General Adams didn't smile. He glared at the slaughter on the screens as if it were his troops being massacred. "Indeed," he muttered softly.

"What is it, Sir?" Major Sanders said, as he eyed the display critically, as if searching for whatever it was that the general didn't like. "Everything is going according to plan."

"Exactly," General Adams scowled. "It is too easy." He turned to one of his aids. "Did they send scouts ahead of the vanguard?"

"Yes, Sir," the aid replied confidently. "All enemy scouts were eliminated by our sniper teams."

The general nodded as if he had expected that very answer. "And they didn't change course when none of their scouts reported back?"

"No, Sir," the aid said with less confidence this time. "They maintained their heading and continued through the gorge."

"Surely this Destroyer be no fool," King Varnir rumbled thoughtfully. "Mayhaps with such a large horde, word o' the lost scouts has no reached him yet?"

"Perhaps," Stratigos Valerian muttered, "but I agree with the good general. Something about this doesn't feel right."

The dwarf king snorted. "Elves an' their *feelin's*."

"Scoff all you like, your Highness," Valerian said with a hint of steel in his voice, "but intuition is a reliable and necessary instinct."

Arch Battlemage Gwydion abruptly pushed forward and pointed to a wooded area on the screen. "What is going on there?" he asked from the depths of his hood.

The other commanders all leaned in, examining the area that the Battlemage was pointing to. It was a large, wooded section of hillside behind the line of B Company.

"It be nothin' but the wind in the trees," King Varnir rumbled, as he leaned back, satisfied with his observation. "Even an old mountain dwarf like me knows what the wind be lookin' like."

"If that's the wind," General Adams squinted at the drone feed, "then why is it only blowing in this area?"

"It's not." Valerian pointed to another part of the hillside. "It is moving there as well."

"That's no wind." Gwydion pulled a small, multi-sided cube from inside his robe. The strange device started to glow in the Arch Battlemage's hand and gave off a faint, bluish light as he held it up to his mouth. "Battlemages," Gwydion said into the cube. "Dispel Aura. Now."

Almost immediately, a shimmering pulse radiated out from the elf mages that rode with B Company. Like the ripples from stones cast into a pond, the spells flowed out and around the line of firing battle tanks.

The glittering wave cascaded down the hill and when it came into contact with the strangely rustling areas that Gwydion had first noticed, there was a faint flicker as the aura encountered another spell and destroyed it.

"My God..." Major Sanders breathed at the sight revealed before them.

B Company was no longer alone on the hill.

Sweeping up the hill were two massive herds of centaur. Armed with short bows, the beasts only paused a moment in surprise as their cloaking spell was dispelled before roaring lustily now that the need for stealth was over and they resumed their charge.

"Contact!" suddenly crackled over the radio. "Hostiles incoming at 7 and 5 o'clock." Calls of "affirmative" hissed over the radio as the B Company expertly adjusted to the new threat.

Thankfully, two battle tanks and several support vehicles had been stationed behind the main line as a precaution for just such an eventuality.

The two cannons thundered to life as each tank targeted a different herd of charging centaurs. Explosions ripped through the tightly packed beasts, but they quickly spread out through the trees, making the next cannon salvo far less effective. Mike estimated the herds to be well over two hundred yards away, much too far to use their short bows, but they were rapidly closing the distance.

On the other side of the hill, the kefali legion was making slow but steady progress through the storm of gunfire. They, too, had spread out and were using trees and boulders for cover as they pushed up toward B Company.

"We need to get them out of there," Mike said, as he recognized the danger of the tanks becoming trapped between the approaching forces.

"Aye," Lord Aurvang rumbled his assent. "Yer machines are goin' ter be surrounded if ye don't get 'em out."

General Adams watched impassively as the battle unfolded before them.

"I thought centaurs couldn't use magic," Mike said. "How did they cloak themselves?"

"They don't. It must have been applied to them before they left the main force," Valerian answered thoughtfully. "This must have been planned before they left the forest."

Explosions and heavy gunfire ripped into the kefali on both sides of the hill and scores of the beasts died with each passing moment. But still they came on in an unending sea of monstrous warriors. The two groups of centaurs were closing the gap between them, and soon B Company would be caught in a deadly vice.

"Stratigos Valerian," General Adams said, while not taking his eyes off the battle. "You say the centaurs have no wizards of their own?"

The tall elf nodded. "As a race, they have almost no Gift for the Art."

"So, they must rely on their bows," General Adams concluded.

"General," Valerian stepped forward earnestly, "the centaurs are master archers, second only to elves in skill. They will surely kill anyone that-" The tall elf's eyes grew wide in alarm as a huge black cloud rose up from beyond the gorge.

The dark mass moved strangely as it rapidly expanded and moved toward B Company at an alarming rate.

"What the hell is that?" General Adams demanded in alarm.

As the dark cloud billowed forward, Mike realized in horror that it wasn't a cloud at all, but a swarm of living creatures.

As the living cloud drew closer, Mike began to make out details of the individual beasts. They had the bodies of women, but their arms and legs were covered in feathers. Large wings sprouted from their backs and their legs ended in large, bird-like talons.

Stratigos Valerian cursed at the sight of the flying creatures. "Order the retreat, General. Now!"

General Adams didn't need to be told twice. He spoke urgently into his microphone. "B Company, this is General Adams. Execute Operation Tailspin. Repeat; execute Operation Tailspin."

A moment later the message was passed across B Company and the vehicles started moving. Slowly at first, but with growing speed, the battle tanks and support vehicles gave up their positions along the ridge and started moving toward the increasingly narrow gap between the charging centaur herds. With the main body of the Horned Legion still coming up the other side of the hill, B Company turned its full might on the approaching centaurs. Freed from the bombardment, the Legion surged ahead, eager to chase down their fleeing prey.

But none of the commanders were watching the engagement on the ground. They were focused on the dark swarm of feathered beasts that was now blotting out the sun from the warriors below them that were still flowing through the gorge.

The winged creatures were deceptively fast and the living cloud quickly flew the length of the gorge and was above the valley in moments.

"What are those things?" Major Sanders asked worriedly.

"Those," Stratigos Valerian eyed the fast-moving swarm, "are harpies."

CHAPTER 17

Jack had never felt so alive!

He bound through the trees on all fours, his paws churning up the soft soil as he raced beneath the leafy canopy. A whole new world of sounds and smells greeted him and he reveled in the flood of new sensations. But he was getting tired.

Not physically tired, he was sure he could run for days, but his mind was becoming sluggish as he fought to suppress the ever-present hunger that was building up inside him. He had allowed himself to transform several times in the hopes of dispelling the hunger, but instead it became harder and harder to grab the wolf inside him and force the change. And when he did master the wolf, the hunger would come back even greater than it had been before.

Jack glanced over at Emily who was running along nearby. He ran much faster than her, but she more than made up for it when she fell behind by leaping into a tree and popping out several trees ahead of him. Seeing her racing ahead of him spurred him on even faster. If only he could catch her and clamp his jaws on her soft throat-

Werewolf Jack shook his shaggy head as he pushed the unwelcome thought aside. Rangvald had been right. The hunger was taking all of his strength to control and he was afraid of what would happen if he lost it.

A new scent suddenly caught his attention.

Jack tasted the air and discovered it wasn't one scent that he was smelling, but several different ones all swirling together. At first it was hard to distinguish them, but the longer Jack smelled them, the easier it became to tell them apart.

One was sweet and flowery while another was similar yet different, but both were drenched in fear. Mixed around them were several eerie odors that brought to mind death, decomposition, and... At first Jack wasn't sure what to call the putrid odor, but then he realized what it was.

Corruption.

The huge werewolf came to a stop and bared his long fangs in a snarl as the cloying scent grew stronger.

Emily heard the growl and looked back to see Jack crouched in the brush, hackles raised as he seemingly snarled at nothing. She took a quick step into a nearby tree and stepped out of one right beside her growling friend. "What is it?" she asked and looked around the forest curiously. "I don't see anything."

"You won't." Jack forced the instinct to growl aside long enough to answer. "I smell it."

Emily experimentally sniffed the air and wrinkled her nose. "Smells like something died down over the hill."

"It's more than that." Jack tasted the air again. "Something evil is down there. It tastes like corruption... and it is chasing something."

"Then we better go check it out," Emily said cheerfully, as she knocked an arrow.

The thought of a fight made Jack's heart race. To chase down his prey and sink his jaws into its soft flesh filled Jack with desire. The taste of blood in his mouth as he devoured the warm meat was almost too much to bear. And if Emily was there...

"No," the huge werewolf growled angrily as he shook his head, trying to clear the bloodthirsty thoughts from his mind. "I can't go like this. I don't know if I could control myself."

Emily looked at the towering beast before her. "You aren't made for control, Jack. And this evil needs killing."

"I know," Jack snarled, "but the hunger is growing. I cannot guarantee your safety if I go down there like this. Everything looks like prey to me."

Concern filled Emily's face. "Then change back."

A short bark of laughter came from Jack. "Naked and unarmed is not how I like to start a fight."

"Good point." Emily put her arrow back in her quiver. "Don't go anywhere. I will be right back."

"Where are you-" Jack started to ask, but Emily jumped into a tree and vanished before he could finish. Jack's wolf-like features scowled. "Going," he finished with a sigh.

Jack's ears perked up as a soft scratching sound reached them. It was faint, but he could tell that there were several somethings moving swiftly away from him near the base of the hill. He was sure it would only take a minute for him to run down there and see what it was. He only wanted to look. Surely, he could be back before Emily got back.

Making up his mind, Jack leapt over a fallen log and bound through the woods.

"Hey!" a voice shouted. "Where do you think you're going?"

Jack came to a halt and turned back guiltily to see Emily walking toward him with a large bundle in her hands.

"I thought I heard something," he answered lamely.

"Sure, you did," Emily smirked. "Now, take this and get changed." She held the bundle out to him, but Jack just looked down at it. "Drop the shaggy dog act and put this on before your evil thing gets away."

The huge werewolf took the bundle in its huge, clawed hands and gave Emily a strange look and she laughed. "Don't be silly. I am not turning around." She crossed her arms under her breasts and grinned. "There isn't anything I haven't seen before."

Jack scowled down at her but didn't argue. If she wanted to think that he was nervous about being naked in front of her then he was more than happy to let her believe that. In reality he didn't want to let go of the wolf. It was like losing a part of himself. He felt incomplete without it. But the scent was quickly fading and he knew they had to get going.

With a deep breath, Jack reluctantly released the wolf. His vision dimmed and his other senses seemed to fade away. Even though his human senses were heightened, being human again still felt like becoming a frail old man, blind and deaf.

Jack was glad to see that his katana was strapped to the bag and he carefully leaned it against a tree before opening the bundle with his now-human hands. Inside were his black combat fatigues, bulletproof vest, pistol, and several daggers, but his samurai-like orc armor was missing.

"Where did my armor go?" Jack asked, as he quickly began dressing.

"Ted took it," Emily answered with a shrug. "He said he was making some improvements or something."

"Wonderful," Jack moaned, and he quickly pulled his boots on and laced them up.

Fully dressed, Jack jammed his pistol into the holster and slid the katana into his belt. "Let's go."

Emily and Jack set a quick pace through the woods as they hurried down the gently sloping hill toward the foul stink that got stronger as they raced on.

It didn't take them long to discover signs that something had come this way. Sticks and leaves were scattered and broken where something had passed by not long ago.

They followed the trail and the stink through the forest for several minutes as it led them to the bottom of the hill and across the wooded valley floor.

An eerie scream suddenly exploded from ahead of them and the trees swayed violently as if caught in some terrible storm.

Emily and Jack shared a quick look before they raced toward the cry. Together they charged down a steep bank and leapt across a small stream as they raced through the trees. Panicked shouts and chilling, raspy laughter grew louder as the pair scrambled over a large pile of boulders.

As Emily and Jack hopped across the tops of the boulders, Jack realized that the huge stones formed a kind of maze below them and that was where the shouts were coming from. The massive rocks gave a strange echo that made it difficult to pinpoint where the sounds originated, but Jack's enhanced senses let him pick out the pounding of feet and the scratch of claws on rocks, allowing him to lead Emily swiftly across the tops of the boulders and catch up to whatever was below them.

The stink of rotten flesh was overpowering as the pair caught their first glimpse of movement between the rocks.

Three figures darted through the maze, but they shambled along with a strange gait that didn't seem quite right. There was something off-putting about the way they moved and Jack quickly realized why.

The creatures were gaunt and looked like little more than grey skin stretched over bones as they raced along on all fours as often as they did on two legs. Like corpses fresh out of the grave, the monsters' decaying flesh stank of death.

Two other figures raced just head of the three undead monsters, but it was clear that these two were very much alive and that the unnatural creatures were chasing them.

Without hesitating, Emily drew and fired an arrow in one fluid motion as she leapt from one boulder to another. The arrow punched into the back of the skull of the leading monster and drove out the other side and into the stone, pinning the creature's head to the boulder.

The other two monsters ignored their comrade and darted around a huge stone in pursuit of their living quarry and were lost from sight.

To Jack and Emily's horror, the mortally wounded creature thrashed and clawed at the arrow in its head as it tried desperately to escape. As the pair raced overhead, Emily dove three more arrows into the undead thing's body, further pinning it to the boulder.

Leaving the trapped creature, Emily and Jack raced across the huge stones and quickly spotted the other two creatures as they closed in on their prey. The undead things moved unnaturally fast and were swiftly closing the gap.

"Oh, no," Emily breathed, just as the fleeing couple came to an abrupt halt. They had struck a dead end. Trapped on three sides by towering boulders, the figures turned to face the approaching creatures. It was then that Emily and Jack got their first good look at the fleeing couple and to their surprise they discovered that it was a pair of female elves. One had long golden hair that was tied back with a slim band of leather and the other had short brown hair.

The undead things cackled with glee and slowed their pace as they realized their prey was trapped.

Jack cursed as he recognized that there was no easy path across the boulders. They would have to go around if they hoped to reach the trapped elves in time.

Dressed in soft leathers and with no obvious weapons between them, the elves boldly faced their corrupt enemies. The creatures' scratchy laughter echoed eerily between the stones as they attacked.

The blonde elf held up her hands and as one of the creatures descended on her, roots shot out from between the stones and wrapped themselves around the creature in midair.

The other undead thing avoided the roots and drove at the dark-haired elf. The thing extended its bony claws and pounced. The elf abruptly vanished in a swirl of autumn leaves and the creature fell right through it. The brunette elf reappeared a moment later and raced away as the undead thing charged after her.

The trapped creature violently thrashed in the binding roots and somehow managed to free itself. It fell to the ground on all fours and hissed angrily at the surprised elf maiden. It charged at her as more roots shot out of the ground, but the undead thing avoided them as it scrambled toward her. The blonde elf reached over and yanked at a root that was growing over one of the stones and as she did the root broke off and formed a hard, wooden staff just as the creature's claws reached for her. She swung the staff and just barely managed to knock the undead thing away.

The brunette was weaving through the boulders as fast as she could, but the creature was gaining on her with every step. As she darted down a narrow passage, the creature scrambled up onto a smaller boulder and shrieked as it pounced at her exposed back. She turned just in time to see a large shape crash into the leaping monster and bear it to the ground.

Jack drove his tamahagane blade into the creature, but the undead thing didn't seem to notice. It slashed and bit at him, and he was forced to pull the sword out and back away. Jack held his sword at the ready as he put himself defensively between the undead thing and the brunette elf.

"Stay behind me," Jack ordered without taking his eyes off the creature. Its bloody lips hissed as it eyed him balefully with eyes that glowed a sickly yellow and were sunken deep into its emaciated skull. The foul stench of decay that emanated from the creature was overpowering.

The monster shrieked and leapt at him, and Jack's blade bit into the thing's arm, but didn't cut through. The creature didn't stop and its other hand lashed out and the clawed fingers racked along Jack's face.

Jack growled in agony and violently knocked the clawing creature away. Blood ran freely from the five gouges in the side of his head, but Jack was no stranger to pain and he pushed the discomfort aside.

The creature sprang at him again, but this time an arrow punched into its head and threw it off balance. Jack seized the opportunity and his blade bit deep as it scraped against the bones of the creature's neck. To Jack's surprise, the undead thing's head didn't come off and instead it reached for him with its claws. Expecting an easy kill, Jack was unprepared for the attack and he just barely got away from the claws that slashed at his throat.

Jack slammed hard into a boulder, but surprisingly the undead thing didn't pursue him. Instead it bounded toward the elf again. Jack slashed at the creature's back as it rushed away, but again his sword only scraped ineffectively off its spine.

A bolt of green energy slammed into the creature, but somehow it still didn't fall. Emily dropped down and landed lightly on her feet between the skeletal monster and the elf. Emily raised her scepter again and another fiery bolt slammed into the undead thing, but it weathered the blast and took another step toward them.

Panic grew on Emily's face as another emerald bolt struck the creature and had little effect. The monster weathered the storm and continued its slow advance.

Jack slashed at the creature's exposed back, but his blade barely scored a line on the monster's bones. Apparently aware that Jack's sword wasn't a threat, the undead creature ignored him and moved toward Emily and the elf.

Jack's mind raced. How was this skeletal thing defeating his soul sword? It could cut through just about anything. There was no way simple bone should be able to withstand his strike. There must be more to this creature than simply undeath.

Then Jack had an idea. He wasn't thrilled with it, but he didn't have any other options. He had considered joining the wolf, but if his tamahagane blade couldn't cut the creature, then his normal claws surely wouldn't either.

So, Jack opened himself up to the soul sword and allowed the sentient power in the blade to join with him. He wasn't really sure how he did it, but after his experience with the wolf sprit, it almost seemed to come naturally to him.

Power flowed through him and he became one with the possessed blade. The energy of the sword threatened to overwhelm him, but Jack squashed the torrent of power and brutally harnessed it to his will. Burning symbols flared along the length of the blade and a hellish red glow radiated from the black weapon.

With a lusty roar, Jack swung the sword with all his might. The burning blade left a trail of black ash in the air as it carved through the creature's neck. The undead thing released an unworldly howl as its head fell to the ground and the body remained upright for a moment before it disintegrated in a cloud of dust.

"Thank you." The dark-haired elf eyed Jack with a mixture of fear and awe. "That must be a truly powerful weapon to have defeated the wendigo."

"So, that's what it was," Emily muttered, as she kicked the pile of dust.

A cry of pain suddenly echoed through the maze of boulders.

"Nualla!" the elf cried, and then dashed off back in the direction of her companion. Jack and Emily wasted no time in following the dark-haired elf back through the forest of stone.

After a mad dash between the monolithic stones, they came upon the blonde elf seated on the ground with her back against a boulder and one arm held out above her. A broken staff lay nearby and a wall of leaves swirled beyond her outstretched hand as two wendigo slashed wildly at the leaves in mindless desperation. Somehow the leaves withstood their sharp claws better than a normal leaf had any right to, but even as they arrived, more and more of the leaves were shredded and fell to the ground. Soon, the barrier would be gone and the wendigo would reach the trapped elf.

One of the monsters had a hole through its head and body, and Jack recognized it as the wendigo that Emily had pinned to the stone. Obviously, it had escaped and was now slashing at the leaves with reckless abandon.

The burning characters on Jack's sword glowed with even more intensity as he charged the distracted wendigo. Before the howling monsters could react, Jack came up behind them and with two swift strikes, decapitated them both.

They screamed and burst into dust as their skeletal bodies hit the ground.

As the burning symbols faded from his blade, Jack took the blonde elf by the hand and helped her to her feet.

"Thank you," the pretty blonde elf breathed, as she looked up at Jack gratefully. "My name is Nualla and I owe you my life."

"We both do," the brunette elf said, as she put her arm around Nualla protectively. "I am Kyli." She nodded to Jack and Emily. "We are grateful for your assistance against the wendigo."

Emily returned her scepter to her belt as she inspected the pair of elves. "I'm Emily," she said carefully, "and this is Jack." He nodded to the elves. "What is a pair of Druids doing all the way out here? I thought Belenos called everyone back."

The Druids' surprise was obvious. "High Druid Belenos is here?" Kyli asked with disbelief evident in her voice.

"Of course," Emily replied in confusion. "He is in the Glade of Pittsburgh like he always is."

"Pittsburgh?" Nualla wrinkled her nose as if she didn't like the taste of the word. "Is that the name of this world?"

Realization struck Jack and instead of answering he asked, "How long have you been here?"

"A few days," Kyli answered.

"Ever since the mist brought us here," Nualla added.

A raspy howl of a wendigo bubbled up from beyond the trees and was answered by what must have been dozens more.

"We need to go," Nualla said nervously, as her eyes darted around like a frightened deer. "Now."

"Yes," Emily agreed. "We can treewalk to the Glade."

Nualla looked at Emily skeptically. "You are a Druid?"

"In training," Emily replied testily. She didn't like the elf's tone. "But I can treewalk."

But Kyli shook her head. "We cannot," she said nervously, and unconsciously touched a pouch on her belt. "We have an... artifact that does not allow for such travel."

Scratchy laughter was getting closer all around them.

"Well, that's unfortunate," Jack said quickly, as he sheathed his sword and then put his hands on the two elves. "But I suggest we talk about this more after we are safely away from here," he said as he herded them swiftly through the maze of boulders.

****

The centaur screamed as the speeding tank dragged the poor beast under its tracks, but the cry only lasted a moment before the centaur was crushed beneath the mighty vehicle. The mutilated corpse was spat out as the tank roared by, unnoticed by the tank's crew as they poured gunfire into the dark cloud behind them.

All through the woods the scene repeated itself as the centaurs were being run over by fleeing tanks and armored vehicles as the mechanized company tried to escape the swarm of harpies. But as fast as the tanks were, the flying beasts were faster and they descended on the fleeing troops with horrible screeches of bestial glee.

B Company's gun crews pumped countless rounds into the swarming harpies as the drivers struggled to maintain their speed as they weaved through the trees and were constantly pelted by arrows from the teeming centaurs all around them.

The two herds of centaur that had tried to sneak up on them had joined forces into one massive herd just as the first armored vehicles crashed into them. Now the battle lines had been lost, with each vehicle racing along on its own as harpies swooped down and tried to snatch soldiers away.

A few of the tanks were safe inside protective magical spheres created by the mages onboard, but most were not so fortunate and had to weather the storm alone.

Bullets ripped into the harpies as they dove through the trees and clawed at the soldiers. The feathered bodies fell like rain around the fleeing vehicles, but for every one that fell, five more took its place.

A harpy swooped down and grabbed a soldier by the shoulders with its large talons and viciously pulled him out of the gun turret. The unfortunate soldier vanished into the screeching cloud before he could make a sound.

As more harpies pulled soldiers from their guns, the stream of fire slowed and more of the flying beasts found their way to the exposed gunners. The centaurs took advantage of the distraction and fired arrows with remarkable precision at the racing vehicles.

"We need to do something!" Mike growled, as another soldier was pulled from his armored Humvee and shot with three arrows before he had cleared the turret.

"There is nothing we can do," General Adams said somberly. "We don't have any other units in the area. They are on their own."

Just then, one of the video feeds spun crazily as the drone was hit by something. There were flashes of color before it crashed to the ground. Upside down, the screen showed centaur hooves racing by until a moment later when the huge form of a tank appeared. The guns of the mighty machine roared as it barreled down the hill, directly toward the crashed drone. The screen filled with the whirring treads and then the screen went black as the drone was crushed.

Major Sanders cursed. "Now, we only have the Predator left."

The other screen displayed a view high above the battle, so high that very few details could be seen through the trees and soaring harpies. But what could be seen was the sea of kefali that rolled up and over the crest of the hill where B Company had been positioned earlier. The vanguard of the Horned Legion flowed down the other side of the hill in pursuit of the fleeing company.

There was a sudden flare of light and the video shook as something exploded beneath the trees.

"What the hell was that?" General Adams demanded.

"Perhaps somebody threw a grenade," one of the aids offered lamely.

"No," Major Sanders shook his head, "that was far too large to have been a grenade."

"It isn't doing us any good guessing," General Adams snapped. "Look," He pointed to the screen. "They are almost clear of the centaurs. Then they will cross that bridge and be free of the beasts."

Stratigos Valerian eyed the screen dubiously. "How will crossing the bridge be of assistance? Surely the Legion will follow."

"Once our men are across, they have orders to blow the bridge." General Adams answered grimly.

Lord Aurvang nodded approvingly as the live UAV feed showed the boxy shapes of the armored company finally push through the last of the centaurs to emerge from the trees and onto the road near the bridge.

The swarm of harpies fell behind like an angry storm cloud as the vehicles picked up speed and roared down the road.

Mike breathed a sigh of relief as B Company pulled farther away from the pursuing kefali. It was a short drive from where they had exited the forest to the foot of the bridge and in no time the armored convoy was barreling across all four lanes.

The live video abruptly flickered and became jumpy with intermittent static. One of the command personnel touched his earpiece and listened to something for a moment before turning to the general. "Sir, we are having difficulties communicating with the Predator."

"I can see that," General Adams growled. "Fix it!"

The tech began working furiously on the small tablet in his hand, but the screen only became more scrambled.

The battle tanks and armored support vehicles of B Company were nearly half way across the bridge when gunfire and panicked shouting suddenly erupted on the radio.

"What's going on?" General Adams demanded into his headset.

"Hostiles!" the scratchy voice on the other end shouted over the thunder of gunfire. "….coming up …. underneath!" The radio went in and out. "…. everywhere!"

The drone's feed jittered and faded in and out, but it was clear enough to see the hundreds of small, dark shapes that were suddenly swarming around the bridge. Like the jaws of some titanic beast, the figures boiled up over both sides of the bridge. B Company raced ahead, guns blazing as they desperately tried to escape the swiftly closing trap.

The drone hesitantly zoomed in on the bridge and the dark figures took on more detail. It was hard to make out over the nearly constant static interference, but these new attackers bubbled up out of the river and slithered up the bridge supports. At first glance they appeared almost human, until the camera zoomed in more and it became obvious they were not. Instead of legs, the creatures' lower halves ended in a long, snake-like tail and their skin was covered in dark scales.

"Naga," Gwydion hissed angrily, when he recognized the serpentine beasts.

Suddenly, darts of black energy and crackling bolts of power erupted from hordes of naga and pounded into the racing convoy. Two Humvees erupted and burst into flame while an armored Stryker drove into a glowing orb and simply vanished.

B Company returned fire and cut down large swaths of naga, but for each one killed, another remained safe behind a protective, magical shield.

Mike watched helplessly as a blistering volley of destructive magic hammered into the battle tanks as they plowed onward. The Battlemages joined in and lashed out at the beasts with deadly spells of their own. Muffled shouts of pain rang out over the radio amid the thunder of gunfire. One tank abruptly ground to a halt as its engine was struck by a powerful kinetic blast.

The video flickered and then went black for what seemed like an eternity before returning a moment later with a haze of grain over it. When the screen cleared, the damaged tank was swarming with the serpentine creatures as they slithered over the tank's armored hull, trying to find a way in.

The convoy was now completely surrounded by the naga and the lead vehicles were slowing down as they tried to plow their way through the scaly throng. With progress slowed, the dark cloud of harpies was again closing in, and the rest of the kefali Legion was streaming onto the road and picking up speed as they raced toward the besieged convoy.

Another tank was rocked by a devastating barrage of silvery beams that seared through the mage's spell shield and pierced the armored hull. The superheated beams must have hit the ammunition stored inside, for the battle tank suddenly erupted in a brilliant explosion.

The video screen filled with static and then went black as the sounds of battle on the radio were drowned out by the hiss of static.

One of the aids looked up at General Adams. "We have lost contact with the Predator."

"Radio communications are also out," another added.

General Adams ripped his headset off and threw it to the ground. "Damn it!"

The general turned away as he tried to regain his composure. "Get the coms back up. Now." He took a deep breath. "Can't we use a spell or something to see what they are doing? And what the hell were those things?"

"We tried," Gwydion answered grimly. "They are blocking all of our scrying spells."

"We call them naga," Stratigos Valerian added. "They are a reptilian species of kefali that have the distinctive characteristic that instead of legs, they have the body of a serpent. As you saw, the naga are cunning warriors and extremely gifted in the Art."

"Yes, I noticed," General Adams growled. "And now my men are dead."

Arch Battlemage Gwydion's eyes flashed angrily. "So are my Battlemages," he hissed with a dangerous edge in his voice. "This whole mission was folly. I should never have agreed to this."

"Aye," King Varnir abruptly rumbled, "but ye did, and there be no takin' it back."

Gwydion rounded on the stocky dwarf king and Mike was afraid things were about to get out of hand. "I didn't see any of your dwarves out there dying."

"That be true," the king rumbled easily. "O' course that be because me clan be makin' war with the orcs in the east, or did yer pointy-eared self be forgettin' that?"

The Arch Battlemage's features softened as he realized the dwarf was right. Gwydion had only granted a bare handful of his Battlemages to assist the human company, while King Varnir had devoted countless Anvilborn warriors to harass the growing orc horde.

"Besides," King Varnir continued, "their sacrifice has given us valuable information on our adversaries."

"How so?" Major Sanders asked. "All I saw was our boys getting killed out there."

"King Varnir is correct," Stratigos Valerian said thoughtfully. "We now know that the Legion isn't merely made up of land-based infantry, but they also have numerous aerial units and aquatic forces."

"Aye," King Varnir rumbled approvingly. "The question now be this; what will we do about it?"

General Adams ran a hand over his shaved head as he regained his usual level of calm. "The harpies won't be a problem. After that surprise attack by the orcs, I'm having machine gun nests and anti-aircraft batteries placed on every possible rooftop. There aren't as many as I'd like, but at least we will be more prepared when the time comes."

"I will see to it that these locations have at least one mage to protect them from magical attack," Gwydion said. "Surely our enemies will target these installations in the hopes of simply flying over our walls."

King Varnir rumbled his assent, "A Guardian will be joinin' each o' them as well."

"Thank you," General Adams nodded gratefully to both the elves and dwarves, "but what about these naga creatures? We don't have any defenses in the water."

"Fear not," Stratigos Valerian said. "Our walls will keep them at bay. However," he held up a slender finger, "we must be wary of launching any kind of counter attack. If your troops march out, the naga will surely come out and cut off any retreat like they did today."

Mike didn't like the sound of that. "So once the battle starts, we are truly trapped here?" he asked.

"Unless ye know o' a way ter clear the rivers," Lord Aurvang rumbled.

"I would say we could plant mines," Mike answered, "but I don't think we have any…" He looked to General Adams as he said it. The general shook his head and Mike sighed. "I didn't think so."

"We wouldn't have time to plant them anyways," General Adams said. "These Isfet are thirty miles away right now and at their current speed, if they march all day and through the night, they will arrive at our walls by dawn tomorrow."

"Will the defenses be ready by then?" Mike asked.

"They will have to be," the general answered grimly.

Mike didn't like the sound of that either. "What about these shadow elves to the south? What do we know about them?"

"Very little," Major Sanders admitted. "We know they are headed toward us, but we don't know their numbers or what kind of troops they have. We are blind."

"The Shadowed Ones will not reveal themselves until they are ready to strike," Gwydion warned.

"Bah," King Varnir rumbled scornfully. "We hold the Mount and Varnirborg below. No army o' undead, pointy-ears be takin' it away from us."

"These are no mere undead," Gwydion replied sharply. "These are Aos Si that have fallen from the Light and embraced the Shadow. Many of them were master mages and among the most gifted in the Art. They became obsessed with power and immortality and embraced any means to achieve their selfish desires. And now their vampiric powers make them even more formidable."

King Varnir snorted in disdain. "I have been makin' war fer over three hunnerd years, elf. This foe does no frighten me."

"It should," Stratigos Valerian rounded on the dwarf king. "I have been leading armies for over *two thousand* years, dwarf. So, trust me when I say that the Shadowed Ones are the greatest threat we face."

If King Varnir was impressed by the elf's revelation, he didn't show it. Instead the dwarf king crossed his muscled arms across his broad chest defiantly. "And what would ye suggest then?"

A flash of surprise crossed the elf's features, but it was so fast that Mike wasn't sure it had really been there. Valerian turned from the blank screens and waved his hand across the small table in the center of room. As his hand passed by, a holographic image of Pittsburgh suddenly appeared above the table, and Mike and the others gathered around it.

"The orcs and their allies will land here." The elf commander pointed to the angled, star fort inspired, eastern walls of the city. "And the kefali will descend on us here." He pointed to the northern wall. "That only leaves the south hills for the Shadowed Ones to come from. But," he pointed to Mt. Washington that ran along the southern edge of the Ohio River, "the dwarves have put their keep upon this ridge, blocking the Shadowed Ones from reaching the southern wall."

Lord Aurvang eyed the hologram critically. "Ye make that sound like a bad thing."

"Your people know how to defeat the orcs and their kin," Stratigos Valerian answered. "They would be of the most use along the eastern wall."

"So ye want us ter abandon the Mount ter fight the orcs?" Lord Aurvang rumbled. "An' I be guessin' ye want us ter let yer kind in ter fight yer kin." The dwarf lord eyed the elf shrewdly and Stratigos Valerian nodded.

"They are our responsibility," the elf answered. "We are the best equipped to defeat them."

King Varnir shook his bearded head vigorously. "Impossible. The Mount an' the whole o' the ridge belongs ter Clan Anvilborn."

Stratigos Valerian looked pleadingly at the dwarf king. "I am not suggesting we keep your fortress, just that you allow us to use it-"

"Perhaps ye did no hear me," King Varnir interrupted with a dangerous edge in his deep voice. "Clan Anvilborn will no be tuckin' tail an' runnin' away ter let some pointy-eared elves do our fightin' fer us."

"That is folly," Gwydion growled. "You jeopardize all of us with your stubbornness! I don't-"

King Varnir slammed his thick fist into the table. "The matter be settled," the king rumbled menacingly. "Clan Anvilborn will no surrender the Mount so long as I be King."

Gwydion sighed regretfully. "You are sending your people to their graves."

King Varnir ignored the Arch Battlemage and instead addressed Lord Aurvang. "Yerself and Brokkr will take' some o' the Clan ter hold the Mount against these stinkin' shadows."

"What o' yerself, Highness?" Aurvang asked.

"I will be leadin' the rest o' the Clan against the orcs," King Varnir grinned eagerly. "It has been too long since the Axe o' Perun has tasted orc flesh."

"At least allow some of my mages to join you against our fallen kin," Gwydion pleaded.

King Varnir looked to Lord Aurvang who gave the slightest of nods. "So be it."

General Adams had watched the exchange in silence up to this point. "What of the rest of the elven forces?" he asked.

"We will split our forces." Stratigos Valerian pointed to the hologram. "You will need our aid against the kefali sorcerers and I will leave the remainder in reserve along the southern wall should the Shadowed Ones overcome the Mount."

King Varnir snorted derisively, "If that be all, I have a battle ter prepare fer." And with that, the stocky king turned and headed for the door with his guards and Lord Aurvang close behind.

"King Varnir!" Mike shouted, before the dwarf had made it through the doorway.

King Varnir Anvilborn turned and glared at Mike in annoyance. "What do ye want?"

The sudden weight of having the mighty dwarf king's full attention on him gave Mike pause, but he quickly overcame the paralysis and answered.

"I would like a word with one of your guards."

"Me Huscarls?" King Varnir looked at the four heavily armored dwarves in confusion. "Which one?"

"Him." Mike pointed to the one dwarf on the end. The dwarf's features were completely hidden beneath a winged helm and elaborate plate mail that was identical to the other three guards. The only distinguishing characteristic was his bushy black beard that stuck out from under his helm, and the magnificent war hammer that pulsed with latent power.

Mike thought he saw a brief flash of surprise on the king's face, but it was gone so fast that Mike doubted it had been there at all. King Varnir regarded Mike for a moment before apparently making up his mind. "Very well, but yer comin' with us," the king rumbled, before turning and continuing toward the door. "Ye will talk in Varnirborg."

CHAPTER 18

The day was passing much too quickly, by Ted's reckoning anyways. He had a great deal of work to complete before the battle began. Thankfully, he wasn't alone. Elves and dwarves came and went throughout the day, each assisting with a particular task that Ted either didn't have the time to do or lacked the required knowledge to perform.

Hot plastic flowed out of the glowing vat as Ted carefully poured the molten material into a large mold. Once the mold was full, he repeated the process on four smaller molds. After a careful inspection looking for any leaks or cracks, Ted gave a satisfied nod before leaving the plastic to cool.

Sparks flew around Ted as he pointed a slender, metal wand at a large steel breastplate. He wore a heavy welding mask and a thick glove on his right hand as he carefully welded several oddly shaped blocks to the breastplate.

Dozens of magnets hovered over a table nearby. Under the magnet table was a pile of what looked like car parts, including industrial springs and shock absorbers. Pieces of plate armor and chunks of metal littered the floor around Ted as the white-hot tip of the wand welded another piece to the breastplate.

As Ted slid several large enameled plates together over and over again, an elf in shimmering yellow robes sat hunched over a length of cloth, softly muttering to herself as she waved her arms, forming arcane symbols above the fabric. Sweat beaded her brow and it was obvious that she had been working there for some time.

Ted scowled at the plates in his hands. "Is there an enchantment or something for the expansion and contraction of rigid objects?"

The elf finished her spell with a flourish and one final word of power. As the enchantment settled on the material before her, she looked at Ted. "There is," she replied wearily, "however, we lack the necessary components. Even if we did have them, and you had the required skill, it would still take several days to prepare. Days that we do not have."

"That's unfortunate." Ted sighed. "I guess I'll just have to do it the hard way."

The two dwarves faced each other and groaned with effort as they pushed with all of their formidable strength. Veins bulged and muscles strained as the two stocky smiths tried to force themselves toward each other.

Both dwarves held a heavy steel plate in their thick hands and each plate was covered with numerous magnets that were attached to the facing sides. The smiths inched the pieces together even though the opposing magnetic fields that tried to repel each other grew stronger the closer they got.

"Just a little further," Ted encouraged excitedly.

Both dwarves growled and pushed even harder, bringing the magnets slightly closer together.

"You almost have it."

Nose to nose, the stocky smiths forced the magnets together until they were almost touching.

"Hold it there!" Ted said excitedly, as he reached into his stained lab coat and pulled out a small pouch. He swiftly opened the pouch and withdrew a pinch of fine sand. Ted muttered a few arcane words as he sprinkled the sand on the magnetic devices.

"Erry it up... wizard," one of the dwarves groaned through gritted teeth.

With the last word of his spell, Ted bent over and exhaled the final syllable. With his final breath on the devices, the grains of sand vanished.

Ted straightened up and the dwarves both looked at him in confusion.

"That it?" one of them growled, still straining to keep the magnets together.

Ted scratched his beard. "I think so."

"Ye think so!" the same dwarf groaned angrily. "If ye even-"

Ted suddenly bent over again and put his hands under the devices. "Let it go."

The dwarf smiths shared a disbelieving look but followed his orders, and they released their respective devices and stepped back. To everyone's surprise, the magnetic devices actually stayed together, even though they weren't touching, and landed in Ted's waiting hands.

Ted sat hunched over a small table with several open scrolls lying across it. A small metal cylinder that contained six cylindrical chambers was cradled in a strange looking device that held the cylinder in the air before him.

Using what resembled a golden ink pen encrusted with twinkling red gemstones and wearing his magnification goggles, Ted carefully inscribed the cylinder with a precise, glowing script. The characters flared white-hot at first and then slowly faded away, leaving the characters cut into the surface of the cylinder.

Ted stopped his writing for a moment to look over at one of the open scrolls beside him. He carefully read over the text until he found what he was looking for. Nodding to himself, Ted put the strange pen device to the cylinder and it flared brilliantly as he continued writing.

Ted rubbed his eyes wearily and reclined in his chair. He took a sip from the mug in his bronze hand. He couldn't remember the last time he had slept. But there were important things here that he needed to finish.

Floating several feet off of the floor before him was a small motor. Ted drank from his mug as he watched the motor lazily rotate in the air. With a wave of his free hand, the motor suddenly broke apart into its component pieces.

The exploded motor parts orbited around each other as Ted stroked his beard thoughtfully. Other pieces floated up from the piles of scrap that littered the room and joined the dancing pieces.

Some of the central components joined together to form a small device while the majority continued their orbit. A large gear flew to the device, but it was too large and clattered to the ground. Another smaller gear flew in and fit perfectly. Springs and other bits of machinery flew around, each trying to find the proper position within the growing device at the center of the miniature solar system.

When several parts wouldn't fit, the device exploded again and all the parts returned to orbit. With a sigh, Ted started over again. This time he used a different configuration to begin his creation.

After several more failed attempts, Ted finally had what he was looking for. Floating in the center of the room, surrounded by countless orbiting pieces, was a tiny motor. Ted grinned as he snatched the fist-sized device from the air. As soon as he had the motor in hand, all of the floating parts fell to the ground in a glorious racket of raining metal.

Ted put the mini-motor on a workbench beside a pile of signet runes, a rusty old cutlass, a length of chain, and a half-written scroll.

A heavy knocking rattled the door.

"Enter!" Ted shouted from his workbench in the center of the lab.

The door swung open and two men stepped in. One was large with thick muscles beneath his heavy leather apron. The other was short and wore the pale grey robes of an apprentice sorcerer. As the pair approached, Ted noticed the large blacksmith carried a small rectangular box.

"They are finished then?" Ted asked eagerly, as he stood and hurried to meet them.

"Indeed," the apprentice replied softly. "These should have the desired effect."

"Excellent!" Ted took the small box and opened it.

Inside was a case containing ten small, glass tubes that were only a few inches long and encased in delicate bronze housings. The casings were covered in fine runic script and the objects gave off a blue light from some unknown source inside the glass tubes. The tops of the glass tubes bubbled out, giving each of them a small dome. Pulling one out of the case and holding it up between his thumb and finger, the glowing object resembled a bullet.

"I made a few improvements to your original design," the apprentice said confidently. "They should perform better than originally promised."

"Improvements?" Ted looked dubiously at the apprentice. "We shall see about that."

Ted was sewing two small pockets on the backs of a pair of fingerless leather gloves when he realized he wasn't alone.

"Yes?" Ted asked without looking up.

A soft rustling announced the approach of someone in long robes. The newcomer walked around the table and stood across from Ted, who had yet to look up from his sewing.

"My master sends his greetings," the newcomer announced.

Ted glanced up and saw a slender elf whose features were mostly concealed beneath a bright red cloak. In her delicate hands was a long, wooden case that she gently sat down on the table and pushed toward Ted.

Ted stopped his work and took the offered case. He opened the lid and inspected what was inside.

"My master has upheld his part of the bargain," the elf said tersely. "He expects you to uphold yours."

"Don't worry." Ted closed the case and looked up at the hidden elf. "Your master will receive his payment before the sun sets."

"See that it is so," the elf replied briskly.

Ted was about to reply when he felt a sudden, yet gentle pressure on his mind. Someone was trying to reach him, but his mental barriers were keeping the psychic intrusion away. Ted closed his eyes and used a technique that he had learned from Dianoia to identify the type of intrusion and who was sending it.

To Ted's great surprise he discovered the sending was coming from the Mistress of the Psionic Cult herself! Dianoia was trying to contact him!

Ted opened his eyes and was about to excuse himself from the cloaked elf, but she had vanished. With a helpless shrug, Ted lowered some of his mental barriers and allowed Dianoia to reach him.

"Your presence is required in the Chamber of the Masters," her silky voice whispered in his mind. *"Immediately."*

The sending ended as abruptly as it had started leaving Ted to wonder at its reason. Certainly nothing good could come of such a message.

Ted grabbed his mug and took a long drink, and then wiped the foam off his beard with his sleeve before heading for the door. *This had better be important*, he thought. *There is so much work yet to do!*

Ted's heart pounded as he entered the Chamber of the Masters.

It was a small, circular room made of stone blocks and a tiled floor. The tile was inlaid with a three-armed spiral symbol that covered most of the floor. Glowing orbs hovered around the room, giving an eerie light to the figures seated at the long table in the center of the chamber.

Five tall chairs lined the table, but only four of them were occupied. The tallest chair in the middle remained suspiciously empty. However, four elves were seated at the remaining chairs.

Seated on the far left was Pars, the bulky Master Combat Magician and Chief Arbiter of Vlaanderen. His chainmail glinted strangely in the light and Ted noticed that the spiral symbol on his crimson tabard matched the large one on the floor.

Seated next to the dark-skinned Pars was the pale Sorceress Supreme. The petite Lady Braelynn looked stunning as always in her form-fitting white gown.

To the Lady's left was the empty seat that was normally occupied by the Archmage. Ted had noticed that Talsin had been absent a lot recently. The excuse was that he was working on some important project and didn't want to be disturbed. But when Ted had gone to see him the other day, the Archmage was nowhere to be found and nobody had any idea where he might be. It could have been a coincidence, but there were also an unusual number of disappearances at the same time as Talsin's mysterious project.

Across from Talsin's empty seat was the Master Wizard, Quillan. His long, brown hair was pulled back in a ponytail and his pale blue robes shimmered in the light as he watched Ted approach.

Last at the table, but certainly not least, to Quillan's left was Dianoia. A bronze diadem held her tightly curled hair away from her eyes and her copper blouse and black corset were as revealing as ever. Dianoia smiled at Ted and he couldn't help but smile back.

"What are you smiling about?" Pars barked. "Do you see something funny?"

Ted's smile vanished, "No, Lord Pars."

"Good." Pars leaned back in his chair. "Now, it has come to our attention that you have been missing your lessons. Is that true?"

"Yes, Lord Pars," Ted answered.

"And why is that, I wonder," Pars looked thoughtful. "Is learning how to control your Gift not of paramount importance? What could be more crucial to your survival than understanding and mastering the secrets of the Arcane Arts?"

"Nothing, Lord Pars," Ted answered quickly, "but Arch Battlemage Gwydion gave me permission to suspend my studies and focus on other projects until the city is safe."

"Did he now?" Lady Braelynn breathed. "I do not recall being informed of such a decision on the part of the Arch Battlemage."

"He did, Lady," Ted said. "I do not wish to sound disrespectful, but I do not answer to you or this Assembly. As an Apprentice Battlemage, my training and education in the Art falls under the jurisdiction of the Arch Battlemage alone."

"Does it now?" Quillan laughed. "I was not aware that such jurisdictions existed."

"What does it matter?" Ted asked, clearly getting tired of the questions. "I am the best in nearly every class. Meditating for hours on the Glyph of Fire is a waste of time. At most, our enemies will be outside our door within days, and you want me to try and meditate?" Ted's laughter was forced. "If we survive the coming battle, I will gladly devote all of my time to study. But until then, I have important work to do that might just save lives."

The gathered masters didn't seem very pleased with his response. Ted could sense something passing between the members of the Assembly and he knew they were communicating telepathically amongst themselves.

Few others would have been able to detect the faint signals, but as Ted was always ready to point out, he was one of the best in his class.

Ted waited for several tense moments as the telepathic debate raged silently before him until finally Lady Braelynn leaned forward. "Very well." She looked Ted directly in the eye as she spoke. "Gwydion tells us that the kefali will be here by dawn tomorrow."

Ted was surprised. He had detected the communication between the masters in the room, but not any outside influence. And to learn that they would be here tomorrow! He had expected a few days at least. Not just today. He had so much to do yet. This was terrible news indeed.

"It is the decision of this Assembly that you will be permitted to continue your personal projects until the matter of the kefali and their allies is resolved," Braelynn finished.

Ted tried not to roll his eyes. Leave it to elves to downplay the possible annihilation of an entire city. But so long as they were off his back, that is what mattered. "Thank you." Ted bowed as graciously as he could before turning and walking swiftly from the chamber.

****

After a brief tour of the Training Rings, Liz led Alex into the Healers Tent. However, it wasn't really a tent at all. It was a small structure that was nestled up against the main tower of the Cathedral of Learning. It was made from the strange white stone that the elven Shapers created and was ornamented with numerous banners of varying styles and colors, representing all of the different religions and orders that trained or maintained healers here.

If there was one place that everyone could put aside their differences and work together, it was here.

Liz spotted the dark grey banner with three, interlocking, silver horns that represented the Church of the Allfather not far from a white banner with the bloody red handprint of the Hands of Tyr. Liz's heart swelled with pride as it always did when she saw the elven and human banners interspersed with the dwarven. The vast majority she didn't recognize, but she did see the Healers Cult of Aesculapius' blue banner with a white symbol of a snake wrapping around a staff and the emerald green banner of the Druids with its elaborate, golden tree made from a dizzying pattern of knotwork.

A small stream bubbled in one corner, giving off the relaxing background noise of water running over rocks. The sweet smell of flowers filled the air and Liz inhaled deeply, enjoying the aroma.

Rows of plain, white cots filled the space, but only a few were occupied. All around the room, elf, dwarf, and human healers moved from patient to patient, tenderly administering to their individual needs.

"Not as busy as I would have expected," Alex noted, as he looked around the pristine room.

"You never have to wait in the Tent," Liz chuckled. "Patients come in and out rather quickly when injuries can be healed in moments."

"Of course," Alex grinned sheepishly. "But why are there people in the beds?"

Liz looked at all the people on the cots and realized that all of them were humans. "They are probably being helped by the Soothers." When Liz saw Alex's blank look, she continued. "They specialize in mental healing like phobias, anxiety, depression, and the like. Some of them take longer than one treatment to cure. The mind is complex and it takes special attention to fix without causing even more damage."

"And you can do that?" Alex asked.

"Well... yes," Liz admitted, "but I'm what's called a True Healer. I can cure wounds as well as disease or mental conditions. It's sort of a jack-of-all-trades. But I'm not nearly as proficient in mental healing as a dedicated Soother. Their expertise lies purely in the mind."

Alex shook his head as he looked around the room. "I'm still surprised there are so few people coming in with injuries. With all the training and patrols, I would expect to see a steady stream of injured coming in here."

Liz shrugged helplessly. "Most people still just go to whatever hospital is closest."

"Hospitals?" Alex looked at Liz in disbelief. "Why would there still be hospitals when anything could just be healed?"

"There aren't enough healers to go around," Liz replied, "and most of the ones we do have are busy working for the military. We still need doctors and nurses to take care of the day-to-day injuries and only use healers for the most serious cases because healing takes energy. Healers have to be careful how much they use or they won't be able to heal until they recover."

But Alex still wasn't convinced. "There must be at least a few hundred thousand people in this city. Surely some of them discovered they could heal."

"Some of them did," Liz answered. "A thousand, maybe two, but only a fraction of them are true healers."

"That's it?" Alex breathed. "Incredible.... I thought there would be a lot more."

"If there are, they aren't coming here to learn how to use their gift." Liz replied flatly.

A fire siren started blaring somewhere in the city.

Alex looked back out the doorway with a look of concern on his face. "I wonder where Mike is right now."

"He's still at HQ," Liz answered, "and he isn't happy about something."

Alex turned back to Liz with a strange look on his bearded face. "And how do you know where he is and what he is feeling?"

A sick feeling filled her as she realized she had said too much. "Oh, just a guess," she replied quickly.

Alex's eyes narrowed skeptically. "That was an awfully confident guess."

"I know your brother pretty well." Liz was telling the truth and she prayed that Alex would accept her answer. Her prayers were in vain.

"I think it's more than that." Alex stepped closer and took her hands in his. He closed his eyes and let out a long, slow breath. Liz wasn't sure what was going on, but she allowed it.

After a moment, Alex's eyes snapped open and a look of concern crossed his face.

Liz pulled her hands away and stepped back, suddenly worried. "What is it?"

"Your pneuma..." he breathed, trying to find the right words. "It's... fractured... yet stronger." Alex's brow furrowed in confusion. "I don't know how that is possible."

"My what?" Liz didn't have a clue what he was talking about, but the panicked look on his face didn't fill her with confidence.

"Pneuma," Alex repeated. "My master calls it the 'breath of life.' It's your life force, the energy stored inside you. Some might call it your soul."

Liz definitely did not like the sound of that. "You're saying my soul is broken?" To which Alex nodded. "How can you tell? Maybe you're mistaken."

Alex shrugged helplessly. "It is possible, I am relatively new to most of this myself. But for these past months, I have been training under Master Chrysippus." When Alex noticed Liz's blank stare, he explained. "He is an elf that arrived not long after you guys left. He started a martial arts school in Clearfield and I was one of his first students. Anyways, he has been teaching us about pneuma and how to channel it."

The large man ran a hand over his smooth scalp. "I don't get it... from what I understand, if your pneuma is incomplete like yours is, then you should be in some kind of pain or something. Yet you seem perfectly normal." Alex shook his head in defeat. "I'm afraid this is far beyond my limited knowledge. We should have one of the healers look at you."

"No, thanks," Liz shook her head. "Like you said, I am perfectly normal. Maybe you just sensed it wrong."

Alex scowled. "I may be a noob at this, but I *can* tell when somebody is missing a piece of their spirit. It's kinda hard to miss." He caught some movement out of the corner of his eye and saw a slender elf in white robes walking through the aisles. The elf looked over and saw Alex looking at her, so he raised his hand and motioned her over.

Liz saw the exchange and scowled as the elf approached. "I told you I don't need any help," she hissed just before the healer reached them.

Liz smiled and greeted the newcomer. "Hello, Febe."

Febe inclined her head slightly. "Greetings Liz and..."

"Alex," Alex offered. "A pleasure to meet you, Febe."

"The pleasure is all mine, Alex," Febe smiled up at him. "What can I do for you?"

"I noticed something... off about Liz's pneuma and I was hoping you could take a look at her." At the mention of pneuma, Febe's eyes grew wide in surprise. "It feels like a piece of her soul is missing... yet her pneuma is still strong; stronger even that I think it should be... I can't explain it."

"How does a human know about pneuma?" Febe eyed Alex curiously. "That is not a common practice, even among the Aos Si."

"Master Chrysippus taught me," Alex answered curtly. "Now, will you please take a look at her?"

"I do not know that name," Febe turned to Liz. "Will you allow me to examine you?"

Liz gave a resigned sigh. "Sure."

"I am confident that it is nothing," Febe reassured her as she placed her hands on Liz, "but let us put your large friend's mind at peace."

Febe was a superb healer and Liz had every confidence in her extensive abilities.

A chill passed through Liz and she fought off the urge to shiver as Febe began her Delving. It was an odd sensation, having somebody rooting around inside your very being. Liz fought the natural urge to fight back against the intrusion, and instead tried to calm her mind and make the Delving easier. Liz knew from experience that it was easier to Delve when the patient was relaxed, or better yet, unconscious.

Febe's brow furrowed in concentration even though Liz wasn't resisting; that was not a good sign. "Interesting…" Febe muttered as she still had her eyes closed and was holding onto Liz. Maintaining the ability to speak while in a Delve was a skill that Liz had yet to master.

A moment later Febe opened her eyes and released Liz. She looked at Liz strangely before she spoke. "It seems your friend is correct." It was as if she was having trouble finding the right words. "It is as if a piece of your spirit has been removed, yet what remains is stronger than before… It is almost as if…" Febe gave Liz a hard look. "Have you attempted to perform a Binding with someone?"

"A what?" Liz asked, utterly confused. "I don't even know what that is."

Febe sat back on one of the cots. "A Binding is a ritual where two people weld a piece of their soul to the other, forming a permanent bond between them. It has many benefits, including increased vitality and stamina; they heal from wounds much more rapidly and have enhanced reflexes. But they not only have physical changes. Those who are bound can sense where the other is and what they are feeling. Also, depending on the strength of the Binding, it is said that some can even share their thoughts."

Now, that got Liz's attention. She hadn't noticed any increased stamina or other changes to her person, but sometimes she did know where Mike was and what he was feeling. But those moments were random; there was no consistency to them. She might go days with nothing, and then suddenly she would know exactly where he was and how he felt. She wondered if he ever felt the same…

Febe was watching Liz's face and leaned forward eagerly. "I see some of that is familiar to you. Tell me, who did you bind with?"

"I didn't *bind* with anybody," Liz answered. "I've never even heard of this before today. But some of what you just described I have been experiencing."

"Like what?" Febe pressed. "And with whom?"

Liz took a deep breath and tried not to think about having a piece of her soul missing. "Mike," she finally answered. "I occasionally get the feeling of what he is thinking or where he is at… but it comes and goes, there is no consistency to it. I haven't noticed any enhanced agility or anything either."

"Mike…" Febe looked up at Alex. "You resemble him."

"He is my brother," Alex said.

Febe nodded as if she had expected that. "For not knowing what a Binding is, how did you manage to, at least partially, bind yourself to Mike?"

"I don't know…" Liz's mind raced, searching for an answer. How could this have happened? She sat down on the opposite cot, completely at a loss.

Febe placed a comforting hand on her knee. "Don't worry my dear. I will get this sorted out. Now, when did these symptoms first start?"

Liz thought back to the first time she had known where Mike was. She had been practicing her sword work and was waiting for him to show up. When she thought about him she had suddenly known where he was. That had been a few days after their battle with…"

"The Nephilim," Liz breathed excitedly, as memories came flooding back. "We fought it inside that horrible fortress… it wanted to use me as a sacrifice to open a portal to the Abyss… and when Mike tried to save me, the nephilim… killed him."

Alex sat down heavily beside Liz.

"Death cannot be healed," Febe said, "and I saw Mike just the other day."

Liz stared at the floor. "By the time I got to him, he had no pulse and wasn't breathing. I tried healing him, but nothing worked. So, I did the only thing I could think of; I Delved into him, searching for some sign of life… and… I found it. The barest spark flickered deep inside but was slowly fading even as I found it…I'm not sure what I did… but I poured myself into that spark and when I came out, he was breathing again."

As Liz finished her tale she looked up to see Febe nodding knowingly.

"What you did was extremely careless and exceedingly dangerous," she said not unkindly. "You could have died as well. If you had been a moment later your soul could have departed with his and been lost to the ether." She took Liz's hands in her own. "What you did, without knowing it, was perform a very crude type of binding. You used a piece of yourself to anchor his spirit, thus allowing for him to survive. But in doing so, you lost the piece of yourself that remains in him."

"Can I get it back?" Liz asked hopefully.

Febe shrugged. "I'm afraid I don't know. Bindings are extremely rare and there are very few who even know how to perform the ritual correctly.

"Why are they so rare?" Alex asked. "From what you said, they make you physically better in nearly every way."

"Because there is one major drawback to the Binding," Febe answered softly. "If one of the pair dies, they take a piece of the other's soul with them. The shock of that loss is usually too much for the survivor to bear, and usually results in madness for the survivor or the death of them both."

"That's just wonderful." Liz slumped back against the wall.

"Perhaps it will not be so bad," Febe offered. "You say that you do not have the benefits of a true binding, so perhaps if something happens to Mike, you will not suffer any severe repercussions."

Liz stared at the floor. "That doesn't make me feel much better." Then she looked over at Alex. "Has he said anything about knowing where I am or anything?"

Alex shook his head. "I'm afraid not, but then I only just got here today."

"It could be that he is not bound to you," Febe said almost to herself.

Liz looked up at her. "What do you mean?"

"I mean that you healed him. It is possible that a piece of your spirit latched on to his and then remained there when you withdrew." Febe shrugged. "I have no idea if that is even possible, but I don't see why it couldn't be… He could be completely unaware of what has happened."

Liz laughed mirthlessly. "He is unaware alright."

Febe suddenly stood. "Remain here," she ordered, before moving swiftly away. "I just thought of someone who may be able to help," she said over her shoulder, as she disappeared deeper into the Tent.

Alex and Liz sat in silence for a time until Alex finally spoke. "You should tell him how you feel."

"Ugh, not you too," Liz moaned. "Em keeps saying the same thing."

Alex smiled. "Emily is not one I would normally go to for relationship advice, but in this case, she is correct."

"Look, I don't want to talk about this right now, okay?" Liz said a little more sharply than she meant to. Alex didn't press the issue and for that Liz was grateful.

The pair sat on the cot in an uncomfortable silence for what seemed like an eternity until Febe finally reappeared, but she wasn't alone. Flowing along beside her in golden robes was Kassandra, the beautiful Priestess of Demeter.

"Greetings, Liz," Kassandra said, as she sat down across from Liz. "Febe has informed me of your situation and I am here to see if I can be of assistance."

"Do you know anything about Bindings?" Liz asked hopefully.

"Some," Kassandra admitted. "I have devoted a great deal of time to the study of the Binding ritual, but I have only performed it once before."

"That makes you the expert," Liz said. "Can you remove it?"

"It could be possible," Kassandra answered, "since Mike's soul may not have joined fully to yours."

"That's good though, right?" Liz asked.

But Kassandra shook her head. "It would be exceedingly dangerous. The Binding ritual is meant to be permanent. I have studied how to bind souls together, not split them apart. It is also possible that you would both die in the effort."

"Is there anyone else that knows anything about bindings?" Liz asked desperately.

Kassandra thought a moment and looked to Febe before answering. "The Druids practice a type of soul binding when they bond with their spirit animal. However, bonding with an animal is extremely different than with another sentient being."

Liz's heart sank. "Then what am I supposed to do?"

Kassandra and Febe shared another look before the priestess answered. "I can ask the Druids for their council, but I believe it would be far safer to just complete the binding. Then you could both enjoy the benefits associated with it."

Alex nodded along. "It would be handy to have those perks when a battle is coming."

Liz couldn't believe what she was hearing. "Are you serious? You want me to purposefully rip a piece of my soul away and trade it with Mike, and then hope that neither of us dies and drives the other insane?"

"Technically, your soul is already ripped away," Kassandra said softly. "All I would do is fill your void with a piece of his."

"And then you would both be stronger and more alive than you were before," Febe added.

Liz stared at the elves in disbelief. "You are both crazy."

CHAPTER 19

Once inside the safety of the Mount's deep halls, King Varnir and three of his guards turned down a side passage while the strangely familiar guard took Mike down a different corridor. It was a long and winding path, with several turns that led ever downward. They made their way in silence, with only their footfalls echoing off the walls for company, until they came to a large, reinforced door.

The door was covered in intricate runes and inlaid with gold and silver. Strangely, for such an impressive door, there was no handle and there were no guards posted outside. Then, Mike noticed the large symbol engraved in its center. It was in a diamond shape and it was very angular, with numerous bent arms turning inward with a smaller diamond symbol inside the top of the larger symbol. Suddenly, Mike realized where he had seen it before.

The dwarf marched up to the door and placed his hand in the center of the symbol. He muttered a word of power in dwarvish and the runes in the door began to glow. The entrance silently swung open and light spilled out into the passage.

Mike followed the dwarf guard through the opening and found himself inside a large chamber. Runes, like the ones on the door, covered the stone walls and snaked across every exposed surface. The sharp clang of metal on metal greeted them and Mike's eye was drawn to the two figures battling in the center of the chamber as the door closed silently behind them.

Power crackled around the pair as arcs of energy crashed against shimmering fields of protective force as all the while blades darted and slashed at each other.

One was a slender elf in emerald green armor that wielded a shimmering spear, while the other was a towering elephant creature armed with a pair of immense scimitars and covered in silver and gold scale armor.

The dwarf guard stepped forward and removed his helmet with one hand as he pounded the head of his hammer into the floor. Waves of multi-colored light radiated out along the runes in the floor and flowed out and up the walls until they flowed across the entire chamber.

The dueling pair ceased their battle instantly and turned to face the newcomers. A brief look of surprise crossed the elf's face, but then she smiled. "Greeting, Michael Strazney. We meet again."

"Hello, Brigit." Mike nodded respectfully to the blonde Warden and then looked up at the huge Hathi. "LuHark," he said, and the tusked Warden displayed no emotion as she nodded slightly in greeting.

The dwarf guard joined his companions and then turned back to Mike. "So, how'd ye know it was me?" Rodan Odinson asked in his gravelly voice.

"That is a rather distinctive weapon you carry." Mike gestured to the impressive war hammer whose head was resting comfortably before the dwarf's feet. "I wasn't sure about it the first time we saw you in the Grove. But then today I realized where I had seen it before."

LuHark gave a disgusted trumpet. "I told you to take a different weapon."

Rodan scowled up at the towering Hathi. "Ukonvasara be mine. I will no be usin' some lesser weapon," he rumbled. "Besides, only the human and his companions saw it."

Neither Brigit nor LuHark seemed pleased with that answer. "And so, you brought him here?" Brigit asked.

"I be thinkin' it best ter have this conversation where we be sure that we will no be overheard," Rodan rumbled.

"Not your worst idea," LuHark muttered grudgingly.

Mike stood his ground before the three powerful Wardens and tried not to be intimidated. "So now that you've got me, what are you doing here? I thought that after you destroyed the fortress you were leaving."

"We may have deceived you," Brigit admitted. "In reality, we have no place to go."

"Aye," Rodan rumbled. "We be trapped on this accursed world."

"Trapped?" Mike asked. "You guys teleported in. Why don't you just teleport back out?"

"It is not so simple as that," Brigit answered. "To cross the Veil requires an immense amount of energy, the likes of which we do not currently have access to. And even if we did, we lack the necessary components to perform the crossover ritual."

LuHark sheathed her massive blades. "But those facts are irrelevant. This world is a nexus within the Ashvattha and therefore of great importance. Whoever controls this world has access to countless others. We would not leave until it has been secured."

"You are talking about the World Tree, right?" Mike asked.

Brigit nodded. "That is one description for it, yes. Most worlds are connected by only one or two branches, but your Earth directly connects to at least six worlds, perhaps more."

"I thought you said they were countless?" Mike pointed out.

"I did," LuHark trumpeted. "Think of the Ashvattha as a spider's web. At the very center is this world and it has six strands reaching out. If you follow any one strand, you reach another world and in turn, that world is connected to even more worlds. All branches end at some point, but you can always go back to the center and take a new path, thus a countless number of worlds may be reached."

"Trees and spider webs, I can understand," Mike said, "but you mentioned this world needed secured." He thought he already knew the answer to his next question but he asked it anyway. "Secured from what?"

"Evil o' course," Rodan rumbled grimly, confirming Mike's suspicions.

"So, you three are going to help us against the armies headed our way?" Mike asked hopefully.

"Indeed," Brigit replied softly. "Yet, we three are a sad defense against the overwhelming forces allied against us."

"Tell me something I don't know," Mike muttered.

Brigit ignored him. "And that is why we have activated the beacon. With any luck, allies will arrive before our enemies do."

"Unless your friends get here in the next twelve hours or so, I doubt they will get here in time," Mike said. "The kefali will be here by sunrise, if not sooner, and the orcs won't be held off for much longer."

"What of the Shadowed Ones?" Brigit asked. "Has there been any word of them?"

Mike shook his head. "No. We know they are still out there somewhere, but they have eluded any direct sightings. We know they are south of here, but we don't know just how far," Mike said in frustration. "They could show up any minute or not at all. We have no idea."

Brigit looked as if that was exactly as she had expected. "The Shadowed Ones will attack at night, as that is when they are strongest, and they will most assuredly wait until the other two armies have committed their forces before joining the battle." Her staff hummed with power. "The Shadowed Ones are likely few in number, so they will be cautious and let their minions probe your defenses for weaknesses before they themselves strike."

"It sounds like you have some experience with them," Mike noted.

"We do," Brigit confirmed grimly, and nodded to her companions. "We have each faced all manner of vile creatures in our time as Wardens. Yet the Shadowed Ones remain among the most secretive and deadly."

Mike looked at each of the Wardens in turn. "If you are here to help us, then what are you doing hiding down here?"

"Our presence must remain a secret," LuHark answered. "It is for that reason we are so far beneath this accursed ground." The huge Hathi looked up at the vaulted ceiling and shivered.

"I take it you don't like being underground?" Mike asked, eager to learn something about this mammoth kefali.

"We Hathi do not like having things above our ears," LuHark admitted. "All of this stone makes me... uneasy."

"I'm not a big fan of being underground myself," Mike confessed, "but why don't you hide with the elves in their Grove or some other place above ground?"

LuHark smiled sadly. "You try being ten feet tall and blending in with a bunch of elves. Besides, the elves are not very fond of any kefali, even after all this time." The large Hathi shook her head, making her huge ears flap. "It is safer here below where few can see. King Varnir has been most hospitable and our stay is as comfortable as can be expected."

"Who else knows you are here?" Mike knew King Varnir did. This was his stronghold after all and Rodan was acting as one of his bodyguards.

"King Varnir and his son, Prince Brokkr, are the only ones who know who we are," Brigit answered. "A few others know of our presence here but are ignorant of our true nature."

"The Warden Order be an Imperial secret," Rodan rumbled. "Only the Kings and their heirs be knowin' we exist."

"And the Council of Archmages," Brigit said.

"Don't forget the Grand Matriarch of the Peacekeepers," LuHark added.

"What about us humans?" Mike asked. "Do any of our leaders know about your Order?"

"Once," Brigit replied sadly. "But after the Veil closed, it became nearly impossible to reach our agents on this world. They were left to their own devices and a few formed their own Orders to continue our mission. As of yet, we have been unable to locate any surviving descendants."

"It is difficult to do any real research," LuHark trumpeted, "when you are trapped in this tomb."

"We are watching for the proper signals." Brigit looked up at the big Hathi. "It wouldn't do us much good to go stomping around this world hoping we stumble across something."

The beautiful elf suddenly rounded on Mike. "Now, what do you want of us?"

"To train with you," Mike replied instantly. That evoked a range of emotions from the assembled Wardens. Rodan snorted in contempt, LuHark looked thoughtful, and Brigit smiled.

"I thought that may be the case," the blonde elf said. "We all sensed your potential when we first met." Brigit was still smiling. "Let me guess; you discovered that your abilities do not align with either the dwarf Guardians or the elven Paladins."

Mike nodded. "I seem to be caught somewhere in-between," he said in disgust. "I can't create barriers as large or as strong as the Guardians, nor can I seem to master the Corona like a Paladin does. But I can do things they can't, like move barriers around after I've summoned them."

"There is a reason for that," LuHark trumpeted. "For those are traits of a Warden."

That was the answer Mike had been hoping for. Ever since he had met the Wardens in that twisted castle, he had felt a connection with them. He couldn't explain it, but he felt a kind of kindred spirit with them he never felt for the Guardians or Paladins.

"Will you train me?" Mike almost pleaded.

The three Wardens shared a look and Mike was afraid they were going to refuse.

Then Rodan spoke. "O' course we will," he rumbled to Mike's vast relief. "We can no be leavin' one o' our own ter stumble alone in the darkness."

"Thank you," Mike sighed, "but we only have today. What can you teach me before the kefali arrive tomorrow?"

Brigit thought a moment before answering. "I know you are proficient in summoning protective barriers and channeling power into a weapon, but can you heal?"

"Heal?" Mike chuckled. "Do I look like a cleric to you?"

"Of course not." Brigit's eyes narrowed dangerously, and Mike's mirth cut off abruptly. "Yet every Warden has at least some healing ability. You have not experienced this?"

Mike shook his head. "Some of the Paladins have tried to teach me, but it never works. I have been unable to heal even the smallest scratch. My prayers never get answered."

"That is concerning," LuHark said. "Perhaps your faith is not strong enough."

"Now you sound like Liz," Mike chuckled humorlessly. "Faith has never been my strong suit."

"Ye had best be findin' some then," Rodan rumbled. "A Warden be a holy warrior, pledged ter seek out evil and destroy it in whatever form it be takin'. But many o' our most powerful skills be drawn from our divine patrons who grant us the blessings we need ter unleash their glorious wrath."

"We are also called to protect the innocent and heal the sick," Brigit added. "But Rodan is right. Without our patron, we would never reach our full potential as Wardens."

Mike groaned. He was going to need to find his faith in a day, which he hadn't been unable to find his whole life. His prayers never got answered and he had no illusions that this would change anytime soon. It appeared that training with the Wardens was going to be harder than he had thought.

****

Liz put her cell phone down in disgust. "It is still going straight to voicemail."

"Well, you said he was somewhere in Mt. Washington," Alex said. "I doubt there is any service down there. Frankly, I'm still amazed that you get any reception at all. After all the satellites fell and the cell towers quit working, I thought all that stuff was gone for good."

"They didn't all fall," Liz answered. "Just most of them. We have regained at least partial control of a few satellites, but interference makes any reliable service impossible."

Alex nodded. "Yeah, I was able to call home once, but every other time I try to make a call all I get is static. What about you? Have you heard from your family at all?"

"I have," Liz nodded. "I talked to them about a week ago. My parents are still in New York with my brothers. They are somewhere around the Finger Lakes with a group of friends," she sighed. "I don't really know much more than that. The phones cut out before we could say too much."

"Same thing in Clearfield," Alex said, "but then again, Clearfield has always had crap for cell service."

"Yeah, it has," Liz smiled. "So, how is Clearfield doing? I know you said the dwarves made a brewery, but how is everything else going?"

"Fine, I guess," Alex shrugged. "The dwarves sure do love their walls. They are working on one that surrounds the western part of town and an even longer second wall that stretches around the eastern half and follows Route 879."

"More people keep moving out from the safety of the walls and going back to their homes and farms, but everyone is now part of the militia and receives training from our soldiers and the dwarves, with even the handful of elves teaching their skills," he continued, "There are a few confrontations between the races, but for the most part they get along well enough."

"The goblins, kobolds, and whatnot have mostly gone. The only thing that has been giving us trouble is those blasted ratmen. It doesn't seem to matter how many times we clean them out of the sewers they always come back. We have even put locks on all the manhole covers, but they still keep popping up."

"Sounds like you need some of those cat-like kefala," she said with a grin.

"As long as they come with a leash," the big man grinned back.

Liz sighed as she looked around at the bustling training grounds around the Cathedral. "I suppose there is no point in just standing around waiting for Mike to call me back. Want me to keep showing you around?"

Alex shrugged his large shoulders. "Sounds good to me," he said, even though he wasn't really concerned about learning anything else. He knew where the important places were and how to get there, but he hoped that showing him around would be enough of a distraction to keep Liz from dwelling on what she had learned in the Healers Tent.

Alex suppressed a shiver; he didn't even want to imagine losing a piece of his soul.

It was unthinkable.

And so, Alex cheerfully followed Liz as she took him to the many sights of Pittsburgh.

The hours passed and the day grew warm as the sun reached its peak and then began its descent. The breeze carried with it a chill that sent colorful leaves swirling and warned of the coming winter.

As the sun began to set, Liz was surprised to hear the faint rumble of thunder. There were hardly any clouds as she and Alex watched a team of dwarves work to equip a group of griffins with dark, runic armor that was fresh out of the Foundry.

Alex looked to the east where the rumbling was coming from. "That is some strange sounding thunder."

"I don't think that's thunder," Liz said grimly, as the heavy booming continued. "That sounds more like cannon fire."

Alex stared in the direction of the sounds as if it would allow him to see the source of the noise. "Do you think it's the orcs?"

Liz shrugged. "That is the right direction." They listened to the sporadic thunder for a few more minutes until Liz nodded to herself. "I think it's getting closer."

Alex watched the horizon. "Our troops are being pushed back?"

"I'm sure we will find out soon enough," Liz replied grimly.

The thunder continued as the dwarves finished their work and the group of armored griffins flew away. A few moments later, a new group of griffins arrived, ready to be fitted for their armor.

As the evening wore on, word spread of the kefali advance in the north and their expected arrival by the morning. Fear and panic began to take hold in the city, as the approaching thunder of battle was a constant reminder that the orc horde was also closing in.

Suddenly, the specter of battle was no longer a distant thought, but soon to be a deadly reality.

Liz and Alex could feel the tension in the air as they made their way through the darkening streets towards the apartments. Large patrols of soldiers marched through the streets and everyone was on edge as the cannon fire still rumbled in the distance. Looking around, Liz wasn't sure what was worse; listening to the sounds of a battle drawing nearer or being in an actual battle.

She thought that the waiting was worse. At least in a battle there was a purpose and an enemy to face. Waiting was just allowing fear and doubt to eat away at you.

Liz knew she wouldn't be getting any rest that night and was in no real hurry to be alone. Mike was still somewhere inside Mt. Washington, Ted was locked in his lab, and she hadn't seen either Emily or Jack all day. Deciding that waiting in her room wasn't an option, Liz led Alex to the parking garage across the street.

"Where are we going?" Alex asked in confusion, as they entered the large concrete structure.

Most of the vehicles were covered in dust from disuse and Liz led him to a sleek black motorcycle. "We are going for a ride," Liz replied, as she took one of the helmets off the bike and handed it to Alex. "I'm going to see what is going on over at the wall."

Alex took the helmet cautiously. "I thought nobody was allowed to drive?"

"We aren't allowed to take any gas," Liz corrected, "so most everybody just leaves their cars sit so that if they really need them, they will be here."

"And this is your crotch-rocket?" Alex asked as he strapped the helmet on.

Liz swung her leg over the bike and started the engine. "It is now."

It was fully dark when they arrived on the battlements and what had once been a distant rumble was now a steady roar of gunfire punctuated by faint flashes of light far beyond the walls as the retreating soldiers made the advancing horde pay for every foot they gained.

Liz and Alex watched for over an hour before Liz realized that the retreat had stopped. Her heart swelled with pride to know that the brave men and women out there weren't simply running away in the face of overwhelming odds, but standing their ground and pushing back.

The night wore on and eventually the faint flashes and rumbles of gunfire drew nearer once more as the retreat renewed. The fighting approached at a snail's pace late into the night

Alex finally turned to Liz. "We should be going," he said with a yawn. "At this rate, it will be dawn before they reach the walls and we need to get some sleep or we will be worthless tomorrow."

Liz knew he was right, but she also knew she wouldn't be able to sleep. Not with an army closing in on them. She looked back out into the darkness. "You're right," she sighed wearily before turning away from the wall. "Let's get out of here."

CHAPTER 20

A grey dawn greeted Mike as he stepped out of the Fort Pitt Tunnel and into the chilly morning air. He knew he was tired after spending all night in a brutal training session with the three Wardens, but his body didn't feel it thanks to Brigit's healing just before he left. He knew the feeling was temporary and that tonight he would need to make up for the lack of sleep, but that was a problem for later. He could hear the rumble of heavy gunfire off to the east and right now he had to find out what was happening across the city.

He hadn't gone five steps when his phone started vibrating madly. He dug it out of his pocket and saw that there was a pile of missed calls from Liz and a few from HQ. All of them were several hours old and he hoped that there wasn't some emergency. Looking out over the city, he didn't see any fires or hear any sirens, so he guessed that whatever they had wanted wasn't that dire.

He called HQ back first and learned that the kefali army hadn't arrived with the dawn like they had feared, but a drone had discovered that the army had split and was using the highways. One force was coming down I-65 and the other I-279. Both should arrive at the North Shore within the next two hours.

The news of the eastern front was even less encouraging. The orcs had pushed A Company out of Monroeville and nearly back to the eastern wall. Soon, the defenders would be forced to pull back behind the relative safety of the walls and continue their bombardment of the advancing horde.

There was still no sign of the Shadow elves to the south, but a few scouts hadn't reported back, giving the commanders an estimate on where they were. It was assumed that they were somewhere directly below the Mount, but the elves agreed that their kin would wait and launch their attack at full dark when their powers would be strongest.

It didn't look like Mike would be catching up on sleep anytime soon. He was just about to call Liz back when his phone started ringing in his hand. He was surprised when the caller ID said it was Ted.

Mike put the phone to his ear. "What's up?"

....

"Yeah, I will be there in ten."

Mike ended the call and put the phone back in his pocket as he changed direction and headed toward the Foundry.

****

Even this early in the morning the Foundry District was as busy as ever. Humans, elves, and dwarves all were hard at work, trying to finish their tasks before the battle began.

Mike made his way quickly through the chaos of the Verkstad and finally pushed open the door to Ted's lab. Inside was the usual mess, only Mike discovered that he and Ted weren't alone.

Liz, Alex, Jack, and Emily were all gathered around the only clean table in the room.

"About time you came out of your hole," Liz grumbled, as Mike joined them at the table. He felt a flare of emotion in the back of his mind, but swiftly pushed it aside.

Mike ignored that and instead asked, "So, what was so urgent that I had to get here when there are multiple armies at our door?"

"For the Dispensing-of-the-Goodies," Ted said cheerfully, as he emerged from behind a pile of rusty scrap. "I have been working on a few projects that will hopefully increase our likelihood of surviving the coming battle, and perhaps even allow us to look marvelous while doing it," he added with a lopsided grin.

Emily rolled her eyes. "More like your inventions will explode and kill us all before we can do any fighting."

"Ever the optimist," Ted grunted, as he busied himself by pulling a large crate out from beneath a cluttered workbench. With great difficulty, he dragged the crate over to the waiting group. He wiped some sweat from his brow and looked at Mike. "You're first."

"Good." Mike rubbed his hands together eagerly. "Just the way I like it."

Ted reached into the crate and withdrew a steel lobster gauntlet. It was of beautiful craftsmanship and Mike could make out the faint runes inlayed into the surface. Ted put the gauntlet on the table and then went back into the crate. With a grunt of effort, Ted stood and placed a heavy cuirass on the table beside the gauntlet.

The cuirass was the strangest design that Mike had ever seen. It was of the same polished steel with inlaid runes like the gauntlet, but that was where the similarities ended. There was a heavy collar to protect the neck, but where the collar was usually riveted down, this one was connected by what appeared to be several small hydraulic cylinders. But that wasn't the strangest thing. The same devices connected the shoulder pauldrons to the cuirass and a curved steel plate floated just above each pauldron.

"What is this?" Mike asked as he inspected the odd armor.

"I call it Impact Armor," Ted said proudly, as he put matching arm and leg armor on the table beside the rest. When he was done, there was nearly a full suit laid out before them. It was only missing a helmet and the other gauntlet.

"Impact Armor, eh?" Mike pressed the plate that was hovering over one of the pauldrons. "So, it's like my mace?"

"The opposite actually." Ted pointed to the cylinders. "These are shock absorbers and these-" he pointed to the pieces that were floating, "are magnetized. I believe that this design should reduce the impact of any strike you may suffer."

"Very cool," Mike said, as he pressed on the magnetic pieces experimentally, "but you are missing a few pieces."

"Ah, yes." Ted pointed to the gauntlet on Mike's left hand. "You made that one with the shield, so I didn't bother making one for that hand." He then reached inside the head opening of the cuirass. "And I know how much you love helmets, so I decided to go with something else." He pulled out a length of dark blue material.

"It's a Deadening Hood," he said proudly.

"A what?" Jack asked.

Ted displayed the hood for everyone to see while it stayed attached from somewhere inside the cuirass. "A deadening hood is a type of cloth armor used by mages," he explained. "It has the strength and rigidity of steel when struck by a high velocity object, yet remains light and flexible to the wearer."

"I like the sound of that." Mike rubbed the material between his thumb and forefinger. "It doesn't feel like much."

Ted laughed, "That is the point." He motioned for Mike to take the suit. Mike quickly obeyed and piled the armor at his feet. As Mike began to remove his current armor, Ted motioned for Jack to come forward. "You're next," he said, as he bent back into the crate.

Jack took an eager step forward and was glad to see Ted remove his orcish armor from the crate. However, it didn't look the same.

"What did you do to it?" Jack asked in annoyance. He had liked how the armor had fit before, but now he saw that Ted had added some additions to it. The steel plates were larger and more tightly packed than they had been and there were other pieces making the suit bulkier than Jack remembered.

"As you can see, I made a few modifications," Ted said, as he set the last pieces on the table. "I realized that your current... affliction wouldn't allow you to wear your armor, and I didn't think that going unarmored into a battle was an intelligent idea. So, I took a few quick measurements from our friend Lorcan and enchanted your armor to expand with your alternate form."

Jack's golden eyes widened in surprise. "You're telling me that I can wear this while I'm a werewolf?" To which Ted nodded and Jack grinned wolfishly. "Now, that's what I'm talkin' about!" He eagerly grabbed the armor and began quickly pulling it on.

Then Ted turned to Emily. "I know you aren't a fan of armor, so I got something else for you." He pushed the now-empty crate aside and went over to another one of his workbenches. He returned a moment later with a long narrow box in hand. He set the box down and slid it over to Emily.

She opened it and found a beautiful scepter laying in the velvety inside. It was a little over a foot long and got thicker near the head. It was made of silver and gold and topped by a large blue-green stone that matched the necklace she wore.

Ted beamed as Emily withdrew the scepter in awe. "I must admit I didn't have time to make you something, so I traded one of my plasma weapons for it instead. I thought you could use something a little more powerful than that crude goblin scepter you've been using."

"What does it do?" Emily asked, as the gem on the scepter began to glow faintly from her touch.

"It is a focus," Ted answered. "My friend assured me that it is attuned to the natural earth energies that Druids wield. Holding it will enhance any spell you are casting, besides providing a much more powerful blast of destructive magic."

"Thank you." Emily withdrew the much larger and more cumbersome goblin scepter from her belt and handed it to Ted before replacing the empty slot with her new elven scepter.

Ted tossed the skull-topped scepter onto one of the piles of junk before rounding on Alex. "I know you said you didn't want any armor, but I found something for you anyway." Alex scowled, but didn't say anything as Ted handed him a bundle of black, orange, and gold cloth. "It is the robes of a Disciple of Apollo," Ted explained, and Alex's scowl grew. But Ted held up his hands in a calming gesture.

"Now, I know you aren't a Disciple of Apollo, but it was the only thing that I could find that would fit you."

"And what does it do?" Alex asked, as he unfolded the cloth and eyed the robes dubiously.

"It is a rare type of Null armor," Ted said grandly. "Luckily, the previous owner won't be needing it any longer."

Alex dropped the robes in a heap back on the table in front of Ted. "I don't want some dead elf's clothes."

"You will when I tell you what it does." Ted pushed the pile back at him. "Null armor is incredibly powerful in that it is extremely resistant to spells. So, it is the perfect armor for fighting mages."

Alex didn't pick up the robes. "If it is so wonderful, how did he die?"

Ted looked down at his feet. "Arrow to the eye," he mumbled, then looked up. "It protects the wearer from magic. It is harder than normal cloth but is not as strong as real armor. So, you had best stay away from swords and the like."

Alex grudgingly picked up the robes and went back to help his brother finish putting on his new armor.

Ted looked at Liz and smiled. "I saved the best for last."

"Oh, no," Liz moaned, as Ted picked up a long tray that had a large cloth over it. Lumps in the material spoke of something underneath and Liz didn't want to guess at what might be under there.

"I spent more time on these than everything else put together." Ted put the tray down in front of her and pulled the cloth away with a dramatic flourish.

There, on the tray, was a pistol and a sword.

The pistol was an old revolver with a white handle that had been finely engraved with elaborate silver markings across every inch of exposed metal. Liz picked up the revolver and was surprised to see a faint glow emitting from inside the six bullet chambers.

"It's a plasma pistol," Ted said proudly. "The plasma charges will replenish after firing, so it will never run out of ammo. However, they do need several seconds to recharge, so you can't just fire nonstop. Even if you could, the barrel wouldn't be able to handle the intense heat. The enchantments should disperse most of the energy, but too much use could see it overheat. If the barrel starts to glow, stop shooting until it cools down."

Liz eyed the revolver with a mixture of wonder and fear. "It's not going to blow up on me, is it?"

"Of course not," Ted assured her. "I put redundant fail safes in place to prevent any explosions."

Liz put the revolver in the holster that Ted handed her. "That doesn't make me feel much better," she mumbled, as she clipped it to her belt. Then she noticed the sword.

If that was what you would call it.

Short and slender, the sword had the curved bronze handle of a cutlass. But just above the guard was a blocky mechanism that attached to a blade that was split into a Y shape on one side, allowing a channel for the distinctive teeth of a chainsaw.

"I call it a chainsaber," Ted gushed. "I know how much you like chainsaws, so I had a dwarf smith forge the blade with the channel so that I could put the modified chainsaw inside it. That gives you a sword on one half and a chainsaw on the other," he said proudly. "It's quite ingenious."

"You're an ass," Liz smiled, and shook her head ruefully as she picked up the so-called chainsaber and hefted it experimentally. It was surprisingly light and well-balanced for having a small motor attached to it.

"I'm surprised there isn't a gun or plasma thing stuck on here too," she teased. Then she discovered a small button near her thumb on the handle, so she pressed it.

The chainsaber growled to life in her hand, teeth whirring rapidly. Liz was surprised that there was no smoke like a usual chainsaw produced. Ted must have read her expression because then he shouted over the roar of the weapon. "There is no gas or oil needed. It is fueled by a power cell that one of my colleagues devised. It should run for several hours before needing recharged."

Liz thumbed the activation stud again and the whining blade came to a stop. "I think you've outdone yourself this time, Ted," she said. "But if any of this stuff blows up on me, I will kill you."

"I stand behind my creations," Ted said solemnly.

Mike finished locking the last clamp on his new armor. "What about you?" he asked Ted. "I don't see any fancy new gadgets on you."

"Ahh," Ted held up a slender finger. "That is because mine isn't quite finished yet." He turned away and disappeared behind a towering metal coil. He reappeared a moment later, pushing a mannequin on wheels that was dressed in glossy grey armor.

Ted planted the mannequin before his friends. "My new armor," he announced proudly.

Mike tapped his knuckle on the grey cuirass. "Is this plastic?"

"As a matter of fact, it is," Ted preened proudly. "But it is as strong as steel and resistant to magical attack."

"If you had to enchant it to be strong as steel," Emily began, "then why didn't you just make it out of steel in the first place?"

"An excellent question," Ted answered. "You see, a mage draws some of his power from inside himself, but the rest is taken from the natural magical essence that lives everywhere. But some materials allow this essence to pass through more easily than others. Most metals are one such mineral that hinders magical flow."

"Different metals affect magic differently, of course," Ted said, "but that is why few mages wear metal armor. Armor also hinders the necessary movements required by some spells, making them difficult or even dangerous to cast. A mage must be a true master of their Art to be able to perform while wearing a full-suit of metal armor."

Jack laced up the last piece of his modified orc armor. "What about those Battlemages? They wear armor and still fling spells around like candy."

"Battlemages are trained in the use of armor," Ted explained. "And they do not wear full suits; most just wear a cuirass, greaves, and arm guards, allowing them mostly unhindered movement. As for the metal itself, most Battlemages use a unique type of elvish metal called orichalcum that is lightweight, has almost no magical hindrance, can hold numerous enchantments, and is extremely durable."

"Why don't you have this... orichalcum armor then?" Emily asked.

"Their method of creation is a highly-guarded secret. A secret known only to the Forgefathers," Ted sighed. "But I did discover that plastic is just as light and has a very low hindrance ratio. It doesn't hold nearly as many enchantments, but I will make do."

"What do you mean, hold enchantments?" Liz asked, as she clipped the chainsaber to her belt.

"Different materials can store varying degrees of magical energy," Ted explained. "For example, dwarf steel can be completely covered in Superior runes, while copper can only take one."

"That doesn't make any sense," Emily said in confusion. "You just said that metals hinder magical flow, but then you say the stronger metals can take more enchantments."

"Both are true," Ted began. "You see, the molecular constitution of-"

"Let me stop you right there," Mike interrupted. "I'm sure the details are fascinating, but we have more important things to do right now than learn about molecular structures."

Mike then proceeded to fill them all in on what he knew the situation to be at that time.

"And so," he finished, "the orc horde is already at the eastern wall, the Isfet will arrive in the North Shore in a little over an hour, and the Shadow elves are likely to wait until tonight to make their move against the Mount."

"Good," Jack growled, and as he talked his body suddenly expanded and morphed into a giant black werewolf. "I'm tired of all this waiting around." The overlapping armor plates slid apart and adjusted to Jack's enlarged form. "It seems your little invention worked," the huge werewolf snarled, as he inspected the expanded armor covering his furry body.

Everyone but Emily stared at Jack in surprise. "Yes, I can talk," Jack growled after seeing all the shocked expressions. "Now, what is our plan of attack?" He put a clawed hand on his Muramasa hilt. "I think we will be going to the eastern wall. Yoma-Ketsueki is hungry for orc and I am in a mood to indulge it." Jack's body seemed to melt and a moment later he was back to his normal self.

"I think I will tag along," Alex said. "I missed out on fighting the orcs last time. I don't plan on doing so again."

"I'm called to the Grove with the Druids," Emily said. "Belenos has summoned everyone there for some kind of emergency meeting."

"I will be commanding the defenses of the northern wall," Mike said.

"Would you mind if I joined you?" Liz asked him.

"Fine by me," Mike answered with a shrug. "Although, I didn't take you for the front-line type."

"I'm sure people will need healing before long," Liz said, "but can we make a short detour? I need to stop at the Healers Tent first."

"As long as it's quick," Mike replied.

"While the lot of you are out being brave and whatnot," Ted said, "I will be here until I have completed my armor. I predict it will be finished before nightfall so I can test my skills against these Shadow elves."

Jack snorted derisively. "They have to get past the dwarves first."

"The elves are confident that they will," Ted argued. "The rumor is that an exceedingly powerful lich must lead them to be able to hide such a large host. It is believed that this lich, or liches, must have trained in Scholomance to command such potent spellcraft."

"Scholomance? As in the devil's school?" Mike asked, to which Ted nodded in confirmation.

"How do you even know that?" Emily asked.

Mike grinned. "Hey, I know things."

"Yeah," Liz added, "stupid things."

"We can argue the importance of the things I know some other time," Mike said. "But right now, we have a city to defend."

****

Mike got a lot of strange looks as he followed Liz into the Healers Tent. Apparently having magnetic armor, reinforced with shock absorbers, was an uncommon sight. Who knew?

Liz spoke a few quiet words with one of the healers before the white-robed elf quickly disappeared into another room. When the healer was gone, Liz directed Mike to sit on one of the cots and then slowly sat next to him. Mike could tell something was bothering her, but he waited for her to speak first.

"We need to talk," Liz started off cautiously.

"Oh, no," Mike groaned in mock dismay. "The last words any guy wants to hear."

Liz's glare shot daggers at him. "I'm serious. There is something I need to tell you."

Mike could see that something was really bothering her and he took her hand in his. "What's the matter?"

Liz stared at the floor between her feet for a long time before she finally said. "Do you remember the fight with the nephilim?"

"Who could forget it?" Mike answered. "Why?"

"Have you ever felt anything… odd since then? Like knowing where somebody is, or how they are feeling just by thinking about them?" she asked with an almost pleading tone.

Mike shrugged his broad shoulders. "Maybe. Why?"

Liz took a deep breath and continued to stare at the floor. "Because I have been able to do that with you," she finally admitted in a rush. "Ever since I healed you in that awful castle, I have gotten glimpses of what you were feeling, or where you were… it was like I could feel what you were feeling… I don't really know how else to explain it."

Mike was stunned. It had been a month since that battle and he had no idea of what Liz had been going through since then. He felt terrible.

Somehow, he should have known that something was off and found a way to fix it. But before he could say anything, Liz barreled on. Now that she had started, everything that she had been holding in for so long came rushing out.

"I talked to some of the healers about what I have been experiencing and they think that I unintentionally ripped off a piece of my soul to keep you alive. So, now I have this fragment of me that's trapped inside you, and sometimes it lets me... sense you," Liz blurted out all at once.

Mike took a moment to digest everything she had said. "What can we do about it?" he finally said. "Can I give it back or something?"

"I don't know," Liz almost sobbed. "The healers don't even know for sure. They have something called a Binding Ritual that lets two people share a piece of their souls. But it's rare and what I did isn't quite the same."

Mike smiled and tried to lighten the mood. "Sounds like getting married." But Liz wasn't amused, so he changed tack. "What is the point of this Binding Ritual then? Can it be reversed?"

"They don't know," Liz sighed. "I guess it allows both people to know where the other is and sense what they are feeling. It also has physical perks as well, like increased healing and faster reflexes and the like."

"What's the catch?" Mike asked suspiciously. Everything sounded good so far.

Liz refused to meet his eye and kept her gaze locked on the ground. "If one of them dies, the other will most likely go insane or kill themselves."

"That's wonderful," Mike muttered. "I take it that since I have a piece of your soul that means if I die you will go crazy or die too?"

Liz nodded mournfully.

"And if you die, what happens to me?"

Liz shrugged. "It might hurt... or maybe nothing."

"That doesn't sound fair," Mike muttered. "So, what do we do about it?"

"The healers can try to separate us, but they don't think it will work." Liz mumbled miserably. "If they fail and can't get my soul to return to me, then I will die. But you should be fine since your soul is still intact. They think that it would be safer to perform the ritual and fully bind us together."

"So, you get screwed no matter what ..." Mike ran a hand over his shaved scalp. "What do you want to do?"

Liz sat there a long time before answering. "I want my soul back."

"I would, too." Mike took her hands in his. "But it sounds like you probably won't survive this. Wouldn't it be better to just leave it alone? I mean, there is a good chance I will die in this battle and that would drive you crazy, but maybe I won't die and you will be fine. It sounds almost guaranteed that you won't make it out of this procedure, so wouldn't it make more sense to take the chance of me not dying over almost certain death?"

Liz smiled sadly up at him. "Of course, I don't want to die. But neither do I want to live with a piece of myself missing. Besides, it's not fair to you. Now that you know about the bond, you are less likely to do what you need to for fear of hurting me." Liz squeezed his hands affectionately. "Making you a little less reckless wouldn't be a bad thing, but if it costs other people their lives, I can't have that on my conscience either."

Mike shook his head in wonder. "Leave it to you to make this about helping me."

"Just let me do this," Liz pleaded gently. "For both of us."

Looking into her eyes, Mike couldn't say no. "Then it's decided." He stood up and pulled Liz up after him. "Let's get you back to normal."

As if on cue, a group of healers entered the room, led by Kassandra. "You have decided?" she asked when she reached them.

"We have," Liz nodded. "Separate us."

Kassandra looked concerned, but she nodded in agreement. "Very well. You understand the risks."

The six other healers gathered around Liz and Mike and held hands, forming a circle around the pair as Kassandra placed a hand on each of their foreheads and closed her eyes. The golden light that Mike associated with the healers filled his vision as Kassandra began.

A strange sensation coursed through Mike as time seemed to come to a standstill. The feeling wasn't painful, but it was extremely uncomfortable. He had to force himself to not push back at the intrusive presence because he knew that it was Kassandra trying to separate them and if he interfered it could cost Liz her life.

"It is as we suspected," Kassandra muttered. "Your soul is attached with his… but it is more entwined than I would have thought possible…"

Through the golden light Mike could see that Kassandra had her eyes pinched shut and was starting to sweat as she tried to free Liz's soul from his own. The unpleasant crawling sensation continued for what felt like an eternity until Mike noticed that Liz had gone suddenly very pale.

Kassandra was muttering furiously to herself as Liz's color drained away and she began to sway dangerously. Kassandra spoke louder and faster in elvish as Liz's condition rapidly deteriorated.

Liz's legs abruptly gave out and she started to fall. Mike caught her before she hit the ground and gently cradled her in his arms.

Sweat was pouring off Kassandra when she opened her eyes. "The separation is nearly complete," she gasped, out of breath, "but I have been unable to rejoin her soul. As soon as I free it, I am afraid it will leave and take the rest of her with it." Kassandra looked at Liz's unconscious form sadly." If I finish, she will die."

Panic nearly seized Mike. "What can you do?" he asked desperately.

"We can perform a true Binding," Kassandra replied gravely. "That is the only thing that will save her. But it will require a piece of your soul to fill the void in hers. And if one of you dies, it will likely result in the death of the other as well."

Mike wasn't about to lose Liz like this. He made up his mind instantly. "Do it."

The golden glow returned, but this time the sensation was different. There was a brief moment of cold shock that filled him with emptiness, but it was replaced a moment later with warmth that made him feel more alive than he had ever been before.

Mike was suddenly aware of a new presence in the corner of his mind. He probed the new awareness and realized it was Liz! He could feel her weariness as he held her, cradled gently against him. It was an odd feeling, sharing a piece of yourself with another, but not completely unpleasant. Mike was actually surprised at how comfortable he was with her being there.

Kassandra breathed a deep sigh and stepped back. "It is done," she proclaimed wearily.

"Thank you," Mike said, as the gathered healers started moving away. Kassandra smiled and gave a slight bow before she too strode away, leaving Mike and Liz alone.

A few moments later Liz's eyes flickered open and a new awareness blossomed in Mike's mind.

She smiled up at him. "What happened?"

Mike's own smile faded away. "It didn't work," he admitted sadly. "If Kassandra had finished separating us, you would have died."

Liz looked up at him in confusion for a moment and then realization suddenly crossed her face. "You performed the binding! That's what I feel…"

Mike carefully set Liz on her feet as she tried to process what had happened. He could feel her confusion followed by a brief spark of anger when she realized her wishes hadn't been obeyed that changed into something else that Mike couldn't place.

Liz looked up at Mike in wonder and he couldn't help but think of how beautiful she was and how afraid he had been of losing her.

"I couldn't let you die," Mike blurted out. "I can't lose you."

A flood of emotions cascaded from Liz and Mike couldn't hope to decipher them all, but then one emotion overwhelmed all the rest. Realization suddenly struck him and Mike knew that he had the same feeling for her.

Liz's eyes were sparkling pools as she stepped closer and put her hands on his chest.

Mike pulled her closer. "Liz, I-"

But she gently put a finger to his mouth and smiled. "I know."

Then Liz reached up and pulled him down to her and kissed him. Mike enthusiastically returned the kiss as one emotion flooded across the bond.

Love.

When Liz finally pulled away, they were both out of breath. Mike was relieved that Liz finally knew how he felt about her, even though he hadn't been able to admit it to himself.

She smiled up at him, happier than she had been in a long time. "I should have done that a long time ago."

But before Mike could say anything, sirens began to wail across the city. They held each other for a long minute, unwilling to let the moment end, for they both knew what the sirens meant.

The battle for Pittsburgh was about to begin.

PART III

CHAPTER 21

Emily stood inside the monolithic stone ring of the Glade with a hundred other Druids and their apprentices when the sirens started.

"Brothers and sisters," High Druid Belenos intoned from the center of the ring. "Today is a glorious day! For today, we have been given a mighty gift!" Belenos held aloft a carved wooden box about a foot square and only a few inches tall. "We have recovered one of the Great Seals!"

The gathered Druids all cheered as Belenos held the box above his head for all to see. When the applause finally quieted, Belenos lowered the box and continued in a more somber tone. "However, this gift comes at a price. For today our enemies surround us and seek to destroy this Seal. As you all know, its destruction would release one of the Harbingers of Shadow."

The High Druid paused a moment as alarmed mutterings rolled through the crowd. "We cannot allow this to happen, for we are the Watchers of the Seals and it is our sworn duty to protect the Great Seals at all costs."

"As you all are aware, as Druids we practice neutrality and seek balance in all things. But today we must make an exception. Today, we must join our kin and their allies in battle to defeat the evil that threatens to devour this world and all other worlds." Belenos raised a slender wooden staff high.

"Today, I call the Druids to war!"

****

Black smoke clogged the eastern sky as the orc horde burned everything they came across on their slow advance toward the city walls. What had once been miles of homes and businesses was now nothing more than charred timbers and black ash.

The army of howling beasts seemed never-ending, seemingly stretching across the horizon as far as Jack could see. Although everyone called it the orc horde, in actuality, less than a third of the "horde" was even made up of orcs. Jack knew that the majority of the massive army was comprised of goblin tribes, kobolds, and other creatures that had been brought under the sway of the orcs with their strange, psychic dominance.

The guns had stopped some time ago after the last of the troops had been ushered behind the safety of the walls and an eerie silence had descended upon the waiting defenders.

"They don't look so tough," Alex noted, as he stared out at the distant horde.

"Of course, they don't," Jack laughed. "They are a mile away and look like ants. Wait until you've got a seven-foot tall green monster trying to split you in half."

Alex didn't say anything right away and continued to stare out over the battlements. "Is it wrong of me to be looking forward to the coming battle?" he asked softly.

"Of course not." Jack put his hand on Alex's shoulder reassuringly. "I look forward to every battle," he admitted. "You will never feel more alive than when you are fighting for your life. There is something almost peaceful about the singular focus you have when it's just you and your opponent."

Then Jack sighed. "That eagerness is tempered with such a large-scale conflict, however. Good people will die, but I know that if they do not, even more will die. It is better to stand and fight than to be hunted down and slaughtered."

"I feel the same," Alex said. "I dread the coming loss of life, but it is eclipsed by my urge to finally strike back at the beasts that have been plaguing us these last months."

Jack nodded his understanding. "It will all be over soon, one way or the other."

****

When Mike finally reached the top of the mighty gatehouse that spanned all five lanes of Veterans Bridge, he was surprised to find Stratigos Valerian.

"What are you doing here?" he asked, as he joined the elf on the battlements. "I thought you would be back at HQ watching over the city."

Valerian adjusted his sword belt. "Your general is an able commander with a better grasp of this city and the capabilities of his forces. I believe my presence here would be more beneficial to our cause."

"Fair enough." Mike looked out over the long bridge and saw the opposite bank was swarming with the kefali of the Horned Legion. "What are they waiting for?"

Valerian clasped his hands behind his back as he surveyed the field. "I believe we will soon be given terms of surrender."

"Why would they do that?" Mike asked. "I thought these Isfet were just out for blood."

"They are," the elf admitted, "but I suspect The Destroyer has plans of eliminating his current allies, and it would serve him better if he didn't have to fight us first."

"Or they are waiting for the Shadow army to arrive tonight so all three can attack as one," Mike offered. "That's what I would do."

Valerian smiled. "As you humans say, time will tell."

It wasn't long until a ripple passed through the gathered Isfet legion. The kefali parted around something large that was slowly moving toward the bridge. Mike made out a flash of gold, but at this distance it was hard to see any details. But as it broke free of the throng and moved alone across the bridge, the details became clearer.

A pair of enormous bulls clad in intricate golden armor pulled an extravagant golden chariot that ran red with blood from the severed heads that decorated its gold spikes. But it wasn't the bulls or the gruesome chariot that drew the eye, but its driver.

The towering beast that directed the chariot was mighty to behold. His upper body was of a golden-haired minotaur of staggering proportions, while his lower half was that of a golden-scaled serpent. The mighty creature was resplendent in gem-encrusted golden armor as he held the reins in one mighty fist and a golden *was* scepter in the other.

The golden figure rode alone across Veterans Bridge and finally came to rest about fifty yards from the gatehouse. Mike switched on his radio as the beast raised his scepter high and spoke.

"Behold, a living God!" the mighty beast roared in a voice that sounded like it had been dredged up from the depths of Hell. "I am Malek The Destroyer, son of the Great Apep, Lord of Chaos! Your doom is upon you, mortals! See me and know fear!"

Maybe it was the new bond giving him courage, or maybe he was just too tired from the night without sleep, but Mike found The Destroyer's proclamation to be annoying.

"No, thanks!" Mike suddenly shouted.

Valerian and everyone on the gatehouse turned and looked at Mike as if he had gone mad.

"Who dares defy the Son of Apep?" the golden beast roared in anger.

"That would be me!" Mike shouted back. *No point in turning back now.* Besides, he had a plan. "I am Mike Strazney, Lord of the Nerds! Slayer of the Digital Hordes! Vanquisher of the Random Baddies. Savior of Stereotypical Damsels in Distress and Commander of this wall. If you want something, you will have to talk to me."

Stratigos Valerian leaned over. "What are you doing?" he hissed angrily.

"Very well, Mike Strazney," The Destroyer boomed. "I have a proposal for you."

"I'm all ears," Mike replied with a grin.

"Throw down your weapons, open the gates, and surrender to me. If you do this you will all be made slaves," The Destroyer boomed. "If you resist, you will all be butchered and your families sacrificed to the Lord of Chaos. You have until nightfall to decide."

"Never going to happen, Malek," Mike shouted back defiantly. "Now, I have a proposal for you. Pack up your little army and piss off before we fill this river with their corpses."

The Destroyer's nostrils flared angrily. "You insolent little worm!" he bellowed. "This world belongs to me!"

"You want this world?" Mike shouted back. "Then come and take it!"

The golden demigod roared in anger. "When I bring down this pathetic wall, Mike Strazney, I will find you and I will devour your soul!"

"Bring it on, you ugly cow!" Mike taunted back. "I'll send you back to your father myself!"

The Destroyer bellowed in rage and violently snapped the reins. The defenders along the wall erupted in cheers as the golden demigod spun his chariot around and thundered away.

"By the Fields," Valerian cursed. "You just drew the wrath of a demigod. What were you thinking?"

Mike didn't say anything and realization struck the elf commander. "You did it on purpose, didn't you?"

"Yep," Mike grinned. "You said they would offer terms, and they did. But you also said that they would wait for their allies before attacking. So, I goaded him in the hopes that he will rush in and fight us alone."

Valerian shook his head in disbelief as Mike leaned over to one of the sergeants next to him. "Why are we not attacking them yet?" Mike asked.

"Sir?" The sergeant looked at him in confusion.

Mike sighed heavily. "Our guns reach across the river, don't they?"

"Of course, sir."

"Then we don't need to wait for them to attack us, do we?" Mike noted.

Understanding lit up the sergeant's face and he smiled eagerly. "No, sir."

"Good." Mike pointed at the Isfet legion waiting across the river. "Light 'em up!"

The thunderous roar of gunfire shook the city as its defenders unleashed the awesome might of their combined firepower against their enemies. Heavy artillery dropped high explosive ordinance into the heart of the kefali and orc armies as tanks and machine guns ripped into the packed masses of warriors. The sudden bombardment caught the kefali and orcs by surprise and they suffered astounding losses in those opening moments.

But the Horned Legion and orc horde were no strangers to battle. The zealots of the Isfet roared lustily and charged across the northern bridges in howling waves of fur and steel as the goblins and other minions of the orcs flooded across the scorched hills toward the eastern wall.

When the beasts had gotten close enough, the soldiers and machine gun nests on the walls opened fire, adding to the carnage. But the kefali and orcs didn't stop. They charged ahead, eager for blood, even as they were cut down in droves.

The Isfet offensive on the bridges was soon stalled as the overwhelming firepower brought against them made each bridge a killing lane. The orcs and their allies had little better luck as they swarmed across the eastern hills and met a barrage of overlapping gunfire.

As the corpses began to pile up and the offensive slowed on both fronts, the enemy commanders finally signaled a retreat. Pulling back cost them even more, but eventually the warriors found refuge inside those abandoned buildings that were still standing. The artillery and tanks continued to pound the enemy forces, but the soldiers and machine guns quieted as the nearest enemies hid from view.

****

The shelling dragged on for some time before Alex asked, "What are they waiting for?"

"That's a good question," Jack replied grimly, as he looked out over the wall at the sea of the orc horde, stretching out into the distance. "But I'm sure we'll find out soon enough."

As if on cue, dozens of huge trolls strode out to the front lines. Each beast pushed a bus or some other vehicle to use as a shield. Goblins and other minions crammed in behind the moving shelters as gunfire erupted anew. The improvised protection worked well until the tanks along the wall targeted them. The tank crews waited until the beasts were halfway to them before opening fire.

The trolls and their vehicular shields were reduced to scrap in an instant as the heavy shells ripped into them. With their shields gone, the horde was easy pickings for the machine gunners. The beasts scattered and retreated, but not before leaving a trail of dead in their wake.

The defenders of the eastern wall cheered as the horde retreated for the second time. Alex cheered along, but Jack remained stoic as he watched the withdrawal.

"What's the matter?" Alex asked merrily. "We are winning!"

"Are we?" Jack growled. "Can't you see how many of them are out there? We may have killed thousands of them, but there are hundreds of thousands more. And the orcs themselves haven't even joined the fight." He gripped his M27 grimly. "They are merely testing our defenses."

****

A similar scenario played out along the Allegheny River.

The kefali stacked ruined vehicles on top of each other and used them as mobile barricades in an attempt to shield themselves from gunfire. But they were similarly destroyed and Mike wondered if the two armies were somehow communicating. It seemed unlikely, but they were allies after all.

Mike's unease grew as the Isfet hid among the abandoned buildings of the north shore and prepared for their next offensive.

Mike reached up and touched the small earbud that was hidden inside his left ear. Ted had supplied the six of them with the devices before they had split up so that they could communicate with each other without needing to rely on phones or radios.

"Jack, what's the situation over there?" Mike asked.

"All quiet over here," Jack's voice said over the thunder of artillery.

"Liz, do you see anything?" Mike asked.

Liz was positioned on a gatehouse further down the wall. "I've got lots of movement, but I can't make out what they're doing."

"Alright," Mike said. "Everyone just keep-"

"Wait," Liz interrupted. "Here they come again."

Mike saw the surge a moment later. The kefali poured down onto the bridges and gunfire erupted once more. But this time, a line of Isfet sorcerers led the way and a wall of protective magic shielded them from the bombardment. The sorcerer's magic couldn't cover everyone and bullets still found their way through, but it wasn't a slaughter like before.

The kefali roared eagerly as the sorcerers rushed ahead and the Legion poured across the bridges and finally reached the walls. Spells lashed out from the Isfet sorcerers, fireballs and lightning scoured the battlements, and arrows fired from the kefali made the soldiers on the walls duck for cover, giving the warriors below more time to throw heavy grappling hooks and bring ladders to the front.

Gunfire and devastating spells from the human mages rained down on the massed warriors and the Isfet sorcerers couldn't protect them all. Kefali died by the score, but there were always more to take their place. Much of the walls were built right up to the river so the only places the kefali could attack were the gatehouses.

Heavy ladders landed along the walls of the gatehouses and Isfet warriors immediately began to climb. But before they got halfway up, streams of liquid fire showered down on them. They howled in agony and fell as the flamethrowers covered everything in burning petrol. The wooden ladders and grappling hook lines crumbled to ash and with their destruction the offensive stalled. With no way to climb the mighty walls and more warriors charging across the bridges, the ones crammed around the gatehouses were sitting ducks.

Liz and the other snipers targeted any kefali that were giving orders, causing even more confusion among the Legion, while the human and elf mages overwhelmed the trapped Isfet sorcerers.

Mike was feeling more confident as he watched the crammed kefali try to escape back across the bridge, but their own troops were blocking their escape. Powerful spells and concentrated gunfire made short work of the confused masses.

Suddenly, the water all along the river began to boil madly. Countless grappling hooks abruptly flew out of the roiling water and found purchase all along the walls. Scaly creatures with the upper bodies of men and lower bodies of snakes dragged themselves out of the water and began slithering up the walls.

"Naga!" Mike shouted into his radio. "Coming up the walls!"

The soldiers on the battlements responded immediately and turned the guns to the new threat. While the naga climbed, lightning and bars of black energy crashed against the battlements as naga sorcerers provided cover from the water.

So engrossed in the new battle along the walls, at first Mike didn't notice the new development along the bridges until something dark caught his eye. Looking back, he saw that the kefali had brought up huge battering rams that were covered in a turtle-like shell of heavy steel shields.

One of the tanks fired on the nearest battering ram and to Mike's surprise, it survived the blast as a flickering shield of magic defeated the explosive round. The tank fired again and this time the blast ripped some of the armored plates away. The shield failed completely on the third shot and the armored battering ram exploded.

But before Mike could enjoy the destruction of one of the battering rams, a dark mass rose up from the north shore like a billowing black cloud. The harpies shrieked madly and dove toward the city.

****

Alex felt worthless as he stood on the eastern wall with his staff and watched as the soldiers fired their rifles and the dwarves used their heavy crossbows to devastating effect.

Off in the distance, the orcs were trying to build siege equipment, but every time a trebuchet or catapult neared completion, one of the tanks would reduce it to kindling. Alex smiled at how frustrated the orcs must be as another siege tower exploded.

A sea of creatures rushed the walls and wave after wave of them crashed into the defenses and were cut down as the soldiers fired down through the machicolations. They attacked with mindless abandon, heedless of their own lives, as if something possessed them onward. Which it probably did, Alex realized. The goblins, troglodytes, kobolds and other creatures were all slaves to the will of the orcs. And if the orcs wanted them to overrun the walls, that was what they were going to try and do. However, dwarves knew what to expect and so the defenders were well prepared for such a mindless assault. But such brutal tactics were short-lived.

When it became clear that their minions wouldn't overwhelm the defenders by weight of numbers, the orcs called in reinforcements.

Hundreds of huge, armored trolls of every size and shape lumbered out of the throng and quickly crossed the distance with their long strides, crushing anything that was unfortunate enough to be in their way.

"Take down the trolls!" Jack shouted and fired at one of the huge monsters.

The heavy guns turned to the trolls and many of the huge beasts fell, but not all of them. The walls were too tall and slick for the trolls to climb, and the ladders and ropes that the goblins tried to use were far too small to support their massive bulk. So instead, the trolls charged the gates and tried to break down the reinforced steel doors.

The heavy gates were not so easily defeated, and the trolls pounded on them ineffectively until boiling oil and grenades dropped from the gatehouse ended their attempt while flamethrowers made sure the trolls wouldn't get back up.

"I expected this to be harder," Alex shouted over the noise.

Jack lowered his rifle. "I wouldn't call this easy," he shouted back, "but we have been preparing for weeks."

"I know," Alex replied, "but it still seems too easy. I thought the orcs were supposed to be these amazing warriors."

"It does seem too easy," Jack agreed, and then raised his M27 again. "But we haven't actually fought any orcs yet," he shouted, before continuing to fire into the mass of creatures that were still trying to mount the walls.

A horn blast from somewhere deep within the horde rattled the air with its call.

The echoes hadn't faded when the first dark spots appeared in the sky above the horde. The battle along the eastern wall raged below and in a few short minutes, the spots had grown into scores of wyverns.

Jack cursed as the wyverns drew closer.

"That's not our only problem." Alex pointed beyond the swarming goblins. When Jack followed the motion, he cursed again. Striding through the throng was an army of giants.

CHAPTER 22

As the reports from the eastern wall came in, Mike was positive the two armies were working together. It couldn't be a coincidence that both sides sent in aerial forces at the same time. They were trying to overwhelm the defenders and Mike prayed that it wouldn't work.

The harpies screeched overhead and crossed the river in moments. The ugly bird-women flew far faster than their awkward flight suggested. When the first harpies flew over the walls, the anti-aircraft batteries opened fire.

The heavy air defense and machine gun nests positioned on the rooftops ripped through the unarmored harpies by the score. Feathered bodies fell like rain around the defenders who were desperately trying to fight off the naga attack from the river as well as the harpies swooping down from the air, all while armored battering rams ground ever closer to the gates.

The tanks along the wall focused on the rams, but it seemed whatever enchantments were protecting them had been upgraded because the shields withstood far more punishment before finally collapsing.

With harpies diving at the soldiers, the rate of fire slackened and some of the naga were able to gain a foothold on the wall. Skirmishes broke out in several places as the defenders tried to push the naga back.

Spells flew back and forth as the human and elf mages unleashed wave after wave of devastating spells into the kefali. But the Isfet sorcerers returned every spell with a curse of their own that scoured the battlements of defenders.

A wall of purple fire suddenly arced down at the roof that Mike was on and at the last moment he summoned a barrier that covered the entire gatehouse from the enchanted flames. His shield must have attracted the attention of the kefali sorcerers because a moment later a flurry of spells crashed into his Svalinn Field.

He withstood the onslaught for several moments, and the defending mages and snipers used that time to find those sorcerers and kill them before they could call up their own defenses.

Mike was breathing hard when he finally released his shield. Maintaining a field over such a large area was difficult on its own, let alone when spells were hammering at it.

Harpies swooped down and clawed at Mike's head, but his hood protected him from their wicked claws. He swept his mace in a high arc and three of the bird-women crumpled around him. Nearby, Valerian was battling a pair of the winged creatures, but he quickly dispatched them before more swooped in.

Looking down the walls, Mike saw skirmishes in several places, but the defenders were still holding. If they could just get the pressure of the harpies off, then the walls could be taken back. Before he could think any more about it, a huge, greyish naga slithered up over the battlements right in front of him.

Without hesitating, Mike slammed his mace into the beast's chest and the force blasted the poor creature over the wall and sent it flying. Another naga started to reach for the top, but Mike struck the grappling hook head and it shattered. The line dropped away, taking a line of hissing naga down with it.

A harpy slammed into his back and nearly carried him over the edge, but he caught himself and shrugged the clawing beast off. A quick strike ended the unfortunate harpy, but no sooner had its feathered body hit the ground than six more descended on him. Mike could feel Liz through the bond and he hoped that she was having a better time than he was.

****

Liz ducked away from a grasping claw and pulled the trigger of her new pistol. A glowing bolt of plasma struck the harpy and blew a fist-sized hole in its chest.

She had been forced to drop her rifle as more and more harpies swooped down at her. An armored battering ram was nearly to her gate, but there wasn't anything she could do about it. Her MK13 sniper rifle was lying at her feet while she fired her sidearm into the swarming harpies all around her.

The tank that had been targeting the ram had been struck by an Isfet spell and was now covered in flames. There were no other tanks available to penetrate the armored shell of the ram, but there were a few holes in the armor plates that Liz thought she could exploit if she could just use her rifle.

The soldier next to her was suddenly yanked off his feet and pulled into the air. Liz shot the harpy that had him and he fell back to the ground in a heap. Liz rushed to his side and found deep puncture wounds around his shoulders and neck where the harpy's talons had dug in. She put her hand on him and muttered a quick prayer. The wounds closed up a moment later and as the soldier opened his eyes she quickly helped him to his feet.

Thanks to Liz's efforts, there hadn't been any casualties on her gatehouse yet, and she planned to keep it that way.

The anti-aircraft batteries were ripping harpies apart, but they didn't seem concerned. Their focus was the defenders on the walls. This seemed odd to Liz. Why wouldn't they attack the guns that were shooting at them? Now, a few did, but they were quickly shot down before they could get close. But if they attacked all at once…

She didn't get any more time to think about it as another of the ugly bird-women swooped at her. Liz twisted away and activated her chainsaber as she did. She swept the whirling sword up and the teeth tore through the harpy's wing, causing the maimed beast to crash to the ground.

Liz planted her foot on the shrieking harpy's chest and a quick plasma bolt ended the beast's misery.

Momentarily free, Liz holstered her blade and grabbed her MK13. She found the armored ram uncomfortably close and had to dial back her scope. She searched for a weak spot as the lumbering siege weapon drew ever closer. Soon, it would be at the gate and Liz didn't know how long the heavy doors could last.

The huge device shifted slightly to better align with the gate and when it did, Liz saw her opening. There were several small holes in the armored shell and she could see the huge minotaurs inside that were pushing the ram forward.

The holes were no bigger than her hand, yet her first shot blew the leg off of one of the minotaurs. Her second dropped two more with holes in their broad chests and a third removed the skull from another. With four of their number gone, the battering ram ground to a halt as the remaining kefali didn't have the combined strength to move the heavy piece of equipment.

Liz breathed a sigh of relief, but she didn't have time to enjoy her small victory. She had been so focused on the ram that she hadn't noticed the ladder set up next to her. She noticed now though, when a snarling lion-woman pounced up onto the battlements beside her. Without thinking, Liz turned and fired at the kefali. The lion-woman vanished in pink mist as the powerful .300 hit her point-blank.

Liz drew her revolver and leaned out over the battlements long enough to fire two shots through the center of the ladder. The wooden ladder held for a moment before the weight of all the bodies scrambling up it was too much and it snapped.

The ladder tumbled away, taking the kefali with it.

To Liz's dismay, she saw that the ram was moving again. Apparently, more minotaurs had found a way inside the armored shell and had taken the place of the fallen.

Liz pulled up her rifle again and found another small opening.

****

Air defense systems roared to life as the flights of wyvern neared the walls. The great beasts soared low and Jack quickly realized why. Each beast was weighed down by the orcs that were clinging to their scaly sides.

The slow-moving wyverns proved easy targets as the heavy guns ripped into them. However, there were far too many of the flying monsters to stop them all. Thankfully, there were few that made it through the storm of gunfire.

Jack cursed as instead of attacking the walls, the wyverns soared right over them and continued on into the neighborhoods beyond. He lost sight of them as the winged beasts landed between the houses and disgorged their orc passengers.

"Don't ye worry," a deep voice rumbled nearby. Jack and Alex turned to find the speaker and they were surprised to discover the impressive bulk of King Varnir standing before them.

The king was resplendent in the most marvelous suit of rune plate that Jack had ever seen. Glowing runes covered every inch of his blued, dwarf steel armor and a matching helm with tall wings made him seem even larger. Gold and silver trim accented the sharp angles and gentle curves of every detailed piece of metal. The mighty Axe of Perun was clenched in his gauntleted fist; its rough, flint-like appearance at odds with the crisp lines of his armor.

"The pointy-ears be takin' care o' 'em," King Varnir rumbled confidently.

"You mean the elves are down there?" Alex asked.

"O' course," the dwarf king nodded. "We expected those stinkin' orcs ter try flyin' over us. But I have a wall ter be defending, so we be lettin' the elves clean up the mess."

Jack noticed the king's retinue for the first time. Ambrosar, Chief Guardian of Thor, stood just behind the king, his great black beard flowing out from a scowling helm and two short-handled war hammers in his thick hands. Beside Ambrosar was the ancient Rune Lord, Eitri Starmantle. He was clad in exquisite armor and his grey beard brushed the ground. Jack couldn't see any weapons on the ancient Rune Lord, but he was positive the dwarf wasn't unarmed. Behind Eitri was a knot of the ever-present Huscarls that accompanied King Varnir everywhere.

"What are you doing here?" Jack boldly asked the king of the dwarves.

King Varnir seemed amused by Jack's forwardness. "Word reached me that the warlord was spotted near here," he rumbled, and looked out over the churning battlefield. Guns still blazed as an army of giants carried huge ladders and pushed siege towers toward the walls.

Artillery and heavy cannon blasts ripped into the giants, but they were spread out and moving quickly across the broken ground. With so many enemies around, it was difficult to decide who was more important to target first. So far, the defenders were keeping the horde from gaining any purchase on the walls, but if the giants and their equipment reached them, then that would be a different story.

Now that their cargo had been unloaded, the wyverns were taking to the air once more. The great beasts screeched and soared back toward the walls, but the air defense systems didn't fire. The wyverns were flying too low and the gunners didn't want to fire into the town.

Jack cursed and raised his rifle at the nearest wyvern that was speeding toward them. But before Jack could pull the trigger, a bolt of lightning shot out of the sky and struck the beast like a hammer blow. The wyvern shrieked in pain and faltered as electricity coursed over its scaly body.

More lightning fell from the cloudy sky and crashed into the speeding wyverns. A moment later, dozens of shapes dove out of the clouds and descended on the beasts with a vengeance.

The griffins streaked out of the sky like meteors and slammed into the unprotected backs of the wyverns as their dwarf riders flung devastating lightning bolts from their long hammers. The wyverns broke off their attack run and wheeled in the air to face this new threat.

Jack tore his eyes away from the spectacular aerial battle in time to see the first giant drop a huge ladder on the walls. Then the giant began to climb. Everyone turned their guns on the climbing giant, but the small caliber rounds only seemed to anger it. As the giant heaved its massive bulk onto the wall, there was a loud crack from behind Jack and the top of the giant's head exploded. Like a felled tree, the giant slowly toppled backward and smashed the ladder as it fell.

Jack turned to see Jason Andrews lowering his smoking AX50 sniper rifle.

He smiled at Jack. "Looked like yinz could use a hand."

More giants reached the walls, but as soon as they crested the battlements, the elite sniper units took them out with well-placed shots to their unarmored heads.

A sudden explosion ripped into a distant part of the wall, followed by another. More blasts detonated along the wall and then sporadic gunfire started striking the battlements.

"Get down!" Jack shouted, and everyone ducked for cover as bullets flew overhead.

"What the hell is going on?" Alex shouted. "Who is shooting at us?"

"Only one way to find out!" Jack poked his head out between the thick merlons and what he saw he couldn't believe.

With no explanation forthcoming, Alex joined Jack at the crenel.

"Is that…?"

"Yep," Jack groaned. "That is an orc with a Gatling gun."

Alex cursed. "When did they learn to use that?"

Jack shrugged. "I suppose when you watch enough of your comrades get blown apart, you figure it out."

Jack and Alex took cover again as bullets sprayed along the battlements. "They must have taken them from the men they killed," Jack mused, "but where are those explosions coming from?"

Alex peered out over the walls again pulling Jack up beside him. "Look." He pointed out deeper into the horde.

There, rolling along with the orc horde, was a line of deformed tanks. And they were firing on the walls.

****

The situation on the northern wall wasn't looking good.

Battles were erupting all along the wall and as soon as one was cleared, two more seemed to take their place. Curses and deadly enchantments flew in both directions and the kefali received the worst of the magical exchange, but that didn't mean the defenders went unscathed.

Healers ran everywhere, pulling fallen soldiers back from the brink of death to continue the fight, but they couldn't save everyone. The dead littered the battlements and a mountain of corpses was piling up outside the scarred walls. Harpies still wheeled around overhead and dove at the defenders, but their numbers had been greatly reduced thanks to the concentrated fire of the machine gun emplacements and anti-aircraft batteries.

The kefali warriors were relentless and their sorcerers proved a match for even the most skilled human mages. Mike wished he had a few more Battlemages to bolster his line, but he had to make do with what he had. There was still no sign of Archmage Talsin or any of his most powerful mages and Mike was worried that something had happened to the formidable elf. But now was not the time to worry about a missing Archmage. He had more pressing matters to attend to.

An explosion of putrid, green acid slammed into the gatehouse and it was only thanks to Stratigos Valerian's Aegis that everyone on the building wasn't killed. Before anyone could recover, however, a trio of Isfet sorcerers flew up and landed on the gatehouse. Fire and black bolts lashed out at the surprised defenders, killing many in that first brutal assault. Mike quickly summoned a barrier, deflecting the magic missiles and charged at the nearest sorcerer.

An ugly beast that looked like some kind of sloth stood before him. Dressed in black robes and armed with a long scythe, the sloth sorcerer reminded Mike of the Grim Reaper. But the specter of death didn't frighten him and he charged the kefali.

Tongues of green flame lashed at Mike, but they couldn't touch him. The sorcerer desperately swept the scythe at him, but that too crashed ineffectively into the protective barrier. Mike made short work of the kefali with a brutal strike that crushed the beast's chest and flung it back over the wall.

Mike turned in time to see Valerian pull his sword from the back of another sorcerer as the last was surrounded and gunned down by a squad of angry soldiers. With the gatehouse clear once more, Mike suddenly realized that the sun was beginning to set. Brilliant reds and oranges painted the sky and he was struck by the beauty, even amidst so much destruction.

A tremor shook the walls.

And then another.

And another.

The steady vibrations made Mike look down the length of wall to see that somehow, one of the battering rams had made it to a gatehouse. The heavy ram crashed into the gate, over and over, but so far, the heavy doors were holding. Boiling oil was poured, but it rolled off the armored shell.

The battlements were a warzone with naga scaling the walls from the water and minotaurs assaulting the gates, all with harpies swooping down and pulling soldiers into the air.

Mike's radio suddenly crackled to life.

"Col. Strazney, do you copy?" came the voice of General Adams.

"I do," Mike shouted into the receiver amidst the thunder of gunfire and explosions. "We could use some reinforcements over here!"

"I'm afraid we don't have any to give you," the radio crackled. "Your walls are ready to fall. Execute Operation London Bridge."

"But sir, we can still-"

"That's an order!" Then the radio went dead.

Mike cursed to himself and changed radio channels. He didn't like this plan, but he also knew that General Adams was right. The walls wouldn't hold out much longer. "All bridge commanders," Mike shouted into the radio. "Execute Operation London Bridge. I repeat Operation London Bridge!"

A tense moment followed as Mike waited to see if his orders had reached the other commanders.

He got his answer a minute later when the ground shook as massive explosions detonated along the Clemente, Warhol, Carson, and McCullough Bridges.

With a shriek of tortured steel and a growl of crumbling concrete, the four bridges tore free of the walls and collapsed into the Allegheny, taking the crammed kefali warriors with them.

Now, only the Fort Duquesne Bridge and Veterans Bridge remained standing.

With the sudden loss of reinforcements, the kefali on the gatehouses were quickly overwhelmed. And then with the gatehouses secured, the soldiers of Pittsburgh could concentrate their fire on the naga that were still pulling themselves up out of the water, although their advance had also been stymied by the sudden destruction of the bridges.

Despite the sudden reversal, the Horned Legion was far from finished.

****

Liz's plasma revolver blazed in the evening light as she fought her way along the length of the wall toward the Veterans Gatehouse and Mike. The tower of the gatehouse she had been on was secured now that the bridge had been demolished. But now all of the remaining Isfet were concentrating on the last two bridges. Mike could use her help and she was eager to be by his side again.

She had her rifle slung across her back and the chainsaber growled in her other hand as she fired another volley into the naga trying to hold a section of the wall. Then Liz caught something out of the corner of her eye and she dove away just in time to avoid a harpy's talons. The bird-woman shrieked angrily as it swooped by and Liz shot it in the back before it could escape.

The naga on the wall were suddenly slammed against the battlements as a force of air blasted into them. Before the half-snakes could recover, arrows punched into their scaly bodies and suddenly that section of the wall was clear.

Liz was surprised to see Emily standing on the other side of the dead naga, bow in hand. "What are you doing here?" Liz asked, as she rushed over and embraced her friend.

"Belenos told us to go join the fighting," Emily said. "So, here I am." She knocked another arrow and fired it into the eye of a naga that dared to poke its head over the wall. "What are you doing here? I thought you were on a gatehouse?"

Liz shot two harpies before answering. "I was, but then they blew the bridges. So, now I'm trying to get to Mike." Liz pointed down the wall to the massive gatehouse off in the distance. The entire length of the wall between them was in chaos as harpies and naga battled the defenders on the battlements.

"Are you crazy?" Emily laughed helplessly. "There is no way we will get through that."

A group of naga broke away from the soldiers they were fighting and slithered toward Liz and Emily. Liz shot one of them, and Emily waved her hand and a swirl of air pushed the other two off the wall.

A series of explosions pounded the distant gatehouse and Liz was relieved to feel that Mike was still alive.

"They will never hold off that many monsters," Emily said, as she watched the legions of kefali storming across the wide bridge, "unless we can buy them some time…"

Inspiration came to Emily and she grinned evilly.

"What are you talking about?" Liz asked.

"Just keep them off me for a minute," Emily said, before setting her bow down. She closed her eyes and took a deep breath. She made a circular motion with her hands and Liz could hear her muttering something under her breath.

A harpy swooped in and Liz dispatched it with a carefully placed plasma round. A grappling hook clanged against the stone as it caught hold, but Liz quickly cut the rope with her chainsaber before anything could climb up. When Liz looked up from cutting the rope, she noticed something strange on the river.

The air above a section of the river abruptly began to swirl and soon it had formed into a twisting waterspout. The tornado of water grew until it was several stories high. The wind began to howl as the mighty vortex pulled water into itself and grew ever larger.

Panic gripped the defenders as the enormous waterspout began to move. Slowly at first and then with growing momentum, the waterspout traveled down the river and plowed into Veterans Bridge.

The mighty bridge quivered in the gale as the kefali were sucked up into the howling vortex. Furry bodies spun through the air as the massive twister carried them off like pieces of trash.

Emily suddenly sagged and Liz caught her by the arm. The waterspout began to fade and within the span of a few heartbeats, it was gone like it had never been, except for the clear space where the kefali had been blown away.

Emily groaned weakly as Liz helped steady her. "I hope that gave them some time," she muttered groggily.

"I'm sure it did." Liz couldn't help but smile. "Since when can you make tornadoes?"

"Turns out Druids can call upon the powers of Nature." Emily picked up her bow, as her fatigue seemed to melt away. "Who knew?" she grinned, then adjusted her headscarf and looked at the good hundred yards of wall that were under siege between them and the gatehouse. "Now, let's go find your boyfriend before we all die."

****

As the sun set, the cannons and artillery of Pittsburgh returned fire on the entrenched orc horde. High explosive rounds sailed back and forth as the goblins, giants, and other creatures scrambled across the killing field to assault the nearly three miles of heavily-defended wall.

The grim human soldiers fired ceaselessly into the coming hordes as the dwarves hacked gleefully at anything that dared crest the wall. So far, the shocking addition of the orc's tanks and firearms hadn't dislodged the defenders. If anything, it aided the human soldiers. Enemies with guns and tanks, they knew how to fight.

The griffins and wyverns still battled fiercely in the air above the walls, neither willing to give any ground. The wyverns still had the numbers on their side, but the griffin riders used fiery spells to even the odds. Fire and lightning streaked across the sky as the white-winged griffins clashed with the leather-winged wyverns for control of the skies.

Alex crouched behind the parapets as more explosions ripped into the reinforced battlements. Thankfully, the strange elven crafted stone and the rune-covered metal bands of the walls resisted much of the heavy shelling.

King Varnir crouched beside Alex with a wild grin on his face.

"What are you smiling for?" Alex hissed, as another explosion rained bits of stone on them.

The king threw his thumb in the direction of the orc horde. "Tis him." A wild light entered King Varnir's eyes. "The stinkin' warlord finally showed 'emself."

The dwarf king peered out from the parapet and Alex joined him. "There." King Varnir pointed out into the horde.

At first Alex didn't see what he was pointing at, but then he saw it. Striding through the churning horde was a red-skinned orc of immense size. Easily head and shoulders above the rest, this orc was even larger thanks to a mechanical exoskeleton that made him tower over even the largest of orcs. A tall banner attached to his back hung proudly above him, showing a dark cloud with a curved horn stabbing out like a lightning bolt.

"Warlord Stormtusk," King Varnir rumbled eagerly. "And an oni ter boot!" the king smiled madly. "It be a glorious day human! It's been an age since a Svartalfar king has met an oni warlord on the field o' battle!"

"We are a long way from you crossing blades with that guy," Alex shouted over the sudden roar of gunfire.

"That may be," King Varnir rumbled. "At first I cursed the gods fer brining' me and me kin ter this strange world. But now I be seein' that it was fer a greater purpose."

"To fight that warlord?" Alex guessed.

"Aye," the dwarf king nodded. "Our blades will cross, don't ye doubt."

****

Mike spat blood as he picked himself up off the ground. That tornado had nearly blown him and the rest of the soldiers off the gatehouse. If he ever found out what crazy mage it was, he would make them regret it.

However, the twister had done one good thing. It had scoured the gatehouse and the area immediately around it clear of kefali.

The radio had blown away in the gale and his earpiece wasn't working. So, now Mike had no way of communicating with HQ or his friends. Not that any of that really mattered. He had to hold this bridge at all costs.

After helping Valerian and the other soldiers get back on their feet, Mike was surprised that the legion wasn't rushing back to the gate. The angry mass of kefali stayed back as if waiting for something.

That something showed up a minute later when The Destroyer rode up in his golden chariot and stopped at the head of his army.

The golden demigod slithered out of his chariot and when he did, a hundred robed acolytes swarmed around him. His bull-like gaze found Mike and he smiled.

"Ah, Mike Strazney. I see you still live," his powerful voice echoed along the wall. "That is good. I will take great pleasure in destroying you myself."

Mike laughed at the glittering monster before him and he hoped it didn't sound too forced. "It will take a lot more than a few mangy animals to kill me," he shouted back.

"That can be arranged," The Destroyer boomed. As if on some signal, all of the gathered acolytes suddenly drew daggers and as one, plunged them into their own hearts.

The Destroyer spread his arms wide and the blood around him began to vaporize. As the red mist grew, it started to swirl around the golden figure before it was finally pulled into the demigod.

Mike clenched his fists and looked around at the gathered defenders who were watching the spectacle in amazement. "Why are we not shooting at him?" Mike shouted, as he grabbed the M4 from one of the oblivious soldiers. He pulled the rifle up and fired at The Destroyer. His shot hit an invisible field, but the noise was enough to break whatever had taken hold of the defenders. Gunfire and spells erupted along the walls once more and crashed into the protective shield around the demigod.

The Destroyer's laughter boomed over the noise. "Foolish mortals! You have provided a great sacrifice for the Lord of Chaos this day! Now, behold the power of Lord Apep!"

The Destroyer's hands began to glow as he moved them around in a strange pattern. Power pulsed around him and his golden form seemed to take on a light of its own. It was as if every move gathered more power to him and soon the air around him pulsed with barely contained power. Explosions detonated around him, but nothing penetrated the barrier. Then, with one final sweeping motion, The Destroyer of the Horned Legion brought his hands together and a beam of blistering red light shot forth.

****

Liz and Emily were still battling their way along the wall and were nearly fifty yards away from the Veterans Gatehouse when The Destroyer struck.

They watched in horror as the column of hellish energy struck the heavily fortified structure.

There was a brilliant flash as the mighty gatehouse exploded.

The walls rocked from the force of the blast, knocking the stunned defenders from their feet.

Liz stumbled as searing pain filled her mind in a flash and then was gone. She gasped in agony as a sudden emptiness filled her and she realized with horror that she couldn't feel Mike's presence anymore.

Emily helped Liz up and saw the pain on her face. "What's wrong?" Emily asked. "Are you hurt?"

"No," Liz managed to say through gritted teeth. With tears in her eyes, she looked up at the bridge and saw the huge, golden Destroyer climb onto his chariot and lead his cheering army forward. Shock and sadness were suddenly replaced by pure rage at the sight of the monster that had taken Mike from her.

Liz brushed Emily's concern away as she stormed along the walls, filled with blinding hate and rage. Her plasma pistol blazed in her grip, punching smoking holes in any creature that got in her way. Her chainsaber growled angrily as she slashed through the air at anything within its deadly reach.

Emily followed behind, afraid of the sudden change that had come over Liz, but unsure of what to do about it. Her only option was to follow along and help in whatever way she could.

With the gatehouse breached, the retreat was called, and the defenders abandoned the walls to form up in prearranged locations within the city.

But Liz wasn't paying attention.

She only had eyes for one thing.

Like a force of nature, Liz crossed the length of the wall, destroying anything that came in her path. She nearly single-handedly cleared that last section of the battlements before she finally came to a stop where the wall suddenly ended.

The broken wall stopped where the gatehouse should have been, but through the choking smoke and fire, Liz could only see a scorched crater where the mighty building had once stood.

They quickly scrambled down the jagged ruins of the wall and found themselves eerily isolated in the crater. Thick, swirling smoke obscured their vision, and if it wasn't for the echoes of battle all around, they could have been alone.

Pieces of charred stone and shattered chunks of concrete littered the ground in all directions. However, Liz didn't see any bodies, but she could hear the clamor of the approaching legion.

Emily grabbed her by the arm and pulled her away from the wall, toward the city. "Come on," she hissed. "We need to get out of here before the kefali show up!"

"I need to find him," Liz growled.

Emily stared at her in confusion. "Who? Mike?" she snorted and swept her arm around the scorched ruins. "He is probably scattered around here in a million pieces." Then her voice softened. "We need to go. We won't be doing anybody any good if we are dead too."

Liz knew Emily was right and she struggled to push her burning rage aside. She had hoped to find a body, and maybe even heal him, but now she wanted nothing more than to make The Destroyer pay for taking him from her. She had finally admitted how she felt about him, and she knew he felt the same way, but now that was all gone. Taken in one blinding instant.

The clatter of hooves grew louder and before Emily could drag Liz away, a huge, golden chariot emerged from the smoke with the screaming Isfet legion close behind.

The Destroyer grinned evilly when he spotted Liz and Emily before him.

He turned to his followers. "Go." He pointed into the city. "Find the Seal before that old hag does and kill everyone you find." Then he looked back at Liz and Emily. "But leave this pair to me."

The kefali cheered and howled eagerly as they flowed around Liz and Emily, then poured down the abandoned city streets in search of prey.

The Destroyer slithered out of his chariot and carefully picked his way toward them through the rubble. A few yards away, he stopped and his wide nostrils flared as he sniffed the air. "I smell the stink of that annoying human on you," his deep voice boomed. "You were his friends," the golden beast sneered. "A pity he perished so soon. I had hoped to devour his soul before I killed him."

Liz's rage flared anew. "You talk too much." She suddenly raised her plasma revolver at the golden demigod and fired.

CHAPTER 23

The shadows lengthened as the sun was nearly hidden behind the distant hills. The battle had been raging for hours and both sides were eager to break the grueling stalemate.

Guardians stationed all along the mighty eastern wall summoned their Svalinn Fields for protection against the newest orc tactic.

The warlocks of the horde had moved to the front, throwing vile curses and devastating dark magic at the weary defenders. The dwarf Guardians had stepped up to the challenge and warded off everything but the most concentrated bombardments.

Most of the orc tanks had been destroyed, but a few still fired from behind the safety of powerful enchantment and hastily constructed fortifications, while the aerial battle had moved west toward the city.

The mechanically enhanced oni warlord had moved toward the front of the horde, surrounded by a huge knot of his cronies, including hulking orcs in elaborate armor, dark-robed priests, and grim warlocks.

There was a lot of movement inside the orc horde and Jack didn't like it. They were up to something, he was sure of it. But when he brought his concern to King Varnir, the dwarf monarch only laughed. "O' course they be up ter somethin'. They be orcs!"

"Silly me," Jack grumbled under his breath at the casual dismissal of his unease.

The battle along the wall raged for some time longer until it suddenly reached a fevered pitch as the horde suddenly surged when the orcs began to chant.

Softly at first, the chant grew into a roar that vibrated through the air. The strange words were painful to hear and many soldiers' hands clasped over their ears in an attempt to block out the racket. But the otherworldly shriek of the words grew louder and caused many along the wall to drop to their knees in agony.

The awful call had the opposite effect on the orcs and their minions, filling them with renewed energy and focus. Thankfully, the dwarves seemed resistant to the orcs' wailing chant and they roared in defiance as they continued to defend the walls while their human allies were incapacitated.

As the malevolent chant reached its excruciating crescendo, walls of purple-black flames suddenly sprung to life throughout the horde like a burning river that flowed between their ranks of warriors.

The dark flames flared as huge figures took shape inside them. The purple and black flames suddenly blazed with an otherworldly darkness and then abruptly vanished. In their place, stood row upon row of misshapen monsters. The orc horde had just successfully doubled its size in a matter of moments.

The hellish creatures were enormous; easily the size of giants, with some even larger. Their soulless eyes burned with the same purple-black fire that had spawned them and the ground burned from their touch. Many of them were vaguely human shaped, but some were little more than lumpy masses of tentacled flesh or abhorrent abominations of different creatures all mashed together.

"I been wonderin' when those buggers would be showin' up," King Varnir rumbled grimly.

"What are they?" Alex asked in horror.

"Unless I be mistakin', those be Muspell," Ambrosar growled.

"Aye," Eitri confirmed with a nod of his ancient head. "Demons."

****

Emily leapt away as the place she had just been standing exploded behind her. She dove behind a large pile of rubble, as another searing bolt from The Destroyer's *was* scepter followed her. A moment later, she heard the distinctive crack of Liz's plasma revolver and she jumped up, bow in hand.

Three arrows sped in rapid succession at the towering, golden monster that was now throwing spells at the large chunk of broken concrete that Liz hid behind. But like all of Emily's other arrows, these bounced harmlessly away just before reaching the cruel demigod.

The great beast laughed as he again turned his attention to her. "Foolish mortal. Your pathetic weapons cannot harm me."

Emily took The Destroyer's words to heart. Perhaps her arrows couldn't hurt him, but she had something else that might. She slung her compound bow across her back and drew her new scepter.

Hopefully, this would work better.

The scepter felt good in her hand and she could sense the superior quality of the weapon compared to her old one as she pointed it at the laughing monster.

The emerald bolt exploded and crackling energies cascaded around whatever shield surrounded the golden beast. The Destroyer's laughter changed to a roar of anger. "Enough of this game," he snarled, and a blade of hellish energy sprang to life along the tail of his scepter. "Time for you to die."

The Destroyer took a step toward Emily and just then Liz rushed out from behind her cover and charged the demigod's back. Her growling chainsaber swept toward the huge monster, but he spun around and deflected the strike with a sweep of his long scepter. Then he countered, faster than Emily could follow, as a long cut grazed Liz's arm as she desperately spun away.

The golden demigod chased after Liz as she tried to put some space between them. She fired her pistol as she scrambled away, but the energy was deflected like all the others. The Destroyer's blade was like a striking snake and Liz couldn't block them all. More cuts appeared and Emily knew she wouldn't last much longer.

Emily aimed her scepter at the monster's back and fired. She wasn't sure what she did, but instead of the emerald bolt, a pulsing, beam of crackling liquid fire erupted from the scepter and slammed into The Destroyer's shield. The beam flowed out of the scepter in an unbroken stream of emerald fire.

The Destroyer spun around and fired a hellish red beam of his own that slammed into Emily's. With the demigod distracted, Liz charged back in, pistol blazing. To her great surprise, the third shot actually struck The Destroyer's golden armor.

His shield was gone!

The demigod roared angrily and a sudden buildup of energy ripped from his scepter and exploded, destroying Emily's beam and flinging her backward. The golden beast twisted away as more plasma rounds whizzed by his ear. He reversed his scepter and charged Liz with the glowing spear tip. Liz met the enchanted *was* scepter with her chainsaber and sparks flew as the weapons collided.

She fired her pistol as they dueled, but The Destroyer was too quick and dodged each superheated round while still managing to land a few strikes of his own.

Emily got to her feet and fired another emerald bolt at the monster's back, but somehow he anticipated the strike and twisted away before it hit. Seeing an opening, Liz drove in hard, chainsaber slashing and pistol firing, but again The Destroyer was ready and somehow deflected all of her attacks.

Liz and the demigod traded blows and danced around each other in a spectacular display. Emily cursed as she tried to find an opening, but they were moving too fast and she was afraid she might hit Liz. So, she slid the scepter back in her belt and grabbed her bow once more.

Arrows slammed into the surprised Destroyer and some found their mark between the plates of his golden armor. The demigod roared and launched a brutal flurry at Liz that left her reeling. She was bleeding from numerous cuts and her arms were getting heavy. With every strike, The Destroyer was getting closer.

But Liz wasn't done yet.

As she parried another of The Destroyer's slashes, she prayed. A moment later, golden light shined down on her and her wounds began to heal. The demigod howled in rage and attacked with renewed fury, but Liz's strength had returned, and she held her ground.

"A priest!" The Destroyer bellowed in surprise. "Your god cannot save you! The Lord of Chaos will consume everything!"

An arrow abruptly lodged in the demigod's shoulder and he roared angrily.

Suddenly, he spun and used his long serpentine tail to wrap up Liz's legs. Liz desperately slashed at the beast's tail, but the whirring blades only scraped off the golden scales.

The huge monster's tail swiftly wound its way up and pinned her arms down. Liz struggled, but the tail only coiled tighter until she struggled to breathe.

With Liz trapped, The Destroyer turned his full attention on Emily. He slithered with amazing speed toward her, despite towing Liz along behind. Emily desperately fired arrows as fast as she could, but the huge demigod easily brushed them aside with a wave of his scepter.

Being inside the city prevented Emily from calling on many of the powers of nature, but she did have a few options.

A column of swirling wind howled to life and buffeted the approaching beast, but the demigod shouted a word of power as he came and the air calmed.

The ground rumbled and there was a loud cracking sound as the pavement buckled and split. A wall of stone suddenly erupted from the road and blocked The Destroyer's path.

Emily could hear laughter from the other side of the stone and a moment later the wall shattered in a violent explosion.

Emily was thrown backward by the force of the blast and slammed into the pile of rubble. She crumpled to the ground in a daze as a shadow loomed over her.

"A priest and a Druid," The Destroyer boomed, as he grabbed Emily by the neck and pulled her up to face him. "An odd pairing." Emily's vision swam as she hung in the air with the demigod's huge hand clamped around her throat. "But then you *are* humans," The Destroyer's bull-like visage grinned. "I will enjoy devouring your souls."

"Just kill us already," Liz gasped, as the coils drew tighter, "so we don't... have to hear you talk... any more."

"Oh, no," The Destroyer laughed. "There is no hurry." He held both

Liz and Emily out before him as he gloated. "Soon, this city will fall and I will possess the Seal. Then I will claim this city as my own and recover my losses by converting those heathen green-skins to the glory of Chaos," the demigod laughed, as the shadows grew long. "That scheming lich and her bloodthirsty elves will need to be killed, of course, but once they are removed, this world will be mine for the taking."

Emily gasped for breath, but the demigod's grip was too tight. Spots filled her vision and she thought she saw snow swirling around, but she knew that it was still too warm for snow. Her sight blurred as she began to lose consciousness and blackness threatened to engulf her.

Suddenly, she was falling.

Emily landed hard on her back and coughed violently as she inhaled greedily. It was only after her vision cleared that she heard the heavy thuds and strange roars. Gingerly, she sat up and was shocked at the scene before her.

Liz was free and shooting at The Destroyer while the golden demigod was locked in a titanic struggle with an enormous white tiger. When she saw Emily sit up, Liz rushed over and helped her to her feet. Healing energy flowed into Emily and she took a deep breath as her wounds vanished.

"We need to get out of here," Liz said.

"Ya think?" Emily hissed.

The mighty tiger's claws raked the golden armor, but The Destroyer seemed unconcerned as he drove the *was* scepter into the great cat's side. Kiba'Nadare cried out in pain and backed away, giving Emily the opportunity she needed.

She called the wind and a column of swirling air took shape. Then, using the fissure in the road, Emily pulled stones into the roaring vortex.

The growling rock tornado shot forward and slammed into the golden demigod as he prepared a final spell to finish the wounded Great Cat.

The Destroyer was hammered backward under the onslaught and buried under a pile of heavy stones.

Kiba'Nadare bound over to Liz and she wasted no time in climbing up onto its broad back. "Come on!" Liz cried, as she held her hand out to Emily.

The Destroyer burst from the rubble with a terrible roar as Emily swung up behind Liz. The powerful tiger did not delay and immediately bounded away.

When Emily looked back, she could just make out The Destroyer climbing into his chariot right before the smoke and dust obscured him from sight.

****

The last rays of sunlight vanished behind the hills and when they did, the Muspell's hellish cry reverberated across the city. The huge demons surged forward as if a dam had broken and the whole of the orc horde charged with them.

Heavy gunfire and streaking spells hammered the assaulting army, but they came on in an unrelenting tide.

Surprisingly, some of the demons sprouted wings and leapt into the air, but instead of attacking the walls, they flew away into the city. The air defense batteries sprang to life and pounded the flying demons, but some of the Muspell shrugged off the hits and flew on.

When the fire giants reached the fortifications, the runic bands on the walls flared brilliantly and the demons screamed in pain. The rest of the horde continued their assault, climbing ropes and setting ladders, but the glowing runes repelled the huge demons.

Eitri laughed as the Muspell tried climbing, but they were burned each time they got too close to the walls. "Take that ye overgrown imps!" the Rune Lord bellowed gleefully. "Go back ter whatever cesspit ye crawled outta!"

Alex shook his head in amazement.

Trust a dwarf to taunt an army of gigantic demons.

The Muspell screamed in frustration that they couldn't go near the walls, and then began launching vengeful incantations at the battlements. But those fizzled out as they touched the walls, defeated by the power of the Warding Belts.

Alex stabbed a goblin in the chest as it appeared over the parapet. The small, green body slid off the icy blade and Alex wasted no time in cutting the rope that the little monster had used before any of his companions could follow, hearing a satisfying chorus of screams as the rope fell away.

But Alex didn't get to enjoy his small victory. When he looked out across the raging battlefield, his heart sank.

Spread out across the field, there must have been nearly half a dozen burning portals facing the walls. A hellish light spilled out of the demonic gateways, and as he watched, they continued to grow.

When they finally stopped expanding, each was easily large enough for several Muspell to walk through.

Something moved inside the hellish opening and as it drew closer, Alex realized that it was far larger than any of the fire giants.

Suddenly, a beam of pure white light shot out from a distant section of the wall and struck one of the burning portals. There was a blinding flash followed by an otherworldly squeal and tearing sound as the massive rift collapsed into itself.

Alex searched the walls and found the source of the beam. A dwarf War Priest stood atop the parapet with a glowing symbol in her outstretched hand. But before the priest could fire another holy beam, a troglodyte grabbed the dwarf by the ankle and with a vicious tug, pulled her over the wall.

Looking back at the portals, Alex saw a massive dark shape begin to slither out of each of the huge openings. The flexible tubes were thick bands of muscle that expanded as flowed out of the rifts and soared high into the air.

Massive suckers the size of cars covered the bottoms of the huge structures and Alex realized with alarm that they were colossal tentacles.

Each of the impossibly huge appendages was a deep purple color and was so thick that they filled the entire gateway. The limbs crawled toward the sky and stretched hundreds of feet into the air as they continued to flow out of the rippling gateways, and Alex hoped that they all didn't belong to the same creature. Such a titanic monster was impossible to comprehend.

Alex craned his neck to look up at the limbs that swayed in the darkness like living skyscrapers over the tiny figures that battled desperately below them.

"Um… I think we should go," Alex shouted over to Jack who was dueling with a trio of kobolds. Jack finished the three of them off with two quick slashes that decapitated two with one stroke and split the last one in half. He looked up at the titanic appendages and nodded vigorously. "I'm not usually one to run away, but I'm willing to make an exception."

The other defenders must have reached the same conclusion as the humans and dwarves began to flee the walls. "Where ye goin'?" King Varnir shouted. "We can take em!"

"I must side with the humans, me king," Ambrosar rumbled. "We should retreat."

"Retreat?" King Varnir's copper beard bristled in agitation. "Dwarves do no retreat!" he bellowed grandly. Just then, one of the mammoth tentacles descended like a felled tree, slowly at first, and then with growing speed. The earth heaved as the gigantic tentacle completely flattened a fifty-foot section of the wall and everything around it.

King Varnir's eyes bulged. "Retreat it be!"

Alex and Jack rushed down a nearby staircase built into the back of the wall with King Varnir and his retinue close behind. The walls emptied of defenders in moments as the other arms began to descend.

The earth shuddered violently with each colossal strike as the city's defenders tried to get safely away. Not everyone was successful, as hundreds were pulverized by the falling towers of muscle.

The tentacles tore huge rents in the earth as entire swaths of wall and buildings behind them were reduced to rubble. The horde cheered and roared in victory, even as countless numbers of their own warriors were crushed beneath the hellish appendages.

The giant Muspell rushed through the breaches as the rest of the horde flowed over and through what remained of the fortifications. The surviving defenders scattered into the neighborhoods, weary and battered, desperate to find some kind of safety from the terrors they had just witnessed.

Once the fortifications were breached, the entire three-mile length of the great eastern wall quickly fell to the might of the orc horde.

But the armies of Pittsburgh weren't done yet.

All across the rural neighborhoods there had been barricades, traps, and other fortifications put in place for just such an emergency. It was at one of these rally points that Alex, Jack, King Varnir, and his retinue found themselves. Alex guessed that there were about a hundred survivors scattered around them, not to mention the few dozen guards that had been stationed at the barricade.

"Well, now what?" Alex gasped, as he tried to catch his breath from their mad flight from the walls.

"We must find the warlord!" King Varnir growled without hesitation. "He be the key. Cut off the head, an' the body dies."

Jack laughed mirthlessly. "And just how do you propose we do that? If you haven't noticed, we don't know where he is and even if we did, there is still an entire orc horde and an army of giant demons between him and us."

"Ah," King Varnir winked, and touched the side of his nose slyly. "We be makin' him come ter us."

****

Darkness fell quickly on the backside of Mt. Washington. Thus far, the southern defenses had been quiet and the dwarves of the Mount were eager to join their kin in battle. It chafed all the dwarves to be forced to wait and watch as the city battled desperately below them.

They looked on in dismay as the Veterans Gatehouse was destroyed in a brilliant explosion, and later it was hard to miss the impossibly huge tentacles as they pulverized the distant eastern wall.

Gunfire and explosions rang throughout Pittsburgh as the kefali of the Horned Legion flowed down the city streets and were met by the repositioned defenders.

The fighting had moved from one long battle across the wall to dozens of smaller skirmishes between the towering buildings. Harpies and wyverns still wheeled through the air, but their numbers had been decimated by the heavy fire from the air defenses that still targeted anything that came within range. But as the darkness closed in, a host of huge demons soared in from the east.

"We be needin' ter help 'em!" Prince Brokkr rumbled, as the demons landed inside the city and were lost from sight.

"No," Lord Aurvang growled. "Our duty be ter guard the south from these evil pointy-ears."

"And where they be?" Brokkr rumbled and waved at the empty darkness around the Mount. "I be seein' no enemy here. Me thinks the elves deceived us."

Aurvang snorted. "And what would the point o' that been? Ye think they wanted ter die?"

Brokkr scowled. "I'm no fer knowin' what a bloody elf be thinkin'!

They be deceitful creatures by nature."

"True enough, me prince," Aurvang rumbled, "but they be our allies in this. There be no point in deceivin' us."

"Perhaps," Brokkr rumbled his assent, "but I still no be like it… it be feelin'… wrong."

Aurvang nodded as he looked out into the night. "I be feelin' the same."

The pair stood on the inner wall of the Mount and impatiently waited as the rumble of battle echoed up behind them.

The night grew and the dwarves lit torches along the walls to ward off the cold and deepening darkness. After a time, Lord Aurvang realized he couldn't see beyond the outer curtain wall despite his natural dwarven night vision.

The dwarf lord was just about to mention this when a pair of glowing eyes appeared at the edge of the unnatural darkness.

Shouts of alarm spread across the heavily fortified keep as the warriors became aware of the lone pair of eyes in the darkness.

"Finally," Brokkr rumbled eagerly.

Lord Aurvang's brow furrowed as he peered over the battlements. "Could just be a lone creature, er some sort o' forest spirit."

Just then, another pair of eyes appeared next to the first, followed by another, and then another. Suddenly, there were thousands of eerily glowing eyes watching the Mount from the unnatural darkness just beyond the walls.

"Ye were sayin'?" Brokkr rumbled, as he hefted his mighty war hammer.

The eyes stared unblinkingly at the dwarves upon the walls as a rustle sounded behind the pair of dwarves. Brokkr scowled when he saw Battlemage Regulus striding purposefully toward them in his sculpted silver armor. "Yer late," the dwarf prince growled, as the blonde elf joined them upon the battlements.

"A mage is never late," Regulus replied without looking at the dwarves and stared impassively at the army of eyes. "You should be glad we are here at all."

"Glad?" Brokkr snorted derisively. "Ye an' yer cronies be lucky ter be permitted on the Mount," he growled, in reference to the dozen or so

Battlemages that were scattered across the fortifications. The elves had pleaded for more, but the dwarf prince would hear none of it. The Brokkr was confident in his warriors' abilities and the strength of their defenses.

Regulus ignored the jab. "What is the situation?"

"Ye can see the situation, elf," Brokkr growled.

"That I can," Regulus replied smoothly, "and it appears they are coming closer."

The Battlemage's words were proven true as Brokkr watched the countless eyes draw nearer.

The defenders got their first look at their elusive enemy when the front row of figures stepped out of the enchanted darkness.

They were humans, Brokkr saw with surprise. Both men and women, young and old, flowed out of the darkness in a seething mass. The people shambled forward as if drunk, and it was then the dwarf prince noticed their appearances. Grey skin stuck to their cadaver-like bodies as dried blood caked nearly all of them; many were missing limbs or had suffered from some other grotesque injury. There was no possible way any of the humans below should have been able to walk with such grievous wounds. It was then that Prince Brokkr Anvilborn realized what he was seeing.

An army of the undead.

The warriors on the walls came to the same realization and there was a sharp *thwang* as hundreds of flaming crossbow bolts shot into the shambling mob. The bolts themselves didn't cause much damage to the undead since they couldn't feel pain or be killed by anything but a strike to the cranium. However, the elves had provided one important bit of information that the dwarves now used to marvelous effect.

Fire.

The animated corpses' desiccated flesh burned like dry parchment when exposed to the flames.

Hundreds of undead humans burned brightly as they continued their unsteady march up the steep hill toward the dwarven keep. But despite the constant hail of burning crossbow bolts, the army of undead seemed never-ending as more shuffled out of the darkness every moment. Soon, the hillside was covered in them.

The dwarves' rate of fire couldn't keep up, and within minutes the undead had reached the curtain wall.

Prince Brokkr's despair turned to amusement a moment later when he saw the undead clawing futilely at the smooth walls. "Those foolish creatures dun be havin' any siege equipment with 'em!"

The dwarf prince looked up at Regulus and he saw the Battlemage's face turn pale with fright. "What's yer problem? Yer 'Shadowed Ones' don't seem so tough."

"That is because they are *not* the Shadowed Ones." Regulus pointed out at the milling mob with a quivering hand. "Those are."

Brokkr looked back down the hill and immediately saw what the shaken elf was pointing at.

Dozens, perhaps hundreds, of black-cloaked figures were gliding through the growing throng of undead toward the keep. Wisps of darkness trailed along behind them as they moved with an unnatural grace. The crammed undead parted as the shadowy figures passed by.

When the shadows were nearing the walls, the night erupted with brilliant flashes as the Battlemages unleashed a volley of destructive spells at the approaching shadows. A few of the enchantments found their mark and the shadows vanished under the sudden onslaught, but most were either defeated by counter spells or simply avoided with unnatural speed.

When the first shadows reached the walls, they leapt impossibly high to land on the battlements in a single bound. But as they crossed over the wall, the runes set into the stones flared and the shadows that had been clinging to the figures were banished.

Pale elves with glowing eyes and dressed in all-black armor landed gracefully on the walls, apparently unarmed, and were immediately set upon by the dwarven warriors. But the Shadow elves, despite being severely outnumbered, moved with impossible speed and tore into the helpless dwarves with claw and fang.

Fire was no use against the creatures and even a successful strike failed to incapacitate any of the fluid attackers.

Prince Brokkr stared in horror as his warriors were cut apart with ease. "Odin's Beard," the prince cursed. "What manner o' creature be that?"

Regulus drew a slender sword and wand from his belt. "Vampires."

The elf vampires moved along the outer curtain wall like cats surrounded by mice. A few of them fell to brave War Priests and Guardians, but the average warrior had no chance against such creatures.

Battlemages held their ground against the vampires, but there were too few to stop the dark tide and they were forced to retreat.

The gatehouse fell soon after the vampires entered and the undead rushed in as the gates were thrown open.

The undead now swarmed before the inner walls just below Prince Brokkr and his companions on the inner gatehouse.

With the curtain wall fallen, that left only the inner walls and the great keep itself. The warriors were reeling from their sudden defeat, but the loss only seemed to anger the stubborn dwarves.

Dark spells crashed into the inner walls, but the engraved runes protected them from the worst of the damage. The Battlemages fired back with a blistering barrage of their own.

The inner walls were higher than the outer curtain wall and the vampires couldn't leap onto them, a fact that made Prince Brokkr immensely grateful.

He couldn't afford another repeat of the outer wall.

The vampires jumped as high as they could, but were unable to find purchase on the warded walls. Angry, the Shadow elves targeted the heavy gates with their dark spells. The gates were similarly warded and the destructive spells only had moderate effect.

"Get er'y priest an' Guardian; we have ter hold the gate," Brokkr ordered. "That door will no last forever." His warriors were quick to obey and soon there was a large force gathered behind the reinforced door as enemies' spells hammered into it.

"My mages will give you as much time as they can," Regulus said, as a pair of Battlemages approached the gate and some kind of spells flowed into it. Brokkr wasn't sure what they were doing, but whatever it was seemed to be resisting the vampires' spells and the battered door stopped taking damage.

"How long 'el that hold?" Brokkr rumbled.

"A few hours I should think," Regulus replied.

"Loki's balls," Lord Aurvang suddenly cursed as he looked out into the darkness. "We don't be havin' hours."

Brokkr followed his gaze and his heart sank.

Six immense, black shapes, nearly invisible in the darkness, soared toward them on huge, leathery wings. One of the beasts was more than twice the size of the others and its baleful gaze glowed with a hellish light.

The dragons swooped down and torrents of blistering green flame poured out of their fanged mouths as they descended on the Mount.

****

Ted finally stepped out of the Verkstad and into the darkened street wearing his new, plastic armor. His eyes were sore and his back hurt from being bent over his worktable all day. But despite that, he had never felt more confident. The armor had turned out better than he had hoped and he felt ready to take on anything his enemies could throw at him!

Ted jumped as a massive explosion of green fire suddenly erupted on the hill behind him. He looked up to see the Mount bathed in evil green flames.

Thick smoke billowed up from the emerald inferno and an immense black dragon landed on the burning fortress. The colossal beast released an ear-splitting roar and sprayed a gout of green flames high into the air as it bellowed in victory.

Ted stared, dumbstruck, as more dragons swooped out of the roiling black smoke and descended on the embattled city.

CHAPTER 24

A large banner that was bathed in light from several spotlights and depicting the royal heraldry of Clan Anvilborn waived atop a tall flagpole.

Jack didn't like the dwarf monarch's plan, but you couldn't argue with a king, especially a dwarf king. *Besides*, Jack thought as he cut down another troglodyte, *the plan seemed to be working*, just not in the way they had intended.

Creatures had been swarming toward the banner in droves for some time now, but so far there had been no sign of the elusive warlord. King Varnir was confident, however, that the huge oni would find them before long.

A company of dwarf warriors blocked all of the streets around the banner, with human soldiers stationed behind each line of dwarves. Any hostile forces that appeared out of the smoky darkness were immediately riddled with gunfire, until they reached the living barricade of bearded warriors.

Roving bands of goblins, troglodytes, kobolds, and other monsters were all drawn to the brilliantly lit banner, but none of the beasts survived the encounter; that is until a band of misshapen demons appeared.

All of the demons were horrid abominations. Some looked like giant spiders with blades for legs, while others had huge crab-like claws for hands or bodies that were covered in needle-like spines that dripped poison. One exceptionally large demon had four arms and wielded an enormous double-bladed axe in each huge fist.

The stocky warriors created a shield wall as bullets riddled the charging demons. But the bullets had little effect on the hellish creatures and the demons crashed into the dwarves with blade, claw, and fang.

Jack wished he was on the street with the demons as he gutted another poor troglodyte. The gang of alligator-faced monsters pressed in all around, but the indomitable dwarves held their ground as they carved into them. Alex was at his shoulder, stabbing the crested troglodytes with his spear that had a long blade of ice at the tip.

A massive AC-130 gunship suddenly roared overhead as a stream of blistering tracer rounds streaked through the darkness.

Jack was just about to bemoan the pitiful battle when a chorus of gurgling shrieks echoed down the street. He looked up to see a group of bulky demons that resembled enormous toads emerge from the darkness. Their skin was dark red with bladed spikes protruding from their backs and shoulders, and a wide mouth with rows of razor-sharp fangs was set into their chests. Powerfully muscled arms ended in wide, three-fingered hands, tipped with huge claws.

The demon toads charged down the street and as they got closer, a horrible stench wafted before them. Many of the soldiers gagged and the dwarves wrinkled their noses at the odor as they tried to fight off the troglodytes.

The demons reached the back of the troglodyte throng and tore into them with their huge claws. The demons didn't slow as they ripped the poor monsters apart in their haste to reach the defenders.

A troglodyte sorcerer tried to use a fireball to clear a path through the dwarves in a desperate attempt to escape the trap, but the fireball rebounded off a shield summoned by one of the humans. The ball of flames struck the sorcerer and engulfed him in searing flames.

The troglodytes were quickly exterminated, caught between the unmoving wall of dwarven warriors and the raging demons. As the last troglodytes fell, the bloodthirsty demons threw themselves at the dwarves in a frenzy.

The hellish monsters used their wide bulk and thick hide to barrel through the dwarven shield wall and scatter the defenders' line. Chaos erupted as all semblance of order broke down and the street became a free-for-all.

Jack lost sight of Alex as a demon lunged at him. He parried the blow with his oversized katana but was forced to stay on the defensive as the demon slashed at him faster than Jack would have thought possible for such a stocky beast.

The bark of gunfire and the clash of steel were like music to Jack's ears. The energy of the encounter flowed around him and he breathed in the sweet smell of blood and sharp tang of gunpowder that mixed with the cloying stink of the demons. His heart raced and adrenalin flowed as the excitement of battle coursed through him.

Jack danced to the sweet sounds of battle even as a second demon charged in beside the first. He flowed from one stance to another, in time with the music, expertly avoiding the sweeping claws of both demons. His blade bit deep into the arm of one demon and its blood splashed across Jack's face.

The taste of blood sent a shiver through Jack and his golden eyes dilated with pleasure. A terrible hunger filled him and Jack didn't fight it, he embraced it.

Jack's body suddenly expanded and in a matter of moments, a huge werewolf had taken his place.

Jack slashed one of the demons across the face and he suddenly realized that his sword now fit perfectly in his enlarged hands. The weapon sang to him and the wolf responded.

Jack howled lustily as the spirit of the soul sword and the wolf spirit became one. Power, like Jack had never experienced, flowed through him. Time seemed to slow around him as his perception changed.

The blade glowed hungrily as Jack sliced the demons apart before they realized what had happened. The huge, armored werewolf left two piles of twitching flesh behind as he charged through the battle like a tornado, driving his blade into every demon that crossed his path.

Nothing could stop his crazed bloodlust and soon every demon lay dead or dying. Stinking blood covered Jack and he howled hungrily, eager for more. His heightened senses caught movement in the darkness down the street and he charged ahead, heedless of the danger. Several shapes moved through the smoky night and Jack lunged at them.

The obscured shapes became a group of battered humans as Jack's blade sliced through the air. Sudden realization struck him and Jack just barely managed to shift his momentum in time to avoid decapitating one of the men.

Horror filled the surprised humans and they all immediately raised their weapons as the huge wolfman in orcish armor with a hellishly glowing blade appeared before them. But before the terrified humans could fire, a voice shouted from the darkness. "Wait! Don't shoot!"

The humans paused, just long enough for Alex to come rushing out of the smoke to stand beside Jack. "He's on our side," Alex said, as he put his hand on the big werewolf.

"Well, he almost killed us!" one of the humans shouted.

Jack bared his fangs. "You're lucky it was almost," he snarled, and the humans all took a frightened step back. Jack put on a good show, but deep down he was horrified that he had nearly killed his allies and fellow humans. He put a clamp on the wolf inside him and vowed to never let it take ahold like that again.

Such vows were easier made than kept.

"Come on." Alex beckoned them to follow him and the group hesitated until a roar in the darkness motivated them to move. Jack brought up the rear, keeping an eye, and nose, out for any possible dangers.

There were fires burning all over the town as the horde burned everything they came across. Jack could see other points of light out in the darkness that told him where the other strongholds were, but none were close and trying to reach any of them through the roaming warriors of the horde would be suicide.

It looked like they were stuck here.

They made it back to their outpost without incident, but when they arrived, several other streets were struggling to hold off a large group of hobgoblins. Jack resisted the urge to rush over and join the fray as Alex took them to the lone cleric in the center of the outpost.

As the cleric administered to the wounded, Alex asked them questions. "How does the rest of this section of the city fare?"

One of the survivors shrugged helplessly. "Burning mostly. And crawling with monsters," she shuddered. "Our outpost was overrun and we're the only survivors."

"What happened to you?" Alex asked with concern.

The woman rubbed her eyes wearily. "We were holding the lines just fine against the smaller monsters, but then the orcs arrived. They came with sorcerers and the largest orc I have ever seen. He was huge and red, and he had this… like mechanical suit or something."

Nearby, King Varnir perked up. "Did ye say big 'n red?"

"Yes…" the woman replied curiously, "and he had a big flag on his back with an ugly storm cloud or something."

"Stormtusk," King Varnir breathed eagerly. "He be close!"

"Then let's go get him," Werewolf Jack snarled.

But the dwarf king shook his bearded head. "No. We will be remainin' here."

"But why?" Jack whined. "If he is close we can disrupt his whole horde!"

"Because dwarves defend," King Varnir rumbled dangerously. "It be foolish ter go wanderin' off in the hopes o' findin' our quarry. He will be comin' ter us, don't ye doubt."

****

The Mount burned with malevolent green flames as corpses rolled down Mt. Washington in a putrid tide. It was to Ted's revulsion that he realized the bodies weren't actually dead.

The undead lurched to their feet once they stopped rolling and continued to shamble, unopposed, across the Fort Pitt, Smithfield Street, and Liberty bridges.

With the northern wall broken and the Isfet striking ever deeper into the city, the southern wall had been abandoned and the defenders repositioned to strong points throughout the city. But not everyone had reached those locations and skirmishes were being fought all across the streets.

Ted had hurried away from the deserted wall and found a company of elven Hoplites on the march that he gladly joined up with. They were headed deeper into the city where they had heard that a group of human soldiers had become surrounded by kefali.

Scattered groups of harpies and a few wyverns still battled the griffin riders in the skies above Pittsburgh as the anti-aircraft batteries made short work of any approaching aerial threats. The midair battle was steeply in the defenders' favor until the gigantic dragons swooped in.

Heavy fire riddled the enormous beasts as they soared between the skyscrapers, but the dragon's scales were proof against much of the gunfire.

Ted looked up to see one of the dragons, which was easily twice the size of the largest wyvern, breathe a gout of white-hot flames onto a rooftop and incinerate the weapons platform stationed there. The platform erupted in a series of explosions as the ammunition cooked off and the dragon swooped away, already searching for another target.

The ring of small-arms fire brought Ted's attention back to the ground and as they rounded a corner, they came upon a sprawling battle.

The plaza they entered had once been surrounded by beautiful glass and steel buildings, but now most of the glass panels were broken from the bullets and spells being traded between the opposing forces. A double line of elven halberdiers anchored the center of the line while Steel City Guards held the flanks against an overwhelming force of kefali warriors.

The Isfet were mostly enormous minotaur warriors armed with oversized swords and battleaxes with several of the cat-like Feloran Lector Priests providing magical support that countered the elven mages and gifted humans.

Tight ranks of halberdiers used their long weapons to keep the huge kefali at bay. They stabbed with the halberd's long spike and when they withdrew, they used the concave axe blade to hook the minotaurs and pull them forward, making easier targets for their comrades. The strategy was sound and would have decimated any other foe. But the minotaurs were not easily moved and used their great size to try and bull their way into the lines in an attempt to break the tight elven formation.

The Hoplites and Ted quickly formed a solid phalanx and leveled their spears as they advanced on the occupied kefali's rear. Ted and the elves caught the kefali completely by surprise and drove hard into their flank, killing scores of the monsters before the Isfet realized the danger behind them.

Ted pulled his darkened safety goggles down to protect his eyes as he took aim. His plazmax blazed to life as he fired into the packed masses of minotaurs. The smell of burnt flesh and singed hair filled the air as the scorching bolts seared through the horned monsters.

Caught between the two forces, the lightly armored kefali were easy prey for the stabbing spikes and spears of the disciplined elves. The Isfet fought wildly, desperate to escape, but to no avail. The elves and humans closed the vice and slaughtered every last Isfet. The Lector Priests and their guards were the last to fall, wielding their magic frantically. But they, too, were cut down by spell and blade.

The fight was short but intense, and the blade of Ted's plazmax glowed white hot, despite the flexible pipes running a constant stream of coolant to regulate the temperature. Ted grinned as the last kefali fell and he carefully pulled up his goggles. The plazmax had performed remarkably well for its first official field test.

The two forces met in the middle of the ruined plaza atop a pile of furry corpses. But the victory was short-lived as a shout from the rear caused everyone to turn.

A shuffling mob of undead lumbered toward them down one of the connecting streets, but Ted wasn't concerned.

There was only one group of them after all.

Another shout from the other side made everyone turn again. Ted groaned as he saw another mob of shuffling undead coming down the opposite street.

Now, they were caught between two forces.

Yet Ted still wasn't concerned. The mindless zombies would be easy pickings for the tightly packed ranks of skilled defenders. Combined with the mages and gifted humans, there was little to fear.

That was until more shouts of warning sprang up from all around as more undead were spotted coming down other roads. Within moments, it became dreadfully apparent that all six streets were filled with undead as they converged on the plaza.

One of the elven commanders, a Paladin named Roxana - Ted thought was her name - began shouting orders and the combined forces immediately took action. They formed a compact circle that alternated spears and halberds around the outer edge like a giant porcupine, and Ted found himself in the second row since his plazmax was technically a polearm. He didn't mind, however, since his time in the SCA had prepared him well for the grind of polearm combat.

The undead came to an abrupt halt some twenty yards away and remained eerily silent as their dead eyes stared at the surrounded defenders.

"What are they waiting for?" Ted growled after a tense minute.

His question was answered a few moments later when, starting at the back of the mob, their eyes began to glow a sickly yellowish green.

"What is going on?" Ted breathed at the strange sight.

Many of the elves gripped their weapons tighter as the strange light flowed forward and infected every undead around the plaza.

"The Shadowed Ones have arrived," a nearby mage muttered grimly.

At first Ted didn't see anything different, but then he noticed the dark shadows gliding through the throng. Wherever the shadows passed, the eyes of the undead became alight.

The undead became visibly agitated as their eyes lit up, almost as if they strained to move. Within a few heartbeats, every undead creature's eyes were glowing and they twitched erratically in place.

"What does it mean?" Ted whispered, half afraid of the answer.

"Normally, the undead are mindless constructs that only exist to kill," the mage answered softly. "But when a vampire nears, they can exert their will on the undead and give them strength and purpose." The mage nodded toward the silent mob. "It is the vampires' will that you see causing the eyes to glow. The dead creatures are now being controlled."

"Lovely," Ted groaned.

As if normal undead weren't bad enough.

****

Kiba'Nadare dashed down the dark boulevards with Liz and Emily clinging to her back. Bodies littered the streets and signs of battle were everywhere. But the fighting had moved away from this section, leaving only ruins behind.

A few streetlights were still working, providing islands of illumination. Liz glanced back over her shoulder and to her relief she didn't see anything behind them. The Destroyer had given chase after they had made their escape, but he was nowhere in sight.

"I think we lost him," Liz shouted over the rush of wind in their faces as the huge tiger raced along.

"Good," Emily shouted back. "He was starting to annoy me."

Liz chuckled, "Everyone annoys you."

"That's because people suck," Emily hollered over the wind. "Besides, we have more important things to do."

"Oh, yeah?" Liz asked in mild surprise. "And what is that?"

"We need to get to the Grove and warn Belenos that The Destroyer is sending his goons to find the Seal," Emily answered grimly.

"I thought the Seal was still lost?" Liz asked in confusion.

"It was," Emily admitted, "until earlier today when Jack and I found a pair of Druids in the woods beyond the walls. We rescued them from a gang of wendigo and escorted them back to the Grove. It was only after we brought them to the High Druid that we learned they carried the Seal."

Liz looked over her shoulder and glared at Emily. "Why am I just learning about this now?"

"Because we were sworn to secrecy," Emily answered. "The less people to know about the Seal, the safer it would be. Or so we thought…"

"That's just wonderful," Liz growled. "Somehow they know we have the Seal and now we have to ride the whole way to Frick Park and warn somebody."

"No," Emily said. "After the Druids answered the call to war, the Grove moved to Schenley Park so that -"

Her words were cut short by a sudden clatter of heavy hooves and a rumbling growl that echoed down a nearby street. The noise grew into a thunderous racket as an enormous golden chariot pulled by armored bulls burst from the intersecting street just as they were racing by.

Liz and Emily were nearly flung off the tiger's back as the huge cat leapt aside to avoid the chariot, barely missing the spinning blades protruding from the wheels.

Liz held on for dear life as she bent over the cat's neck and willed her to run faster.

It could have just been coincidence, but the great tiger did get a burst of speed and bound ahead of the chariot.

The Destroyer roared as he eagerly gave chase once again.

Emily released her grip on Kiba'Nadare's thick fur and drew her bow. Using only her legs to hold on, Emily turned and fired at the pursuing Destroyer. But she cursed as the arrows bounced harmlessly off a magical shield surrounding the chariot. Her next shot was aimed not at The Destroyer, but one of the huge bulls pulling the chariot. To her dismay, she discovered that a magical field protected them as well.

"Seriously?" Emily growled, as she slung her bow and drew her scepter instead.

The Destroyer saw the movement and laughed as he aimed the long *was* scepter at his prey. A searing red bolt flashed from the eyes of the stylized animal head on the staff. Emily got her scepter up just before the red bolt and it exploded against a shimmering emerald field.

Emily stared in surprise at the unexpected development. "Well, that was new," she breathed, as The Destroyer howled in rage at his shot being defeated. Another red bolt leapt from The Destroyer's staff, but this time the huge tiger sprang away.

Emily and the golden demigod traded blows while they raced down the ruined street.

Suddenly, Kiba'Nadare took a sharp turn and bounded down a side street. But instead of another abandoned road, they found a huge battle filling the avenue.

To Liz's surprise, the battle was being fought between a legion of kefali and a sea of undead. She didn't really want to go near that confrontation, but with The Destroyer coming up from behind, they didn't have much choice, so they charged into the fray.

The huge tiger darted through the melee like an eel and jumped onto abandoned cars and rubble whenever possible. The Destroyer, on the other hand, plowed straight into the combatants, heedlessly trampling his own Isfet and undead alike. The spinning blades on the chariot's wheels carved a wide swath through the warriors, leaving a trail of dead in his wake.

Kiba'Nadare darted through the chaotic battlefield, while Liz used her plasma pistol to remove any creature that got in their way. They made rapid progress and gradually outdistanced The Destroyer as the sea of bodies slowly bogged him down.

In the darkness above, a dragon was suddenly hit by a spear of light and the gigantic beast crashed into the skyscraper above them. Huge chunks of concrete and glass rained down around them as Liz and Emily clung to the tiger's back as she dodged through the falling debris. But despite the great cat's amazing agility, a large block of concrete slammed into Kiba'Nadare's hindquarters.

The huge tiger howled in pain as she tried to keep running but was forced to slow down. Liz quickly whispered a soft prayer and the healing light flowed into the great cat. The injury faded and the tiger roared gratefully before bounding off again.

They escaped the last of the falling debris and when Liz looked back she didn't see the golden demigod anywhere. Hopefully, they escaped him for good this time. But they still needed to reach the Grove and warn them that the Seal was in danger from more than just the Shadow elves.

There was a loud bang and then an explosion suddenly ripped into the warriors, so close that pieces of debris pelted them.

Liz looked down the street and saw that a tank had pulled up into the next intersection with a platoon of soldiers and had blocked the road ahead.

Flames billowed out from the tank's main cannon as it fired again and another explosion ripped into the packed warriors. Liz briefly considered heading toward the soldiers, but she realized that they probably wouldn't recognize the giant tiger running at them as a friend and would likely open fire on them.

So instead, Liz guided the great cat toward a nearby parking garage. They raced through the last of the battling factions and ducked into the garage apparently just in time, for a moment later the line of soldiers opened fire and a hail of bullets ripped into the kefali and undead.

They rushed through the parking garage and out of the other side but came to an abrupt halt when they saw an enormous demon striding down the street. It was headed for another tank that had blockaded the road similar to the one on the other side of the garage.

The tank fired and an explosion cleaved into the side of the hideous demon. But the demon ignored the gruesome wound and continued its charge.

Caught between the charging demon and the tank, Kiba'Nadare spun around and scurried back into the relative safety of the garage. With both entrances blocked, the great cat bound up the spiral ramp and eventually emerged on the roof.

The darkness above was a riot of colors as spells cascaded through the air and struck beasts and buildings alike. It was pure chaos as packs of harpies clawed at both wyverns and griffins while the gigantic dragons soared between the buildings, killing indiscriminately.

A griffin rider came into view as it banked around a building and a moment later, a pair of wyverns appeared as they chased the griffin. The wyverns proved faster and more agile and were quickly catching up. But before they could reach their quarry, a dark red dragon dove out of the darkness.

The dragon dwarfed its smaller wyvern cousins as it slammed into the back of one of the beasts. Huge claws raked the wyvern's back and one of its leathery wings was ripped off. The smaller beast shrieked in pain as it plummeted from the sky. The other wyvern turned to face the new threat, but the dragon breathed a cone of fire and the wyvern was engulfed in flames.

Before the charred wyvern could hit the ground, the dragon turned its attention to the griffin. The rider released a volley of multicolored darts that slammed into the dragon's face, but the gigantic monster didn't slow. The griffin banked hard and disappeared behind another building with the dragon close behind.

A series of bright flashes and loud bangs in the sky from the opposite direction drew Liz away from the scene unfolding before her. She heard Emily gasp just before she laid eyes on the battle unfolding in the darkness above the city.

An immense black dragon, far larger than all the others, landed heavily on top of the largest skyscraper in the city and the huge building groaned under the strain as thick claws dug into the steel beams. A pack of griffin riders darted around the titanic monster like a swarm of angry bees.

The dragon breathed gouts of brilliant green flame that incinerated one of the griffins in a heartbeat. Spells from the riders slammed into the dragon's huge body, but nothing seemed to harm the behemoth.

One of the griffins dove in and tried to rake the dragon with its claws, but the griffin's claws couldn't penetrate the heavy scales. The dragon swiped the pesky griffin away like it was brushing off an insect. The griffin and rider flew through the air and slammed into a building, shattering glass and vanishing inside.

A pair of griffins dove at the dragon's huge head, but the beast simply unleashed its fiery breath and the smoking corpses plummeted to earth. More griffins swooped in and spells hammered the dragons face and body, but the monster remained unharmed and crushed another griffin with a lazy swipe of its huge tail.

"We have to do something!" Emily cried in dismay at the ease at which the dragon killed the brave griffins and their riders.

"Like what?" Liz replied sullenly. "What could even hurt that thing?"

"Another dragon?" Emily offered, as she stared up at the mighty black dragon and clutched the pendant around her neck.

Liz laughed darkly. "I don't suppose you have one of those in your pocket, do you?"

"No," Emily replied, "but I know where to get one."

"What!?" Liz rounded on her friend. "What are you talking about?"

Emily took a deep breath and carefully unwound the headscarf that she hadn't removed since coming back from her travels with the Druids. Her black hair cascaded passed her shoulders in tight ringlets as the scarf was pulled away.

Liz gasped.

Protruding from Emily's brow above her temples, were two small horns! They swept back and were a strange, transparent blue color, almost like glass.

Liz stared, dumbstruck.

"Well," Emily asked anxiously. "What do you think?"

The great black dragon on the skyscraper roared and incinerated a group of wyverns that had gotten too close.

The roar shook Liz from her paralysis. "Are you telling me you're a dragon?"

"Of course not," Emily replied. "But I can call one..."

"Then do it," Liz ordered, as another griffin rider was knocked from the dark sky.

A strange roar erupted from behind them and Emily smiled. "I already did."

Liz spun around and looked up to see four new dragons flying toward them. Where the ones currently attacking the city were either black, red or green in color, these four were quite different. Two of them were a deep bronze, while the third was a brilliant silver. But the fourth and largest dragon had bluish metallic scales streaked with various colors that had the same glassy appearance as Emily's horns.

The three smaller dragons soared over the garage and engaged the colossal black dragon. Lightning erupted from the bronze dragons and the silver dragon exhaled an icy blast.

The lightning and ice crashed into the immense black dragon and it roared angrily as it leapt into the dark sky, its great wings vibrating the air with the powerful beats. The three smaller dragons took off away from the city and the black behemoth followed, eager to make its smaller kin pay for daring to attack it.

The glassy dragon landed on the garage and the sturdy building groaned under its weight. Only slightly smaller than the colossal black dragon, this dragon still cut an impressive figure. The crystalline scales reflected the light from the fires burning across the embattled city as the dragon spoke in a powerful voice.

"It is good you called, Kaolru," the dragon boomed. "Phlebolith must be dealt with."

Liz fought hard to keep Kiba'Nadare from running away as the huge dragon crouched down to where its massive head nearly rested on the ground.

"Come," the mighty dragon ordered. "We are stronger together and it will take us both to overcome the Blightwing."

Without hesitating, Emily slid off the uneasy tiger and scampered onto the mighty dragon's back. She looked tiny, perched on the dragon's broad back as it stood and stretched its immense wings.

The tiger backed up nervously as Liz struggled to keep the big animal calm.

"Get to the Seal!" Emily yelled from the dragon's back. "Don't let those monsters have it!"

"I will," Liz shouted back, as the massive dragon suddenly jumped, and its heavy wings beat the air as it took to the sky.

Liz watched the dragon fly away over the city in disbelief over what had just happened.

Emily had a dragon!?

How did that happen?

When? Where did it come from?

There were so many questions tumbling around in her mind that it took her some time to realize the other sensation she was feeling.

It started out faint at first, but the knot of emotions in the back of her mind grew stronger with every passing moment and Liz's heart filled with joy.

He was alive!

CHAPTER 25

There was only darkness and pain.

A great weight pressed in around him, pinning his arms and legs and making it impossible to move. Then, there was a heavy scraping sound and a flickering firelight suddenly pierced his vision.

Mike groaned as the rubble was pulled off him by a pair of enormous grey hands. He blinked rapidly to clear his sight and found the huge Hathi Warden, LuHark, smiling down at him.

"You humans are tough little creatures," she trumpeted happily, as she grabbed Mike by the shoulders and pulled him out of the rubble. A faint wave of healing passed through him and took away nearly all of his aches and pains.

"Thanks," Mike groaned, as he stood up beside the elephant-like kefali. Looking down, Mike saw that his new armor was a battered wreck. One of the magnetic pauldrons had been ripped away and several of the small shock absorbers around his high gorget were either broken or missing. But despite the missing pieces and numerous dents, the armor had survived the explosion surprisingly well, and more importantly, it had helped to keep him alive.

"What happened?" Mike asked, as he looked around and saw that night had fallen. The other two Wardens stood nearby and he saw that they were on the edge of a huge crater where the Veterans Gatehouse had once stood. He could hear the sounds of gunfire and explosions coming from deeper within the city but saw no other sign of life.

Panic filled him for a moment before he realized he could still feel Liz in the back of his mind and knew that she still lived. She was deeper within the city and moving away from him. He could tell she was desperate and confused, but at what, he couldn't tell. Relieved that she was safe for the time being, Mike looked over the ruins with a critical eye. "And how did you even find me in all this?" He motioned to all the rubble and debris scattered around the crater.

"Malek lived up to his name and destroyed the gatehouse, allowing the Isfet to enter the city," Brigit answered, as she carefully picked her way toward him through the debris. "And we found you with this." She held up a pendant bearing the strange angular symbol of the Wardens, identical to the one that hung around Mike's neck.

"Aye," Rodan rumbled close behind the blonde elf. "All the walls have fallen. The city be lost."

"All is not lost," Brigit retorted sharply. "There is always hope." She stepped closer to Mike and held Rikr Foerah out to him. "You will be needing this."

Mike took the offered impact mace gratefully. "What do we need to do?"

"We sensed the presence of a Demon Lord entering this plane," LuHark answered grimly. "It must be destroyed."

"Then let's go find it," Mike said eagerly. He turned and headed into the city, but Brigit placed a firm hand on his shoulder and stopped him. When Mike turned back in confusion the elf smiled. "I have a better idea."

Brigit brought two fingers to her lips and whistled four times. At first nothing happened, but then a few moments later, four griffins swooped out of the dark sky.

"Oh, dear," LuHark sighed mournfully.

Rodan scowled at Brigit. "Ye know we don't like ter fly," he growled in annoyance.

"I know," Brigit replied curtly, "but we do not have the time to fight our way to the demon. We must kill it quickly and then reach the Seal before the Shadowed Ones do."

"We found the Seal?" Mike asked.

"Indeed," LuHark answered. "It was actually two of your friends, Emily and Jack, that secured it."

Mike stared at her in confusion and Brigit waved it away. "We will explain on the way."

"Very well," Mike shrugged indifferently. He knew that learning how his friends came to possess the Seal was secondary to them protecting it, although he was annoyed that they hadn't told him. "Why don't we split up?" he offered, as the four griffins landed beside them.

"Split up?" Rodan laughed mirthlessly. "Foolish human. A Demon Lord alone be more than a match fer the four o' us. An' trust me, it will no be alone."

Mike scowled, not liking being called foolish, but the dwarf was right. He was far out of his element here and the best he could hope to do was help the Wardens with their quest. It was then that Mike actually looked at the four griffins that now stood around them and he was surprised that he actually recognized two of them.

One was the mighty Longmane, pale leader of the griffins, and the other was Eagle Feather. Mike wasn't sure how he knew who it was, since most griffins looked remarkably similar, but somehow, he recognized Eagle Feather. All four griffins looked resplendent in their new armor and each had a reinforced saddle strapped securely to their broad backs.

Brigit wasted no time and quickly pulled herself up onto one of the griffins. Rodan grumbled to himself but followed Brigit's lead and mounted another of the griffins. But LuHark eyed Longmane dubiously and the mighty griffin didn't seem thrilled at the prospect of carrying the large Hathi.

"Oh, just get on already," Brigit snapped. "We haven't got all night."

LuHark muttered something under her breath as she carefully hauled herself onto Longmane's back. The leader of the griffins didn't complain as the towering elephant-like Warden settled into the groaning saddle.

Mike had started to pull himself onto Eagle Feather when he had an idea and dropped back to the ground.

"What are ye doin'?" Rodan rumbled in annoyance, but Mike ignored him and began a hurried search of the ruins around them. He quickly found what he was looking for and pulled an M4 carbine from a dead soldier's grip. Mike then stuffed as many magazines of ammo into his belt pouches as would fit before returning to Eagle Feather and hauling himself up.

With everyone mounted up, Longmane leapt into the air despite his heavy burden and the other griffins followed his lead. The four griffins and their riders soared away, heading deeper into the city and vanishing into the darkness.

****

The last human soldier fell and Alex suddenly realized he was alone.

He twisted away from the slashing orc blade and countered with a thrust of his staff. The icy blade tip took the orc warrior in the throat and it collapsed with a wet gurgle.

More orc warriors poured down the dark street, their black armor making them difficult to see. But Alex didn't rely on his sight alone. He could hear the rattle of their armor, the tread of their boots, and even the hiss of their blades slicing through the air. He could feel the vibrations of their footsteps, the breath of air as they moved, and even smell their foul stink that announced their location like a beacon to his honed senses.

Alex channeled his pneuma as the orcs closed in and he lost himself in its power. What he couldn't see, he could hear. What he couldn't hear, he could feel. And what he couldn't feel, he could smell. His focus became razor-sharp and as the first orc reached him, Alex struck the green-skinned warrior before the orc could raise its sword.

The icy blade sliced through the warrior's neck as Alex suddenly stepped forward, directly into the charging orcs and catching them completely by surprise.

That momentary surprise was all that Alex needed as he waded into their midst, his staff a blur. The icy tip scraped ineffectively off their armor, but a few strikes found their mark and two of the orcs fell. The others recovered quickly and Alex suddenly found himself surrounded by slashing orc blades.

He spun, twisted, ducked, and dodged wildly as the orcs hacked at him from every angle. But none could touch him. His enchanted staff whistled through the air as he struck back when the opportunity presented itself. A swift stab under the upraised arm of one orc pierced its heart and it fell dead before Alex parried a slash from another warrior. A quick riposte and the icy blade punctured the orc's eye and buried itself in the warrior's skull. When Alex pulled the staff back, the ice blade abruptly snapped.

A katana sliced at Alex's head and the broken ice blade rapidly melted away as he brought his staff up to block. The orc blade struck the staff and when it did, Alex called upon its powers.

Lightning sparked at the point of contact and traveled up the sword. The electric shock entered the warrior and the power of the discharging energy threw the orc backwards. His twitching body crashed to the ground and spasmed uncontrollably.

Their friend's electrocution didn't deter the other orcs in the least. They drove in harder than ever and the electrified staff sent many of them crashing to the ground in twitching heaps. The shocks weren't necessarily fatal, however, and several of the warriors got back to their feet and rejoined the fight, although they were now more cautious in their approach.

The orcs slashed and stabbed from all sides and it was everything Alex could do to keep them at bay. He kicked one in its ugly face and, continuing the motion, brought his staff around in a wide arc that knocked several orcs back.

Desperate for some room, Alex planted his foot on a stunned orc's back and leapt high into the air. He brought his enchanted staff over his head and as he landed, he slammed the staff into the road. A shockwave of asphalt and stone radiated outward, sending orc warriors flying in a spray of debris.

Dust and smoke obscured his vision and Alex seemed suddenly alone in the darkness. But the crunch of gravel and creak of armor told him otherwise.

A huge orc wielding a tall naginata appeared out of the smoke and rushed Alex. The pole weapon was longer than his staff and the nearly two-foot-long blade made the orc's reach even greater.

The icy spearhead reformed on the staff as Alex spun out from the naginata's path. He slashed at the warrior as he danced away, but the orc was quick and easily blocked the strike. They traded blows and Alex came to realize that this was a far more skilled opponent than the others, and when another orc appeared out of the smoke, Alex suddenly found himself in trouble.

It took all of his skill to keep the naginata-wielding orc at bay, and now even more orcs were appearing. Alex realized he had to end this contest quickly, before he was overwhelmed.

The next strike that landed on the staff, Alex summoned the electricity and it traveled up the blade, but it ended there as Alex realized to his dismay that the naginata pole was wood. But Alex had a sudden idea and called on the staff's power once more.

The opposite end of the enchanted staff began to glow a cherry red as what appeared to be lava abruptly bubbled up and formed a crude blade. Alex reversed his grip and attacked with the burning blade with a flurry of quick slices.

The orc's wooden shaft began to smoke and char where the superheated blade touched it.

Realizing Alex's strategy, the orc adjusted his tactics and on Alex's next strike, he raised his arms in order to lower the blade so that it caught the burning weapon instead of the shaft, just as Alex had hoped.

Reversing his swing before it struck, Alex stepped in close and came in under the orcs upraised arms. Seeing the feint, the orc tried to recover but Alex was faster. The icy blade came in low and sliced up, catching the orc warrior in the groin and continued until it ripped through his chest. The orc's insides spilled out onto the shattered road and a moment later the gutted warrior collapsed.

Alex didn't have time to savor his victory as another orc slashed at him before the dying warrior had hit the ground. He ducked the blow and stabbed the orc in the leg. The orc bellowed in agony and tried to rush him, but the wounded leg slowed its movement and Alex easily sidestepped the clumsy charge. As the orc barreled by, Alex spun the staff around and sliced the warrior across the back, carving through the armor and severing its spine.

Four more orcs charged through the smoke and before they could reach him, Alex whipped the staff around him and icy darts erupted from the tip. The darts flew through the air and slammed into the surprised orcs. All four fell with spears of ice sticking out of their chests and Alex was alone again.

An eerie howl echoed down the street and a moment later a menacing creature bound out of the darkness. The huge, armored werewolf stopped beside Alex and eyed the carnage around him.

"I'm impressed," Jack growled. "I didn't think you would make it after we got separated."

Alex smiled as he wiped sweat from his brow. "Your faith in me is… encouraging."

"No time fer small talk," Ambrosar rumbled, as he followed Jack's path out of the darkness. The Chief Guardian stomped through the smoke and a group of armed dwarves and humans followed him.

A building suddenly exploded a few houses away and the light of the fire illuminated a gang of huge orcs surrounding a massive monster with red skin that was connected to a mechanical exoskeleton.

They had found him!

The warlord had arrived.

****

The tide of undead crashed into the circular phalanx of elven steel.

Ted had never seen such complete disregard for one's safety. Even the creatures under the sway of orcs at least tried not to get hit. But these undead had no such concerns, Ted realized.

They were already dead after all.

Spears and halberds stabbed and slashed the charging throng, but the undead just kept coming. Ted's shorter plazmax glowed cherry red as the heated blade carved into any undead that pressed in too close.

Stabbing the creatures had little effect, but it did keep them from getting any closer. Bullets whizzed through the air, but only those rare impacts with a skull resulted in a zombie that didn't get back up. The real damage came from the beams of holy light and arcing fireballs from the priests and mages that scoured the undead ranks. However, the sheer weight of numbers was preventing the phalanx from retracting their weapons and the bodies began dragging the weapons down.

The undead surged forward and threw themselves into the bristling rows of polearms, successfully skewering themselves and trapping the long weapons inside them.

Shouts of alarm spread through the defenders as the impossibly dark shadows suddenly flowed through the masses of undead and converged on the besieged forces.

The shadows moved with otherworldly speed and before the defenders could react, the vampires struck. Like death incarnate, the Shadow elves ripped into the phalanx with spell and claw. Clouds of noxious red mist choked anyone caught in their path, and black ropes entangled arms and legs making easy prey for the ravenous undead. Purple lightning charred brave warriors alive inside their armor and swarms of bats served as distractions, allowing the enemy precious time to get in close.

The phalanx broke apart under the onslaught and the warriors dropped their spears and halberds and drew short swords. The undead howled and rushed in, eager for blood.

All order broke down as it became everyone for themselves. Ted obliterated scores of undead with several blasts of his plasma cannon before the battle became too chaotic and he risked hitting his own men. The first zombie to cross his path got a searing blade to the skull and the next was swiftly decapitated.

Ted lashed out in all directions, caught in the middle of the swirling battle. Claws and fangs reached out from every angle and Ted needed every ounce of skill he could muster to fend them off.

His arms were getting heavy as he fought off the reaching claws of undead for what seemed like an eternity.

Was there no end to these cursed creatures?

Ted saw the soldier beside him get his throat ripped out and then, to his horror, the fallen soldier arose a moment later with glowing eyes. The undead soldier lunged at Ted and he quickly summoned a wall of flames that consumed the poor creature.

Ted suddenly realized why defenders couldn't seem to gain any ground. As soon as one of them fell, they got back up as zombies! How could you fight against an enemy that used your losses against you? Now, Ted understood why the elves had been so adamant that these Shadowed Ones were the most dangerous. Defeating an enemy that grew stronger as you grew weaker would be nearly impossible to overcome. *But there must be a way,* Ted thought. *The elves had defeated them once before.*

He saw an elven priestess nearby that had a blazing holy symbol clenched in her fist. Any undead that came close were reduced to ash when exposed directly to the light. Ted hoped that she could help him. "How do we stop them from rising again?" Ted shouted over the noise of battle.

The priestess grabbed a wounded soldier that had his arm ripped off and healed it with a touch before she looked up at Ted. "We must kill the lich that is resurrecting them," she shouted back. "That is the only way to stop them."

A group of zombies rushed Ted and the battle quickly swept him away from the priestess. He hacked away at the undead with his plazmax, unwilling to waste any more energy than he had to on spells. He needed all his strength if he was to find this lich and kill it. The only problem was, he had no idea what this lich looked like.

A monster suddenly leapt out of the swirling battle and raked its long claws across Ted's plastic breastplate. This creature wasn't the usual undead. Its flesh was a pale grey and its limbs were elongated. Its fingers ended in extended claws and a mouth that was too wide was filled with rows of needle-like teeth. Its eyes burned with a wild hunger and an unnaturally long tongue hung out of its mouth.

Ted recognized the undead creature for what it was; a ghoul.

The ghoul shrieked madly as it came at him. Ted dodged the first two swings and he used the butt of his plazmax to knock the ghoul off balance. But this creature was more agile than it appeared and before Ted could strike, the ghoul dove away on all fours before pouncing at him again.

Ted was unprepared for such a quick counter and he just got his weapon up in time to hold the ghoul at bay. The creature shrieked and its tongue lashed out and scored a long cut on Ted's cheek. Ted cried out and flung the creature away as he recoiled from the surprising attack.

The ghoul hissed gleefully as it licked the blood from its tongue and prepared to pounce again. But before the creature could strike, a figure in silver armor appeared out of the raging battle and with a sweeping stroke of a glowing sword, parted the ghoul's head from its shoulders.

The body hit the ground and began to bubble and hiss as it decomposed within moments. Ted looked up from the puddle and had enough time to nod his thanks to the female elf Paladin before more undead charged in.

Ted fought his way through the undead and the battle carried him toward the outer edge of the plaza. So far, he hadn't seen anything that looked like a lich.

He was breathing hard as he had just split a zombie in half when he saw a strange green glow moving down a parallel street.

As he dueled another pair of mindless zombies, he watched the glow get closer.

A knot of shadows floated into view, but it wasn't the vampires that drew Ted's attention. It was the skeletal woman who glided in their center.

It was hard to make any details out from a block away, but Ted could see that it was her eyes that blazed with the malevolent jade light that he had noticed. Her eyes, combined with the knot of vampire guards surrounding her, told Ted that he had just found what he had been searching for.

But the lich didn't turn down the street. Instead, she continued down the parallel road and disappeared behind the next building.

Desperate to find the lich, Ted tried to cut his way through the mob, but there were just too many undead. He took several scrapes before he stopped his wild charge and quickly considered his options.

He knew the lich was the key. If she died, the undead wouldn't be able to rise up anymore. But she was headed in another direction. Obviously, she had someplace else she wanted to be, and Ted was sure he didn't want the lich to reach wherever that was.

He had to stop her.

Making up his mind, Ted pulled a small vial out of one of his pouches. He quickly put the vial to his mouth and drained the contents in a single swallow.

It only took a moment before a chill passed through him and his form began to fade. A heartbeat later, Ted had become transparent and his outline started to break apart. The undead around Ted suddenly ignored him and ran by as if he wasn't even there.

Ted had to move quickly and his gassy form swiftly floated alone through the mob and out onto the empty street beyond. He floated behind a large dumpster just as his potion wore off. As quickly as it had happened, the enchantment faded and he was solid once more.

Ted felt around his body and breathed a sigh of relief when everything was still there. Then he peered over the dumpster and saw that none of the undead had noticed him. Now alone in the dark alley, Ted snuck away down the passage, toward the place he had last seen the lich.

Gunfire and screams echoed down the streets as Ted peered around the corner.

There, already several blocks down the street and swiftly moving further away, was the lich and her vampire escort. Lightning and fire flashed in the sky above as dragons and griffins battled in the air. A pack of minotaurs suddenly appeared from a street across from the lich, but she didn't slow as two of her vampires peeled off and easily cut the hulking kefali apart.

Ted swallowed nervously and gathered his courage before stepping out into the dark street to follow the master of the undead.

CHAPTER 26

The dragons roared as they battled in the night skies above Pittsburgh and Emily couldn't help but notice the almost dance-like quality of the aerial struggle.

The three smaller dragons darted around the enormous black one, scoring its armored scales with their breath attacks. Streaks of frost and electric burns marred the great black's pristine coat, but all of the damage was superficial and only managed to enrage the mighty Phlebolith.

Emily rode her majestic crystal dragon, Lru, through the darkness to aid the other good dragons. But before they could reach them, a pair of red dragons rose up before them. Lru banked sharply and Emily had to hold on tightly as the crystal dragon avoided the twin gouts of flame that erupted from the reds.

Now, Lru was a Great Wyrm, making him far older and larger than most other dragons. But even though he dwarfed the pair of reds, there were still two of them and he couldn't watch them both at the same time. The reds knew this and split up to attack the big crystal from different directions.

Their fiery breath followed Lru through the dark skies and it was all he could do to keep the flames from touching him. But Lru wasn't worried about the flames hurting him. His brilliant scales were resistant to the heat of their flames, but his rider was not.

As another jet of flames flew over her shoulder and struck Lru's tail, Emily realized that the reds were targeting her.

Not one to sit idly by, Emily pointed her scepter at the nearest red dragon. The emerald bolt streaked through the air, but the dragon easily dodged the spell. She unleashed a barrage of emerald bolts at the soaring dragons, but none of them found their mark.

Having an idea, Emily drew her bow as another breath of searing flames arced by. She nearly lost her grip on the dragon as he banked hard to avoid the fire. When Lru righted himself, one of the reds dove at him from above. The crystal waited until the last possible moment before twisting away and lashing out with his front claws as the red dove past. His claws scored long gashes in the red's underbelly and the smaller dragon roared in pain as it fell from sight.

The other red took the opportunity to sweep in from Lru's back, but Emily was waiting for it. As the red dragon darted forward, Emily loosed a stream of arrows.

The red simply turned its head to avoid the small missiles so they would bounce harmlessly off its thick scales. But Emily had anticipated such a move and called the wind. Just before the arrows reached their target, a strong gust of wind sprung up and pushed the arrows in a new direction.

Caught by surprise, the red didn't have time to react before the first arrow slammed into its huge eye. The dragon bellowed in pain and two more arrows slammed home beside the first before the red pulled back, abandoning its attack.

Heavy antiaircraft fire suddenly pounded into the wounded red dragon and Emily was surprised to realize that the chaotic struggle had carried them closer to the city. In the distance, she could see the three smaller dragons of Lru's Flight still harassing the mighty black and Lru increased his speed, eager to confront the other Great Wyrm.

Before the crystal could close in, a red dragon shot out from between two buildings and flew up at the crystal like a spear. Lru saw the danger and turned to face it.

Panic filled Emily as she realized the red planned on slamming into them. She was about to shout a warning when Lru roared and a rippling wave of concussive force thundered out.

The red was caught in the blast and hammered into the side of a building. Chunks of concrete rained down and Emily hoped that the battling figures far below weren't friendly. Another barrage of force pounded the red further into the building like the blows from some titanic jackhammer.

Lru inspected his handiwork, and apparently satisfied, turned away from the wreckage and resumed his pursuit of the mighty black.

As Emily watched, one of the bronze dragons darted in too close and Phlebolith lunged forward, biting down on the smaller dragon's wing. She could hear an agonized shriek as the great black violently shook its huge head. The bronze's wing ripped off with a horrible tearing sound and the dragon was flung through the air like a rag doll. The wounded bronze slammed onto the roof of a tall building and then struggled to rise.

Lru beat his wings furiously, desperate to reach the wounded bronze in time, but Emily could see that they would never make it.

Phlebolith descended on the stunned bronze and landed on the rooftop. The silver and other bronze tried to distract the mighty beast, but the black ignored their efforts. Planting his huge front claws on the smaller bronze and digging his claws in, Phlebolith lowered his huge head to the trapped bronze. The pinned dragon spat a bolt of lightning in defiance that crackled across the black's snout and elicited a slight wince of pain.

The bronze thrashed under the black as Phlebolith's jaws opened wide. Green flames erupted in a scorching torrent and slammed into the pinned dragon. The bronze shrieked as the green flames engulfed its head and neck, but the cry faded as its flesh melted. Within moments there was nothing left but a charred skull.

Phlebolith roared in victory as the scorched corpse tumbled from the building and Lru bellowed an angry challenge. The mighty black's head snapped up at the challenge, and when Phlebolith saw Lru rushing toward him, Emily could have sworn the monstrous black dragon smiled.

But before the enemies could meet, a small, dark green dragon darted out of the city and spat a stream of foul acid at the large crystal. Lru swerved aside, but a little splashed on his tail, causing those scales to hiss and bubble.

Heavy gunfire unexpectedly struck the green from above and Emily looked up to see a pair of attack helicopters descending toward them with guns blazing. Scales were ripped from the green dragon as the concentrated fire took its toll. The green peeled off and hurried away from the assault by flying low and darting between two buildings. The helicopters roared overhead as they pursued the fleeing dragon.

Two smaller black dragons abruptly shot out of a burning section of the city and crashed into the bronze and silver that were still flying around the mighty black. Phlebolith took to the air once more as the smaller blacks distracted the battered good dragons, giving the monstrous black a clear path to the charging crystal.

Emily braced herself as Lru bellowed another challenge that was accepted with an earsplitting roar from monstrous Phlebolith. Gunfire and explosions lit the sky above the embattled city as griffins, wyverns, harpies, and dragons clashed in a titanic struggle that went largely unnoticed by the two Great Wyrms as they barreled toward each other.

****

Liz's bloody chainsaber growled hungrily as she rode through the expanding battlefield. She had crossed through the war-scarred heart of downtown and was now wading through a pitched battle between a combined force of humans and elves that was being slowly pushed back by a tide of vicious kefali. The battle was being waged across several city blocks and everywhere she looked, Liz saw war and death.

The beasts fought as if possessed and threw themselves at the defenders in a berserker rage. A tight phalanx of elven Hoplites blocked off one street while a rigid shield wall of elite Steel Legion Knights held another; the center was filled with gifted humans, elven auxiliary, soldiers, mages, and healers who tried to stem the tide of Isfet warriors that filled the wide avenue.

Liz knew she was getting close to the Grove, but there were several blocks of battling warriors between them. She briefly entertained the thought of trying to rally the defenders to push toward the Grove, but she quickly dismissed the idea, as it was obvious that they were being pushed away from her goal, not toward it. They had no reason to follow her orders anyway. Now, if Mike had been here… but he wasn't, she reminded herself.

She was on her own.

Liz could see the mighty Cathedral of Learning looming in the distance and she knew that Schenley Park was just beyond it. With nearly all of the Druids out fighting, there were few left to actually guard the precious artifact. With any luck, the Grove would still be where Emily had said, and she could deliver the warning before it was too late.

A huge minotaur suddenly jumped out at her, but Liz managed to parry its heavy sickle sword. Her mount's huge claws ripped into the beast's throat and it fell away as more monsters pressed in.

Liz and Kiba'Nadare were a whirlwind of death as they moved through the swirling battle. Liz fired her plasma revolver and slashed with her chainsaber as the white tiger clawed and bit at anything that came within its reach.

Liz saw a wounded elven warrior struggling to stand as a lion-like Feloran closed in. She tried to shoot the beast, but she had fired too many shots too rapidly and the revolver wasn't charged back up yet. Unwilling to let the elf die, Liz jumped off her tiger and rushed the Feloran.

Sparks flew as her screaming chainsaber bit into the long scimitar of the kefali warrior. They traded several swift blows, and Liz was surprised at the speed and agility of the lion-like kefali. The growling beast pressed hard and Liz was forced backwards.

Liz bided her time until she saw her opening. Knocking the sweeping blade aside, Liz stepped in close and buried the chainsaber in the Feloran's chest. Chunks flew as she ripped the growling blade back out in a spray of flesh and blood.

Liz pressed through the throng and found the wounded elf still struggling to rise. Her tiger plowed through the kefali, rending limbs as it came, until it stood protectively beside her.

Liz crouched down and a moment later the grateful elf stood. There was no time for thanks as more kefali pressed in and the defenders were forced back.

A herd of centaurs charged into the fray and they were met by a barrage of gunfire from a platoon of Marines that had just rumbled in behind a pair of M1A2 Abrams battle tanks. The heavy machine guns on the tanks thundered to life and ripped into the masses of kefali.

Scores died in moments and the Isfet offensive sputtered under the devastating bombardment.

Liz used the slight reprieve to quickly move through the defenders and heal everyone she could. But her healing was cut short when one of the adjacent buildings suddenly exploded and a mangled tank rumbled out of the ruined building.

At first, she couldn't understand why the driver had driven through the building, but then it became horribly apparent that this wasn't a friendly tank. Graffiti of strange symbols covered the battered hull and Liz was shocked to see the tusked face of an orc manning the machine gun. Orcs and their minions swarmed out from behind the tank and crashed into the surprised defenders.

The orc tank plowed ahead and drove deep into the heart of the allied forces, nearly cutting them in two. But before the orc tank could bring its main gun to bear, the Marines fired first.

The orc tank erupted in a ball of fire and secondary explosions ripped the armored vehicle apart. The humans cheered as the stolen tank's ammunition cooked off, but the victory was short-lived.

Out of the darkness of the ruined building strode a colossal demon. Taller than the largest giant Liz had ever seen, the demon towered over the battlefield with tree-trunk sized legs. Its eyes were black pools and its skin was pure white but covered in malevolent brands that oozed black blood. An impossibly large cleaver was clenched in the demon's fist that was connected to it by a length of chain that encircled its wide wrist.

In three huge strides, the demon reached the Marines as they fired on the massive monster. But the bullets seemed to have little effect on the hell spawn and with a roar, the pale demon drove its cleaver into one of the Abrams tanks. There was an awful shriek of tearing metal as the abominable cleaver sheared the tank in half.

The demon howled lustily and ripped its weapon out of the wreckage before turning toward the other tank. Bullets hammered into its branded flesh, but many of the rounds couldn't penetrate the white skin and the ones that did only scratched the surface.

A pair of orcs charged Liz and two rapid shots dropped them both. When she looked back, there was a pretty, blonde elf in pale blue robes standing atop the tank facing the gigantic demon and Liz recognized High Priestess Ipheto immediately.

Ipheto stood her ground and boldly raised a wheat-tipped staff up before her as the towering demon advanced. A brilliant white light burst from the wheat, and the demon shrieked and shielded its eyes from the dazzling light. Ipheto shouted something, but Liz couldn't hear it over the sounds of battle, and the demon's skin began to smoke and sizzle wherever the light touched it.

Now, when the bullets struck the blistering white flesh, they burrowed deep.

A wounded soldier propped up against a ruined car called for help and Liz rushed to his side. When Liz stood again the demon was howling in agony as the brilliant light charred the demons flesh and pieces of its skin began to flake away.

A few mages added their powers to the attack and pieces of the demon were ripped off and crumbled into ash. The huge cleaver fell to the ground with a resounding clang as the demon's hand was blown apart by a barrage of magical darts. The pale hell spawn roared and pushed toward Ipheto in desperation, but before it could reach her, the High Priestess shouted a word of power and an explosion of light burst from the staff, disintegrating the demon into a billowing cloud of ash.

As the light faded from the staff, Liz caught a flash of reflection from atop the ruined building where none should have been. Looking up, she saw an orc leaning over a piece of ruined wall with a large, cylindrical object on its shoulder.

Too late, Liz realized what it was. She shouted a warning, but Ipheto was too far away to hear. The rocket launcher roared to life and the missile streaked through the air. The RPG struck the tank she stood on and the High Priestess vanished in the resulting explosion.

The Abrams survived the blast and its main cannon returned fire, vaporizing the offending orc and most of the remaining building. Debris rained down across the swirling battle and Liz didn't have the time to mourn the loss of Ipheto as the orcs and kefali pressed in from every side.

Liz could see another group of tanks rumbling down a different street with Arch Battlemage Gwydion and several Army commanders directing their troops as they tried to stem the tide before the defenders of Pittsburgh were overrun.

A sudden roar filled the air and a row of windows shattered overhead as bullets from somewhere crashed into them. A huge, green dragon suddenly swooped around a building and sailed overhead. A moment later, a pair of attack helicopters appeared with machine guns roaring as they pursued the dragon down the street. But Liz didn't have time to marvel at the sight above her as an ugly little ratman shot out of the melee and lunged at her.

Liz easily dodged the creature's hasty attack and a brutal chop of the snarling chainsaber removed the ratman's head from its shoulders. The small creature fell next to the body of an elf Blade Dancer and Liz bent over to see if she was still alive. Kiba'Nadare stood guard as Liz carefully rolled the elf over.

The glazed eyes gave Liz her answer before she saw the ragged gash in the Blade Dancer's neck. Liz laid the body back down and moved to close the staring eyes. But when Liz tried to gently pull the eyelids down, they wouldn't budge and the dead eyes remained open. Curious, Liz leaned in closer to see what was causing the eyes to stay open when the corpse suddenly reached out and grabbed her by the throat.

Liz fell backwards in surprise and the undead elf landed on top of her. Gasping for breath, Liz tried to pry the cold hands from her neck, but the zombie opened its mouth and tried to bite her. Releasing her grasp of the undead hands, Liz pushed the undead's snapping jaws away just in time. Her vision began to fill with spots and Liz knew she was running out of time.

Her mind raced as she tried to think of a solution before she suffocated or was bitten. She could grab her pistol or chainsaber that lay nearby, but in doing so she would have to let go of the zombie and it would bite her before she could use either weapon. Her sight blurred and Liz started to lose consciousness when the pressure around her throat suddenly vanished and the weight of the corpse was lifted from her.

She inhaled greedily and her vision returned. She saw Kiba'Nadare holding the undead elf in its massive jaws by the back of the zombie's head. Liz sat up and grabbed her weapons as the tiger snapped its jaws shut and the zombie's skull collapsed like a shattered egg.

Liz looked around and was horrified to see that the dead were rising all across the battlefield. Human, elf, orc, and kefali, it didn't matter, all were brought back in the dreadful state of undeath.

The already chaotic battle was thrown into even more confusion as the undead rose up and attacked everything around them. The few battle lines that remained quickly deteriorated under the new undead assault. Kefali battled orc, orc fought human, elf confronted kefali, and the undead attacked them all.

Liz realized that the presence of the undead could only mean one thing.

The lich was getting close.

She was running out of time.

Liz hauled herself up onto the great tiger's back and urged the mighty beast forward. Kiba'Nadare barreled through the swirling melee, knocking undead, orc, and kefali aside as it responded to Liz's unspoken command. They charged down the avenue and Liz slashed and shot at anything that got too close.

Seeing a shattered storefront, Liz angled toward that and they charged through the opening and into the relatively quiet of the inside. They rushed through the building as fast as the great tiger could navigate the narrow corridors before they finally came to a large door of the loading dock at the back of the building. Liz pressed the button on the wall to open the door and she was relieved when it actually worked.

They charged out of the door before it had opened the whole way and found themselves on a quiet alley. The sounds of battle echoed off the buildings all around, but back here seemed like stepping out into a different world. Kiba'Nadare bound down the street and was nearing the exit when a group of centaurs suddenly appeared from around the corner.

The great cat didn't slow and plowed into the surprised centaurs with teeth and claw. Liz unloaded her revolver and hacked at the creatures before they had time to recover. Within moments, all of the centaurs were dead, and the tiger bound down the next street, leaving a trail of bloody paw prints.

They crested a small rise and down below them Liz could see the high walls protecting the towering Cathedral of Learning complex and beyond that was Schenley Park. Liz and her huge mount hurried down the slope toward a line of distant trees where Liz hoped the Grove remained safely hidden.

****

The griffins stayed low, just below the level of the buildings so as not to get caught in the turmoil of the battle that raged in the skies overhead. As they flew, Mike was in awe of the sheer scale of the war raging both above and below him. The city was a warzone and everywhere he looked there were either battles being fought or the scatted remnants of one.

It wasn't long before they passed beyond the city center and left the skyscrapers behind. The structures here were smaller and Mike immediately saw where they were headed.

At first, he thought there had been a landslide, but they were already on the top of a hill so that couldn't be. Then he realized that what he had mistaken for a landslide was actually an army of rock-like demons.

The tide of stone demons rolled along, crushing everything in their path. A group of battered Scadian mercenaries desperately fought against the unstoppable wave, but they were slowly being overwhelmed.

"Loki's balls," Rodan cursed, as they sailed closer. "Lithopedions."

"And that can mean only one thing," Brigit scowled, as she studied the churning avalanche of rock demons below. "Asag is here."

"Well, let's fly down there and kill it!" Mike shouted over the wind in his ears.

"No!" Brigit shook her head. "We must land and face Asag from the ground."

"What?" Mike couldn't believe what he was hearing. "Are you crazy? Why would we do a thing like that when we can just swoop down and attack him from the air?"

"Because he be indestructible from above," Rodan growled in disgust. "The only way ter defeat him be ter strike the soft sections under the folds o' his hardened skin."

"Naturally," Mike groaned under his breath, as griffins dived toward the battle.

The four griffins landed swiftly behind the battered line of defenders and only paused long enough to allow the Wardens to get off before taking wing once more.

As the griffins flew off, Mike raised his looted rifle and took a shot at the head of the nearest stone demon, but the bullets simply bounced off the rocky skin.

"That will avail you not," Brigit said. "Their form is proof against such weapons."

"Of course, it is." Mike threw the rifle down in disgust. "So, what will kill these things?"

"Explosions can shatter them," LuHark offered, "and water will wear them down, but a blessed weapon is the most effective."

"Good" Mike drew his ancient mace and gripped it tightly. "That, I have."

As Mike and the Wardens rushed to join the beleaguered forces, the line of defenders suddenly broke. The mercenaries abruptly shattered before the Wardens could reach the opening and the stone demons ripped into the defenders.

The demons went wild and charged in a frenzy, attacking at random. Soldiers threw grenades and fired rockets as mages flung spells in all directions. Druids found that their powers of nature had little effect on the demons, who seemed able to merge any earth or plant that touched them back into their own bodies. Paladins and clerics fared better, but there were too few of them to have much of an impact.

Mike and the three Wardens drove into the chaos eagerly, cutting deep into the rocky monsters with amazing skill and precision. Their enchanted and blessed weapons sliced through the gravelly hide of the demons with relative ease. But the demons were large and there were many, and wading through them would be no easy feat.

The Lithopedions needed no weapons or armor, preferring to use their rocky hide and heavy stone fists to overcome their enemies. They pummeled anyone who dared stand in their way, but the arrival of the Wardens slowed their rolling advance and gave the defenders a renewed sense of purpose.

Mike crushed the leg of one tall demon as another Lithopedion slammed its heavy fist into Mike's upraised shield. Mike was knocked backward by the force of the blow and landed on his back as the demon advanced. The stone monster balled its huge fist and prepared to pound Mike into oblivion when a flaming axe slammed into the back of its small head. The Lithopedion crumpled as a dwarf with a brown mohawk rode the dying demon to the ground.

The dwarf's armor was dirty and dented, but the white scapular with the bloody handprint was plain to see. "Glad ter see me?" the captain of the Hands of Tyr grinned madly.

Raenods ripped his burning axe out of the demon's head and spat on the corpse as Mike got to his feet.

"I had everything under control," Mike grumbled.

"Sure, ye did," Raenods chuckled. "Ye humans like ter fight on yer backs, eh?"

More members of the Hands of Tyr fought their way through the demons to join their leader until over a dozen of the sturdy warriors were gathered in a ragged ring around them. Mike recognized Ingemar with his unruly hair and lightning-wreathed war hammer alongside the Guardian, Astrid, with her blonde hair tied under her chin.

Mike ignored the jibe. "We need to kill their leader, a Demon Lord named Asag."

"Do we now?" Raenods rumbled.

A stone demon exploded and Rodan stepped out of the dust, his war hammer throbbing with power. "Aye, we do," the dwarf Warden rumbled, and stepped into the ring to face the captain. "The lad speaks the truth. Asag must be destroyed. He be growin' stronger with every passin' moment."

Raenods eyed Rodan with a curious eye. "And just who do ye think ye be, tellin' me what ter do?"

Rodan scowled at the Captain of the Hands. "I be Rodan Odinson, Warden o' the Imperial Order."

Raenods' eyes bulged as he took in the stocky Warden's armor and the other Hands muttered in amazement. Obviously, they had not expected a figure out of legend to step into their midst, especially on a battlefield of a different world.

Two stone demons lost their heads and LuHark emerged from the swirling melee. The Hands raised their weapons uncertainly as the huge Hathi approached, but a sharp bark from Rodan stayed their weapons. Brigit followed LuHark into the ragged circle. "What is the delay?" Brigit demanded.

Raenods stared up at the huge kefali Warden. "And what sort o' creature be ye?"

"All questions will be answered," LuHark trumpeted, "but now we must move. Asag's power grows."

The three Wardens abruptly charged out of the ring and dove into the swirling battle with Mike close behind. Raenods stared in wonder for a moment before he roared a battle cry that was picked up by his Hands and they charged after the Wardens.

The Wardens and Hands formed a tight wedge and cut into the raging Lithopedions with LuHark acting as the tip of the spear with Rodan and Brigit flanking her. As they drove into the melee, others joined their formation and their numbers swelled the further they traveled.

"How we be knowin' this Asag if we be seein' him?" Raenods bellowed, as another Lithopedion fell before his burning axe.

"Trust me," Brigit shouted, and sliced the head off of a wounded demon with her shimmering spear. "You will know."

The dead and dying grew thick around them as they pressed ever onward. They suffered losses, but the urgent pace of the Wardens kept them moving and the formation simply tightened and continued on, refusing to slow down.

Their tenacity was rewarded when a foul stink filled the air and Mike saw the most horrible creature imaginable. The Demon Lord hurt his eyes to look upon, but with a supreme effort of will, Mike beheld the awful majesty of Asag.

Larger than his children, the Demon Lord had three thick legs and three heavily-muscled arms that protruded from a round body made of a similar rocky texture as the Lithopedions.

Asag had no neck and numerous eyes spread across his entire bulk. Four curved horns twisted out of his wide head and scaly wings sat upon his broad back, but they seemed much too small to support the demons' mass. Thick, stony skin covered nearly every inch of the Demon Lord, but there were cracks between the overlapping plates where a sickly, greenish yellow puss constantly oozed out.

"Asag is a plague demon," LuHark trumpeted as they drew closer to the horrific fiend. "Do not touch the mucus he excretes."

Some of the attacking force couldn't handle the sight of the Demon Lord and they stayed behind, unable to move any closer. The spear's numbers dwindled the closer they got, and soon only the purest of heart and mind remained. The Wardens led the charge and Mike was surprised to see that a trio of Druids were dueling the repulsive Demon Lord.

Punishing sprays of water and gale-force winds hammered the Demon Lord, but he seemed unaffected. Thick roots sprouted from the ground and wrapped around the demon's legs while huge chunks of stone were ripped from the ground and flung at the mighty monster. But Asag cackled gleefully as he easily tore through the ensnaring roots and crushed the flying boulders with a wave of his mighty arm. Nothing the three Druids threw at him had any effect and it was only a matter of time before the Demon Lord overwhelmed them.

The Druids struggled against the huge demon and as he got closer, Mike discovered that he recognized the three Druids. They were Emily's mentors, the elf brothers - Rubadub, Robadoo, and Rabidad.

The Wardens punched through the last Lithopedions in their way and finally came face to face with Asag. The Demon Lord eyed the newcomers with a mixture of amusement and eagerness.

"So." Asag's voice sounded like many voices all talking at once with a strange, wet quality, as if he were underwater. "The legendary Wardens have come to stop me." His heavy body shook as he laughed. "I will enjoy watching you wither away as pestilence consumes you."

Mike and the three Wardens responded by brandishing their weapons and charging the Demon Lord.

CHAPTER 27

The darkness was nearly complete as Ted snuck down the deserted alley. He wasn't sure how long he had been following the lich and her vampire cronies, but it seemed to him that he had been scrambling through the shadows forever.

He lost them several times as they slipped from shadow to shadow, but using a trick he learned from Master Pars, he was able to pick up the "scent" of their dark magic and follow the faint trail.

The undead master kept a swift pace and had stayed relatively close to the abandoned southern wall. Ted found this curious and wondered why they remained so close to the fortifications. The only answer he could think of was the wall provided a quick escape route to the nearest bridge. Not a bad idea, Ted mused, considering there was such a small group of them. But that didn't make sense either. He had seen the small band rip apart much larger forces of kefali and orcs that had happened across their path. They were up to something and Ted was determined to figure out what.

The distant shadows detached from the wall and slipped around the corner. Ted followed as quickly and quietly as he could and reached the intersection a minute later.

But when he peeked around the corner there was nobody in sight.

He stared down the dark street for several long moments, hoping to see some movement, but none ever appeared.

The undead had vanished.

Ted cursed under his breath and muttered the cantrip to reveal their faint necromantic trail. He hated to use any power at all if he could help it because he knew he would need every ounce of strength he could muster when he finally confronted the lich and her vampires.

The hazy trail appeared in the air and Ted followed it for a few steps until it abruptly vanished. Ted scowled and tried the cantrip again, but to no effect.

The trail was gone.

Ted snuck down to the end of the road and hid in the darkness of the intersection as he searched for any sign of the undead master. But he didn't see anything or detect any trace of their passing. It was if the night had swallowed them up. Which, Ted considered, might be the case. After all, he didn't know the first thing about what powers a lich did or didn't have. His only knowledge was from ancient mythology or from fantasy books and games. None of which could be called reliable.

The roar of gunfire and clash of weapons echoed through the darkness and Ted considered abandoning his mission and returning to the fighting. The thought was a brief one as Ted quickly discarded the idea. Finding and destroying the lich was far more imperative to the survival of the city than fighting off the hordes of enemies that swarmed through the streets. At least that's what Ted told himself as he ducked back down the street to where the trail ended.

He tried a *detect magic* spell and a *reveal invisibility* charm, but neither showed him anything new; the trail still disappeared into thin air. Desperate now, and out of helpful spells, Ted began to search for any physical clues as to where they might have gone. But he was no tracker and quickly abandoned the effort. If only he knew where they were going... A soft rustle behind Ted made him spin around, plazmax raised. But there was nothing there. Just a dark, empty alley.

Ted's heartbeat pounded in his ears as he slowly lowered his charged weapon. *False alarm.* Ted shook his head ruefully at his own jumpiness.

An idea suddenly stuck him. *Jumpiness.* Ted hurried back to the place where the trail vanished and looked up. Sure enough, hanging several feet above his head were the faint remnants of the trail.

Now, he just needed a way to follow.

Ted looked back down to discover a dark, hooded figure standing before him. Ted jumped back in alarm, away from the stranger, and raised his plazmax defensively.

"Very good," the shadowy newcomer hissed softly. "Your dedication is commendable, if misplaced." The figure reached up and carefully lowered his hood, revealing a pale elf with unnerving red eyes. The elf saw Ted's discomfort and smiled, displaying a pair of long fangs.

"Allow me to introduce myself." The elf vampire bowed low without ever taking his eyes off Ted. "I am Count Otho, a humble servant of Mistress Sabine. And you are…?"

Ted eyed the vampire count distrustfully but decided it wouldn't hurt to try and learn a little more about his enemies. "Battlemage Ted Koldun" *Now, that had a nice ring to it.*

"Interesting." The vampire's eyes widened slightly in surprise. "I never imagined my former kin would accept a human into their ranks." Count Otho looked thoughtful for a moment before he waved a hand dismissively. "But that is not why I am here. My mistress was impressed at your skill and determination at following us. So, she has asked me to offer you a place in her court."

Ted tried to hide his shock. "And what does that mean?"

"It means," the vampire slid closer, "that our great mistress has given me permission to grant you the Blood Gift. You will become one of us."

"You mean a vampire," Ted said.

"Yes," Count Otho hissed eagerly. "Think of it; you will never grow old, never feel the creeping ache of age catching up on you. As the centuries pass, your powers will only grow, until nothing will dare to stand in your way. You will be faster and stronger than you ever thought possible and the blood magic…" the vampire sighed in ecstasy, "is intoxicating."

"And what would I need to do for this to happen?" Ted asked cautiously, as he slowly lowered his weapon.

Count Otho smiled and his fangs gleamed in the faint light as he slid even closer. "A simple bite," the vampire hissed seductively. "One brief moment of pain followed by an eternity of power."

Ted had to admit that did sound nice. Getting old was secretly a fear of his. "What's the catch?"

The vampire reached out and placed a slender hand on Ted's shoulder. "Your powers will be weakened in the daylight, but at night you will be unstoppable."

"You say I won't age," Ted said carefully, "but can I still be killed?"

Count Otho hesitated a moment before smiling reassuringly. "Sunlight will harm us, but it would take the removal of our head or heart to fully destroy us." The vampire leaned in close. "But with your new powers, none will be able to get that close."

Ted tilted his head and presented the vampire with his neck as he smiled. "I did," Ted whispered.

Count Otho paused and looked at Ted in confusion. Then a sudden spasm rocked the vampire as a beam of superheated plasma burst out of his back.

The shocked vampire stumbled back a step, revealing a gaping hole burned in his chest as steam rose from Ted's plazmax.

"No…" Count Otho gasped, before he abruptly burst into flames and swiftly disintegrated into a small pile of sparkling dust.

"A nice offer," Ted said, as he detached a small pouch from his belt and knelt down beside what remained of the vampire count. "But I will take brains over brawn any day of the week, you stupid bloodsucker," Ted chuckled, as he quickly scooped up the dust and put it in the pouch. Vampire dust was extremely versatile and extraordinarily rare, so he wasn't about to let it go to waste.

With the dust-filled pouch secured to his belt once more, Ted found a ladder that led to the roof and set off after the fading trail once more.

****

Smoke from the burning buildings obscured much of the battle, but Jack could see the towering warlord easily enough. The huge, red-skinned oni was hard to miss with his mechanical exoskeleton adding to his fearsome visage.

Humans, elves, and dwarves battled the various monsters and demons of the orc horde all across the rolling hills of the sprawling neighborhood. The power had gone out some time ago and the only light came from the burning buildings and the flashlights carried by human soldiers.

The black werewolf howled lustily as a pair of burly orc warriors charged out of the swirling smoke. Jack's blade met the first orc's katana with a shriek of metal and a flash of sparks. The second orc's sword slashed at his head, but Jack ducked, and the blade hissed by just above his ears.

More heavily armored orcs rushed out of the smoke and crashed into the ragged group of defenders. A cheer went up from somewhere behind him and when Jack stole a glace behind, he saw a company of human Knights entering the fray. Leading the elite company was an exquisitely armored Knight with a distinctive plumed helm. Duke von Jensin led the charge as the Knights crashed into the orcs and drove them back. With help on the way, Jack turned his full attention back to the pair of orc warriors.

The huge werewolf wielded his large katana in one hand and clawed at the orcs with the other. Jack rushed one orc and tried to overwhelm it before the other one could come to its aid, but these orcs were not your average warriors. These were the warlord's personal Sohei guard and they were not so easily defeated.

Jack found this out the hard way when he nearly lost his head to the orc's skillful counter attack. The werewolf disengaged just before the second orc reached him and the pair of orcs circled Jack cautiously.

Nearby, the light of a burning building showed Alex working his way through the orcs with marvelous staff work. Jack was impressed at the level of martial skill that Alex possessed. He practically danced through the sea of enemies and despite not wearing armor, the large man didn't seem to bear a single wound. A fact that Jack found slightly annoying, considering his dented and scratched armor, and several shallow cuts. But Jack didn't have time to worry about Alex when he had a pair of skilled orc bodyguards circling him.

Stormtusk bellowed something in the orc's guttural language as he lumbered through the growing battle. A knot of the warlord's commanders and advisers huddled around the oni's colossal form, and a ring of guards protectively surrounded all of them as they waded into the defenders.

King Varnir and his Huscarls were too far back, but the nearest dwarves went wild at the sight of the warlord. They formed a rough wedge and drove into the orc guards. They split the protective ring, and the warchiefs and sorcerers leapt to the warlord's defense before any of the dwarves could reach him. Until an opening suddenly appeared in the orc line, and Ambrosar the Thunderer charged through and faced the warlord alone.

The Chief Guardian of Thor's runic tattoos glowed fiercely as he faced the towering oni.

"Odin's Breath," Ambrosar bellowed. "Ye sure be an ugly bastard."

The oni warlord laughed deeply and waved away his warriors before they could attack the Chief Guardian. "You da king?" Stormtusk growled eagerly, as he stepped closer to Ambrosar.

"No," Ambrosar rumbled, as he hefted his pair of rune hammers. "I be his Chief Guardian."

Stormtusk scowled at the news, but then shrugged. "Close enough me guess. You grubs all die da same." A huge circular saw attached above the left hand of the warlord's exo-suit suddenly growled to life. The spinning blade was a monstrous disk similar to an industrial saw that would be found in a lumber mill. The immense blade was being powered by a smoking generator that was strapped to the warlord's back.

Stormtusk advanced on Ambrosar as the battle raged around them. To the dwarf's credit, he didn't balk as the huge oni bore down on him.

The Sohei lunged in unison at Jack from opposite directions and the werewolf parried one strike and barely avoided the other. The orcs worked together to keep Jack on his toes and he quickly realized that he was outmatched.

The wolf within was howling to be fully released and Jack gladly opened himself to it. The soul sword sang in his grip as the wolf Spirit overtook him.

The roar of battle was music to Jack's enhanced ears and he quickly fell into the harmony of war. Black ash suddenly erupted from the glowing blade of Yoma-Ketsueki and trailed after the sweeping katana, surprising the orcs and giving Jack a much-needed advantage.

Stormtusk roared and drove the deadly saw at Ambrosar, but the Guardian didn't budge. The whirring teeth slammed into a protective field just inches away from the dwarf's bushy black beard. Sparks flew and the saw screamed as it ground into the Chief Guardian's Svalinn Field.

Ambrosar shouted and his voice thundered with power. The force of the shout knocked the warlord back a step and Ambrosar charged the stunned oni. His heavy hammers swung at the monster's knees, but a sweep from the warlord's long, iron club knocked them aside.

The knobbed club was longer than Ambrosar was tall, and the oni wielded it with ferocious precision despite it being a two-handed weapon and he was only using one. The power of Stormtusk's strikes forced Ambrosar backwards and the dwarf barely managed to keep the heavy iron club from reaching him.

The warlord roared lustily and swung his massive saw at the Guardian's back while Ambrosar deflected another blow from the club. Just in time, Ambrosar saw the spinning blade coming and dove aside, but not before the hungry teeth ripped a chunk out of his fine, rune armor.

Stormtusk pressed his advantage and hammered the dwarf with both saw and club. Ambrosar was sorely pressed and used a combination of protective shields to keep the worst of the assault at bay. What his shields couldn't block, he either parried with his hammers or dodged aside. But even his considerable skill couldn't hold back the terrible might of the oni warlord and more blows made it through to hammer the besieged Guardian.

The black werewolf danced between the slashing blades of the orc guards. He danced to the sounds of war and the harmony gave his wild rage a focus. To Jack, it was as if the orcs were moving through jelly; their movements slow and lacking energy. He knew the feeling wouldn't last forever as he glided between their lethargic swings and drove his blade into the chest of the first orc.

Yoma-Ketsueki gladly devoured the soul energy of the orc and screamed for more.

Jack was happy to comply.

The second orc lost its head a moment later and Jack wasted no time in charging through the battle toward the dueling Guardian and warlord.

A knot of dwarves blocked his path and Jack realized it was King Varnir and his guard as they tried to punch through the orc defensive line. The dwarves recognized the huge werewolf as Jack joined them and found Alex at the king's side as they pressed into the warlord's elite Sohei guards.

"Forward lads!" King Varnir bellowed as he urged his warriors onward.

Ahead of them, the duel raged on, but it was clear that Ambrosar was in trouble.

Stormtusk laughed as he slammed the Guardian to the ground with a brutal blow of his huge iron club. Ambrosar picked himself up and spun aside just as the saw chewed into the ground where he had been a moment before.

Ambrosar limped away, trailing blood, as he desperately tried to get some distance between himself and the powerful oni. But Stormtusk charged after him and another swing of the long club sent the Chief Guardian crashing to the ground.

On his back, Ambrosar raised his hammers as if to ward off the approaching warlord, but then lightning suddenly erupted from his hammers and the twin bolts crashed into the oni's muscled chest. The exo-suit sparked and shuddered as the electricity threatened to overwhelm its systems and the mighty Stormtusk was suddenly locked in place. Ambrosar scrambled to his feet and charged the warlord that was trapped inside his short-circuiting exo-suit.

Stormtusk roared in anger and thrashed around inside the skeletal metal frame as Ambrosar neared. But as the Chief Guardian closed the gap, the suit suddenly came back online and the oni exploded into motion. Caught by surprise and too battered to respond quickly enough, Ambrosar was helpless as the whirling saw blade ripped into him.

"Noooo!" King Varnir shouted in disbelief as he watched Ambrosar be cut in two by the laughing warlord. The dwarf king roared and brutally hacked his way through the last Sohei with Jack and Alex close behind.

Finally, King Varnir Anvilborn came face to face with Warlord Stormtusk.

****

The darkness under the trees was nearly complete as Liz and her great white tiger made their way through Schenley Park. Liz didn't know where the Grove was and hoped that Emily's instructions would get her there.

The sharp *crack* of a breaking stick somewhere behind her urged Liz onward.

Things were moving through the forest and she wasn't about to wait around and see what it was. The great cat responded to her unspoken command and bound forward, eager to be away.

Kiba'Nadare moved surprisingly quietly for her size and they quickly outdistanced the rustling noises.

They had been moving through the darkness for some time when the great cat suddenly stopped. The tiger's fur stood on end and a low growl rumbled deep in its chest. Liz strained her senses in the gloomy darkness but couldn't hear or see anything unusual. She urged her mount forward and the big cat took two steps before refusing to go any further.

"Oh, come on!" Liz moaned when she couldn't get the huge tiger to budge. When she tried to urge the beast, the huge tiger actually whimpered like a scared little kitten! Surprised, Liz slid off the cat's back and stood beside his massive head. "What's the matter, Kiba?" she asked softly, as she stroked his thick coat.

The cat sniffed the air and shook its head as if it smelled something terrible. Liz didn't smell anything, but she knew the tiger's senses were far better than her own. Something truly dreadful must be up ahead if it caused such a reaction from the mighty tiger.

Making up her mind, Liz raised her pistol and headed deeper into the woods in search of the tiger's distress. She hadn't gone a step past the tiger when an unnatural feeling of dread began to well up within her. Liz recognized the sensation and suddenly realized the cause of the tiger's fear. They had reached the Panic Line.

They had found the Grove!

Liz took a step back and the fear drained away. "We have to cross this to reach the Grove," Liz said to the distressed tiger. "It will be-"

Kiba'Nadare perked up and Liz froze. A moment later she heard it too, the rustling of many bodies approaching through the forest.

They were out of time.

Liz knew she wouldn't be able to coax the great cat across the Panic Line in time, so she did the only other thing she could think of. She focused her thoughts and willed the tiger to return to her bracelet.

It might have been her imagination, but Liz could have sworn Kiba looked sad before she vanished in a swirl of snow and was gone.

Putting the cat out of her mind, as the crunching grew louder, Liz took a deep breath before she charged ahead into the Panic Line.

The fear started out faint and quickly became an all-consuming terror that threatened to overwhelm her. But Liz had faced the Line before and she knew that the fear was only in her mind. However, that knowledge didn't help much as Liz struggled to put one foot in front of the other.

After what seemed like an eternity, the terror suddenly faded away as if it had never been and was replaced by the peaceful calm of the Grove. That calm didn't last when a heavy crunching of leaves and twigs rustled behind her.

Liz hurried away but did glance back to see several large groups of figures moving beneath the trees. Gold flashed in the faint beams of moonlight that penetrated the leafy canopy as the figures moved through them. Fur and horns covered the creatures and large sickle swords were clenched in clawed fists.

The Isfet stomped through the forest and stopped as they came upon the Panic Line. Liz smiled to herself. *Let's see them stomp across that!*

But Liz's smile faded as a white-sashed Lector Priest came to the front of each group. She couldn't make out what they did, but each priest raised an object above their head and chanted something in their slippery language as they stepped into the Line. The other kefali gathered tightly around them and like little islands of fur, they rushed across the Panic Line and entered the Grove.

Liz cursed under her breath as she bound through the underbrush and away from the kefali. She had to reach the High Druid and get him to take the Seal away before it was too late. She was planning what she would say to Belenos when two dark shapes lunged out of the shadows and slammed her into a tree.

One assailant pinned her arms to her sides while the other held a hand over her mouth and a curved dagger to her throat. Liz thrashed in their grip, but she was held fast. She couldn't make out much in the shadows, but her captors had dark hair and long snouts with long fangs that practically glowed in the darkness.

A third figure emerged from the shadows and when Liz saw who it was she ceased her struggling. Seeing the recognition in her eyes, the hand was removed from her mouth.

"Pipaluk," Liz breathed in amazement. "What are you doing here?"

A signal from the old shaman saw Liz released and the two Baribal warriors faded back into the shadows. Pipaluk smiled. "The Druids have given us the honor of protecting the Seal while they are out making war on our enemies."

"That's why I'm here," Liz said urgently. "They know we have the Seal and they are coming for it. The Isfet are coming this way as we speak."

"We know," Pipaluk replied softly, and she directed Liz to join her behind a large tree. "That is why we are here. Watch."

Liz hid behind the tree with the old shaman and soon the crashing of many feet echoed out of the darkness. It wasn't long before the lumbering forms of the Isfet appeared out of the shadows and headed straight for them. Liz wanted to run, but Pipaluk kept a firm grip on her shoulder.

The leading Isfet were nearly upon them when a storm of arrows sailed out of the darkness and slammed into the unsuspecting monsters. Shouts of alarm rang out as a second volley punched into the Isfet forces. Dozens fell in those first moments and no sooner than the last arrow slammed home, then dark shapes detached from the trees and carved into the surprised Isfet.

The Baribal warriors moved through the Isfet like specters of death, wielding long knives with savage efficiency. Within moments, over half of the Isfet were dead and more fell every second.

"You see," Pipaluk smiled, as they watched the slaughter unfold, "we are prepared for-"

The shaman's words were cut short when the dead Isfet began to stir. All across the woods, the fallen warriors began to rise up, many with arrows still sticking out of them and blood running freely from their wounds.

"Impossible," Pipaluk breathed, as the undead began attacking the astonished Baribal warriors and their fellow Isfet alike.

"Oh, no," Liz moaned. "They're here."

Pipaluk's eyes were wild with fear and confusion, as their carefully planned ambush became a full-on battle. "Who is here?"

"The Shadow elves," Liz breathed.

Every warrior that fell arose a moment later in undeath and joined in the slaughter of their former fellows. The Baribal began to pull back as the numbers of undead kept increasing and threatened to overwhelm them. The remaining Isfet formed tight groups and fended off the undead, and somehow pressed onward, fanatical in their intent on completing their mission no matter what got in their way.

"Do you know where the High Druid is?" Liz asked desperately as the first retreating Baribal overtook them.

"Yes," Pipaluk answered distractedly, as the battle moved closer to them. "He is within the stone ring at the heart of the Grove." The old shaman dumped a bag of bones on the ground and muttered something under her breath. The bones rattled around and suddenly formed three small skeletal creatures. The skeletons charged the nearest undead and jumped upon it, ripping it to pieces with their boney claws.

"Go now," Pipaluk ordered. "We will hold them as long as we can."

Liz gave the old shaman a grateful nod before turning and hurrying away. As she drove deeper into the Grove, Liz realized the sounds of battle were coming from all directions, not just behind her, and she feared she was already too late.

All across the Grove a battle was being fought. The Ma'at kefali and the few remaining elves fought a retreating battle against the Isfet and growing numbers of undead. As Liz ran past them all, she could have sworn she even spotted a group of orcs trudging through the trees.

It was like a living nightmare.

Liz ran as fast as she could through the dark forest with the roars of monsters and the cries of the dying all around her. Undead rose up and reached for her, but she carved through them with her growling chainsaber. Isfet appeared in her path, but her plasma revolver cleared the way. Flashes of light lit the darkness as spells were brought to bear and the forest shook with the power of their release.

Breathing hard, Liz stumbled out of a dense patch of brush and found herself in a large clearing. Her heart leapt at the sight of the colossal stones that formed a ring in the center of the grassy field.

She had made it!

Out of breath but with her goal in sight, Liz sprinted across the field and charged between two of the monolithic standing stones.

Inside the ring, Liz found four Korybantine Guards standing protectively around the huge stone altar at the center of the circle. A lone

Druid in heavy, bark-like robes stood behind the altar with a small wooden box resting on the heavy slab before him.

The Korybantes didn't try to stop Liz as she approached the High Druid. "We need to get out of here," Liz wheezed, as she stopped before the altar. "They are coming for the Seal!"

CHAPTER 28

Rubadub, Rabidad, and Robadoo stood before the might of Asag and hurled everything they had at him. Fire and lightning, ice and stone, water and air, even binding roots, but nothing harmed the impenetrable monster.

The weary Druids redoubled their efforts as Mike and the Wardens charged by them to challenge the demon lord. Rabidad's war cry turned into a mighty roar as his body swelled and was replaced by a massive brown bear. Robadoo leapt into the air and transformed into a very large and very ugly bird. Rubadub aimed a gnarled staff and a stream of emerald energy cascaded across the demon's rocky form.

LuHark's long strides outdistanced the others and her blessed scimitars flashed as the demon lord was rocked by the Druid's emerald impacts. The twin blades scraped across Asag's rocky skin and scored his stony hide but failed to do any perceivable damage.

Asag's gurgling laughter thundered around them as Mike, Rodan, and Brigit joined LuHark against the mighty demon lord. Asag carried no weapons, but the mighty demon didn't need to. Snotty streams of disease oozed from between the rocky plates and his three fists were like granite battering rams.

One of those boulder-like fists suddenly crashed into LuHark and slammed her to the ground. Asag raised one mighty fist to crush the stunned Hathi, but Robadoo swooped at the demon's wide head and clawed at some of Asag's many eyes. The demon lord swatted at the nimble Druid but couldn't hit the darting bird. The distraction was enough for LuHark to get back to her feet and resume her attack.

Then, Lithopedions came to their father's aid in an avalanche of demonic stone monsters.

Raenods and his Hands, along with the other defenders, were suddenly beset on all sides by roaring demons before they could reach Asag.

Rodan was knocked away by a swift backhand, but before he could charge back in, a pair of hulking Lithopedions blocked his path.

An explosion suddenly ripped one of the demons apart.

Rodan found the large elven Arbiter that had cast the spell and gave him a swift nod of thanks before the Warden charged the other demon.

Mike slammed his mace into the demon lord over and over, but all he managed to do was to chip away small fragments of stone. Ducking under one of Asag's thick arms, Mike saw a large opening in the rocky armor near the demon lord's abdomen where a thick ball of puss was oozing. But before Mike could get close, a heavy fist slammed into his back and knocked him to the ground.

The next blow was about to crush him when LuHark jumped in front of him and warded off the demon's strike. Mike scrambled to his feet, but a moment later Asag stomped the ground and a shockwave knocked everyone from their feet.

With a moment's reprieve, Asag turned his attention on Robadoo who was still dive-bombing his eyes.

All three arms swiveled unnaturally and lashed out at the flying Druid. Robadoo managed to avoid the first two fists, but the third found its mark.

Feathers exploded around the fist and the bird's broken body crashed to the ground.

Mike and the others regained their feet, but more Lithopedions were charging in and none of them could reach the stricken Druid. Asag laughed as he raised a massive foot above the crippled bird.

"No!" Rubadub shouted and twisting roots ripped out of the ground and wrapped around the raised leg. But Asag only laughed louder and slammed his heavy foot down, crushing Robadoo in an instant.

Rubadub and Rabidad cried out in dismay as their brother disappeared beneath Asag's boulder-like foot. The massive brown bear howled and rushed the demon lord, but Asag pivoted away and knocked the angry Druid away with an almost casual slap.

The Wardens and their allies were slowly being pushed further away from Asag as more of his dreadful children joined the fray. Challenging the Lithopedions was like fighting a rockslide, and soon Mike found himself back to back with Brigit, surrounded by a sea of stone demons.

The duo was being hammered from all sides when suddenly there was a brilliant flash and a huge revolving ball of crackling energy burst into existence nearby. The pulsating orb flared once and then abruptly vanished, leaving behind two figures in the center of a burned circle.

"Thank the gods," Brigit breathed at the sight of the identical warriors. "Our call for aid has finally been answered."

The newcomers were large and muscular, and they both wore a unique style of armor that made them look like ancient samurai. Their armor was exquisitely enameled in white and gold with intricate symbols painted upon each interlocking panel. Tall golden crests stood proudly upon their wide helmets.

Mike stared in confusion as the new Wardens raised their silvery katanas and charged into the surprised Lithopedions. "Aren't those-" Mike started to say, but Brigit cut him off.

"Yes," she growled, as she stabbed a Lithopedion in the neck with her shimmering spear. "That is Daijiro and Shojiro Yabuki. And yes, they are orcs." Her mighty spear carved through their rocky skin with ease as she sliced the blocky arm off of another demon. "And two of the most skilled Wardens you are likely to encounter."

Orc Wardens? Mike couldn't believe what he was hearing, but he wasn't about to argue with Brigit. She was a Warden after all. Besides, he had more important matters to consider, like not having his skull bashed in.

A very round demon abruptly rolled toward him and Mike summoned an Aegis Shield before it ran him over. The Lithopedion bounced off the shield and roared angrily as it pressed up against the invisible barrier, trying to force its way through.

The shield abruptly vanished and the demon stumbled forward and fell. Mike split the demon's skull with a brutal chop of his mace before another

Lithopedion came charging in.

The orc Wardens had arrived astonishingly close to Asag and they carved a path through the Lithopedions to reach him. Brigit and Mike followed their lead and slowly forced their way toward the demon lord.

When the last demon blocking the orc's path fell, Asag laughed as his three rocky hands morphed into immense, razor-sharp stone blades. A coating of sickly green ichor covered the blades as the orc Wardens swept in.

Their swords glowed in the darkness as they slashed at the impregnable demon lord. Asag's enormous blades met their katanas with a shriek of grinding stone and tortured metal. The orcs dueled the three-armed demon lord in an amazing display of skill. They flowed around the heavy strikes like wheat in the wind while scoring numerous cuts to the demon's rocky body.

Growing angry at his inability to hit the elusive Wardens, Asag spit acid and flung globs of pestilence at the pair. But the orcs were prepared and the vile projectiles struck shimmering barriers and splattered harmlessly off of them.

Quick as a snake, the Wardens struck at the nearly imperceptible cracks in the demon lord's armor. The glowing blades bit hungrily into the rocky skin as they searched for an opening.

Brigit and Mike finally cut down the last Lithopedion in their way and joined the orcs battling Asag. The wounded demon lord howled in rage as they approached and suddenly stabbed all three arms deep into the ground, creating a stone barrier between himself and the Wardens. Asag growled something in a foul language that hurt Mike's ears, and his muscles bulged as he fought to pull his arms back out of the ground.

The earth beneath Mike's feet heaved and they were forced back as the demon lord pulled something out of the ground. Asag's arms erupted from the dirt in a shower of debris and clenched in his huge hands were more Lithopedions. The stone demons dropped out of their master's hands and formed a living wall before him. Despite their ponderous appearance, the Lithopedions flew into action and crashed into Mike and the three Wardens with savage eagerness.

Mike was quickly separated from the others as the Lithopedions swarmed around them. Several of them surrounded him and it was only thanks to his training that he was able to hold the shields up around himself as the demons' heavy fists pounded away at them.

A battered Hand of Tyr abruptly stumbled out of the swirling battle and a surprised Ingemar suddenly found himself beside the towering demon lord. In a show of spectacular bravery, the dwarf didn't hesitate as he slammed his lightning hammer into Asag's thigh. Pieces of stone chipped away and the demon lord turned his baleful gaze on the burly Hand.

Mike wanted to help Ingemar, but he was surrounded by Lithopedions and was barely holding out against the rocky demons. He crushed one ugly skull and blocked a heavy swing with his shield before summoning two barriers and using them like a wedge to push the demons away. Mike charged through the opening and raced toward Ingemar. But before he could get there, the demon spat a glob of green puss into the dwarf's face.

Ingemar howled in agony and dropped his hammer. He clutched at his melting face and pieces of it peeled off in wet chunks.

Mike skidded to a halt as the Hand collapsed before him. The poor dwarf's cries faded away as the corrosive puss ate away the last of the flesh from his skull. Mike stood beside the smoking corpse and suddenly realized he was alone before the hideous demon lord.

One of Asag's hands reformed into a long blade and stabbed directly at Mike, but Mike twisted away and stepped in close to the putrid demon. The sickly stench nearly overwhelmed him, but Mike pushed the nausea aside and swung his mace with all his might at the large weak point in Asag's impenetrable hide.

The powerful runes that had been forged into the ancient weapon activated as the mace struck the oozing hole and a tremendous impact ruptured the demon lord's abdomen in a violent spray of foul puss and pulverized stone.

Asag howled in agony and reeled backwards, clutching at his ruined chest. The pain in his hideous face quickly vanished and was replaced by pure rage. "You will pay for that little mortal," Asag roared.

Despite clutching the grievous wound with one huge hand, the demon lord lunged at Mike with the other two bladed arms. Mike rolled away as the blades stabbed into the ground where he had been a moment before. He charged back in, but before he got close enough a glob of acid splattered against Mike's hastily summoned barrier. The acid stuck to the shield just in front of his face for a few precious moments, blocking his view as a huge fist smashed into him. Mike crashed to the ground in a heap as the demon lord lumbered toward him.

Mike groggily rolled onto his back and looked up at the terrible visage of the demon lord as Asag loomed above him.

"Die knowing that this world is mine," Asag laughed, as he raised an enormous blade above Mike's chest.

A brilliant beam of hellish red energy suddenly slammed into Asag and exploded.

"This world is mine!" another voice thundered, as Asag was knocked back by a second blast.

Still on the ground, Mike craned his neck to find the source of the surprise attack and when he found it he couldn't believe his eyes.

Moving through the battlefield was a knot of hulking warriors surrounding a towering golden monster.

The Destroyer had his golden *was* scepter raised and pointed at Asag. The animal-headed staff glowed with an evil light as another beam of blistering energy erupted from the staff's eyes and ripped into the reeling demon lord.

The orc Wardens finally cut their way through the Lithopedions and pounced on the wounded demon lord. Asag's one arm clutched his ruined chest, while another morphed into a wide stone shield as another barrage from The Destroyer slammed into it, leaving only one arm to fight the pair of orcs.

Then, Brigit and Rodan emerged from the swirling battle and attacked the demon from the rear. The one-armed demon spun around but couldn't keep up with the skilled Wardens.

A Lithopedion suddenly exploded and LuHark burst through the demon. Trumpeting grandly, the huge Hathi joined her fellow Wardens and surrounded Asag.

Mike scrambled to his feet and hurried to join them. A beam of pure white light from Brigit's spear tore through a weakened joint on one of the trunk-like legs and Asag howled as he toppled over.

Daijiro and Shojiro ran up the floundering demon and together they drove their blades into charred fissures created up by The Destroyer's scepter on opposite sides of the demon lords' hideous face. Asag screamed as the glowing blades drove home and then both orcs ripped their blades clockwise, slicing all around the demon's stumpy head.

With an awful sucking sound, Asag's head ripped away from his body and a fountain of putrid gore flooded out of the gaping hole.

Asag's head continued to spit curses even as his body began to consume itself. The sickly yellow puss sizzled as it ate away at the black, stony skin, creating a foul smelling green smoke. Within moments, the monstrous body had dissolved, leaving only Asag's repulsive head.

"This world will be mine!" Asag's head gurgled as it too began to deteriorate. "You have not seen the last of the Mighty Asag!" The demon lord's name hung in the air as his head melted away into a foul mist that was swept away by a sudden breeze.

Mike stood before the acid-burned ground where the demon had once been. An awful wailing filled the night air as demons all across the hillside began to deteriorate like their master.

Powerful laughter cut through the wailing and Mike found The Destroyer laughing as the Lithopedions evaporated around him.

As the demons vanished, Mike suddenly realized that The Destroyer wasn't alone. Spread out behind him was what appeared to be the majority of his Horned Legion. Unknown to Mike and the others, the kefali must have attacked the demons from the opposite side of the hill. Now that the Lithopedions were gone, there was nothing left to separate the two forces.

The battered defenders suddenly found themselves with a new enemy before them, and to their credit, they quickly formed up behind Mike and the Wardens as the Horned Legion did the same behind their golden master.

The mighty demigod slithered toward Mike with his army at his back. "I am glad you survived the destruction of your pitiful wall," The Destroyer boomed in his powerful voice. "Now, I will devour your soul!"

The demigod raised his *was* scepter and pointed it directly at Mike. A blistering red bolt erupted from the staff's eyes and shot toward him. Mike raised his shield and everything vanished in a brilliant explosion.

****

Emily desperately clung to the wide crystal scales as the two Great Wyrms clashed high above the burning city. The huge dragons performed a breathtaking aerial ballet of death with claw and fang as they tried to outmaneuver each other to gain any advantage.

The two dragons tore into each other with amazing fury. Emily could feel every scratch and bite as if they were her own, and she was doing everything she could to hold on. She willed Lru to be faster and strike harder as she hung there, gasping in pain at every wound her mount received.

It may have been her imagination, but she thought the mighty crystal dragon responded to her silent plea and, for a short time, landed several more strikes on the mighty black. But Phlebolith was larger and Lru's claws did far less damage than Emily would have liked.

The monstrous black released an earsplitting roar and suddenly launched himself at Lru. Phlebolith slammed into the crystal and the pair began to spiral out of the air in a tangle of scales and claws. The world spun crazily as Emily fought to maintain her grip as Lru twisted beneath her.

The battling dragons plummeted out of the darkness and soon Emily caught dizzying glimpses of fires and buildings as they neared the swiftly approaching ground.

Lru abruptly released a concussive roar that hammered into Phlebolith and blasted him away. The mighty black crashed into the side of a skyscraper and disappeared into the billowing cloud of debris.

Emily finally released her death grip as Lru righted himself and a sweep of his mighty wings stopped their descent.

"Did you kill him?" Emily asked breathlessly as she eyed the jagged opening where the black had vanished. The skyscraper groaned and began to lean dangerously as the stricken building became unstable.

"It will take more than that to defeat the Blightwing," Lru rumbled, as he glared at the ruin.

A sudden chorus of screams caused Lru to briefly look away and when he did, Phlebolith shot out of the building like a titanic black arrow. A torrent of blistering green flames led the way and Lru jerked aside, barely avoiding the living missile, but crying out in pain as the passing flames caught one of his wings.

With the horrible screech of tortured metal and shattering glass, the stricken skyscraper groaned as it lost its structural integrity and began to collapse. The towering steel building toppled forward and Emily screamed as the skyscraper fell toward them. Lru tried to get away, but his injured wing made maneuvering difficult.

Phlebolith saw his enemy's struggles and eager to finish the kill, the mighty black didn't notice the building falling toward them.

Phlebolith dove back in and Lru wasn't able to avoid him this time. The Great Wyrms collided and the force of the barreling black carried them all out from under the falling skyscraper. The broken upper half of the building crashed onto the roof of the smaller structure across the street, creating a bridge of twisted steel and shattered glass.

Emily was nearly flung from her perch when Phlebolith slammed into them, but she somehow managed to hang on as the monstrous black tore into Lru. Emily cried out in agony as she felt Phlebolith's claws viciously rip through Lru's crystal scales.

Suddenly, a brilliant flash lit the night as something exploded against Phlebolith's titanic body.

A brave griffin darted perilously close to the embattled Great Wyrms and an elf mage stood boldly in the stirrups as he pointed a slender wand at the huge black dragon. Regulus's flowing blonde hair and silvery armor gleamed in the light as another dazzling magical bolt erupted from the wand.

Phlebolith shrieked as four more bolts found their mark and detonated against his scaly hide. But the mighty dragon didn't turn from his battle with Lru. Instead, Emily caught a glimpse of movement upon the black's back and she realized that she had forgotten about Phlebolith's rider.

The dark-skinned elf was nearly invisible in his black armor as he drew a small object from somewhere and pointed it at the darting griffin and its rider.

Emily tried to shout a warning, but there was no way Regulus could have heard her over the roaring dragons and deafening explosions.

A beam of utter blackness shot out of the shadow elf's hand and there was a crackling of discharging energy as the beam punched through the Battlemage's shields and struck Regulus full in the chest. The elf was blown from his saddle and his body plummeted to the city far below.

Emily drew her scepter with one hand as she held on to a large scale with the other and fired several emerald bolts at the shadow elf.

But her shots flew wide as the jostling dragons fought beneath them. Emily cursed and put her scepter away before clinging to the dragon's back once more. She knew there was no way she could hit the other rider while the dragons knocked her around. So, she closed her eyes instead and focused on lending whatever strength she could to her dragon.

Lru desperately clawed at Phlebolith's softer underbelly, but the huge black swung his heavy tail and slammed into the crystal's shoulder. Lru was knocked off balance as he desperately tried to right himself, but his injuries were slowing him down. The massive black struck again before Lru could compensate.

Phlebolith's titanic jaws clamped around Lru's leg and the crystal dragon screamed.

****

"Never fear," Belenos replied softly from behind the stone altar, his face hidden in the darkness of his cowl. "This Grove is well protected."

"Not well enough," Liz shot back. "They know that we have the Seal and they are coming for it."

The High Druid didn't move. "Of course, they know we have it," he said softly. "It was rescued from some of their agents just the other day."

Liz slammed her chainsaber and pistol down on the altar as she angrily leaned toward the High Druid. "Then why are you still here?" she hissed in exasperation. "Why didn't you hide it someplace safe?"

"Safe?" Belenos hissed from the darkness of his cowl. "Where on this god's-accursed world would that be?" The High Druid leaned in toward Liz. "The Grove *is* the safest place for the Seal until the Archmage has completed his project. Besides," Belenos said waving a dismissive hand, "they know we have it, but they do not know where it is."

Liz stared at the elf in disbelief. "You're just going to stand here and... what? Wait for them to figure out where it is?"

"Of course not, girl," Belenos growled. "The Seal will be moved whe-" A tremor suddenly passed through the High Druid and as one, all four of the Korybantine Guards drew their blades.

"By the Mother..." Belenos cursed under his breath. "They are here."

"Who is here?" Liz asked.

Belenos clutched a small pouch on his belt and paused a moment as if considering something before he answered. "The Shadowed Ones have crossed into the Grove," Belenos replied grimly. "A powerful lich must accompany them to have defeated Pan's Line."

Liz readied her weapons as she faced the darkness beyond the stone rings. "What does that mean?"

"It means that they know where it is," Belenos replied grimly.

"But aren't the Druids the protectors of these Seals?" Liz asked. "A Druid's Grove is the first place I would look."

Belenos grimaced. "We never keep the Seals in Groves for exactly that reason. Whoever is searching for it must know that. So, they are either very lucky or they have some means to track it…"

"Is that even possible?" Liz asked.

"I only know of one way…" Belenos muttered distractedly as he absently touched the silver torc around his neck. "It should be impossible to track… unless… it's her…" Belenos hissed.

The High Druid suddenly made up his mind and hurried around the altar to stand before Liz. "The other Druids would kill me for this, but I don't suspect that I will live long enough to worry about it."

Belenos removed his silver torc. "You will need this," he whispered, as he placed the cold, metal device around her neck. A strange sensation came over her as the torc settled into place, but the High Druid's next words took her attention. "Do you swear to watch and protect the Seven Seals of the Dagda for as long as you live?"

Liz was too shocked to move at first and she had no idea what was going on, but she could see the intensity in the High Druid's face and she knew what was at stake. Her choice was an easy one. "I do."

Belenos bent down and grabbed a pinch of dirt and grass, then he ground it together between his thumb and forefinger. He muttered something in elvish as he smeared the mud onto her forehead in a tight swirling pattern. Finally, he pulled the small pouch from his belt and handed it to her. "Take this and find the Archmage."

"What about you?" Liz asked as she took the pouch and saw him wince as she quickly stuffed it into her pocket.

"We will hold off the Shadowed Ones for as long as we can," Belenos replied with a sad smile. "You are now a Watcher. It is your duty to protect the Seal at all costs." The High Druid pointed to the dark tower just beyond the border of the park. "Get to the Cathedral and find the Archmage." Belenos urged as he gently ushered her away. "The fate of this world depends on it."

"No pressure then," Liz muttered, as she stepped out of the stone ring and into the darkness.

Belenos watched until Liz disappeared into the trees, then he went back to the altar and waited. He didn't have long to wait, as only a few minutes later several shadows materialized out of the darkness.

A withered woman flanked by four cloaked figures stepped into the ring. A thought from Belenos stopped his guard from attacking the newcomers as they approached.

"Belenosss," the woman hissed. "It has been a long time."

She may have once been pretty, even beautiful, but now she was little more than a walking corpse. Her skin was stretched tight across her body and in some places it had torn away, revealing the white bones beneath. Only patches of wispy hair clung to her rotten skull and where her eyes should have been there were only two points of eldritch light that pulsed with an otherworldly power.

Belenos lowered his hood as he faced the lich. "Not long enough, Sabine."

Sabine's laughter was like the rustling of dry leaves. "Oh, Bel, are you still mad that I killed your master?"

"He was your master too!" Belenos snarled with surprising fury. "How could you have betrayed us like that?"

"My reasons are my own," Sabine hissed back. "Besides, what should you care? I see you have been raised to High Druid, as I know you always wanted."

"But not like that," Belenos snarled. "I wanted to earn it."

"Come now, Bel," Sabine hissed. "It has been over five hundred years. Surely you would have been made a High Druid by now. I just did you a favor by speeding things up."

"Is that what you think? That you did me a *favor*?" The High Druid stared at the lich in amazement. "You are a monster."

"Yesss," Sabine cackled gleefully, "and one that will be here long after your bones have turned to dust. But if you give it to me, I will let you live out the rest of your pitiful life."

"Never," Belenos growled. "You always were more gifted than I, Sabine, but I will *never* surrender the Seal to you. I will protect it with my last breath."

Sabine eyed the wooden box on the altar hungrily before turning her undead gaze back to Belenos. Her eyes suddenly blazed with eldritch power. "So be it."

CHAPTER 29

Wisps of steam rose from Mike's armor as crackling red energy dissipated around the faint blue Aegis Shield surrounding him. A brief look of surprise crossed The Destroyer's bull-like features at the sight of Mike still standing there.

The opposing armies faced each other anxiously, neither side sure of what they should do as Mike and The Destroyer faced off.

"I've had just about enough of your little death bolts!" Mike shouted with much more confidence than he felt. "Is the mighty Destroyer afraid to face a 'mere mortal' in combat?"

"I fear nothing!" The Destroyer bellowed angrily.

"Then prove it, ya jagoff!" Mike taunted. He prayed that the demigod would take the bait because he was sure that his shield wouldn't take another shot from that staff. If Liz had been here, she would have called it reckless, but Mike called it "not getting blown up."

The Destroyer roared and slammed his tail on the ground in rage. The golden demigod suddenly surged forward and the rest of the Horned Legion bellowed a war cry and followed.

Mike raised his mace and the rest of the weary defenders extended their weapons and charged ahead, shouting wild challenges of their own. Despite his heavy armor, Mike easily bound across the rocky ground like a deer as he headed straight for The Destroyer.

As the distance between the two rapidly closed, Mike waited until the last possible moment to summon another shield. But this shield was horizontal to the ground, leaving only a nearly invisible, razor-thin edge exposed.

The Destroyer rushed ahead, eager for the kill and didn't notice the faint shield.

Just as Mike had planned, the demigod charged right into the shield and his neck slammed into the razor-thin edge.

But instead of decapitating the monster like Mike had hoped, the shield shattered like glass and vanished, leaving nothing between him and the enraged demigod.

The shield in his gauntlet sprang to life and Mike deflected the first swing of The Destroyer's staff as the two finally met. All around them the armies clashed and the battle was joined.

The defenders were a ragged bunch that represented a mixture of all the different groups that now called Pittsburgh home, including the Wardens, Hands of Tyr, Scadians, ACL Knights, Marines, Battlemages, various orders of clerics, dwarf warriors, elven legionaries, and human soldiers. They battled the warriors of the Horned Legion that was made up of kefali from all manner of animal species, including bulls, horses, lions, tigers, snakes, birds, monkeys, and even a few massive beasts that resembled hippopotamuses.

Mike dueled the demigod alone but was forced back by the sheer strength and ferocity of The Destroyer's strikes.

Suddenly, the demigod shifted and his heavy tail snapped around and slammed into Mike, knocking him to the ground. Mike rolled away just in time as the fork-like end of the *was* scepter stabbed the ground where he had been a moment before.

Mike caught movement out of the corner of his eye and saw Rodan charging out of the swirling battle. The dwarf Warden roared as he swung his pulsing hammer and slammed it into The Destroyer's back.

The war hammer detonated against the golden armor with a thunderous impact that knocked the demigod into one of his warriors. The Destroyer flung the poor kefali away as he roared angrily and rounded on Rodan.

Mike climbed to his feet as Rodan again charged the demigod. But this time as Rodan pulled back his hammer, The Destroyer's scepter blazed with power and a crackling beam shot out and caught the Warden full in the face. Rodan's helmet was ripped off as the explosion flung his body to the ground.

The Destroyer laughed as Mike rushed in and the demigod unleashed a volley of crackling bolts before he could get close. The barrage slammed into Mike's hastily summoned barrier that defeated most of the bolts, but the last few made it through and ripped into him.

Mike withstood the blasts, but then collapsed to his knees in the dirt before the mighty demigod.

"Finally, you know your place," The Destroyer boomed, as Mike struggled to stand, but couldn't find the strength. His armor had several holes ripped into it and the flesh beneath was burned and broken.

Then, two shapes moved between Mike and The Destroyer.

"Aye," a deep voice rumbled. "An' it be between ye and this world."

Mike looked up and to his surprise he saw Captain Raenods and Astrid standing there, blocking the demigod from him. The two Hands of Tyr seemed tiny before the towering Destroyer, but they faced him without fear. Raenods' axe burst into flames as the leader of the Hands launched himself at the golden demigod. But The Destroyer struck first, and his staff lashed out faster than the eye could follow and severed Raenods' right hand at the wrist. Blood fountained from the ruined stump as the flaming axe landed on the ground with the severed hand still clamped around it.

The Destroyer struck again, but this time Astrid was there, and she pushed the stricken Raenods to the ground as the glowing scepter shattered her Svalinn Field and punched through her chest.

"Is that the best you can do?" The Destroyer taunted, as Astrid's corpse slid off his staff.

"No," Mike growled, as he stood up and faced the towering demigod. As he stood there, the cuts and burns across his body began to mend and a moment later his skin was whole once more.

"Neat trick," The Destroyer growled, "but your soul is still mine!" The monster roared and suddenly rushed Mike.

Mike dove aside and struck with his mace, striking the demigod in the shoulder. The Destroyer spun and launched a series of brutal attacks that

Mike was hard-pressed to avoid. The monster was far too quick, and Mike took several hits as he was forced back.

Mike knew he couldn't hold out much longer and so he desperately fell into the Zone. The world seemed to slow around him, and he was able to block The Destroyer's next strike. Mike struck back and actually managed to hit the demigod, and the elaborate golden armor cracked beneath the heavy impact. But The Destroyer seemed unharmed.

The advantage didn't last long as The Destroyer entered a similar battle trance and once again struck faster than Mike could defend.

A brutal series of blows knocked Mike off balance and before he could recover, The Destroyer plunged the forked scepter into Mike's chest.

Mike gasped in surprise and pain as the spikes punched through his back and he was lifted up into the air.

The Destroyer laughed as he held Mike several feet off the ground. "Now, you die."

****

Ted wearily stumbled out of the dark woods and into a clearing. As he tried to catch his breath, he was again reminded why he hated the outdoors. "Bloody nature," he grumbled, as he set off once more.

The magical trail had led him across several rooftops before entering a dingy stretch of woods. That was when he discovered the rotten path and gratefully released his spell in the hopes of saving his powers.

Now, Ted was no tracker by any stretch of the imagination, but the trail was so obvious that he didn't even need magic. Wherever the lich passed, plants died, leaving a wide trail of death that even a city dweller like Ted could follow.

Torchlight flickered from between the enormous stones in the center of the clearing as Ted followed the trail toward the monolithic structure.

When he stepped into the ring of stones, a scene of carnage greeted him.

The bodies of four Korybantine Guards lay scattered and broken across the rotting grass while a Druid was slumped against one of the standing stones. A broken wooden box was scattered across the huge stone altar in the center of the ring, but there was no sign of the lich.

Ted hurried over to the Druid and when he knelt down, he was surprised to discover it was the High Druid Belenos.

He felt for a pulse, but it became clear that the High Druid was dead.

Ted immediately began rummaging through the dead Druid's pouches and looting anything that he thought might be of use. Surely Belenos wouldn't have any need of it any longer.

Ted was crouched beside the body, stuffing his pockets when Belenos abruptly opened his eyes and lunged at him. Ted fell backwards in surprise as the undead High Druid clawed at him. There was a sudden thrum of power and a two-foot blade of plasma sprang to life on Ted's artificial arm. With a desperate swipe, the blade seared through the zombie's neck and Belenos' head tumbled from his shoulders.

Ted quickly scrambled to his feet and found himself surrounded by four undead Korybantes with blades drawn.

"I should have seen this coming," Ted muttered under his breath, as the undead drew closer.

The Korybantes' eyes glowed with an inner light and Ted knew what that meant. The shimmering blade of the plazmax rippled into being, and the light from the two plasma weapons cast a faint radiance around him.

"Come on out," Ted shouted to the darkness. "I know you're there."

The undead elves didn't respond and continued to close in around him. Ted put his back to one of the huge stones and with a slight shudder he realized it was the same place that Belenos had originally fallen.

The undead suddenly stopped and a shadow moved in the darkness beyond the stones.

A pale elf in black robes glided into the torchlight and she gave him a predatory smile that revealed her long fangs.

"You are persistent," the vampire purred. "I like that in a pet."

"I am nobody's pet," Ted replied carefully.

"We shall see about that," the vampire hissed hungrily. "I am Countess Tatiana and I assume that I have you to thank for destroying Count Otho?"

Ted didn't know what the vampire was after, but he was willing to play along until he found a way out of this mess. "You didn't like him?"

"Like him?" the Countess laughed. "Otho was a fool and was undeserving of the title of Count."

"And you are?" Ted asked.

Tatiana's eyes flashed dangerously. "I am. That is why the Mistress granted me this task."

Ted didn't like the sound of that. "And what task is that?"

The vampire smiled again and her fangs sparkled in the faint light as she glided closer. "Why, to turn you of course."

"I'm afraid that's not going to happen, my dear," Ted replied, as he reviewed the spells he had stored in his mind.

"Oh, didn't I tell you?" the Countess purred, as the undead Korybantes took another step closer to him. "You don't have a choice."

****

Alex and Jack followed the enraged dwarf king as he barreled toward the enormous warlord. But before they could reach the deadly oni, a pair of hulking orcs blocked their path. The one in front of Alex was nearly as large as the warlord and encased in a suit of exquisite armor with a hideous demon's mask covering his face. The other one stood before Jack and was nearly as large as the first but wore no armor at all. Instead, the orc was wrapped in black cloth from head to toe and armed with a pair of three-pronged sai.

Alex stared at the massive armored orc before him as Jack judged the ninja he faced. Alex and Jack shared a brief look and then hastily switched places.

The orcs looked confused for a moment before the pair charged the ugly beasts. The orcs rushed to meet them, and the humans and orcs crashed together as King Varnir barreled past them to face the warlord alone.

The enchanted staff twirled through the air as Alex tried to confuse the orc ninja. But when he struck at the orc's head, the ninja easily blocked it and countered with a lightning quick strike at Alex's exposed arm. He pulled away, just avoiding the stabbing sai, and the orc followed.

Each sai moved like it had a mind of its own and Alex was hard-pressed to defend against the stabbing weapons. Then, one of the sai caught the staff between its prongs and the ninja tried to rip the trapped weapon out of his grasp. But Alex rotated along with the orc's motion and was able to maintain his grip as he pulled the staff free.

Realizing his danger, Alex remembered what Ted had told him about the enchanted weapon. He twisted the center of the staff and it broke apart with a length of chain connecting the two halves. Alex called forth the power of the weapon and one baton glowed white-hot as the other crackled with electricity.

A sai caught the first baton strike, but to Alex's disappointment, the weapon didn't transfer the electrical charge to the orc and he realized it must have been insulated somehow. The sai may be protected from electricity, but Alex was sure the orc was not, and the duel began in earnest.

The weapons rang out each time they met and the speed of the duel was so fast that it seemed as though it was just one long note hanging in the air. Alex and the orc ninja spun around each other in a deadly dance, each seeking the smallest advantage.

Then, when Alex swung a double strike with his linked batons, the ninja twisted aside and put Alex slightly off balance. The ninja lashed out and Alex was just able to block them. Unfortunately, both batons got caught in the prongs of the sai and the ninja swiftly twisted the weapons and brutally ripped the batons out of his hands.

The enchanted staff clattered across the road and Alex suddenly found himself unarmed as the skilled orc ninja advanced.

The werewolf snarled as the two black blades crashed together with a shrill wail. Jack pressed the warchief hard, but the huge orc countered him at every turn. Thick curtains of ash flowed out of the hellishly glowing weapons and soon even Jack's enhanced eyesight couldn't penetrate the increasingly thick dust.

Although he couldn't see, Jack could still hear the orc's blade slicing through the air and he was able to continue fighting in the ash cloud. To everyone outside the cloud, they could only see flashes of movement and bursts of sparks within the ash.

Jack parried a slash at his head and returned with a lightning quick jab at the warchief's gut, but the orc stepped agilely away and easily knocked Yoma-Ketsueki aside. Jack heard the faint hiss of the orc's blade passing through the ash and he deflected the strike with a turn of his own blade.

The warchief suddenly launched a brutal series of slashes at Jack and he was hard pressed to defend them all. Sparks flew as the blades bit into each other and then as Jack parried the next swing, he heard a different sound. Too late he realized what it was. An enormous green fist suddenly appeared out of the ash and slammed into Jack's face.

Everything went black.

The next thing Jack knew he was on his back and a huge shape lumbered toward him. As the wooziness cleared, the world seemed duller, less alive than Jack remembered and he felt as if he had been struck blind and deaf. He also felt strange... like something was missing... Confused, it took Jack a moment to realize what was different.

He was human again.

The wolf was gone.

King Varnir ducked under the whirling saw blade and drove the Axe of Perun into the metal brace of the exo-suit attached to the warlord's tree trunk-like leg. The blade bit deep, but the brace was thick and withstood the mighty blow.

Stormtusk snapped his long, iron club around and forced the dwarf king to roll aside. The huge oni rushed the dwarf and lashed out with both club and saw but King Varnir proved surprisingly agile as he avoided the warlord's furious assault.

The enormous circular saw ripped into the asphalt and sent pieces flying through the air as the iron club left deep indentations where its powerful blows landed. King Varnir flowed around the vicious blows in uncanny dexterity for a dwarf in such cumbersome armor. The king moved like he had no armor on at all, and managed to land several more strikes on the warlord's exoskeleton.

Stormtusk bellowed angrily as the king dodged another killing blow. The warlord bellowed a word of power and the air shook with its command. King Varnir suddenly froze. The enchanted paralysis only lasted a moment, but it was long enough as Stormtusk brutally slammed his heavy club into the immobile dwarf.

King Varnir flew through the air and smashed into a nearby wall. Somehow, he landed on his feet and a thick stream of blood ran from his wide nose as the angry dwarf king raised his axe and again charged the powerful oni.

King Varnir swung the Axe of Perun with all his might as Stormtusk drove his monstrous saw at the charging dwarf. The two leaders met with a thunderous crash and there was an awful grinding sound as sparks cascaded around their deadly weapons.

Stormtusk brought his heavy club around and began pummeling the dwarf king with both saw and club. The strength and speed of the warlord's ferocious attack was awe-inspiring, but King Varnir defended the powerful attacks with a masterful display of martial skill.

Then, as the mighty oni slashed with his growling saw, King Varnir drove his axe into the smoking mechanism strapped to the warlord's arm. The device shattered and the whirling saw sputtered and died. The victory was short-lived as destroying the saw had exposed him and Stormtusk swiftly slammed his heavy club into the king's back.

King Varnir was knocked to the ground by the force of the blow, and before he could recover Stormtusk hit him again. The heavy iron club was relentless as it crashed into the dwarf king over and over again. The mighty oni even used the ruined saw as a weapon by raking the sharp teeth across the stunned dwarf.

The powerful blows rained down until a swift uppercut from the club caught King Varnir and lifted him off the ground. The battered king landed heavily and struggled to get back up.

"Tough lil bugger…" Stormtusk snorted, as he kicked King Varnir over with his mechanical boot, "fer a grub." The oni laughed as he stomped a heavy foot into the king's chest and raised his iron club.

CHAPTER 30

The signs of a recent battle became more pronounced the closer Liz got to the Cathedral of Learning complex. As she approached the high walls surrounding the structure, Liz was forced to walk over a virtual carpet of kefali bodies that littered the ground.

To her vast relief, she saw that the walls were still intact and that soldiers were patrolling the scarred battlements.

A sudden stabbing pain flowed through the bond and Liz stumbled as a sliver of the agony Mike was experiencing made its way into her mind. With great difficulty, Liz pushed the feelings aside and concentrated on the task before her.

She was worried for Mike, but she knew that if she didn't get the Seal away from the Shadow elves, then they would all die.

The guards upon the gatehouse eyed her warily as she approached. "Who goes there?" one of them shouted from his high perch.

"Liz McAllister," Liz shouted back, as she stopped before the immense steel doors. "I'm a healer and have an important message for Archmage Talsin from High Druid Belenos."

The soldier's eyes narrowed suspiciously. "And what is a lone healer doing out in this?" the soldier asked, as he motioned out into the darkness.

Liz realized she must look a sight, appearing out of the shadows, covered in gore and armed with a bloody chainsaber and an old revolver.

She wouldn't have let herself in. But she needed this guard to trust her so she could deliver the Seal before the lich found her.

The soldier scowled and looked about to argue more when a second figure appeared beside him. The newcomer was an elf clad in exquisite silver armor and armed with a short spear. "I will vouch for her," Leandros said, as he flashed her a brilliant smile. "She is a friend."

The soldier wasn't convinced. "And how do ya know she ain't some evil sorcerer in disguise?"

"I am a Paladin of Athena," Leandros replied hotly. "It is my duty to see through the illusions of the Shadow."

But the soldier didn't budge. "I ain't abaht ta open this her' gate unless I have some proof."

"Very well," Leandros sighed. "This will reveal her true nature." He pointed his spear at Liz and a beam of brilliant light shot out. The light hurt her eyes and she raised her arm to block out some of the glare.

After a moment the light faded away.

"There. You see?" Leandros huffed. "She is who she says. Now, let her in."

The soldier muttered something under his breath but didn't make any move to open the gate.

Then there was a sudden commotion within the complex and all the guards began muttering at once. Everyone upon the battlements moved away and Liz lost sight of them.

She suddenly felt very alone in the darkness amidst the sea of dead as the echoes of battle filtered through the cool night air.

A loud clang made her jump as the huge reinforced doors abruptly began to swing open. Leandros and the soldiers reappeared upon the walls, as the opening grew wider. Liz was surprised when she saw that someone was actually coming out of the complex.

She was even more surprised when she discovered that it was Archmage Talsin!

The elf's midnight blue robes billowed out around him as he hurried through the gatehouse and strode up to Liz. "Do you have it?" he asked urgently.

"Yes." Liz reached into her pocket and withdrew the pouch Belenos had given her.

"Excellent." Talsin breathed a sigh of relief.

Liz offered him the pouch, but he held up a hand. "No," he said. "It is not my place. The Seal was entrusted to you."

"But I'm not a Druid," she argued, with the offered pouch still resting in her outstretched hand. "It will be safer with you."

"I cannot," Talsin repeated, as he gently took Liz's hand and closed it over the pouch. "Belenos ordained you as a Watcher and by rights it is yours until another Watcher can protect it."

"Ordained?" Liz stared at the Archmage as if he had grown a second head. "Is that what he did to me with the dirt?" Liz stuffed the pouch back in her pocket. "How do you even know about that?"

Talsin's eyes sparkled mischievously. "Because I'm an Archmage," he replied slyly.

But Liz wasn't in the mood for games. "Well, if you won't take it, where should I go?"

"Ah," Talsin smiled. "I believe I have just the place."

"Well, you had better hurry up and tell me," Liz said, as she pointed back down the street, "because the lich is here!"

Talsin looked to where Liz was pointing and saw a skeletal woman flowing toward them with a gang of shadows surrounding her.

"So, she is," the Archmage sighed. "Best be on your way then, my dear. The time has come." He looked back toward the gatehouse and waved his arm in a grand gesture. The huge section of the sky alongside the Cathedral began to shimmer like heat radiating off of pavement. Then the veil fell away and Liz gasped in surprise at the sight before her.

There, floating in the air was a flying castle.

The walls were tall and angled and made of the same strange, white stone with thick steel Warding Belts like all of the defenses across the city. The fortifications were in a square, star-fort pattern and they sat upon a huge chunk of stone as if the entire fort had been ripped out of the ground.

But Liz could see that this was no medieval fort.

This was a mobile weapons platform.

The entire structure was covered with a variety of armaments. Enormous cannons and advanced laser batteries poked out from the rough underside of the fortress. While electromagnetic railguns, enclosed machine gun nests, and missile silos lined the walls.

Talsin waved his arm again and a glowing door appeared in the air beside him. "Quickly now," he advised, as he gently herded her toward the door.

But Liz resisted his gentle urging. It wasn't that she didn't trust the Archmage, but she had been around Ted enough to know that you don't just step into a magical portal when one appears in front of you.

"And where does this go?" she asked sharply.

"Why, to the *Duquesne II* of course," Talsin said, as he motioned up to the flying fortress.

Liz glanced back and saw the lich was less than a block away and closing fast. Making up her mind, Liz held her breath and stepped though the shimmering doorway and disappeared.

A moment later the portal vanished with a faint pop.

Just then, guns of the airborne *Duquesne II* opened fire and the city shook with the thunderous power of the distant guns.

"Close the gates!" Talsin ordered the guards upon the wall before he turned to face the lich and her gathered vampires.

"But sir, you need to get inside, the enemies are approaching!" the guard shouted, as the gate began to swing closed.

"Yes," Talsin muttered grimly, as the heavy doors banged closed behind him. "I know."

****

Emily cried out in pain as Phlebolith's fangs dug into Lru's shoulder and nearly knocked her off the battered dragon's back. Emerald bolts exploded along the mighty black's long neck, but the scepter did little damage to the mighty behemoth.

The elf upon Phlebolith's back hurled spells at Emily, but the thrashing dragons made targeting the other rider nearly impossible. Emily had tried returning fire, but she quickly abandoned that idea and focused her attacks on the dragon itself. But even with Emily's magic, it became clear that Phlebolith was just too strong.

Lru fought valiantly, but even without the injured wing and crippled leg, defeating the monstrous black would have been a challenge. Now, it was all Lru could do to keep the black from ending the duel.

The fight was no longer about killing Phlebolith; it was about simply staying alive.

A sharp slap from the black's tail sent Lru and Emily spinning through the night and when Lru finally managed to right himself, Phlebolith slammed into them again. In the brief moment between dizzying tumbles, Emily saw a strange shimmering in the air nearby but didn't pay it much heed as she had more immediate concerns.

The two Great Wyrms crashed together again and got locked in a fierce struggle for superiority, one that Lru was swiftly losing.

Emily knew that it was only a matter of time before Phlebolith found a weak point and ended the aerial battle once and for all.

In desperation, Emily unloaded a stream of searing bolts into the black's scaly bulk.

Suddenly, the night lit up and a deafening roar split the air.

Emily looked around wildly for the source of the noise and was shocked to discover a heavily armed fortress floating in the air nearby.

The impressive abundance of weaponry unleashed a torrent of death in all directions.

Heavy cannons pounded enemy ground positions as searing laser beams carved through packed ranks of hostile troops. Machine guns and anti-aircraft batteries ripped into the flying monsters and the night sky began to rain harpies and wyverns. Even the evil dragons were knocked from the air by the powerful assault.

With the unexpected support, the griffin riders were able to form ranks and target the larger packs of enemies while some even swooped down to help the soldiers on the ground.

Emily saw movement on the flying castle and discovered that several of the guns were tracking them!

Panic grabbed her before she realized the guns weren't firing.

At first, she was confused, but then she realized that they were waiting for a clear shot.

Emily tried to get Lru's attention, but the crystal was focused on the huge black that was trying to claw his eyes out. Not knowing what she was doing, Emily dug deep into her connection with Lru and tried to mentally pass along the message.

When there was no reaction, Emily tried again, stronger this time. But still the crystal didn't respond and they continued to spin through the air.

Emily decided to try one more time. She knew what Lru needed to do, if she could only get him to do it. She reached down as deep as she could into the strange current of feelings that she knew was her bond to the majestic dragon and willed Lru to break free.

The wave of concussive force ripped out of Lru's jaws and slammed into Phlebolith, pushing the two dragons apart.

The moment there was some distance between them, the cannons of the flying castle unleashed a hail of fire that peppered the stunned black and ripped into his thick scales.

Phlebolith roared in pain and rage as the unrelenting gunfire tore into his immense bulk. Not even a mighty beast such as he could withstand the awesome might of such furious combined firepower.

The titanic Great Wyrm howled in rage once more before it dove away and beat his tattered wings madly in a desperate attempt to get away. The gunfire followed the retreating black dragon until the mighty beast vanished into the night.

"How did you do that?" Lru asked, as he limped through the hazy air and slowly made their way toward the strange flying castle.

"What do you mean?" Emily asked.

"Summoning my breath to separate us." Lru groaned, through gritted teeth.

Emily knew he was in agony and she was proud that he was still in the air after the beating he had taken. But his words surprised her. "I didn't do anything," she replied. "When I saw the castle's guns, I knew we needed to get away and I had tried to tell you, but you couldn't hear." Emily shrugged helplessly even though Lru couldn't see her. "I dunno... I just used the bond to try and tell you what to do."

Lru's chuckle made him cough and wheeze in pain. When he recovered, Emily could still hear the amusement in his voice. "You certainly told me what to do," he rasped weakly. "You took control for a moment and summoned my breath. That should not be possible until our bond is much stronger."

"I never was much for rules," Emily replied airily, as Lru carefully settled down upon a large helipad attached to the flying fortress. "And I hate when people tell me I can't do something."

Lru chuckled weakly and began to cough again as Emily quickly slid off his back and looked around for help. A lone figure came rushing out of a nearby tower and Emily was surprised to see Liz running toward her.

Emily ran down the ramp and met Liz on the wall.

"What are you doing here?" Emily asked, as she and Liz embraced. "Did you warn the Druids?"

"Yes, it's safe." Liz pulled back and looked her over critically. "Now, how are you?" A faint golden light flowed from Liz's hands and a cool sensation passed through Emily and she suddenly felt refreshed and energized.

"I'm fine," Emily replied, "but Lru needs your help." She grabbed Liz by the arm and dragged her back up the ramp.

The battered Great Wyrm was curled up on the helipad and appeared to be sleeping until one huge eye popped open as they approached. But Lru didn't make any move.

Liz was appalled at the gruesome wounds that covered the majestic creature's body and she couldn't believe that the dragon had been able to reach the *Duquesne II* at all.

She hurried up to the injured dragon and put her hands on his crystalline scales. She muttered the words of a prayer and the soft light spilled into the dragon. The bleeding of the worst wounds slowed, but nothing else happened. Liz furrowed her brow in concentration and tried again, but there was little change.

"I am impressed," Lru sighed. "It takes a powerful healer to mend a dragon."

"But it's not working," Liz growled angrily.

"Do not worry little one," Lru replied calmly. "We dragons are resistant to such things. The fact that you managed any at all should be commended." He looked over to Emily who was nervously watching. "Never fear, my Kao. I will heal, given enough rest." The Great Wyrm closed his eyes. "Now, go. My part in this is over. Your city still needs you." Emily and Liz knew a dismissal when they heard one and the two of them left the dragon to his rest.

Liz led Emily across the walls that shook with the constant thunder of the guns all around them and into the relative quiet of the tower she had ran out of earlier.

"What is this place?" Emily asked, as she followed Liz through the tight corridors.

"I'm not really sure," Liz admitted. "I only got here a few minutes ago myself. But what I do know is that Pittsburgh is nearly overrun and we need to move fast before there isn't a city left to save."

****

The undead Korybantes proved much harder to destroy than Ted would have thought possible. The powerful enchantments on their armor defeated his spells and their swords withstood his plasma blades.

They even moved with the deadly grace that they had been renowned for in life. Ted assumed the latter was due to the vampire's influence more than any retained skill, but that didn't change his situation.

Magical darts erupted from Ted's hand and rammed into the face and neck of one of the undead guards. As Ted swung his plazmax at a different elf, Ted's spell shield deflected another Korybantes' swift thrust. With his back pressed against a huge stone, Ted dueled the four undead warriors as the vampire watched from the shadows.

Tongues of flame lashed out, but the fire vanished when it came into contact with the Korybantes' armor. However, the undead warriors' pallid flesh was not so protected, and their faces and other exposed parts blistered under the fiery assault.

The undead ignored the damage and continued their unrelenting attack. Ted used every ounce of skill he had learned in the years of fighting in the SCA and since, but he was no match for the undead Korybantes. Their blades continuously clashed against his shields and Ted knew they wouldn't hold out much longer.

He had to end this quickly.

He knew he couldn't beat them with his blades; he would need to use magic. But his list of memorized spells was being depleted and there was only so much sorcerous power he could draw on. His brilliant mind raced for a solution as the undead wore down his shields a little more with every strike.

A stream of ice froze one of the Korybantes' feet to the ground and a sticky glob of green goo pinned the arms of another undead creature, giving Ted a slight reprieve. The other two elves came on and Ted's plazmax was a blur as it twirled around, deflecting many of their lightning-quick attacks.

A word from Ted and a cone of force slammed into one of the creatures, and it flew back and slammed into the altar. With only one Korybantes before him, Ted swiftly rammed the spike of his plazmax into its chest. The plasma spike barely broke through the enchanted breastplate, but it was all Ted needed.

A beam of superheated plasma burst from the plazmax and ripped through the undead warrior's chest. The Korybantes' chest melted and the undead creature collapsed in a smoking heap of liquefied flesh.

The zombie that had been knocked into the altar sprang at Ted, but a handful of dust and a quick word froze the creature in midair. But before Ted could finish it off, the ice holding the other creature shattered and the undead elf lunged at him. The enchanted blade rammed into Ted's magical shield and finally broke it. The shield exploded into shards like golden glass and Ted smiled grimly as the flying slivers punctured into the undead around him.

His smile quickly faded, as the Korybantes trapped in the goo suddenly broke out. The flying blades had cut through enough of the sticky material that the undead creature was able to rip free.

Now, the second undead creature cut him off from the stone he had been up against and Ted found himself surrounded. Their blades flashed in the torchlight and Ted blocked one of them with his wrist blade. But the other Korybantes' sword found its mark as it drove at Ted's back.

The blade suddenly clanged against Ted's robes like it had hit a brick wall. Ted ignored the creature behind him, confident that his stoneskin spell would withstand at least a few more blows. So instead, he focused on the undead elf before him.

Ted shouted a word and made a quick motion with his free hand. An enormous fist of burning power howled into existence above the undead warrior and with a swift downward motion from Ted, the fist descended like a comet and slammed into the Korybantes.

The undead creature vanished as the fiery fist exploded into the ground.

Ted was breathing hard as a blade clanged against his arm and another scraped across his back. Turning, he saw that the Korybantes that had been locked in midair had escaped and now both of the remaining undead were on him.

His head pounded and his arms felt heavy as he tried to keep the monsters at bay. But they never slowed and he felt as though he was moving through mud. That last spell had drained him more than he thought it would and now he was paying the price.

He felt a sharp stinging in his side as his stoneskin spell failed and the Korybantes' blade bit into his plastic armor. Like striking snakes, the undead flowed around him, lashing out with their deadly blades that Ted was helpless to stop.

Soon, he was bleeding freely from numerous cuts all over his body. He tried to summon another spell, but the words kept slipping from his mind.

Ted cried out as a slash to the back of his leg brought him to his knees. The undead raised their blades above him and Ted knew it was over.

But the blades never fell.

Ted looked up in confusion.

The undead creatures had frozen with their swords poised just above Ted's neck. The shadows moved and Countess Tatiana glided into the light.

"Very impressive," she purred as she drew closer. "Mistress Sabine was correct. You will make an excellent addition to our ranks."

"What is your deal?" Ted wheezed, as he spat blood and glared up at the vampire. "Why are you so obsessed with turning me into a vampire instead of just killing me and making me another one of your zombies?" He covered his mouth as he coughed.

Lightning flashed and thunder rumbled surprisingly close as the Countess came to a stop before Ted. "You know, I was once a Battlemage like you," she sighed almost wistfully. "I was full of foolish ideas and dreams. But then I learned the power of the Shadow." Her eyes blazed lustily. "And that power lies in dominating others to your will. Could I make you a mindless minion? Of course," she purred almost to herself. "But you will be of greater benefit to us with your mind and powers intact. It would be foolish to destroy such potential."

"And what if I refuse?" Ted groaned defiantly.

The vampire laughed. "You do not have a choice. Once you receive the Kiss, you will be my slave for all eternity. Besides, nobody said being my pet couldn't be enjoyable," she purred suggestively.

Ted found it difficult to stay focused. The thunder was far too continuous to be natural and it only seemed to be coming from one place. *Strange.*

"But you're dead," he wheezed. "That sort of thing needs blood flowing to work." Ted groaned as he sat back on his knees. "It's basic biology."

"We are not dead," Tatiana huffed. "We are merely… preserved. You could call it a form of suspended animation. Our blood still flows and our desires remain."

Ted swayed as he looked up at the sky. "I don't want to be anybody's slave," he breathed dreamily. "I would rather die." He placed his artificial hand up to the side of his head and pressed the hot metal device against his temple.

"No!" Tatiana cried, as she swooped down to pull his arm away before he could activate the plasma blade. The Countess was amazingly quick and surprisingly strong as she jerked his arm away.

As the vampire stood over him with his artificial arm safely immobilized, Ted burst into motion. First, he activated the plasma blade on his arm that successfully distracted the vampire and then he triggered the plazmax that was still clutched in his other hand. Ted heaved with all his might and drove the plazmax into Tatiana's chest.

The Countess screamed as the superheated blade impaled her. Suddenly freed from her grasp, Ted brutally rammed the plasma wrist blade up under her chin and into her brain.

He held her there as wisps of smoke trickled from Tatiana's open mouth before her body burst into flames and disintegrated into a pile of dust.

Two dull thuds made Ted turn and he saw that the two undead Korybantes had dropped their swords. The creatures stared dumbly and Ted noticed that the eerie glow had left their eyes. The undead quickly recovered from their confusion and abruptly lunged at Ted with their bare hands.

He easily avoided their mindless attacks and with a sweep of his plazmax, both creatures were quickly decapitated.

Ted took a deep breath as he regarded the ruin around him. His wounds were mostly healed and the corpses of five elves lay scattered across the grass, much like they had been when he arrived. Only now they were all truly dead. He looked down at a tiny syringe that rested near his feet and Ted was glad a friendly medicus had given him the healing potion as payment for his help.

The sky was alight as thunderous explosions crackled through the night. In the distance, gunfire flashed across a huge shape in the sky that floated beyond the Cathedral of Learning.

Ted didn't know what to make of the amazing spectacle, but he did know that the lich's trail moved in that direction.

He set off once more, eager to end this chase, but dreading what he might find at the end.

CHAPTER 31

The battle raged around them, but Alex was oblivious to everything except the orc before him. The ninja's slender sai gleamed in the flickering firelight as the black-clad orc cautiously circled him.

The ninja suddenly sprang into motion and launched a furious assault. Alex stepped in close to nullify the slightly longer reach of the sai and blocked the striking attacks with his hands and arms.

The orc abruptly spun around and kicked Alex in the side and he doubled over in pain. The ninja thrust both sai at Alex, but with a painful twist, Alex grabbed one of the orc's hands and ripped the sai away.

The orc pulled away and thrust with the remaining sai and the razor-sharp tip grazed Alex's neck. Alex pulled away, but the ninja pursued, slashing wildly with the sai.

Alex sprang into the air and a spinning kick knocked the sai out of the orc's hand. The ninja came on in a flurry of punches and kicks that Alex countered with desperation. The pair traded blows, but neither could land a solid hit on the other. They were evenly matched, but Alex was growing tired and the orc seemed to have limitless energy.

Alex needed to end this contest quickly, but he knew hand-to-hand wasn't going to do it. He needed a weapon.

Lying nearby was one of the orc's sai, but it was out of reach. The ninja must have come to the same conclusion because the orc suddenly broke off the fight and cartwheeled over to the discarded sai and scooped it up before Alex could get there.

Armed once more, the ninja charged.

Alex dodged the first thrust and using the orc's momentum, he caught the ninja's arm and flipped the heavy beast, slamming it into the hard pavement. The shock of hitting the ground dislodged the sai from the orc's hand and Alex swiftly straddled the stunned ninja and rained blows down upon it.

The ninja recovered quickly and assumed a guard position that protected its head while Alex tried to find an opening.

Suddenly, the orc heaved itself upward and with incredible strength managed to flip around and slam Alex into the ground, successfully reversing their positions. The ninja's heavy fists pounded against Alex, who now found himself trapped under the bulky orc.

The huge warchief advanced as Jack tried to summon the wolf, but the Spirit eluded him. His mind was still foggy from the powerful hit as he lay helpless before the mighty orc warchief. His sword was beyond his grasp and if he tried to get it, the orc would surely gut him before he could get close.

But then he had an idea.

The warchief loomed over him and raised his heavy black sword for the deathblow. But before the stroke could fall, Jack yanked the hidden pistol out of his boot and unloaded it point-blank into the orc's masked face.

The mask exploded as the shots ripped into it and the warchief rocked backward as the sudden barrage tore into him. Surprisingly, the orc stood for several moments with its sword still raised before finally toppling over.

Jack scrambled to his feet and retrieved his sword. Nearby, both Alex and King Varnir were pinned down. "Do I have to do everything?" Jack grumbled, as he rammed a fresh magazine into the pistol.

Looking between the two, Jack wasn't sure who to help. Alex was closer, but saving the king was decidedly more important. However, Jack wasn't about to let his friend die when he could do something about it.

Decision made, Jack raced across the battlefield, but fired his pistol at the enormous warlord as he ran to his friend's aid. He just hoped he wouldn't be too late.

King Varnir spat blood defiantly as the warlord's heavy bulk pressed him into the ground. The thick, iron club was about to crush the life out of him when a spray of gunfire pelted the warlord. Most of the shots sparked off the mechanical exoskeleton, but a few found the oni's tough hide. Stormtusk growled in annoyance as he searched for whoever dared to attack him.

The distraction wasn't much, but the oni released enough of the pressure that King Varnir was able to get his hands under the mechanical boot. With a mighty heave, the dwarf king roared as he pushed the oni's foot off his chest and lunged back to his feet. Stormtusk stumbled backwards and growled angrily as King Varnir hefted his legendary axe once more.

The long, iron club lashed out, but King Varnir ducked under the swing and barreled toward the warlord. Stormtusk drove his immobile saw blade at the charging dwarf king, but King Varnir jumped over the blade as he slammed into the ground and bound up the oni's arm.

"Fer the Emperor!" King Varnir bellowed, as he leapt into the air.

There was a horrible cracking sound as the Axe of Perun split the exoskeleton and buried into the oni's chest. King Varnir kept his grip on the axe as Stormtusk fell backwards and he rode the dying oni to the ground. Blood trickled out of the warlord's mouth as he stared up at the dwarf king in disbelief.

King Varnir ripped the axe out of Stormtusk's chest with a wet, sucking sound. The huge oni gurgled and struggled weakly as the dwarf king walked up his broad chest. Varnir raised the Axe of Perun once more and with a brutal chop, drove the blade deep into the warlord's skull.

Blood ran into his eyes and Alex couldn't see as the orc's heavy fists repeatedly slammed into him.

Suddenly, the beating stopped, and the weight vanished from his chest. Alex wiped the blood from his face and looked up to see Jack standing over him with gore dripping off his black sword.

The ninja lay dead at his feet.

"That ninja was mine." Alex growled thickly.

Jack offered him a hand. "Well, you were taking too damn long," Jack said, as Alex gratefully accepted and was hauled to his feet.

Alex quickly retrieved his staff with Jack beside him when he noticed that the sounds of battle had suddenly stopped. The ring of gunfire could still be heard in the distance, but everyone around them had come to an eerie halt.

Looking around in confusion, Alex saw that all the orcs and their minions had frozen and were staring dumbly into space. The humans and their allies had stopped fighting as well and stared at the stupefied horde in disbelief.

"Kill them now!" Jack bellowed and drove his sword into the chest of an immobile orc. "Before they wake up!"

That seemed to break the allies' hesitation and they began to slaughter the horde with wild abandon.

At first, Alex was confused at what was happening, but then he saw King Varnir pull his axe out of the warlord's skull and he realized what had transpired.

The mental link the orcs used to control their forces had broken with the death of Stormtusk. Alex had heard about such things but had never seen it firsthand.

A few moments later, the horde began to wake up from their mental shock, but by then their numbers had been decimated and there were few left to put up any kind of resistance.

Alex and Jack joined King Varnir as he hopped off the warlord's corpse.

"What happens now?" Alex asked.

"This battle be won," King Varnir rumbled, "but the war be far from finished. Now that the orcs an' their minions be freed from the warlord, the Lore says they will go wild."

"And that means lots of prey," Jack grinned, and he suddenly transformed back into a werewolf. "Let's go hunting."

****

The pain was gone.

Now, he only felt cold.

Mike hung here before the victorious golden demigod as his lifeblood pooled beneath his feet. He gasped for breath, but his punctured lung made breathing difficult.

His vision swam as he fought to remain conscious.

But then, a sound like thunder penetrated through the growing fog. Mike looked up beyond the gloating face of The Destroyer and saw the most unbelievable sight.

I must really be dying, Mike thought. *Now, I'm seeing flying castles.*

The Destroyer ignored the noise behind him as he drew Mike closer. The demigod inhaled deeply. "Ahh," he breathed. "Your spirit is surprisingly strong. Once I devour your soul, my powers will be greater than ever before."

"Ugh," Mike gasped. "Just... kill me already... so I don't have to... listen to you anymore."

"Why do you still resist!" The Destroyer howled in rage while violently twisting the spear causing Mike to cry out in pain. "I am a god! Surrender your soul to me and the pain will end!"

Mike's vision blurred as he struggled to stay conscious and his strength was quickly fading. The pain was overwhelming and a piece of him wanted to give up and let it end.

The Destroyer laughed as Mike's body sagged and his eyes closed. But another stronger piece of him wanted to live. Through the haze of pain, Mike saw a light in the corner of his eye and he desperately moved toward it.

The Destroyer's laughter abruptly cut off when Mike's eyes suddenly sprang open and blazed with blue flames.

Mike raised his mace as blue-white flames coursed over the ancient weapon. A beam of brilliant energy erupted from the mace's head and slammed into the demigod. The spear was ripped from Mike's chest and he fell to the ground as The Destroyer was blasted backwards.

Blue flames of the Holy Fire filled the wound in Mike's chest as he stood and unleashed another powerful beam at The Destroyer. But the brilliant lance struck a shimmering red energy field before reaching the stricken demigod.

"You think you are the only one that can call upon the powers of the Ether?" The Destroyer boomed.

As he stood, a nimbus of hellish light radiated from the golden demigod and his eyes burned with abyssal power. "You are but a babe before the awesome might of Malek The Destroyer!" he bellowed with thunderous power.

"He may be," a musical voice replied, "but we are not."

Brigit stepped up beside Mike as all of the Wardens joined him. Each of the legendary warriors glowed with power, even Rodan, despite missing an eye.

As one, Mike and the Wardens charged the towering demigod and The Destroyer roared a challenge as he surged toward them. Before they met, a beam of blistering red power erupted from the *was* scepter and burst across a glittering shield around LuHark.

Brigit reached the golden demigod first and her shimmering spear was met by the golden *was* scepter. Daijiro and Shojiro split up and flowed around Brigit, attacking from either side. The Destroyer spun the *was* scepter as he expertly defended all three Wardens and the shining weapon stretched until it was as long as a spear.

Then Mike, LuHark, and Rodan joined the fray and surrounded the mighty demigod. The Destroyer's tail lashed out as the extended scepter twirled through the air as the demigod moved with impossible quickness. A beam of hellish power knocked Shojiro back and LuHark was slammed to the ground by a sweep of the serpentine tail. But the Wardens pressed in and The Destroyer couldn't defend against them all.

Brigit's spear slashed at The Destroyer's head and the demigod swiftly pulled away, but the glowing blade sliced cleanly through one of his curved horns.

Mike slammed his mace into the demigod's back and the mighty being's golden armor cracked under the tremendous force.

Rodan's powerful hammer pounded the scaly lower body as LuHark's scimitars wove a deadly dance against The Destroyer's twirling scepter.

The demigod howled in pain as a second hit from Mike's mace shattered the armor's golden back plates and crushed the flesh beneath. Brigit's spear rammed into The Destroyer's shoulder and LuHark slashed a deep cut along the beast's golden snout.

The Destroyer bellowed in rage and pain as more strikes found their way through and overwhelmed his defenses. Bleeding freely, the powerful demigod couldn't match the combined might of Mike and the Wardens as he was assaulted from every angle.

The Destroyer abruptly shouted a word of power and slammed his tail onto the ground. The earth rolled beneath him and knocked his attackers back for a moment.

Clutching his wounded shoulder, the mighty demigod still blazed with abyssal power. "This isn't over," The Destroyer spat. "This world will be mine!" Then his hellish glare rested on Mike. "As will you." And with that, The Destroyer abruptly vanished in a shower of crimson flames.

Most of the Isfet considered The Destroyer to be their god, and seeing their god defeated by a group of mortals shook them to their core. Many threw down their weapons and fled, while a few became enraged by the sudden loss of their beloved patron. Those that fought were quickly overwhelmed and soon the entire hillside had become a rout.

Mike found Rubadub and Rabidad staring at the bubbling pile of melting rock that was all that remained of Asag.

"I'm sorry," Mike said. "He died bravely."

Rubadub smiled sadly. "Yes, he did."

A small cockroach scurried up Rabidad and perched on his shoulder. "Eww." The hulking Druid made a face and disdainfully flicked the little bug off.

"There will be time to mourn after the battle," Rabidad growled, as the persistent cockroach scampered onto his broad shoulder once more. Another flick sent the tiny bug sailing away. "Cursed insects," Rabidad muttered with disgust.

"My brother speaks true," Rubadub nodded. "There is no time for sadness."

"Don't be sad, sad," a small voice chirped.

"Ugh," Rabidad growled. "I can still hear his annoyingly squeaky voice."

Rubadub perked up. "So can I!"

Everyone turned to the tiny cockroach that jumped back up onto Rabidad's shoulder. The little bug suddenly bulged and expanded as feathers sprouted across its body.

A few heartbeats later and an ugly bird was perched where the bug had been moments before.

"Robadoo!" Mike exclaimed in surprise. "We thought you were dead!"

"I am not," Robadoo chirped. "Nope. Nope."

"But how?" Mike asked in confusion. Nobody could have survived being crushed by the massive demon lord.

"I changed into a cockroach just before I got stepped on. Everybody knows you can't kill a cockroach," Robadoo chirped happily.

"Nope. Nope."

****

Archmage Talsin stood impassively before Cathy's locked gates as the skeletal lich and her vampires stopped several paces away from him.

"Ah, if it isn't Archmage Talsin," the lich hissed. "I should have known it would be you."

"Sabine," Talsin nodded. "You never give up do you?"

"Never," Sabine smiled, but her rotten face made it look more like a grimace. "And why should I? I have all eternity to pursue my every desire."

"You know…" the lich added, "my offer still stands."

"I have no desire to become your thrall, Sabine," Talsin replied. "The answer will always be no."

"Pity," Sabine sighed. "You would have been a marvelous addition to my court. No matter. Just give me the Seal and I will spare you."

"Do you take me for a fool?" Talsin replied. "Besides, I have sent the Seal away, where even you cannot reach it."

Sabine's eyes flashed angrily, but then she looked into the distant sky and smiled. "You think hiding the Seal on that flying rock will stop me?" Her laughter was like the rustling of dry leaves. "My powers have grown since our last meeting, Archmage. You cannot stand against me."

"Yet here I stand," Talsin taunted. "I defeated you once before and I shall do so again. Or are you afraid?"

"Ever the fool," Sabine hissed angrily.

Glowing black chains abruptly appeared in the air and descended on Talsin. The Archmage didn't move and as the chains touched him they suddenly vanished.

"Your power astounds," Talsin sneered.

Sabine shrieked in rage and with a slight motion, a hail of black darts shot toward the Archmage. The darts sped toward him, but at the last moment Talsin suddenly vanished only to reappear a few steps away as the darts slammed into the gate. Another wave of darts shot toward him, and again he disappeared and reappeared before they could strike.

Talsin opened his hand and a twirling ribbon of multi-colored light twisted through the air and shot toward the lich. The pulsating streamer slammed into the lich and detonated in a brilliant rainbow explosion.

But when the smoke cleared, Sabine was still standing and she shouted a terrible word of power that crashed into Talsin and slammed him into the wall.

A putrid cloud of disease and death boiled up around the lich and flowed toward the stunned Archmage. Talsin swiftly steadied himself and took a deep breath. He exhaled and a gust of wind flowed out and blew the killing fog away.

Talsin then clapped his hands together and then raised his hands, palms out, toward Sabine.

Twin rays of glaring sunlight shot from his outstretched hands and blasted the lich. Sabine howled as her parchment-like skin blackened and blistered beneath the withering rays.

With a sweep of her skeletal arm, a wall of utter blackness sprang to life and cut off the shining beams. Smoke wafted from her charred body as she uttered a string of painful words.

Suddenly, all of the kefali corpses piled before the walls began to move. Hundreds of undead picked themselves up and surrounded Talsin. Gunfire erupted from atop the walls as the defenders fired into the growing army of undead, but there were far too many for the soldiers to stop.

"Kill him," Sabine hissed, and her Shadow elves moved to obey.

The vampires spread out and glided through the ever-growing mob of undead that now encircled the trapped Archmage.

Talsin calmly drew a slender wand from his robes and faced the undead throng. He performed a quick pirouette and scattered some kind of sparkling dust as he spun around. Muttering the words to a spell, he waved his wand and shouted the last syllable as he finished the incantation. The dust flared brightly and suddenly there were a dozen Archmages standing before the gate.

The undead came on in a wave and all of the Archmages unleashed spells into the swarm. Fire and lightning crashed into the undead as beams of light and waves of blistering power erupted all around them.

Dozens of undead were reduced to ashes in those first moments, but the vampires countered the spells with curses of their own. One by one, the overwhelming press of undead was destroying the Archmage's clones.

Then, four flickering points of light appeared in the dark sky above and swiftly grew into blazing orbs of fire that plummeted toward the ground. The four meteors crashed into the swarm around the last three Archmages and obliterated countless undead.

However, the undead were numberless as more appeared out of the darkness and joined the throng.

Ted rounded the corner and froze.

The lich was right in front of him and she had her back to him. Beyond the lich, a battle raged and Ted was caught by the impressive display of arcane power.

In the center of a blasted ruin before the tall Cathedral gates, three Archmage Talsins battled an army of undead that swarmed toward them from all sides. Vampires threw dark spells at the Archmages and directed the undead toward their prey. Fire and lightning flashed and explosions detonated all around the Archmages as they defeated spell after spell with remarkable skill while simultaneously destroying waves of undead.

The lich was focused on the battle as she hurled vile enchantments of her own. Half of her body was charred from some kind of fire and Ted hoped that meant she was weakened. His list of memorized spells had been mostly depleted and his arcane reserves were limited. He needed to destroy the lich quickly because he knew he didn't have a chance with a prolonged duel.

A purple spear shot from the lich's hand and one of the Archmages exploded in a shower of sparks. Ted realized he had to act fast or even the magnificent expertise of the Archmage wouldn't hold out much longer against such overwhelming forces.

"Hey lich!" Ted shouted.

The lich spun around and as she did, Ted reached out and summoned his force of will. He focused on the burned-out building beside the lich and pulled crumbling wall down upon her.

The lich disappeared beneath the wall of bricks and Ted congratulated himself on defeating such a formidable foe with such a modest amount of power.

He began picking his way across the rubble to aid the Archmages when he heard a rumbling beneath the mountain of debris.

Ted turned to see what the noise was when the lich suddenly exploded out of the rubble.

Eldritch green light burned within her charred corpse as the lich radiated ethereal power. Her blackened jaw opened and a ray of sickly light shot out.

Ted hastily wove a spell and the ray abruptly struck a shimmering mirror. The ray bounced off the mirror and deflected right back at the lich. The sickly light hit the lich square in the chest but seemed to be absorbed back into the skeletal body and caused no evident harm.

Orbs of eldritch fire appeared in the lich's gaunt hands and she threw them at Ted. Before the first orbs had made it half way to him, the lich threw two more. The volley continued as the first burning orbs exploded against Ted's shield. When the second pair detonated, his shield shattered, sending pieces flying everywhere. But the lich easily deflected the slivers and continued lobbing fiery spheres at him.

Ted tried to deflect the projectiles, but they were coming too fast and he couldn't stop them all. He was knocked down as the orbs exploded against his last stoneskin spell.

His mind raced as he searched for a solution.

He had just gotten back to his feet when another orb made it through his desperate counters and knocked him down again.

Ted grimaced in pain as that last hit had nearly broken through. Desperate now, Ted had one option left open to him, but he was hesitant to use it. It was the most powerful combat incantation he knew, and if he survived the casting, in his current state, he would surely be rendered unconscious at least.

But it was a risk he had to take.

Summoning up every ounce of magic he could hold, Ted called the spell to mind and uttered the words of power. Eight multicolored rays of light flashed from his outstretched hand. Each ray was a different color as they shot toward the lich.

The rays stabbed toward her, but Sabine countered the rays with mighty incantations of her own. Bursts of multicolored light exploded around her as one by one the rays were destroyed, and when the last ray vanished, the lich still stood atop the rubble in all her terrible glory.

Ted collapsed to the ground, dismayed that his most powerful spell had been defeated. His head pounded and blood ran from his nose and ears as his vision swam, but he remained conscious.

So much for being a hero, he thought groggily.

The moments ticked by as Ted waited for the spell that would kill him. But after several moments, Ted summoned the strength to lift his head. The lich still stood atop the rubble, but she was thrashing around as if she were struggling to move.

At first Ted was confused, then he noticed the greyness flowing over her skeletal body and whatever turned grey became immobile and he realized what was happening.

Each ray had a different power and one of them could petrify the target. It seemed as though that particular ray had made it through the lich's defenses and was now slowly turning her to stone.

The lich's arms and legs had frozen, but as Ted watched, the creeping stone slowed and then stopped before beginning to recede.

It seemed that the lich was overpowering the petrification and pushing it back. Soon, she would be free, and Ted would be dead.

Suddenly, there was an immense explosion of golden light, like a small sun, that burst to life near the Cathedral gates. The golden rays seared into the swarming undead and burned them to ashes. The vampires caught fire and screamed as they fled the burning light for the safety of the darkness. The lich wailed as what little flesh remained on her was burned away and the bones blackened and cracked from the bombardment of brilliant sunlight.

Then, as quickly as it had appeared, the light faded and everything seemed even darker than it had been before.

Archmage Talsin strode out of the burned ruin that had become of the undead army and stopped when he saw the lich still struggling against the petrification.

The Archmage pointed at the trapped lich and a thin green ray sprang from his pointing finger and struck the lich.

Sabine howled as her skeletal body began to disintegrate. Eldritch fire pulsed within her as her blackened bones crumbled to dust. Within moments she was nothing but a floating skull, wreathed in ethereal power. But that too disintegrated and when there was nothing left, the last of the eldritch light faded away with a ghostly wail.

"That was invigorating!" Talsin said, as he made his way across the rubble. "I had forgotten how much fun a good fight could be!"

"I'm glad you enjoyed yourself," Ted groaned, as Talsin helped him to his feet. Ted could barely hold himself up, but a word from Talsin and a wave of strength infused him. "Is she dead?"

The Archmage's face fell. "I'm afraid not," he sighed. "Her physical form was destroyed, but her soul is still bound to her phylactery. I trust that it will take her some time to find a new body, but she will return."

"I was afraid you were going to say that," Ted groaned. "Stupid liches."

"Then again..." Talsin looked thoughtful for a moment. "Her phylactery is most assuredly hidden on Gaea. Since she was destroyed on Earth, it could be possible that she cannot reach her phylactery."

"How will we know?" Ted asked.

Talsin shrugged. "We won't unless she returns."

"That's encouraging," Ted muttered.

A surge of heavy gunfire from the flying fortress drew their attention.

"Come," Talsin said, and with a wave of his hand, a shimmering portal opened up beside them. "We still have a city to save."

CHAPTER 32

The sky began to lighten as dawn approached and Liz found herself looking out over the embattled city from the safety of the battlements upon the *Duquesne II*.

In the few hours since the skies had been cleared of airborne threats, the flying fortress had become a mobile hospital.

Helicopters, griffins, and even the few good dragons ferried the wounded warriors to the healers that had turned the courtyard into an infirmary.

Liz was exhausted from a taxing night without sleep and there was no reprieve in sight. The flow of wounded seemed never ending and her healing powers would be needed again soon.

She loved helping others and was glad that she could save lives, but weariness threatened to overwhelm her and in between healings she found it hard to keep her eyes open.

"Go get some rest," Emily said from nearby, where she was tending to an injured griffin. "You look terrible."

Liz shot Emily a mock scowl. "You sure know just what to say to make a girl feel better."

"I know," Emily smiled happily, as she wrapped a bandage around the griffin's leg. "There. All better," she said to the griffin. "Now, don't scratch it or you will get an infection." She wagged her finger in the beast's face. "I don't want to hear that you went and opened it back up or you will answer to me." Somehow the mighty griffin managed to look repentant before it bound into the air and flew away.

Emily joined Liz and together they watched as the skies grew lighter and more details began to emerge of the ravaged city below. Central downtown looked surprisingly unscathed from the air. The only major damage was the skyscraper that had split and partially collapsed onto an adjacent building. But the further out they looked, the more fires burned. Whole neighborhoods had been reduced to rubble and explosions still flashed in the distance.

A deep rumbling filled the air and soon four enormous C-17 Globemaster II aircraft from the 911th Airlift Wing roared into view. As the mighty transports sailed over the stricken city, their large rear hatches opened up and dozens of paratroopers descended from each of the powerful aircraft.

Looks like reinforcements have finally arrived, Liz thought, as she watched the falling soldiers' parachutes open precariously close to the buildings.

Just then, Liz felt a growing presence in the back of her mind and she smiled as she turned around. "Thought you could sneak up on me, eh?" she teased, as Mike, Alex, and Jack strode toward them.

Mike and the Wardens had arrived by griffin not long after Liz and the healers had begun treating the wounded in the courtyard. Jack and Alex had hitched a ride on a chopper with King Varnir when the dwarf monarch had been summoned to the *Duquesne II* after the death of Warlord Stormtusk.

Liz had learned that General Adams had moved the Command Center to the *Duquesne II* after the north wall had fallen. But the fortress hadn't been flight-worthy until just before Archmage Talsin revealed it.

The castle still wasn't fully operational, but enough of the armaments were in place that it had been activated as soon as possible.

"Sneaking is not my style," Mike answered with a grin, as he, Alex, and Jack joined Liz and Emily upon the heavy battlements.

"No kidding," Emily teased.

"Hey, Em." Jack pointed to a spot above his temple. "You got something right there."

"Oh, yeah." Emily touched one of the blue crystal horns poking out from her hair nervously. "You like it?"

"Sure do," Jack said with a wolfish grin. "You look sexy as hell."

"Why, thank you," Emily grinned wickedly. "Maybe we can play *dragon rider* later."

"Eww," Liz groaned. "That's just nasty."

"What's nasty?" Ted asked, as he sauntered up and joined the group.

Liz noticed that Ted's impractical lab coat was a tattered ruin and his ridiculous plastic armor wasn't in much better shape. *He looks like a wreck,* she thought, as she noticed everybody else. *But then again, we all do.*

Mike's armor hung in pieces and an awful-looking hole was ripped in the chest plate. She didn't even want to know how that happened.

Jack was a bloody mess, no surprise there, and Alex had a fair amount of blood staining his robes.

Everyone, that was, except for Emily. She looked as pretty as ever and that annoyed Liz. *How did she make it through an entire battle and still look that good?*

Liz looked down at herself and couldn't believe it. There she was, covered in mud and gore with her hair matted with dried blood that wasn't even hers, while Emily didn't have hardly a scratch on her. *I need a dragon,* she mused. *That must have been easier than being on the ground.*

But then Liz felt a pleasant sensation coursing through the bond. She looked at Mike as he stepped in close and put his arm around her. "Don't worry," he whispered. "You are beautiful," he said as if he had been reading her mind, which Liz reminded herself he kind of was. "And a total badass," he added with a grin.

Liz blushed at the praise and was surprised at how much she liked it. Screw Emily and her skimpy little outfits. She would rather be a badass any day!

"These two are nasty," Alex waved in the direction of Jack and Emily. "The battle isn't even over yet and they are planning extracurricular activities."

Ted scowled at the pair. "Now is not the time for *that*."

"Don't be such a prude," Emily teased. "I'm sure there are plenty of secluded places in this flying castle," she said, as she looked around at her surroundings. "Where did this crazy thing come from anyways?"

"Dr. Cooper," Ted answered. "He was looking through some old documents about Pittsburgh and found the schematics for an old fort. He didn't think much of it at the time until he told Archmage Talsin about it," Ted said, thoroughly enjoying his tale. "You see, unknown to Dr. Cooper, the Wardens had removed the gravity stones from the nephilim fortress and had given them to Talsin for safe keeping. So, when Dr. Cooper told him about the schematics, the Archmage had an idea."

"They began building this fort in secret a few months ago," Ted said excitedly. "Turns out there were so many gravity stones left over, they are planning a second, bigger fortress. And I have been invited to assist in the development!"

"Congratulations, Ted!" Liz said. "I'm sure you will make it amazing."

"That's great. We're gonna need it," Mike said. "But that will have to wait. I just got done meeting with General Adams and the other commanders. They are planning a counter offensive to push the enemy out. Within the hour, they want to have every available fighter at the Point. From there, they are going to press out into the city and clear it, block by block."

"Sounds fun," Jack growled.

"Don't you ever get tired of fighting?" Liz asked, but Jack only stared at her as if she had asked the dumbest question ever. She sighed. It looked like she wouldn't be getting a rest anytime soon.

"There can't be that many baddies left," Emily said. "A lot of the Isfet gave it up once The Destroyer ran away, the dead aren't rising up anymore now that the lich has been destroyed, and the orcs and their minions don't have a leader anymore and are just roaming about."

"Exactly," Mike replied. "The horde is just roaming around and pillaging everything they come across. There are still tens of thousands of creatures down there and it will take a long time to clear them out to make the city safe again."

"But it might be getting easier," Jack added, to which Mike nodded his agreement. "I don't know if it's the higher elevation or what, but the comms are greatly improved here," Jack said. "Word from Clearfield says it's still safe and we have made contact with several other nearby towns that have promised to help however they can."

"At least we aren't alone," Liz breathed a sigh of relief.

"Right," Jack replied, "but the news isn't all good. The word is that D.C. is completely unreachable. Philly and New York City are battlegrounds and the whole of Ohio is a ruin. A few cities to the south seem to be in relatively good shape, but there is no word at all from the west coast. As for the rest of the world," Jack shrugged helplessly, "who knows?"

"We can't worry about the rest of the world," Mike said. "We have to take care of us first."

"Agreed," Liz said. "And as soon as Pittsburgh is free of the monsters, I will be leaving."

"What?" Emily cried. "And go where?"

"New York," Liz answered, "to find my family and bring them back."

Emily shook her head in disbelief. "But Liz, that's suicide. You don't know what could be between here and there."

"I know," Liz admitted, "but I have to try. Besides, it should only be a few hours' drive."

"Yeah," Emily scoffed, "if you don't run into a pack of centaurs or a dragon or something. You don't even know for sure where they are."

"I agree with Emily," Mike said. "Driving there would be suicide." Liz scowled and was ready to argue when he continued. "That is why we will be flying."

"We?" Liz asked in surprise.

"Of course," Mike answered. "You don't really think I would make you go alone, do you?"

"Well, you never know with you," Liz teased, but she knew Mike could feel her appreciation. She hadn't been that keen on making the journey alone and she was glad to have company.

"I'm sorry," Emily said, "but I have to stay here. Once the city is cleared out, there will be a meeting of the surviving Druids to elect a new High Druid and decide what to do with the Seal."

"And I will be going back to Clearfield," Alex added, as he looked at Mike. "That is where our family is, and I plan on staying with them, at least for now," he said, and Mike nodded his understanding.

"Good luck," Ted said. "I must get back to my lab and make some adjustments to my weapons systems before I begin work on the new fortress."

Mike looked at Jack and he shrugged. "I don't really have any reason to stay here," he admitted. "I just don't want to go."

"That's fine," Liz laughed. "I'm sure Mike and I can handle it." Honestly, she was relieved that none of the others would be going. She was looking forward to spending some quality time with Mike. They hadn't had much time together in the last several months with all the changes that had been happening and she was eager to explore their newfound connection.

"What will you do once you bring them back?" Emily asked.

"I dunno," Liz admitted. She hadn't really considered what would happen then. "I suppose they will want to return to Clearfield, but they might move here instead. Either way, I plan on staying in Pittsburgh at least until spring."

"Same here," Mike said. "I plan on riding out the winter here and we'll see how things stand come spring."

"What about Pipaluk and those kefali that helped us?" Emily asked. "What happens to them?"

"They will be allowed to stay here," Mike answered. "And they may even get a representative in the Council if the other members agree to it."

"They'd better," Liz said passionately. "It was the kefali that protected the Seal when all of the Druids were out fighting across the city."

"I agree," Mike said, "but I don't get to choose. That will be decided after the city is secured."

"Speaking of that stupid Seal," Ted asked. "Where is it?"

"Locked away in a special vault, deep inside this fortress," Liz answered. She had placed the Seal inside the heavily enchanted chamber herself shortly after arriving through the Archmage's portal. "It will be safe there until the Druids decide what to do with it."

"I'm surprised the Wardens didn't take it," Jack added. "I thought they were some kind of 'universal protectors' or something."

"The Seals belong to the Druids," Emily said. "The Wardens have no authority to claim any of them unless a Druid Council gives them permission."

"That's just silly," Jack argued. "Aren't they on the same team? As long as the bad guys don't get their hands on them, isn't that the important thing?"

"It's not that simple-" Emily began, but Jack cut her off.

"You know what," Jack interrupted sharply. "I really don't care."

Everyone laughed as the first rays of sunlight peaked out over the distant hills.

"I wasn't sure we would ever see the sun again," Liz confessed, as she nestled into Mike.

"Me either," he admitted.

Liz sighed contentedly. "I'm glad that's over."

Mike looked out over the burning city and held her close.

"I'm afraid it's not," he replied grimly. "It's just beginning."

EPILOGUE

Dr. Francis Burkhalter watched in awe as the masked wizards did their work.

The old physicist didn't know what else to call them besides wizards since the powers they displayed could only be described as magic.

Francis did not believe in magic. However, he could think of no logical explanation for what he was seeing. Thus, wizards.

Francis and his young assistant, Alicia, who seemed to be the last scientists still alive following the cataclysmic disaster at the Large Hadron Collider, led the three masked wizards to another entrance to the particle collider. As they had done several times already, the wizards muttered strange words and waved their gloved hands in intricate patterns as they chanted before the colossal machine.

Each time the writhing anomalies that crackled in the air would lessen and eventually vanish before the strange display, but no sooner had the last one vanished than more appeared. It was a never-ending cycle that the three wizards had battled for several minutes before giving up on the first room and moving to the next. Now, they targeted and destroyed the largest anomalies or any sizable clusters before moving swiftly to the next area that Francis directed them to.

The facility was deep underground and the collider had a circumference of 27 kilometers. At their current rate of travel, it would take the small band several days to make one circuit. At that pace, the anomalies would grow out of control before they returned and who knows what damage that would cause.

Francis was surprised that the immense collider was holding up as well as it was, even with the constant tremors and collapsing passageways. The facility had not been built to sustain such extensive damage, but Francis was filled with pride that such a magnificent machine was holding on, despite the fact that its still being operational was putting the entire planet in danger.

There must be a way to shut it off and repair this "Veil" that the strange wizards kept talking about, but so far there seemed to be no stopping it. They were only slowing the torrents of dark energy that were spewing through the anomalies and threatening to tear the facility apart.

A tremor shook the passage and a huge block of concrete fell from the ceiling directly above one of the masked wizards. Francis shouted a warning, but the wizard proved more agile than any person had a right to be and he avoided the colossal block as it crashed harmlessly to the floor where the wizard had been standing only a moment before.

"We are running out of time," Kadir, the dragon-masked leader of the wizards hissed angrily. "There must be a central fracture point that is spawning all of these rifts. We must find it… and close it."

"We've tried," Dr. Francis answered testily. "The readings are all off the charts and we can't make sense of most of it."

Kadir snorted in disgust. "This is what you get when you play with forces beyond your comprehension," he sneered. "I should have expected as much from *humans*."

Francis didn't like the way Kadir said the word "humans," but there were more pressing matters to attend to. "The most likely source for a conduit of that magnitude would be at the ATLAS detector," Francis replied. "That is where we got the strongest readings."

"Then lead us to this… Atlas at once," Kadir snarled from behind his hideous dragon mask.

Francis nodded and without another word, he and Alicia started off down the dust-choked passage with the three wizards following more slowly behind.

When there was sufficient distance between them, Alicia leaned in close to Francis as they walked. "I don't trust them," she whispered nervously.

"Neither do I, my dear," Francis replied softly, "but I do not see how we have much choice in the matter. Without them, these anomalies would have torn this place apart by now."

"I know," Alicia grumbled almost to herself, "but I can't shake the feeling that they are up to something."

"Of course, they are up to something," the old physicist muttered. "The question is, what?"

Normally, it was a short walk to the ATLAS detector, but the tunnel was in ruins, and traversing the rubble and fissures made the journey more perilous.

Eventually, they made it to the huge steel doors of the ATLAS chamber. Light flickered beneath the doors and the hairs of Francis's arms stood on end as he slowly approached.

Francis looked back questioningly and Kadir motioned him forward.

Francis took a deep breath and placed his hand against the scanner beside the door. A light turned green and a small panel opened up above the hand scanner. The old physicist bent down and looked into the new device as the retina scanner verified his identity.

"Welcome, Doctor Burkhalter," a feminine robotic voice chimed, followed by a metallic clang of unlocking bolts and a hiss of escaping gasses as the doors slid open.

Inside, was a cavernous room that enclosed one enormous machine. The ATLAS detector was a vast cylindrical device of pipes and cables measuring 46 meters long, 25 meters in diameter, and weighing about 7,000 tons that dominated the entire room.

Light coursed within the monstrous detectors as arcs of power danced across its vast bulk. An eerie wailing filled the air and a strange wind whipped around the chamber. But it wasn't the marvelous ATLAS that drew the eye, it was the towering maelstrom of multicolored energy that crackled angrily in the center of the detector. The rift was immense and dwarfed all they had previously encountered.

Francis led Alicia and the wizards into the howling gale as electricity arced around them until they came to a stop a safe distance before the swirling vortex.

"Finally," Kadir breathed eagerly. "We have found it," he hissed, as he and his companions moved past the scientists to stand before the mighty vortex.

The wizards raised their arms and began to chant as one. Raw power flared around the angry maelstrom and it began to writhe wildly as the wizard's voices grew louder. A crackling arc of pure energy suddenly struck one of the wizards and he burst into flames.

The unleashed power reduced the unfortunate wizard to ash and was swept away by the gale.

Kadir and the remaining wizard continued as if nothing had happened. Their voices grew ever louder until they thundered over the wailing and even shook the chamber. The rift flared angrily and lashed out, but as the chant grew louder, the tempest began to fade.

The booming chant painfully hammered within the chamber, and Francis and Alicia were forced to cover their ears.

Energy flared within the vortex, but its strength was waning. As the moments passed and the powerful chant continued, the rift lost its wild rage and began to calm.

As the wailing died away, the maelstrom morphed into a towering portal with an almost glassy sheen. One final booming syllable from the wizards echoed around the chamber before their chant ended and they slowly lowered their arms.

A strange tranquility filled the chamber as the slowly revolving portal hung in the air.

"It is done," Kadir gasped breathlessly. "The rift has been healed and the Veil is open once again!"

"What is the Veil?" Francis asked.

"Ah," Kadir turned to face them. "The Veil is the barrier that separates our worlds. It has been inaccessible for millennia, but thanks to your little device here, the way is now open."

"So, that is a portal to another world?" Francis asked in disbelief.

"Indeed," Kadir hissed. "Unfortunately, now that we have secured the Veil, your service is no longer required."

A pair of black bolts suddenly shot out of Kadir's gloved hand and slammed into the two surprised physicists.

The bolts burned through their chests and they were both dead before they hit the ground.

Kadir turned his back on the corpses and a moment later the mirror-like gateway grew hazy. The smooth surface rippled as a figure suddenly stepped out of the portal.

The newcomer wore a coat of heavy chainmail with a circular disk set across the chest. A snarling wolf-head helm obscured his face and a pair of slender scimitars were clutched in his gauntleted fists.

"Kadir, report!" the armored warrior barked.

"Our mission was successful." Kadir replied. "Inform The Cabal that the Veil has been secured. We can now reclaim this world and restore it to the Divine Order," Kadir hissed fervently. "All glory to the Eternal Ma'at!"

THE END...

AUTHORS WANTED

Entanglement Interactive is looking for new and experienced authors to help us expand the ever-growing DarkEnergy universe!

No experience? No problem!
We love to hear from first time authors.

INTERESTED?
Visit: **www.entanglement-interactive.com/submissions**
OR
Email: **submissions@entanglement-interactive.com**

About the author

N. J. Colesar enjoys ancient history, mythology,
playing games, and painting miniatures.
Raised in Clearfield, Pennsylvania, N. J. Colesar currently
resides in Pittsburgh with his wife and children.

STEEL CITY SERIES

THE SHEARING
ORIGINS OF MYTH
BIRTH OF LEGENDS

CPSIA information can be obtained
at www.ICGtesting.com
Printed in the USA
LVHW031726200421
685029LV00003B/504